Peter MacKenzie was born in the UK in 1956 but has spent more than half his life living and working overseas in Switzerland, Germany, Japan, India, Tanzania and Namibia. He has visited more than fifty international schools, worked in six, been the head of three, and has sat on the board of one. *Mr In-Between* is his second novel set in the imaginary International School of Ndwalowe.

He lives in Windhoek, Namibia.

Peter MacKenzie

MR IN-BETWEEN

AUSTIN MACAULEY PUBLISHERS

LONDON * CAMBRIDGE * NEW YORK * SHARJAH

A CIP catalogue record for this title is available from the British Library.

Ac-cent-tchu-ate The Positive
from the Motion Picture HERE COME THE WAVES
Lyric by Johnny Mercer
Music by Harold Arlen
© 1944 (Renewed) HARWIN MUSIC CO.
All Rights Reserved
Reprinted by Permission of Hal Leonard LLC

ISBN 9781035896745 (Paperback)
ISBN 9781035896752 (ePub e-book)

www.austinmacauley.com

First Published 2025
Austin Macauley Publishers Ltd®
1 Canada Square
Canary Wharf
London
E14 5AA

You've got to accentuate the positive,
Eliminate the negative,
Latch on to the affirmative,
And don't mess with Mr In-Between.

– Johnny Mercer

Prologue

After Anna Street had left his office, Peter Corby made some brief notes on a writing pad and locked it in a desk drawer.

He then walked next door to his secretary's office and handed her the letter from the Ministry of Education.

'Chiamaka, please scan this for me. I need to send it to the board. Well, some of them.'

'Of course. And the email from the US Embassy?'

Peter sighed. 'I'll reply to them.'

A few minutes earlier, he had felt like celebrating. The International School of Ndwalowe had successfully completed its first year of operation and he had completed his first year as a school head. Inevitably, minor dramas had come and gone but no one had died (an early rumour to the contrary notwithstanding) and, a little more than a year after the shock of bankruptcy, the school appeared to be back on an even keel. More or less.

In a thatched and slightly shabby, but always popular, bar a short walk from the school, some of the teaching staff were enjoying an early afternoon beer, their jobs done for another year and a long holiday stretching ahead of them. Others were already on their way to the airport. A few remained in their classrooms, sorting, tidying, and just enjoying some moments of solitude. But they too would shortly be joining their colleagues for a drink or going home, quite happy to be leaving behind the stresses and challenges of their jobs, at least for a few weeks.

Peter had been rather looking forward to enjoying a cold beer (or three) himself but a social drink and a few laughs with his colleagues would perforce have to wait. Back in his office, he dialled a familiar number.

'Carola, hi. I think we need to talk.'

★

July

The city of Ndwalowe straddles the Lowana, a broad and stately river that meanders slowly across the northern half of Awanza. Such hills as there are rise only gently from the surrounding plains. The climate is benign, the pace of life unhurried, and the city's inhabitants (at least those with money) enjoy a standard of living found in few other cities in southern Africa. There is little or no heavy industry, the air is clean, and pollution is not a major concern (the ubiquitous drifts and tangles of discarded plastic bags excepted). Drinking the tap water would not be prudent but the region's altitude and latitude mean that malaria and dengue are virtually unknown. First-time visitors who express anxiety about gastroenteric illnesses, infectious diseases, or even – much to the amusement of locals – the danger of being attacked by a lion or a crocodile are advised that, as is the case throughout much of sub-Saharan Africa, the most dangerous thing they will do in Awanza is get behind the wheel of a car.

The centre of Ndwalowe remembers better times. Still imposing, though often neglected, colonial edifices loom over boulevards, plazas and parks that were once the pride of the city but are now ill-kept and unkempt. Where the wealthy used to promenade and picnic, street vendors now importune passing shoppers and office workers. Lawns and flowerbeds are largely untended; paving stones are cracked; benches are mostly broken; and too many cars are parked on streets that were never designed for so much traffic.

More modern buildings, some ugly and already dilapidated and others that are mostly attractive and well-built, house government departments (ugly and already dilapidated), the head offices of banks, insurance companies, airlines, and the country's major commercial enterprises (mostly attractive and well-built). A couple of international hotel chains have a presence in the city centre and a number of restaurants continue to do business, though more at lunchtime than in the evening. But life has slowly been draining out of the centre of Ndwalowe. Most people prefer to live and shop and eat and relax closer to the outskirts of the city. Though never quite as far as the very edge.

Those who do venture to the city's farthest corners will find what are quaintly referred to as "informal settlements". Shacks constructed of wood and shiny corrugated-iron sheets, some with electricity and some even with running water, nestle and jostle along irregular streets that are unmade and, in the rainy seasons, run red and brown past and, as often, into the ill-made homes. Children play in the roads; dogs, timid and underfed, scavenge as best they can; chickens risk their lives under the wheels of the surprisingly numerous vehicles; and everywhere people are on the move, going somewhere or nowhere.

Most such communities have grown along the major arteries that run in and out of the city and are plainly visible to anyone who will see. But the drivers of the Land Cruisers and Land Rovers, Fortuners and Freelanders, Tiguans and Tuaregs, Prados, Pajeros and Patrols that barrel up and down these broad highways either do not see or prefer to look the other way. They are driving to or from the affluent residential suburbs of Ndwalowe where they live behind razor wire and electric fences and where their homes are cleaned by and their gardens are tended by people who live in these unseen and ignored settlements.

The homes in these wealthy suburbs are mostly two- or even three-story buildings and they commonly occupy the greater part of the available plot. Only on older properties has space been left for rockeries and shrubs, fruit trees, palm trees, cactuses, terraces and, in rare and optimistic cases, what might pass for a lawn. But space has always been found for a pool, rectangular or kidney-shaped, perhaps just long enough to dive into but usually just a feature in which to cool off rather than take serious exercise.

Homes on the gentle slopes sometimes have a view (though usually only of other houses) but many, however airy, imaginatively designed, and expensive, are surrounded by high walls and solid metal gates. They do not feel like and, indeed, are not part of a neighbourhood. Those who live next door or two doors down may or may not be waved to as cars pass on the street but immediate neighbours rarely socialise, and lives are led anonymously behind imposing barriers of brick, concrete and metal.

Wealthy Awanzans, often those with close relationships to the governing party, live on these prosperous streets but just as many residences are occupied by expatriates who are in the country to represent their country, NGO or IGO (Awanza is a much sought-after posting within the EU and SADC), UN agency, multinational company (Awanza's telecoms and brewing industries are European-owned), Christian missionary charities (mostly from the United States), or sundry poverty reduction or health education initiatives.

And, for those foreigners who have pitched up in Awanza on two- or three- or four-year contracts and have children, the obvious choice is to enrol them in the International School of Ndwalowe. The school has its critics ("no discipline", "no uniform", "too many locals", "too many privileged expats") but it is widely acknowledged as providing the "best" education in the country (though, what "best" necessarily means is seldom unpacked). It is also the most expensive school in Awanza and, for some, that is good enough reason to enrol their children.

'And where do your children go to school …?' (Sometimes asking the question and sometimes answering it, there follows an almost imperceptible smirk.)

In truth, ISN is as good a school as many and better than some. The international schools with the best facilities (and they can be jaw-dropping) are mostly found in Asia but a number of schools in Africa have no need to apologise for the age, quality, or variety of the venues in which they teach sports, the creative arts, the sciences and much else. ISN, formerly Ndwalowe International School until bankruptcy brought a rather abrupt end to its existence, would not consider itself one of Africa's marquee international schools but students are mostly successful and parents are mostly happy. On the international school circuit, few people have a bad word to say about the school. Equally, it enjoys no particular celebrity. It sits, perhaps, a little below the radar.

And in his second year as the school's director and still with much to learn, that suited Peter Corby just fine. A number of enjoyable and successful years as a secondary school principal in a modest but authentic international school in Japan had tempted him to apply for similar positions elsewhere in schools that were certainly bigger if not necessarily better. Suitable vacancies in Turkey and India had briefly excited but, when he had visited Istanbul and Mumbai for interview, neither had appealed and he had not been sorry when the jobs were offered to others. The position in Ndwalowe, however, had most certainly appealed, both the description of the school in the advertisement and the reality he had discovered when invited for interview, and all parties had been delighted when he was asked to become the new secondary principal and had immediately accepted.

Well, almost all parties. Peter's wife, Sheila, had been supportive of a move in principle but was openly ambivalent about exchanging the predictability and security of Japan for the many uncertainties and unknowns of Africa. Her doubts seemed to have been confirmed when, as Peter was winding up his job in Japan, shippers had been booked, a buyer had been found for their car, and, not least, Peter's replacement had been appointed, he had received the message that the school had been declared bankrupt and that his contract was, therefore, worthless.

★

'That's unfortunate,' the director of Peter's school had said when she heard his news. 'What are you going to do?'

It seemed to Peter that "unfortunate" didn't quite capture the gravity of the situation he was facing but as he and his soon-to-be ex-boss talked through his options, he concluded that all may not be lost.

'It's the only international school – or IB school – in Awanza?' she asked.

Peter had nodded.

'Well, those students have to go somewhere. Everyone needs the school. You say there are attempts to reopen the school, perhaps under a new name?'

'That's what I'm being told.'

'Well, you must, of course, start looking for other jobs but I wouldn't give up just yet on Awanza.'

It was good advice. Peter had indeed looked to see what suitable jobs were being advertised this late in the school year (answer: very few) but he was also in daily contact with the now bankrupt Ndwalowe International School, mostly exchanging emails and the occasional phone call with Saskia Kakonje, the business manager, and Valli Agnelli, the primary principal. The members of the board appeared to have gone missing in action and the director, John Conway, Peter was alarmed to learn, had abruptly left the country.

Peter had endured an anxious few weeks, not entirely helped by his wife's rather tight-lipped silences. Ostensibly, Sheila supported and encouraged Peter's continuing dialogue with Awanza but he sensed that she would not have been terribly unhappy to hear that they would not, after all, be moving to Africa.

But if Sheila was ambivalent (at best), Peter was becoming ever more committed. He had liked enormously what he had seen of the school and the country when he visited for interview and was increasingly determined that he would work there. Moreover, with every passing day he felt greater and greater respect and admiration for Saskia, Valli and the few others who appeared to be keeping the school going. He was not yet – and never would be – an employee of Ndwalowe International School but as he questioned Saskia and Valli about the latest developments and offered such advice as he could, Peter realised that he had somehow slipped into suggesting what 'we' needed to do. He had spent only a few days at the school some six months ago and he no longer had any contractual relationship with NIS. But, quite to his surprise, he found that he was feeling a sense of responsibility, an almost proprietorial concern for the future of the school.

Those in Ndwalowe gave Peter regular updates, informing him of hastily convened meetings of senior diplomats, concerned parents, and worried school employees; decisions (some encouraging and some alarming) taken by banks, creditors, and the City of Ndwalowe; and a moment of surreal humour. (A contractor had not been paid for a drainage ditch that had been dug around part of the school perimeter so had pointedly sent a team of men to fill it in again.)

And then Valli contacted him to say that he would shortly be receiving a call from Carola Lasser, mother of a girl at NIS, wife of the German Ambassador and chair of a newly constituted board of directors.

'I bet I'm going to be told that they no longer want or can afford me,' Peter had predicted to Sheila.

In fact, Peter was quite wrong.

★

'Faansie, good morning. How are you?'

'Very well, Peter. I hope you are too.' The two men shook hands warmly.

'Faansie, I'd like you to meet Carola Lasser, the chair of the board.'

Carola stepped forward. 'Mr Burger, it's very good of you to see us at short notice.'

'Oh, please call me Faansie. It's a pleasure to meet you. Take a seat, please.'

'So,' Peter began, 'you read my email and you saw the copy of the letter we received?'

'Indeed. And you say that this Mrs Prosper Luhanga ...' he consulted his notes. 'Assistant Deputy Executive Director at the Ministry of Education ... You say she is also a member of your board?'

Carola and Peter exchanged the same exasperated look. 'Yes.'

'Extraordinary. And she's never brought this up before?'

'No.'

'Well, I may have some good news. The Access to Education Act does not apply to schools in their first three years of operation.'

The look that Carola and Peter now shared was an appreciably happier one. 'Really?'

'Yes. But wait. Our problem is going to be convincing the Ministry that ISN is really a new school.'

'But of course it is. I mean, legally ...'

'Yes. Legally. But, as we all know, the school – whatever it was or is now called – has been around for fifty years or so. If they choose to, the Ministry could make a pretty good argument that the school is certainly not in its first three years of operation.'

Peter's face fell.

'That will be our first line of attack,' Faansie continued, 'but let's see what other cards we have to play. Prior to this letter, what communication did you have with the Ministry about ATE?'

Peter frowned. 'Nothing.'

'Nothing?'

'No. Well, I received nothing. The new school – the International School of Ndwalowe – received nothing. Nothing in the past twelve months. But when the Act was announced, John Conway, my predecessor, wrote to the Ministry for clarification. That was about two years ago. But it doesn't look like he ever received a reply.'

'Well, well. That could be helpful. Will you send me a copy of that letter?'

'Of course.'

'So why would Mrs Luhanga bring it up now?'

'I don't know, Mrs Lasser ...'

'Carola, please.'

'Thank you. I honestly have no idea. But the fact that there has been no communication until now could work to our advantage. Look, you need to acknowledge her letter, of course, and I think we must refer them to Article 14.8 of the Act. That's the bit that exempts new schools for three years. With your permission, I'll draft something for you.'

'Yes. Please. Thank you.'

'Your other problem, of course, is ... Mrs Luhanga.'

'The thought had occurred to us.' Peter said a little sourly. 'Can she stay on the board? I mean, isn't this a conflict of interest or something?'

'Not in the conventional sense. She isn't using her position to benefit personally. At least, as far as we know.'

'Could we remove her? There is a provision in the Articles of Association for the board to remove a member in certain circumstances.'

'These circumstances? Anyway, I don't advise doing anything to further antagonise her.'

'Would it be helpful ...?' Carola spoke hesitantly. 'Would it be a good idea if I, as board chair, met with her over a coffee to, erm, see what she ...?'

'I think it would. Yes. But you need to make it absolutely clear that you are meeting her as a board member and not in any way in her capacity as ...' Faansie looked again at his notes. 'As Assistant Deputy Executive Director.'

'Of course. All right, I'll reach out to her.'

As they left the stylish building in which Faansie's office was located, Peter and Carola shared their thoughts.

'He seems nice, Mr Burger.'

'Yes. I thought you'd like him. And he knows what he's doing. He told me that John Conway was in and out of his office quite often.'

Carola scowled. 'I don't like the sound of that. How often should a school need legal advice?'

'More than we assume, it would appear. Anyway, we have a plan of sorts.'

'I'll contact Mrs Luhanga today. The sooner the better, I suppose.'

'Good. Please let me know how it goes. I do wonder what she's up to.'

Carola nodded slowly. 'Yes, indeed. What?'

★

Before marrying Peter, Sheila had studied and worked in the UK, the US, and a number of Asian countries. She considered herself cosmopolitan and well-travelled but her career had never taken her to Africa and, if she was honest, it was not a continent that much appealed to her. She had lived in Japan twice, initially as a teenager and now as an adult woman, and she associated strongly with the order and efficiency that characterised a country that was her second home or even, she sometimes thought, her first. What she knew of Africa – which, she acknowledged, was not a great deal – suggested that order and efficiency were perhaps less common than she was accustomed to.

'What about Thailand?' she had proposed to Peter early in the recruitment cycle. 'There are some good international schools there, aren't there? Or Singapore? I've always liked Singapore.'

'She, you know it doesn't work like that. You can't pick a country and decide that's where you want to live and work. At least, not in the international school world. Look, there aren't that many positions advertised each year. We are ruling out some countries and other schools will be very American or British and I wouldn't fit in there – even if I could get an interview. Of course, if there are promising options in Thailand or Singapore, I'll apply. But we just have to wait and see where the vacancies are and then decide if it's a place where we could live.'

To Sheila's alarm, the first vacancy that seemed worth going for was in Mongolia. Peter had applied but, to Sheila's relief (and, actually, Peter's too), he had not even been offered an interview. The possibilities in Turkey and India had come and gone (Sheila would have been quite happy with either) and then Peter had told her of a vacancy for a secondary principal in Awanza.

'Africa?' Sheila could not keep the disapproval out of her voice.

Peter shrugged. 'Why not? The school looks about right – six hundred kids, genuinely international, three IB programmes. I think I'd have a good chance of getting it.'

The position that Peter had applied for and been interviewed for and been offered and accepted was secondary school principal. But the phone call he took from Carola Lasser rather changed all of that.

'They want me to be director.'

Sheila had been working when Peter talked to Carola. She had come home hoping (though somewhat guiltily) that Peter was right when he predicted that the call was to tell him that the school no longer wanted him. Instead, she discovered that the school certainly did want him and wanted him, moreover, to assume the now vacant position of director.

'Seriously? What did you tell her?'

'I said I'd need to think about it. And discuss it with you.'

'Do you want it? The position?'

'I don't know. But I can't help thinking I'd be mad to turn it down.'

'Oh, absolutely. A job you didn't apply for in a bankrupt school. What a golden opportunity.'

'She...'

'Why you? Why not the American? The primary principal?'

'I don't know. She said it was the recommendation of the new board after talking to some of the old board.'

'The old board that allowed the school to go bankrupt and then all resigned?'

Peter sighed. 'Look. It's a gamble. I know. But it's a great school...'

'Was a great school.'

'It will be again. And I'm being offered the headship. This could be an amazing career move.'

'It could be a lot of things.'

They looked at each other, each feeling a range of emotions but both wanting this painful exchange to be over.

'Do you want to live in Africa?' Sheila asked.

'I don't know. I was only there for a few days last October. But, yes. Yes, I think I do. Well, I think I want to give it a try.'

Sheila said nothing.

'She, Germany, Japan – Scotland, even. Let's try something different. It's an amazing opportunity.'

'How long is the contract?'

'Two years. Same as the one I had as secondary principal.'

'Two years ...'

'Two years is nothing. If it works out, that's great, and if not, what have we lost?'

Marriage is an endless series of compromises. Many are quite inconsequential. To eat in or eat out? What colour to paint the spare bedroom? Who to invite for a celebration? Others have rather more riding on them. But, whether trivial or weighty, decisions need to be made, ideally by mutual agreement or, if not, then at least some kind of acquiescence on one side or the other.

And so Carola Lasser received the news she had been hoping for and informed the board that Peter Corby, previously engaged as secondary principal, would be coming to Ndwalowe in July to assume the position of director.

★

Peter's contract included a clause noting that he was entitled to twenty-five days of paid leave each academic year in addition to Awanzan public holidays and the period over Christmas and New Year when the school was closed. Such leave was required to be taken during scheduled school holidays. The clause irked Peter no end. The problem was not that he wanted, or felt entitled to, or would even have taken more leave, but that quantifying the days when he was at work or not at work seemed hopelessly out of touch with the reality of Peter's job. The clause that required him to be on school premises from seven am to four pm Monday to Friday was still more irritating.

'I hear what you are saying, Peter, and I tend to agree but some of the board members insisted that we include these things in your contract.' Carola did indeed look as if these clauses annoyed her almost as much as they did Peter.

'So, what? After four pm they don't expect me to answer my phone or reply to emails? Or at the weekend? Carola, in a sense, I'm never not at work. It's the nature of the job. These people are living in another age.'

Peter's point had been underlined during the brief trip he and Sheila had taken to the UK in the last week of June. The application for a work permit for one of the newly hired teachers had been rejected and Peter had spent a full day in their Edinburgh hotel liaising with Julia Rweyemamu, the school's HR manager, receiving, signing, scanning and sending documents, and corresponding with the by now distraught teacher. Sheila was frustrated but Peter accepted that he had little choice and, indeed, took pride in being able to reassure the teacher and, ultimately, resolve the situation successfully. He was doing his job. That he was supposedly on holiday was irrelevant.

The flying visit to England and Scotland to see friends and family had been part pleasure and part obligation but what Sheila and Peter were really looking forward to was an expedition to the remote and arid south-west of Awanza.

There are no perennial rivers in the south of Awanza but rains do fall and four seasonal rivers feed a small lake in an otherwise barren and rocky landscape. A number of small salt pans in the region suggest that in former times there were other such lakes. The lake, named *!Kha* by the desert people who live in the region, and the nearest reaches of two of the four rivers sustain impressive stands of makalani palms. Small islands, incongruously lush and home to an astonishing numbers of birds, are dotted through the lake. Crocodiles populate the waters. For those with deep pockets, chartered flights will deliver visitors to Lake !Kha but its impact is yet more impressive for those who have made the seven-hour drive from Mwenozi through xeric plains and stony valleys on the intimidating roads that wind through mostly lifeless hills.

Their journey began at a ridiculously early hour. Awanzair flew the route twice a day but taking the afternoon flight would have allowed insufficient time for the long drive ahead of them and would have meant spending a night in Mwenozi – a town, Peter was assured, with very little to recommend it and limited options when it came to accommodation. Bleary-eyed and both irritable, Peter and Sheila arrived at the check-in counter shortly before 6am. A family of four, the children whiny and the parents snapping at each other, was already there.

'The romance of air travel,' Peter whispered to Sheila.

The flight to Mwenozi was scheduled to depart at 7:30am and Awanzair sternly instructed all passengers to arrive at the airport no later than two hours before departure. But Peter and Sheila had guessed they would probably be all right allowing ninety minutes and friends and colleagues had concurred.

Indeed, 6am came and went and three more passengers, yawning and clutching containers of coffee, arrived to stand in line but there was no sign of anyone behind the counter. As the queue slowly grew, Peter and Sheila joined those checking their watches, sighing and tutting loudly.

'It's always the same with Awanzair. They're bloody useless.'

Peter glanced back to see who was speaking. A man wearing a suit and tie was talking to no one but himself. He looked familiar. A parent?

'Peter, go and ask someone. It's nearly twenty past. The flight goes in an hour.'

Peter nodded at his wife. 'Yes. This is ridiculous.'

Finding personnel wearing the slightly garish red and yellow uniforms of Awanzair was not difficult. Finding someone who could answer Peter's questions was a good deal harder. He was passed from one not-very-interested member of the ground staff to another and then to a desk where he had to wait for a couple of minutes while the agent completed a phone call that Peter suspected was personal rather than official. And when reluctant eye contact was made and Peter's query considered, the answer did not please him at all.

'Delayed.' He reported to Sheila and to the dozen or so others waiting in the line. 'Apparently, it's now scheduled for 10am.'

'What? Why?'

'She didn't say. Well, "operational reasons", whatever that means.'

'Why did no one tell us? Surely they can see us all standing here?'

Peter shrugged. He could hear the man in the suit swearing quite liberally.

'So now what?'

'Fancy a coffee? We've got at least an hour to kill.'

In fact, several of the would-be passengers were already making their way over to the Slowtown counter.

'But we get a voucher or something. For the delay. Don't we?'

'Sheila, I didn't ask. I doubt it.'

'But they have to give us something. Why didn't you insist?'

'Sheila, it's a twenty Awanzan dollar cup of coffee. A pound. Not even. I'm not going to waste time over that.'

'It's the principle.'

Peter shook his head. 'Are you coming or not?'

With pursed lips and saying nothing, Sheila marched off towards the small cafeteria. Peter sighed and followed. They drank their coffee in silence.

★

The 10am departure had turned out be closer to 11am and by the time they had landed in Mwenozi, retrieved their luggage, and queued to collect the vehicle they were renting, it was almost two o'clock.

'There's no way we're going to reach the lodge today,' Peter said. 'It's seven hours if nothing goes wrong. We'd be mad to end up driving in the dark.'

'Makes sense,' Sheila agreed reluctantly. 'So, where's the Mwenozi Hilton?'

The "Mwenozi Hilton" turned out to be a surprisingly large but painfully dilapidated hotel that seemed to date from the 1970s and may have been quite something in its day.

'Someone told me that there used to be a lot of quite lucrative mining in the area,' Peter mentioned to Sheila as they checked in. 'But I think that's all gone now. You wonder how a hotel like this survives these days.'

Whatever the answer to Peter's question, it certainly wasn't the food. Having checked in, they had taken a stroll around downtown Mwenozi, hoping to find an appealing bistro or pizzeria. Such few eateries as they had found had not been at all appealing and they had returned to their hotel, made straight for the bar (where the beer was at least draught and pleasingly cold), and then, with misgivings, taken two seats (two unmatching plastic chairs in faded colours) on the hotel terrace. The menus they were given confirmed to Peter that they had indeed fallen through a tear in the space-time continuum and were now in the 1970s.

'Chicken in a basket? Really?'

'Don't be such a snob. Look, they also have chicken Kiev. You like chicken Kiev. In fact you make it.'

'Fish fingers?' Peter continued reading. 'I didn't even know they still made fish fingers.'

'That's the kiddies' menu. Come on, we need to be positive.'

Peter snorted.

'Perhaps they could do you a pizza with chips?' Sheila said with a sly grin.

Peter gave the suggestion due consideration. 'Yes, could be. But only if it's as good as Alfredo's.'

Sheila laughed. 'Oh no, nothing can match Alfredo's *pizza patate*! In fact,' she looked at the menu again, 'his pizza with chips would probably fit right in here.'

They ordered a bottle of red wine before they ordered food, teased each other a bit more about their eating habits, clinked glasses, and, without saying anything, agreed that the frustrations of a long and disappointing day should be put behind them. No, they weren't in the !Kha Makalani Lodge enjoying the view and the renowned cuisine but neither of them was to blame and, as Sheila had observed, they were seeing another side of Awanza, far off the usual tourist circuit. It would be a stretch to say they enjoyed their meals (a tough pork schnitzel, chips and salad for Sheila, two dry burgers, chips and salad for Peter), but as they returned to their room, they did so hand-in-hand, reflecting more on their mutual good fortune than the day's misadventures.

★

They rose early, excited about the drive ahead of them (and, in truth, in a hurry to see the unlovely town of Mwenozi in the rear-view mirror). As was their usual routine, Sheila returned the room keys and paid the bill while Peter brought the car round to the front of the hotel.

'That isn't the car we collected yesterday.' Sheila had been about to toss her overnight bag on the back seat but now hesitated. 'It isn't even a Toyota. It's a VW.'

'Of course it's yesterday's car. How else would I be driving it? Anyway, since when have you been interested in cars?'

'I'm not. But I know that isn't a Toyota. We hired a Toyota Hilux.'

'No. We requested a Hilux – or equivalent.'

'So, what's this?'

'It's a VW Amarok. A perfectly acceptable alternative.'

'An Anorak?'

'No. An Amarok. Look, are we going or not?'

And so they set out on their drive, Peter concentrating on the road and Sheila delightedly texting all her friends to say that they were driving a Volkswagen Anorak.

The street was tarred only as far as the last petrol station on the way out of town and, with a small bump, the car dropped an inch onto a wide gravel road. It was barely a track but, slightly to Peter's disbelief, the satnav he had attached to the windscreen happily informed him that they were, as they should be, progressing on the C26 and would be for some time.

'In a hundred and eighty-three kilometres, turn right.' The Home Counties accent of the woman's voice was reassuring but, driving through such a vast and empty landscape, it seemed completely out of place.

Or maybe we're the ones who are out of place, wondered Peter.

He was driving a large and almost new car that must have cost many times the average annual income in Awanza. He had a wallet full of cash and a number of credit cards. On the reverse of his medical insurance card was a number to call for emergency evacuation and the small silhouette of a helicopter. Yes, he and Sheila were far from home and driving through scenery that was as inhospitable as it was spectacular and, yes, upon their return to Ndwalowe he would no doubt refer to their journey as 'a bit of an adventure' but, he mused, they were really just voyeurs, tourists at best.

'What do people do out here?' asked Sheila as they passed an elderly man slowly riding an equally aged bicycle. 'Where can he be going? There's nothing here.' She waved at the barren expanse on either side of the road.

They sat in air-conditioned comfort observing the occasional hut or small settlement; a young boy herding a flock of brown and white goats; a woman, heavily pregnant and with two toddlers trotting behind her as they walked beside the road. But mostly they saw no one.

The road rose and fell, twisted and turned. Long stretches through sandy plains abruptly delivered them into rocky gulches at the bottom of which there appeared to be evidence that a river occasionally flowed. They climbed through a pass where the road narrowed and signs warned of falling rocks. Of wildlife, there was no sign. Peter had hoped, and in fact expected, to see at least some birds of prey (vultures perhaps?) but the cloudless blue skies were as empty as the lands they drove through.

They shared the driving, stopping now and again to take photographs or admire the view, and ate their packed lunches in the shade of one of the very rare trees that were to be found. The sun that had been bothersome when it was low in the sky and reflected in the car's mirrors was now high above them. Where there had been long and sharply defined shadows, there were now none. It had been quite chilly when they left Mwenozi but by the time they stepped out of the car to eat, the air was warm and, out of the shade of the tree, the sun was fierce.

'Remind me,' asked Sheila, 'this is winter here?'

They drove on, the sun now dipping slowly in front of them. If anything, the landscape through which they were passing was still drier and more barren than they had seen through the morning. They no longer saw the occasional pedestrian or sign of human habitation.

'God, it's like driving on Mars.'

They spoke little. Each was somewhat in awe of the world they had somehow entered and each silently wondered what would happen if the car broke down or some other misfortune befell them.

Actually, thought Peter, *this is a bit of an adventure, even in an air-conditioned four-by-four. Well, it's about as adventurous as I think I want to get.*

Sheila had been dozing while Peter drove. She awoke and stretched. 'Where are we?'

'We just passed through the middle of nowhere. I didn't want to wake you. You'll see it on the way back.'

'It's after three.' Sheila indicated the satnav. 'What's she saying?'

'She's saying another thirty kilometres or so. We'll be there well before four.'

'Phew. I won't be sorry.'

'Me too but … Well, it's been quite something, eh?'

Sheila nodded slowly. 'It's an amazing country …'

They crested a steep incline, turned sharply to the left, and were immediately confronted with an extraordinary sight. In the distance, steep hills rose on both sides of a broad valley. Some were the colour of terracotta, others as pale as sand. A few hinted at shades of purple. On none was there any sign of life. But between them a ribbon lake sparkled blue and green in the afternoon sunshine. Numerous small islands were scattered through the lake, each home to diverse bushes, trees, and brilliantly coloured flowers.

On the islands, and especially on the shores of the lake, tall grey-green makalani palms rose high above everything else.

They were now passing small shacks in front of which chickens and goats scavenged and small children played. Vendors of baskets and wood carvings attempted to flag them down. A hand-painted sign invited them to leave the road and drive to a viewpoint overlooking the lake. (*Later*, thought Peter.)

They passed a couple of campsites, a shebeen or two, a few surprisingly well-appointed bungalows, a general store, and a small school. Here and there vehicles were parked (or in some cases looked to have been abandoned). The road they had been following seemed to have disappeared and they drove slowly, weaving between such buildings as there were, and following the wall of green a hundred metres or so to their right.

'Apparently the lodge is at the far end of the town.'

'Town?'

'Well, whatever it is.'

The !Kha Makalani Lodge turned out to be the last of the various accommodation options they had passed. It sat on a bluff, higher above the river than the other campsites and hotels and giving it the best view of a stretch of rapids that was rather optimistically promoted as the !Kha Falls. A small but quite exquisite garden of tropical plants welcomed them as they passed through the lodge gates. Tall, healthy trees and bushes, succulents and broadleaf, lined the path to the reception. Signs bearing the lodge's makalani palm logo indicated where they would find the pool, a wellness spa and, still higher up the bluff, a viewing platform.

'This is gorgeous!'

'Worth the drive, eh? Oh, look. I'm sure that's a collared palm thrush.'

'Well,' Sheila waved her arms in all directions, 'palms …'

Their room delighted them. An extraordinarily large bed looked out through a panoramic window onto the lake. Cleverly, each cottage (as they were called) was positioned so that it could not be seen from the others. All guests could enjoy the fantasy that the spectacular view they were enjoying was theirs alone. From the bedroom, steps led down to a large and airy bathroom that offered the same sumptuous vista. An oval faux antique bath invited and there were two showers, one inside the bathroom and another out on the terrace.

'Showering *en plein air* with a tropical sun on our backs. They're spoiling us!' Sheila clapped her hands in approval.

'Mmm, it's really great but what would you say to a cold beer after that drive?'

'Don't want to unpack first?'

'Do you?'

'Not really.' (It was the right answer.)

A wooden stairway led down from the reception to the bar and restaurant. Diners ate on a terrace looking onto the sandy bank of the lake. There was no obvious way to leave the terrace and approach the water but numerous signs still warned of the danger of crocodiles.

'Are those just there to impress or are they for real?' Sheila wondered.

'Frankly, I'm not particularly inclined to find out. But look.' Peter pointed to their left.

'Where? Oh!'

'If I'm not mistaken …'

'You're not. Wow. How do they get so big? What do they eat?'

'Apart from tourists?'

'I think I read somewhere they have crocodile on the menu here. I'm going to have to try it.'

The bar was at the far end of the terrace on a raised deck angled towards the Falls. A barman wearing a white shirt and smart red bowtie greeted them with a broad smile. 'Good afternoon, Sir. Good afternoon, Madam. What can I get you?'

'You have draught beer?'

'Of course.'

'Good and cold?'

'Very cold Sir.'

'Excellent. Two, please.'

They took their drinks to a table by the railing. Peter raised his binoculars to scan the banks for birds. Behind him, Sheila muttered quietly, 'I somehow doubt she's here for the wildlife.'

Peter turned to see who she was talking about. On a stool at the far end of the bar sat a woman. Two half-empty glasses of white wine lay on the bar before her. A cigarette smouldered in her left hand. She wore a short skirt of black leather with a zip up one side, a frilly crimson blouse that was open to the third or fourth button, large and very dark sunglasses, and high-heeled shoes of shocking pink.

Peter tried not to stare. 'I think she *is* the wildlife,' he whispered.

'Who'd have thought? In a place like this.'

'Or are we jumping to conclusions? I mean …'

Peter's wife gave him a rather patronising look. 'Seriously?'

'Good afternoon, Sir. Welcome back.' The barman's voice interrupted their whispered conversation. Peter glanced towards the man who was ascending the short flight of steps into the bar.

It was Lazarett Snyman.

Lazarett saw Peter. Peter saw Lazarett. The look on each of their faces was approximately the same.

'Peter …?' Sheila observed his reaction with some concern.

He ignored her and, not quite sure why, rose and walked slowly towards Lazarett. He stretched out his hand. 'Well, hello, Lazarett. I … I didn't know you had an interest in wildlife.'

'No, I …' Lazarett was clearly flustered. 'It's business. I'm only here on business. I don't, erm …'

Was it Peter's imagination or did Lazarett flash a nervous glance at the woman at the bar?

'Ah!' Lazarett tapped his trouser pocket. 'I've left my phone in my room. Please excuse me.' He hurried down the steps. Peter watched him go, his mind full of thoughts that were as shocking as they were hysterically funny. *No? Surely not? Really?*

'Peter?' No longer in a whisper, Sheila called him back to their table. 'Who was that?'

'Who? That was, my dear, the infamous Lazarett Snyman, board member, man of some mystery and a total pain in the arse.'

'That was Lazarett? What's he doing here?'

As one, they both turned and, trying (but failing) to do so surreptitiously, took another look at the woman at the bar. At the same moment, the woman's phone rang. Peter and Sheila swiftly returned their attention to their beers.

Behind them there was a brief and mumbled conversation. Then the woman rose, stubbed out her cigarette, and left the bar.

'Well, well, well …'

★

For children and their parents, the start of a new school year is a date on the calendar, a single event that is anticipated with emotions that range from apprehension to relief. For some teachers, naughtily arriving from their long holiday sometimes less than twenty-four hours before they are due back at work (something that intensely annoyed Peter), there is also an element of jumping in at the deep end. For others, often those who live locally, the new year creeps up on them a bit like Christmas. They know it's coming but are always just a little surprised when it does. As the day nears, some teachers will start coming into school for a few hours to deliver or collect materials, start reordering their rooms, or check on maintenance jobs that may or may not have been done. Not all admin staff will necessarily be at work and those that are may be working reduced hours. They will dress informally, park where they are usually not allowed to, and just enjoy the remaining days of peace before the campus is again, and abruptly, full of life and noise.

Peter, Valli and Mick, the Senior Leadership Team, were necessarily at work before most. On the last Monday in July Peter arrived quite early to prepare for the first semi-formal SLT meeting of the new school year. Mick O'Cheney and his wife had been in the country for a couple of weeks but so far they had mostly been preoccupied with setting up their new home. Mick had been shown the campus by Peter and had dumped a number of boxes in his office but today would be the first day when his attention would be expected to be fully on school matters. As he walked through the car park, Peter wondered how the new dynamic within the SLT would play out. Mostly, he was optimistic. He and Valli had a strong relationship and Mick seemed to have his feet on the ground. *Not a bad little team*, he thought.

'Peter!'

Peter turned and saw Dennis Villiers striding towards him.

'Den, I didn't know you were back already. How was the break?'

'Aw, it was great. The kids had a blast with their grandparents. Could hardly drag them back here. You? A good holiday?'

'Yeah, it was actually. We had some time in the UK and then travelled a bit in Awanza. I've still only seen bits and pieces but it's an amazing country.'

'I guess that's why we've stayed as long as we have. Well, that and the school. Not everyone knows when they've got it good.'

'Indeed. I hope I've got a few more years here ahead of me.'

'Everything ready for the new year?'

'I think so. Valli, Mick and I are meeting in an hour to see where we are. Two of the new teachers have already arrived and I pick up another at the airport this afternoon. The fourth,' Peter scowled, 'will be a bit late getting in.'

'I see the science labs have all been repainted. Thanks for that.'

'Thank Genuine and his team. They've been outstanding. I'll need to confirm with Saskia but I think all the maintenance and repair jobs have been completed. On time and on budget, as they say. I'm pleased about that.'

'And the soccer goals? They'll be back in time?'

Peter frowned. 'What goals?'

'The portable goals we use on the sports fields. They've gone for repair … or repainting?'

Peter's frown deepened.

'We were here yesterday to walk the dogs,' explained Den. 'As we were driving in, a truck was driving out with all the soccer goals on the back. You didn't know?'

'No. And yesterday was Sunday. No one was working here yesterday.'

'Security will know, won't they?'

'I certainly hope so. Thanks. I'll go and check now.'

'No worries. Hey, have a good year, mate.'

'Thanks, Den. Fingers crossed.'

★

Peter had Valli's undivided attention.

'She told you on the last day of term?'

'Yes.'

'Why didn't you tell me then?'

'There seemed no point. Neither of us could have done anything then. And it was only a hunch on her part. But now we are all back, we have to find out.'

'So, go on, tell me. Who does she think it is?'

Peter told her. Valli's face clouded. 'Well, I didn't expect that. I thought you were going to say ... or she was going to say ...'

'Yes?'

'I thought you were going to say Genuine.'

'Genuine? Seriously?'

'He left his wife, you know that?'

'I heard she left him. He has a reputation.'

'He has a reputation and keys to every room and he can be anywhere on the campus and no one would be surprised to see him. Or not see him. The invisible man.'

'You have a point.'

'So now we have two suspects?'

'I think "suspect" is putting it a bit strongly. What do they say on television? "Persons of interest". Look, Anna's back next week. I want her to tell you what she told me. And let's see if she has any reason to wonder about Genuine.'

'Here we go again,' said Valli with a sigh.

✱

The atmosphere in the conference room was distinctly frosty. On one side of the long table sat Peter and Saskia Kakonje. On the other, Clay Hooper and Studious Mwangolo of Awanza Security Services shifted uncomfortably in the seats. The guests had been offered no refreshments. Clay Hooper's writing pad lay in front of him and he fidgeted nervously with his cheap biro.

'I can assure you, Mr Corby, that we are conducting a full investigation. The guards who were on duty have been suspended. And I have ordered an immediate review of our operating procedures.' Clay Hooper looked at his assistant who nodded encouragingly. 'This kind of thing should not happen.'

Peter's face feigned surprise. 'Oh, it should not happen, you say? Well, I'm glad we at least agree about that. But it did happen, Mr Hooper. Four men in a truck drove into the school and stole a load of goalposts while your guards...' He pronounced the word with sarcastic emphasis 'While your guards stood and watched. We have no record of the vehicle registration or the identity of the thieves. We only know exactly when it happened because one of my staff happened to be here.'

'Yes. It is unacceptable. A thorough review …'

'A thorough review will do what? You already have systems. You have operating procedures. It's not complicated. All visitors sign in with a reason for their visit and so on. So, yes, review your systems. But systems only work if your people enforce them.' Peter jabbed his finger at Clay Hooper. 'Look. You aren't even wearing a visitor's badge. Did you sign in?'

Clay looked surprised. 'Well, our guards know us, of course, and …'

'That's not the point. The rules have to apply to everybody. Why were the thieves not required to sign in and get badges?'

Studious Mwangolo coughed nervously. 'The men said they worked for the school. They said they needed to take the goalposts for painting.'

'Oh, don't give me that! Your guards know – or should know – all the people that work here. And if they didn't recognise someone, why didn't they ask for identification or call someone?' Peter indicated Saskia sitting to his right.

'It was Sunday and …' Mr Mwangolo's voice died.

'I've been called on Sundays before,' said Saskia. 'If it's urgent.'

'Mr Hooper,' Peter said with finality. 'One of two things happened on Sunday. Either your guards were utterly incompetent or, I'm sorry to say, they were in on it. I don't want to believe the latter because I know at least two of them have worked here for a long time and I don't want to believe they are corrupt. But, one way or another, Awanza Security Services did nothing while a theft took place in the middle of the afternoon. And I want to know what you are going to do about it.'

Clay Hooper sighed and shifted uncomfortably on a chair that had refused to recline and forced him to sit stiffly upright. 'I … I will need to talk to my boss.'

'Please do. And I don't expect to have to wait long for an answer.' Peter stood. 'Thank you for coming.'

There we no handshakes as the two visitors left.

As the door closed Saskia gave Peter a small smile. 'You arranged those chairs on purpose, didn't you?'

'Of course I did. Hooper had to sit to attention throughout while his sidekick was slumped with the table at chest level. They looked thoroughly uncomfortable. These rubbish chairs do have their uses.'

They both laughed.

'What do you think will happen, Saskia?'

'I know exactly what will happen. They will blame the guards. They will tell us that their review revealed … I don't know … that the guards had been drinking or that they were asleep or something. They'll blame the guards, fire them, and hope that we are satisfied.'

'I can't get over the brazenness of it. The middle of the afternoon.'

'A few years back, we took delivery of ten a/c units. That's twenty boxes. I stood and counted as the delivery men unloaded them all and stacked them in a container by the workshop. Then I signed for them and they drove off. A few days later, when we came to install the first of them, we discovered that all the boxes were empty. I'd watched them huffing and puffing while they stacked twenty empty boxes.'

'No!'

'Yep. The company insisted that the boxes were full when they were delivered and the theft must have occurred here. But they had those tight plastic bands around them. There's no way they could have been emptied and resealed.'

Peter just shook his head.

'I make sure that our own people unload stuff now,' Saskia continued, 'but thefts still keep happening.' She shrugged. 'You do what you can.'

★

In Munich some years earlier, Peter had attended an annual educational conference where, during the closing plenary session, the organisers had apologised for choosing two European venues in succession (the previous year's conference having been held in Nice) and promised that the next conference would be somewhere more "exotic".

The word "exotic" had at first surprised Peter and then bothered him. The speaker, who was Dutch, seemed to be implying that Munich, with all its riches of history, culture, and architecture (not to mention the best football team in Germany) was rather an unimaginative choice compared to, presumably, somewhere like Buenos Aires or Bali. But, Peter assumed, those who had attended the conference but had flown in from São Paulo, Accra, and Beirut (and he had met such people there) had no doubt found Munich extremely … well, exotic.

'Another example of the Eurocentric thinking that seems to pervade the international school world,' he had complained to a colleague on the train home from Munich.

'Oh don't be silly,' his colleague had answered. 'Where would you rather go for a conference? Manchester or Manila?'

'I think you've just made my point. We're both British. And I lived in Manchester for eight years.'

'I don't think anyone would call Manchester exotic,' she had continued. 'I'd love to go to a conference in Asia – or even the Middle East. Dubai must be extraordinary. Bangkok, Hong Kong ...' she stared out of the window lost in wonder.

'Exotic places, you mean?'

'Mmm.'

'You do know what exotic means? I mean, really?'

'Peter, you're doing it again.'

'What?'

'That lecturing thing. I'm not one of your students.'

Chastened, Peter had bitten his tongue.

He was reminded of this exchange as he drove to where Frank Gillespie, his wife and young son had been housed. *When I was growing up in England*, he reflected, *we had hedgehogs in the garden. Squirrels, urban foxes sometimes. A badger once. Slowworms, moles. And the birds! Goldfinches, blue tits, great tits, dunnocks, magpies. Even blackbirds. If you've never seen them before, don't tell me these aren't amazing birds. I took them for granted but if you've spent your life on the other side of the world, all these things must appear – go on, say it – exotic.*

He turned into the street where the Gillespies lived.

Whereas here in Ndwalowe, we have palm trees and giant cactuses in the garden, mongooses and geckoes. Porcupines, for goodness' sake! And amazing birds – weavers, hornbills, canaries, lovebirds, turacos, mousebirds. All pretty exotic to me but just every-day to the locals.

He drove up to Frank's house and parked.

And, of course, scorpions. He grimaced as he got out of his car.

Frank and his wife, Marta, were already striding towards him, Frank carrying their young child in his arms.

'Thank you for coming, Peter. I didn't know who else to call.'

'Absolutely no problem. Did you get a look at the scorpion?'

'Not a good look. It was yay big and kind of glossy brown. Do you know much about scorpions?'

Marta and Frank sat in the back of Peter's car, cradling their son.

'Not much. They are sometimes seen in school and Glory Mthembu – she's the school nurse, you'll meet her – has told me what to look for. It's to do with how thick the tail is, if I remember correctly. They are the really dangerous ones. Most scorpion stings are painful but rarely life-threatening.'

'For adults, I assume?' answered Marta. 'But Nick is barely six …'

'How is he?' Peter asked as he drove.

'I don't know,' said Frank. 'He's stopped crying. I think he's gone into shock.'

Not knowing what else to say, Peter just muttered, 'It's not far. The clinic.' He was trying to reassure Frank and Marta. But he was also trying to reassure himself.

Nicholas was unconscious by the time they reached the hospital. Abandoning the car just outside the main entrance, Peter sprinted into the building looking for signs for the A&E department. Frank followed, carrying Nicholas, who had started to twitch and drool. Marta, ashen, was muttering something that might have been a prayer. A number of people with injuries of various degrees of seriousness were already in the Emergency Room but the nurse who received new arrivals immediately rushed Frank and his son into a treatment room, shouting loudly for a doctor. Marta made to follow but the nurse blocked her way.

'No, ma'am. Please wait outside.' She said, quite firmly.

Peter had put his arms around Marta and steered her to a bank of chairs. They watched as first one and then a second doctor had hurried into the treatment room. In the waiting area, half a dozen patients sat or stood, some alone and others accompanied. Each obviously needed or was already receiving attention but they too had their eyes on the door of the treatment room.

Marta sat in numbed silence, barely conscious of Peter's arm around her shoulders and the empty words of encouragement he was mouthing.

August

The death of Nicholas Gillespie stunned the whole community.

Few people had any idea who Frank Gillespie and his young family were. Still fewer had met any of them. But as the news quickly spread throughout Ndwalowe, tears were shed, prayers offered, messages of condolence sent, and questions asked.

For some, the most shocking aspect of the whole tragedy was its arbitrariness.

'They'd only been in the country what? Forty-eight hours?'

'I've lived here for a decade. I think I've only seen one or two scorpions in all that time. And I've never heard of anyone being stung.'

'We have dozens of species in Awanza and only, I think, two or three are dangerous. What are the chances?'

And, of course, a reaction that was more widely thought than spoken out loud.

'That could have been my son or daughter.'

Peter sent a letter to all parents and staff. A photo of Nicholas was placed in the school reception, softly illuminated by a single candle. Carola sent Frank and Marta a heartfelt letter on behalf of the board. But most people had no idea what to do. Frank appeared in school a couple of times looking dazed and confused. Those who met him introduced themselves and expressed their profound sorrow. He thanked them with a weak smile. They looked mournful.

The necessary preparations for the new school year went ahead but the usual laughter and jollity was absent.

★

Expatriate teachers return to their international schools in August after what has been a summer holiday for most (and is often referred to as such even by those whose employment is south of the equator) with a variety of emotions. Most have enjoyed several weeks travelling or perhaps visiting friends and family. Those who work in more than averagely challenging conditions (because of the climate or politics or corruption or shortages or whatever) will have tasted home comforts and it may be with a sigh they return to privations and power cuts. Others may enjoy a quality of life and standard of living in their adopted home that they could never aspire to in their country of origin and, their familial duties discharged for another year, will return eagerly to their privileged lifestyles. For some, it will be just another year. For others, there may be unknowns to worry about: teaching an unfamiliar Grade or subject; assuming a new position of responsibility; waiting to see how a new principal or director will work out. But all (one would hope) will be looking forward to getting back in the classroom and seeing both familiar and new faces before them.

Meena Nair, for much of the previous year acting secondary principal but now returning to the office of the IB Diploma coordinator, travelled from Kerala to Awanza unable (and mostly unwilling) to shake off the feeling that her eighth year at the school would most likely be her last. There was sadness but she harboured no grudges, felt no bitterness. Eight years was a good run in any school and the past twelve months had helped her clarify where she wanted her career to go. Moreover, she believed – and others had told her – that her brief tenure as principal had been successful. She had left behind the disappointment of the previous November. Indeed, she may now have felt something close to gratitude. A different future awaited her. Meena spent much of the flight into Ndwalowe mentally composing the letter she would shortly be handing to Peter Corby.

Helen and Larry Roper had spoken little on their flight from Toronto to London. Much had been said – perhaps too much – during an unhappy month spent shuttling between concerned parents and siblings. Each now chose to keep their thoughts to themselves. The flight to Ndwalowe was half-empty and Helen had moved to a vacant row of three seats far from where her husband stared out of the window at the vast continent slowly passing beneath him.

Anna Street had more reason than most to wonder what the future would bring as she endured the long journey from New Zealand to Awanza. She had spent a month with her parents and sister, patiently reassuring them that no, she had not lost weight and yes, everything at school was fine. She gently waved away their occasional suggestions that she seemed distracted, promised them that she would of course tell them if anything was wrong … and went to bed each night chewing her lip, longing for her parents' advice but unwilling to worry them. She had arranged to meet her friend, Ruth George, in Dubai for the final leg of their journeys and she was grateful for a hand to hold as the plane started its descent towards Ndwalowe.

'You okay?' asked Ruth.

'I think so, yeah. Mixed feelings. You know.'

'Mmm.'

'I want to come back. You know I love my job. But …'

'Did you hear from Peter over the vacation?'

'A couple of times. He wanted to know how I was. And he wants to see me as soon as I arrive.'

'Does he have a plan?'

'I'll find out.'

Ruth squeezed Anna's hand.

'To tell the truth, Ruth, I'm angry. This is my school, my life. I've done nothing wrong. Why should I feel all chewed up about coming back because … because of some …?'

'Inadequate jerk?'

'I just wish I knew – for sure – who it is.'

'I thought …'

'I was pretty sure when I told Peter who I thought it was. Since then I've started to wonder if I was being unfair.'

'Anna, someone has been leaving those notes for you. Someone in school. One of your colleagues – our colleagues. You had a suspicion. You told me. You had good reason to give his name to Peter. Let him investigate.'

'Yeah. You're right. I just don't know how I'm going to react when I see … you know … him.'

Ruth gave Anna's hand another squeeze.

★

Strictly speaking, July is the coldest month in Awanza but it was in August when school resumed and he had to leave the house before seven each morning when Peter grumbled about the temperature. He was not alone. As he hurried to his car, he observed with some sympathy mousebirds fluffed up and huddled together in whatever patches of weak sunlight they could find.

Shortly after arriving in Japan, Peter and Sheila had been taken to a dealer of second-hand cars who was known to the school and was considered reliable. The showroom parking lot was extensive but, seemingly, not organised according to any obvious logic. Tiny (and invariably white) pick-ups sat beside large SUVs. Stylish sports cars and boxy utilitarian vans popped up here and there. Family cars, compact and basic, luxurious and high-end, were arranged in ranks, each with a printed sheet attached to a side window that presumably detailed the vehicle's age, specifications, and condition. These were, of course, completely unintelligible to Peter. What he could at least read, if not make sense of, were the two- or three-digit numbers each car displayed in its windscreen.

'She? These numbers are the price, right?'

Sheila was admiring a sleek and completely impractical two-seat Mazda but glanced up at her husband and nodded.

'But …' Peter frowned. 'That doesn't make any sense. Look. This one is 110. That can't be thousands of Yen. That'd be far too little. And obviously it can't be millions …'

Sheila had turned her attention to a more sensible Honda but called over her shoulder, '*Man*. It's 110 *man*.'

'What?'

'A *man* is ten thousand. So that car is 110 *man*. Or one point one million.'

'You're joking.'

'Why?'

'Well, that doesn't make any sense. Why count in multiples of ten thousand?'

Sheila gave him a slightly patronising look. 'Why not? A thousand is just ten hundreds. You don't have a problem with that.'

'No, but…'

'And a hundred is just ten tens. Why not have a number for ten times a thousand?'

Peter couldn't think of an answer. 'We don't do it in English or French or German ...' he mumbled.

'So?'

'So, that Honda you're looking at is ...' he looked at the windscreen, '150. So that's one and a half million?'

'Correct. Not a bad price, I'd say. About what we budgeted.'

'A *man* is ten thousand ...?' Peter was digesting this new and curious piece of information.

'You've never been to India, have you?' Sheila decided there was more that Peter needed to learn.

'No.'

'A *lakh* is a hundred thousand and a *crore* is ten million. That's how they count.'

Peter frowned.

'And again, dear husband, why not?'

Why not indeed? Peter quickly felt rather foolish to have assumed that all cultures would count the same way. And, as Sheila had pointed out, there was no more and no less logic in having a word for ten thousand or ten million as there was for calling ten tens a hundred.

'One, ten, a hundred, a thousand, a *man*, a *lakh*, a million, a *crore* ...' Peter laughed out loud. 'Love it!'

'Doesn't travel broaden the mind?' Sheila said, just a little archly.

A somewhat similar realisation had dawned on Peter as his first year in Awanza had unfolded. He was of course aware that north and south of the equator the seasons were inverted but, in so much as he thought about it at all, he had assumed that there would be four more or less distinct seasons as there had been in Germany and Japan. The longest day would be in December rather than June but, otherwise, he expected winter to segue into spring and so on.

Terms like summer and winter were used in Awanza – at least by those of European extraction. But neither was as Peter had expected and spring and autumn seemed ephemeral at best. A typical July day – the equivalent of January in his previous lives in northern Europe and East Asia – might start quite chilly but by mid-morning Peter would be quite comfortable in shirt sleeves and by lunch time the temperature would be expected to be in the mid- to high-twenties. Still more surprising to Peter was that 'winter' in Awanza was characterised by weeks and weeks of cloudless blue skies.

Such cloudy days as there were during the year were features of the 'summer' months – November to March. Even then, the clouds were usually discrete and puffy and rather wonderful to watch. The endless gloomy days of low, grey, featureless cloud from horizon to horizon that Peter had grown up with were simply unknown in Awanza. Overcast was not a word in anyone's vocabulary.

Temperatures rose and fell as the months passed and the days became longer or shorter. But what really defined the seasons – of which there were certainly not four – was the presence or absence of rainfall. Nor did Ndwalowe's trees and bushes offer many clues. They certainly grew vigorously during the months that were hot and wet but very few shed their leaves during the dry months. In their garden only the frangipani did but it was seldom long before new buds appeared and the trees quickly regained their splendour.

'I thought life here would be the same but different,' Peter had said to Sheila on one occasion. 'But sometimes it's just different.'

'Isn't that why we're here?'

★

Peter considered himself fairly open-minded. How other people chose to live their lives was their business. He was only intolerant when people behaved selfishly or cruelly, inconveniencing or offending others. All of which presented him with something of a dilemma when he reflected on his brief but memorable encounter with Lazarett Snyman at the !Kha Makalani Lodge.

Should he tell someone? (If he was honest, he itched to do so.) But who? And why?

His closest confidante at school was Valli but she barely knew Lazarett. Trixi Villiers was at least a board member but why was it any of her business what Lazarett got up to in his own time? Should he tell Carola as board chair? But, again, why? It seemed improbable that whatever Lazarett was (or was not?) doing at Lake !Kha would in any way reflect on the school or the board. And if he told Carola, what did he expect her to do with that information?

On their first evening at the lodge, Peter and Sheila had arrived for dinner early, Peter none too subtly looking for Lazarett or the mysterious woman. Neither, however, had appeared. Nor were they seen at breakfast the next morning. Affecting what he hoped was an air of only mild curiosity, he had enquired at the reception, explaining that he had seen a friend yesterday and hoped to meet him again today.

The receptionist had made a note of Lazarett's name and checked the guest list. However, no Mr Snyman, Peter was told, was known to the lodge.

'Maybe he was staying at one of the other places and just came here for a drink,' Sheila had suggested.

'I'd be more inclined to think he was staying here but under another name.' Peter wanted to question the receptionist further – *had any of the guests checked out prematurely?* – but told himself that was probably going too far. There was a line between understandable curiosity and invading someone's privacy.

The rest of their stay at Lake !Kha was thoroughly enjoyable but, if Peter was honest, somewhat anticlimactic after the drama of the first afternoon. He spent more time than he should have wondering how Lazarett would conduct himself when they next met. It frustrated Peter (and sometimes frustrated Sheila more) that on holiday and far away from school, he found it hard to switch off. He had learned not to talk about school with Sheila when they were 'on leave' (as the locals had it). But that didn't mean he didn't think about it.

★

Carola was waiting for Peter at a favourite table on the terrace of the Italian-Awanzan Cultural Centre. She smiled encouragingly as he approached.

'Hello, Peter. How are you? Bearing up?'

'I'm fine, thank you. And thank you for suggesting we meet here. I'm not sorry to have an excuse to get out of school for an hour or two. It's all very sombre.'

'I can imagine. How's Frank?'

'Still looking shocked. I don't think he's sleeping much. He's been in a few times to sort out some expenses and make a few arrangements. But it's like he's sleep-walking. How's Marta?'

Carola sighed. 'As you'd expect. We have a counsellor at the embassy and I'm trying to get Marta to meet her.'

'I'm pleased there's a strong German community here for her. And thank you for talking to her.'

'I'm a mother too. I can only imagine …' She shuddered. 'Have they got a date yet?'

'Yes. They are flying the day after tomorrow. Down to Johannesburg and up to Frankfurt. The funeral, I think, is on Monday.'

'Will Frank be back in time for the start of the school year?'

'I very much doubt it. I've told him to take as long as he needs.'

'Don't we have policies on this kind of leave?'

'Of course. Bereavement leave. Compassionate leave. But they all allow more time at the director's discretion and I can't see it would be in anyone's interests to get Frank back before he's ready.'

Carola nodded. 'Can you cover his classes?'

'We'll have to. Though I don't immediately know how.'

'Anyway, you said you had something else we needed to talk about.'

'Yes. A couple of things, actually. You remember last year I told you about the notes someone was leaving for Anna Street?'

Carola scowled. 'Of course. *Abscheulich!* You haven't found out who it is, have you?'

'No, not for sure but at the end of last year Anna told me she had a suspicion. There was nothing I could do over the holiday but now we are all back Valli and I are going to follow this up.'

'Who …'

'No, Carola, if you don't mind. I don't want to name anyone just yet. Not till we're sure. But if we can pin him down, you know there will have to be the strongest consequence.'

'The board will be right behind you. I can assure you of that.'

'Thank you. I'll let you know if and when I find out more. Now, the other thing is my contract.'

'Your contract?'

'Yes. I'm just starting the second year of a two-year contract. It's not too soon to start talking about what happens after that.'

'Really? It's just the first week of August.'

'I'm afraid that's how it works in international schools. It's a cycle. If you – I mean, the board – don't want to give me another contract, or if I don't want one, you need to start looking now for a new director and I need to start looking for a new job. And the sooner, the better.'

Carola looked a bit shocked. 'Why would we not give you another contract?'

Peter shrugged. 'I don't know, Carola. But it's not something either party should take for granted.'

'Do you want another contract?'

'Yes. Absolutely. I'm very happy here. So is Sheila.'

'Then I suppose I need to talk to the board. Hmm. I didn't really expect this but I can see your point.'

'And lastly, Carola, how did it go with Mrs Luhanga? You met her, right?'

'Oh yes. It was all a bit strange. I emphasised that I was meeting her as a board member and she completely agreed. And as a board member, she told me, she felt she shared a responsibility to ensure that the school complied with current legislation.'

'Have you talked to anyone else?'

'Well, as you know, after you sent everyone the letter in June there was a flurry of emails and phone calls but it all seems to have gone quiet. I think they are waiting for Ernesto and me to take the lead.'

'He'll be regretting agreeing to be vice-chair.'

'Oh, not a bit of it. I think he enjoys this kind of thing.'

'So, all in all, not an uneventful start to the school year.'

'I meant to ask. The goal posts?'

Peter shook his head. 'We're never going to see them again. The police blame the security company. The security company blame their employees. I'm demanding that ASS cover the cost of new goals but I'm not optimistic. Although I do have an appointment with the CEO tomorrow. Our big threat is that we change companies. Cancel ASS and switch to Awanza 24/7 or another company. But that carries its own risks.'

'Why?'

'Because once the outgoing guards know they are losing their jobs, their incentive to be vigilant ...'

'Never strong at the best of times.'

'Precisely. Even worse, they have a month or so in which to – maybe – invite a few people in under the cover of darkness. After all, they know better than anyone where our weak spots are. Which doors are sometimes left unlocked and so on.'

'Would they?'

'I'm told it's not uncommon. Apparently, the thing to do is to line up the new company on the quiet and only inform the outgoing company a few minutes before the new guys take over. But, of course, we'd have to pay ASS a month's notice so we end up paying twice. Not a huge amount but still annoying.'

'And with no guarantee that the new company would be any better.'

'Quite. I've heard lots of people complain about various different companies. I have yet to hear anyone say how good theirs is.'

'Should we employ our own guards?'

'No. All the advice I've had is that it just creates still more problems. But we might consider a security supervisor. An ex-policeman with experience and connections. Someone at the American Embassy told me that's what they do.'

'Another expense?'

Peter shrugged. 'Maybe better than forever suffering petty thefts.'

Carola could only nod.

★

A part of the job that Peter found he enjoyed a good deal was the hiring of new staff. Arriving in Ndwalowe, he had inherited other people's choices. Now he had the opportunity to appoint teachers who met criteria that he considered important. It has been said that over a number of years a school comes to take on the personality of the leader. If there is truth in this, it must in part be because said leader hires staff with whom he or she shares beliefs, opinions, attitudes, and values. (Or maybe they just have a similar sense of humour.)

Hiring staff is often more of a lottery than most people would like to admit – certainly in the world of education but probably elsewhere too. At a minimum, applications will be scrutinised, references checked, and interviews conducted. Some employers go further. Peter knew of schools that required teaching applicants to submit a video of them delivering a lesson or two. He had also heard of (but was grateful never to have personally experienced) the administering of psychometric tests and even an occasion when the three finalists for the headship of a leading (and very self-important) international school had been required to sit together for a full afternoon working through complex problem-solving exercises and role play scenarios while the members of the board and an industrial-organisational psychologist observed them.

And yet, in Peter's experience, no matter how painstaking and thorough the process might be, all schools that he knew of sometimes ended up employing staff who had greatly impressed during the hiring process but who then disappointed in reality. Similarly, candidates who had been no one's first choice sometimes turned out to be outstanding. This being the case, Peter took the job of recruiting staff – both teaching and non-teaching – very seriously, but he did not sweat it more than necessary. He had colleagues in other schools who would find and interview a very strong candidate at one job fair but delay making an offer until after the next fair a week later.

'I might find someone even better,' was the belief.

No, you won't, thought Peter. *You can't really know how good anyone is until they have been in the school for a few months or more. And you will never know if the candidate you didn't employ would have been better or worse. Meanwhile, the first candidate may have accepted another job.*

There were, in Peter's opinion, no perfect candidates for any position so, once he identified someone he believed would be a good fit for the school he was inclined to make an offer, get a contract signed, and move on to the next vacancy.

Recruiting for the new school year had not been too challenging. Only four teachers had left, quite a small number for a school of the size of ISN. Ruby Cleveland, a long-serving and much-loved Kindergarten teacher, had retired, Carmen Dharani and Denise Cutting had taken jobs in Brunei and Brazil respectively, and Shaun Naismith had left without a job to go to, following his wife's career as an epidemiologist. All had made their intentions known in good time, their positions were advertised, and virtual interviews conducted. Although Peter had been actively involved in the recruitment process while at Hamamatsu, the ultimate responsibility had not been his. Here in Ndwalowe, it was and he was quietly relieved that four good appointments had been made without much complication.

★

Valli listened to Anna repeat what she had told Peter in June. The younger woman was clearly uncomfortable and Valli could only

45

sympathise. Peter observed the conversation but did not speak, preferring that Valli heard Anna's story in her own words. Anna paused more than once to sip from a glass of water. She coughed nervously as she talked. Her manner was almost apologetic.

Valli scribbled a few more notes. 'And the second time?'

Anna coughed again. 'It was just getting dark. I was late getting home because I'd stayed behind after netball practice to finish some reports. He was standing under the big tree in the middle of The Warren...'

'Not in the shadow of the container?'

'Not this time, no. He saw me at the same time as I saw him. He turned away. He looked ... guilty.'

'Did you speak?'

'Yes. We'd seen each other. I could hardly ignore him. I called *hi* or something. He replied and then, without me asking him, he said he was there to meet someone. But he seemed really nervous.'

'He didn't say who?'

'No. And, to be honest, I didn't want to stay and talk. As soon as I got inside my apartment I peeked out through the curtains. He'd gone.'

'You two didn't talk about it again?'

'No. I think he was avoiding me. I was certainly avoiding him.'

'Anything else?'

'No. But the more I thought about it, the creepier it seemed. That's when I told Peter.'

'On the last day of term?'

'Mmm.'

Valli looked at Peter.

'Anna,' Peter began, 'you know we take this very seriously. You know that I'm determined to find out who it is. And stop them. So, thank you. This cannot be easy for you.'

'Yes, Anna, thank you. You've been brave and I'm afraid you will have to go on being brave for a bit longer.' Valli lay her hand on Anna's arm.

'But now we have something to go on.' Peter stood up. The two women did the same. 'I need hardly tell you not to discuss this with anyone.'

Anna nodded.

'But we are going to have to have a talk with him. I don't know what his schedule is but it will be tomorrow for sure.'

'Thank you, Peter. Thank you, Valli.'

Valli gave Anna a tight hug. 'Let's hope this will all be over soon.'

Feeling tears coming, Anna thanked them both again and hurried out of the room.

As the door closed, Peter turned to Valli. 'Well, then. Let's see what Mr Simon Swales has to say for himself.'

✱

If Peter had found that he enjoyed interviewing and recruiting teachers, he took no less pleasure and pride in welcoming them to what was often an unfamiliar and, for some, slightly intimidating country. With either Valli or Mick as appropriate, he collected each of them from the airport, drove them to their accommodation where they were met by Julia, and, depending on their time of arrival, took them out for dinner that same day or no later than the following day. He wanted them to feel welcome and safe. And, since all the interviews had been conducted virtually, he was impatient to meet his new colleagues in person at last.

The new school year started for students in the middle of August. Returning teachers were required to be in school a week earlier and flights were arranged for new teachers to have them in Awanza no later than the first of the month and, ideally, a few days earlier to give them time to register with the Ministry of Home Affairs, open bank accounts, perhaps start the process of buying a car, and generally settle in.

It therefore irked Peter when one of the new hires seemed unable or unwilling to commit to a flight into Awanza. Unfortunately, it no longer surprised him.

'He now says that it's not yet clear when he'll be leaving Korea,' Julia had reported to Peter in late May, 'and he'll need at least four weeks in the US to attend to some matters before he can fly here.'

'The others are all booked?'

'Yes. Frank Gillespie and family and Maeve Dinckles are coming on the same flight on the twenty-eighth of July. Terita Gonzáles arrives on the thirtieth.'

'Then why on earth can't Chuck Collins sort himself out and be here at the same time? This is frustrating. Look, I'll write to him myself.' He cursed under his breath. 'Again.'

The references Peter had received on behalf of Chuck Collins many weeks earlier were fulsome in their praise, so much so that they almost put Peter off.

No, Peter had scowled as he scanned the familiar summary sheet used by a leading recruitment agency, *he cannot be in the top two percent in every one of thirty descriptors*. And how could someone write about the *great privilege* it had been to work with *an outstanding educator of vast experience* when Chuck was only in his second overseas school and was still only twenty-nine?

On the other hand, even the more measured recommendations clearly described a teacher who knew his stuff and seemed popular with both students and peers. Plus, he was single and would be a fairly inexpensive appointment. Moreover, Peter had to admit that he had been quite impressed when he had conducted a virtual interview with Chuck and then Larry and Meena, talking with him a few days after Peter, reported that they thought he'd be a good addition to the Maths department.

'Will he fit in?' Peter had asked. 'He isn't too … Tigger-ish?'

Meena had laughed. 'A bit. But maybe it won't hurt to have some boyish energy about the place.'

So, Peter's slight reservations notwithstanding, Chuck Collins had been offered the position. His reply had been immediate and extremely positive. He thanked Peter, accepted the offer, and assured him that he was hugely looking forward to coming to Awanza. He said how much he had enjoyed talking to Larry and how helpful he had been. He gushed about all the good things he had heard about Peter himself (which Peter found fairly improbable) and reported that all of his friends were sure he'd love living and working in Africa.

As was normal, Peter had then passed the file on to Julia to start arranging for a visa, discussing housing options, and the like. Larry and Meena wrote a few times to confirm Chuck's teaching load and fill him in on what his Grade Twelve diploma class had completed and what remained to be done. Duke Etheridge had introduced himself, pleased that Chuck had indicated that he would love to coach basketball.

Chuck, however, then went quiet.

Julia had been the first to bring her concerns to Peter.

'I sent him the contract three weeks ago.'

'You still don't have it back?'

'After my second reminder, he wrote and apologised. He said it had slipped his mind and he would courier it to me immediately. That was eight days ago.'

'*Slipped his mind*? How can signing a contract for a new job slip someone's mind?'

Larry and Duke also confirmed that their messages had gone unanswered. So, with a slightly sinking feeling, Peter wrote to Chuck requesting, and none too subtly, a virtual conversation in the very near future.

At least he got an almost immediate reply.

Yo, Peter!

Great to hear from you. I hope everything's alright with you.

It's been pretty intense here too. But I guess you know all about busy schools! LOL

I'll get the contract off to Julia this afternoon. Sorry. Just been hectic here.

And yeah, let's talk. That would be great. I'm taking a field trip to Jeju tomorrow – leaving early – but I'll be back at the weekend. Can we hook up then?

Best Chuck

Peter wasn't sure what irritated him more. The "Yo, Peter!" was a pretty bad start but nothing in Chuck's email pleased him. He had been planning to give his new recruit an ultimatum and was already considering withdrawing the job offer. He had written back to Chuck immediately, asking if a quick conversation might be possible there and then but was unsurprised not to receive a reply. He had then tried phoning Korea but his call went unanswered.

In frustration, he had fired off a quick email to the head of Chuck's school. The reply acknowledged that he could sometimes be a bit "random" (whatever that meant) but that he was fundamentally a pretty sound teacher and Peter shouldn't worry.

In any case, quite to Peter's surprise (and not a little to his annoyance), the contract was indeed delivered barely forty-eight hours later and long before Peter had had a chance to talk to Chuck. Withdrawing the offer was no longer an option – a contract is a contract – so Peter had little choice but to hope for the best.

Slowly, painfully, and only extracted after a number of increasingly blunt emails from Peter, Chuck's documents were received, messages from Meena and Duke acknowledged, and preparations for his arrival initiated. His emails included airy apologies and sometimes plausible excuses and he continued to express his eager anticipation of the new adventure ahead of him. Peter did manage to have one Skype conversation with Chuck during which he had tried to impress upon the younger man his definition of professionalism and the expectations and standards of ISN. Chuck had nodded vigorously. He couldn't agree more and that was why he was so excited to be joining Peter and his team. In all communications he was unfailingly upbeat. He said all the right things and, Peter had to concede, appeared to mean it.

So, barely two weeks before the school year was due to end in June, Peter was more than exasperated but no longer surprised to find himself negotiating with Chuck over the latter's arrival in Awanza.

The school year in Korea finishes later than yours, Peter had been told, *and, anyway, I have to stay for the wedding of a close friend in late June.* Moreover, flights back to the US, apparently, were ridiculously expensive in the first week of July but much cheaper in the second. *And it's my grandfather's eightieth on July 24th and after that my mother is going in for surgery.* Peter had also been informed (though, he thought, suspiciously late in the day) that Chuck's passport expired in September and he would need to get a new one as a minimum of six months' validity was required for an Awanzan employment visa. Peter at least knew this to be true but he could not understand why Chuck had not applied for a new passport while still in Korea.

As politely and sympathetically as he could, Peter had acknowledged all of the above but also pointed out Chuck's obligations and responsibilities regarding the new job he had accepted. But, much as he tried to pin him down, Peter in the end had to accept an arrival date almost a week into August and just prior to the staff orientation week.

'I have half a mind to call it unpaid leave,' he had complained to Valli, 'but that's not a great way to start our working relationship. He'd better be worth it, after all this. He hasn't even bloody arrived and he's our highest maintenance teacher.'

Valli could think of a few of the existing staff to whom she might give that award but she said nothing.

✴

Peter met his guest at the door of his office. 'Simon, thank you for coming. Please take a seat.'

Simon Swales noted two other people present, already seated. 'What's this about, Peter?'

'Simon, I need to ask you a few questions and it's important that there's no confusion afterwards about what is said. So I've asked Julia as HR Manager and Odetta as Chair of the Staff Association to be here as witnesses. They're not here to take sides or even join the conversation. But they will later be able to confirm what was and wasn't said.'

Simon frowned.

'It's actually for your own protection as much as anything,' Peter continued. Simon looked unconvinced.

'Simon, let me come straight to the point. You recall the meeting of all staff that I addressed back in February?'

Simon thought for a moment. 'About Anna?'

'Yes.'

'You think I had anything to do with that?'

'I don't think anything at the moment but I do need to clarify a few things.'

'What things?'

'Simon, Anna isn't making any accusations – no one is – but she says that she surprised you a couple of times in The Warren. On both occasions it was her impression that you were – I think she used the word 'loitering' – and that you appeared to be watching her apartment.'

'Loitering?'

'You know what she has been going through. She certainly said that you being there seemed strange. And it made her uncomfortable.'

Simon said nothing but was visibly flushed. Julia and Odetta were making notes.

'Simon, you don't live in The Warren. I just need to ask you what you were doing there. The first time was in late May. Anna thinks it was a

51

Tuesday, early evening. She was taking a bag of rubbish to the bins and saw you standing in the shadow of the container.'

Again Simon said nothing.

'I assume you have friends there. Were you visiting someone?'

'Not exactly. I was … I had borrowed something from Pam Somerscale and I was returning it. Well, I was trying to but she wasn't in. So I was waiting.'

'What, may I ask, what did you borrow?'

'A wok.'

'A wok?'

'I was cooking dinner for a few friends and I needed a wok. Pam said I could borrow hers. I was returning it.'

'But she wasn't in?'

'No.'

'Did you call her?'

'Peter, is this really …?'

'Simon, I'm just trying to get the whole picture. Did you call Pam?'

'She didn't pick up.'

'So you were just waiting?'

Simon said nothing.

'Simon, every year we have to allocate housing to the staff. I know who lives in The Warren and I know where. Pam's apartment is number one. She's right at the entrance. That's nowhere near the container.'

Again, a silence. Julia stared at Simon. Odetta stared at the floor.

'So, how long did you wait?'

'I don't remember.'

'Simon, please understand I'm going to have to ask Pam about this.'

'I gave it to her the next day.'

'What?'

'The wok. I gave it to her in school the next day.'

'All right. As I say, I will confirm this with Pam.'

Simon glared at him.

'The second time Anna saw you there was a couple of weeks later. Again, it was getting dark. She says you were standing under the big tree.'

Simon frowned.

'Do you remember being there?'

'Yes. I was waiting for someone.'

'May I ask who?'

'Peter, is my private life anyone else's business?'

'No, of course not.'

'Because this is feeling like an invasion of my privacy. I can't go and visit a friend without being accused of ... of ... harassment or being a peeping tom or something?'

'No one is accusing you of anything.'

'Well, it feels like it.' Simon's face was now red and his voice was breaking.

'Please just tell me who you were visiting, Simon. That's all I'm asking.'

Simon was chewing his lip and breathing heavily. 'Gordon. I was there to see Gordon Sipple. He and I are ... friends.'

'Underneath the tree?'

'He was running late. He told me to wait.'

'When did he arrive?'

'I don't know. After I spoke to Anna I ... I could see she was uncomfortable. I decided not to hang around. So I drove home.'

'And Gordon?'

'I called him. We met somewhere else.'

Peter tried to exchange a look with Julia but she was scribbling in her notes.

'Simon, this is a question, not an accusation. But I'm going to ask you straight. Is it you that has been leaving these notes for Anna?'

Simon's eyes flared and he half rose out of his seat. 'No.'

'Do you know anything about ...?'

'No, Peter. I didn't give her those notes and I know nothing about it. Can I go now?'

'I'm sorry if this has been uncomfortable but you must see that I have to ask these questions. I want to do this correctly. I'm going to ask Julia and Odetta to write up a strictly factual account of this meeting and I'll give you a copy. If there's anything you disagree with, please tell me and ...'

'I've had enough! I'm out of here!' Simon stood, trembling slightly, and pulled open the office door. He slammed it loudly behind him.

★

Helen Roper watched her husband pour himself another glass of wine. 'Don't you think you've had enough?'

Larry gave her a look that was without warmth. 'Not something you'll have to worry about for much longer.'

Helen slowly shook her head. 'Ten thirty tomorrow?'

'Yes. Chiamaka made the appointment.'

'What do you think Peter will say?'

'I don't know. We'll find out. He won't be happy.'

They sat in silence. Helen pushed the remains of her dinner away and lit a cigarette. Larry nursed his wine glass. His own plate of food was untouched.

'So Chuck has arrived at last?' In truth, Helen had very little interest in Chuck Collins but she couldn't bear the silence.

'Yes, Peter and Mick collected him yesterday. I showed him around today.'

'And?'

'And what?'

'How did you find him?'

'A bit intense. It was as if he was trying too hard. But I don't know. Just first impressions.'

There was another silence.

★

The news that Mrs Luhanga would, regrettably, be unable to attend the August board meeting was greeted with both relief and frustration.

'What is this damned woman playing at?' Ernesto Mayor had exclaimed when Carola had phoned him with the news.

On the other hand, it was widely agreed, her absence meant that discussion of her letter would not be as awkward as it might have been.

Carola opened the meeting with the observation that the International School of Ndwalowe was starting its second year of operation with rising enrolment and an improving financial situation and that the members of the board should take pride in what had been achieved.

'I think an expression of thanks is also due to the director and his team.' Ernesto, sitting next to Peter, patted him on the shoulder.

'Oh, of course,' agreed Carola. 'I mean, we all have a lot to feel positive about.'

Lazarett Snyman snorted a trifle theatrically.

'You don't think so, Lazarett?' asked Grant Guthrie.

'What I think is that the director owes the board a full explanation as to why the ATE Act has not been implemented. This puts the school in a very difficult position.'

'Lazarett,' Carola's voice was measured but firm, 'it is on the agenda, as you know, but we have a few other items to address first. Has everyone had a chance to read the minutes of the June meeting?'

Whether they went well or badly, Peter tended to leave board meetings quite exhausted. They started at six in the evening and were seldom over much before nine. Very occasionally he might go home for an hour or two before a board meeting, but usually he just stayed, working in his office. It wasn't just the fourteen-hour day that left him drained but the fact that there were hardly ever times in board meetings when he could switch off. Individual board members might take a lot or sometimes rather little interest in different items and could – and did – drift away for spells while they discreetly checked their phone or emails. But every item on the agenda demanded the school head's attention and concentration. Very often each item began with Peter making a brief report and then taking questions. At other times, he had to be alert to jump in and correct a misapprehension or attempt to steer a conversation away from dangerous waters. And, of course, it is quite properly the job of the board to hold the head accountable and ask sometimes searching questions.

He was least able to start with good news. He expanded on the email he had sent all board members when the IB Diploma results were published in early July.

'Both our pass rate and average score were well above the worldwide averages. One student missed the maximum possible score by just one point and, so far, about two-thirds of our graduating students have been accepted by their first or second choice universities. It certainly looks like the turmoil of last year had no obvious impact on our academic results.'

'Why isn't the pass rate one hundred per cent?' Catherine Mulbarton was studying the spreadsheet Peter had circulated.

'Well, it is sometimes. I mean, the old school achieved it now and again and I'm sure we will too. But I always worry when every student passes.'

Catherine raised her eyebrows. 'Really?' Other board members looked puzzled too.

'I think a hundred per cent pass rate is the least we should expect,' said Lazarett quite firmly.

Peter wanted to point out the absurdity of that statement but sensibly chose not to.

'We need to remember that we are not a selective school,' he explained. 'We are inclusive. We accept students who are academically very strong and others who … are, um, less academic. Most students in Grade Twelve take the full diploma but some only take certain subjects rather than the whole package.'

'How is that decided?' asked Grant Guthrie.

'The teachers monitor students throughout the two years. Sometimes they move from a higher level course to a standard level – or the other way around. We liaise with the parents. And, of course, we involve the students themselves in the conversation. The goal is always to find the right place for each child. But eventually the decision has to be taken whether a student will attempt the full diploma or not. And that's why a hundred per cent pass rate always raises questions.'

'I still don't understand.'

'Okay. Every year there are kids on the borderline. They might just make it over the line. Or they might just fail by a point or two. But I believe they ought to be given the chance. In a year when we get a hundred per cent, I worry that we may have been too cautious, too conservative.'

'But isn't it better for the school to be able to boast about a hundred per cent pass rate?'

'Violet, I see your point, of course, and we could certainly only enter students who are more or less guaranteed to pass – or even get high scores. I know schools that do exactly that. Every year they can point to a high average score and a hundred per cent pass rate. But we are not that kind of school.'

'You're saying we're not a school that strives for academic success?'

Peter had to bite his tongue. 'No, Lazarett,' he said slowly, 'we of course strive for academic success. But it's a question of how you measure it. The weak student who busts a gut for two years and scrapes through the diploma with twenty-five points is as much a success story – maybe more – than the bright kid who cruises easily to thirty-five. It's a question of getting every child to be as successful as they can rather than manipulating our results for marketing purposes.'

Lazarett was going to reply but Carola hurriedly thanked Peter for his report and announced that it was time to move on to the next item.

Lazarett smirked. Peter simmered.

There was a brief discussion about the theft of the football goals with Peter reporting that his meeting with the CEO of Awanza Security Services had not been productive. Student numbers were reviewed and the need to introduce waiting lists in certain grades agreed. Peter was asked for an update on Frank Gillespie's situation. But the agenda item everyone was waiting for was Mrs Luhanga's letter.

'You have all received copies of the letter from the Assistant Deputy Executive Director at the Ministry of Education,' Carola began.

'You mean from Mrs Luhanga,' Ernesto spoke irritably.

'I think it is important that we keep her two roles separate,' said Carola.

'Agreed,' muttered two or three others. Ernesto looked annoyed.

'As you know, the director and I have been liaising with the school lawyer. On our behalf, he has written to the Ministry of Education. Peter?'

'Thank you, Carola. Our lawyer, Mr Burger, wrote to Mrs Luhanga – to the Assistant Deputy Executive Director – in reply to her letter making a number of points. One is that when the Act was announced, my predecessor, John Conway, wrote to the ministry asking for clarification. It seems he wrote twice but did not receive a reply. The ministry are now saying that they did reply. However, they are unable to provide copies of these letters and we have no record of them in my office.'

'Typical!' Ernesto really seemed to be angry.

'Perhaps interestingly, it is not Mrs – the Assistant Deputy Executive Director who has been corresponding with our lawyer but someone else – someone from the Permanent Secretary's office. We have requested a meeting with this person. We are awaiting a reply.'

'And our argument will be?' Clyde Arthurs asked.

'Firstly, that we showed willingness to comply when John Conway wrote to the ministry …'

'Twice!'

'Yes, thank you, Ernesto. Twice. But the school did not receive replies. Secondly, that this is a new school that has existed for barely a year so the Act does not apply to us.'

'Is that going to wash?'

Peter shrugged. 'Mr Burger seems to think we have a reasonable case. At the very least, it can muddy the waters.'

'It also works to our advantage that the ministry waited until June of this year to enquire about the application of the ATE Act,' added Carola.

'And we think we can get some mileage out of the fact that Mrs Luhanga sat on the board all last year but never once raised the subject of the Access to Education Act.'

'The argument being what?' asked Grant. 'That the board – in fact board members – have a responsibility – and obligation – to ensure that the school is compliant?'

'Nonsense!' Lazarett leaned forward across the table, fixing Peter with an angry glare. 'It is the director's responsibility to ensure that the school is compliant. That is a responsibility we devolve to him. And he failed to do it.'

'Did we? Did we devolve it to the director? I don't recall the subject ever being on the agenda.'

'That's a fair point, Ernesto,' Grant looked around the room as he spoke. 'It's not as if none of us knew about the ATE Act. Did we ever ask for an update? I don't remember one.'

'So we don't expect the director to do anything unless we expressly instruct him to?'

'I was rather under the impression, Lazarett, that you quite favoured the idea of the director doing as instructed rather than exercising his own judgement.'

'Ernesto, Lazarett, everyone. I think we were all aware of the ATE Act but ... well, it's not as if we had no other issues to address. And I do think we must all accept a degree of collective responsibility.'

'Well, I don't. I don't, Madam Chairman. And I think it's not right of you to expect us to.'

'Lazarett—'

'I do. I accept some responsibility,' Clyde spoke to Lazarett but looked at all of his colleagues around the table. 'I can't speak for others but, if I'm honest, I was waiting for Mrs Luhanga to make the first move. It's why she's on the board, after all. If she wasn't going to bring it up ... Well, as Carola says. We had plenty of other things to worry about.'

Grant and Ernesto muttered their agreement. Catherine scowled. Violet just looked miserable.

'I think what matters now,' said Trixi, 'is not how we got here but what we do now.'

Carola looked around the room. 'Well? Anyone?'

'You know what I think,' said Lazarett sourly.

'I don't honestly see how trying to establish who – if anyone – is to blame will really help us. But we have to have a plan going forward.'

'Thank you, Clyde. Anyone else?'

'Well, we do have a plan – of sorts, don't we? Peter and the school lawyer are working on it. I think we just need to wait and see how that plays out.'

'I agree with Grant,' said Ernesto. 'It is what it is. I don't think there's much more to be said.' He flashed a slightly challenging look at Lazarett.

'Then I propose we bring this item to a close.' Carola looked at her watch. 'It's a little after nine. If there is no other business …'

'I have an AOB,' said Lazarett.

'Oh?'

'As you know, I have no children of my own here but several of the people I work with – my, um, associates – have their children in the school.'

Peter wondered where this was going.

'One of them was flying into the country from London earlier this month. He was flying business class, of course …'

Of course, thought Peter.

'… and he was surprised to see in the same cabin his daughter's teacher.'

A couple of people frowned. 'What …?'

'In business class. Do we pay our teachers to fly in business class, Mr Corby?'

'No. Of course we don't. We fly overseas teachers home once a year but always in economy class. But I think I know where this is coming from. Do you remember the name of the teacher?'

Lazarett did not.

'Or which grade your friend's daughter is in? No? Well, my guess is that we're talking about Elsa Mattsson who teaches Grade One. I was in the staffroom the day after she arrived and her friends were teasing her about it. She has no idea why but she was upgraded on her flight from London. It made quite an impression. She'd never flown business class before. Doubts if she ever will again.'

'Sounds like she was just lucky,' said Grant gathering up his papers. 'Is that it?'

But Lazarett wasn't finished. 'Do we think that's right? Is it acceptable?'

'*Acceptable*?'

'I don't think she should have accepted the upgrade.'

'What?'

'Parents don't want to see teachers in the business class cabin.'

'Trixi is usually pretty calm, pretty controlled,' Peter was saying to Sheila over the inevitable bottle of wine once he got home. 'But I honestly thought she was going to lose it with Lazarett. You should have seen her face.'

'I don't blame her. What did she say?'

'She never got the chance. Lazarett was pounced on. Ernesto and Carola. Clyde and Grant. Even Catherine Mulbarton. It had been a pretty tense meeting and I think a couple of people snapped. Lazarett was suddenly very quiet. He made a real fool of himself.'

'You'll miss these board meetings when you retire,' Sheila smiled.

'Hah! If there's one thing I won't miss …'

'You look exhausted. Go in late tomorrow.'

Peter took a deep breath (and another mouthful of wine). 'Ah, no. No, that isn't an option. But thanks.'

'I can assure you, I won't miss these board meetings either.' Sheila pushed the cork into the neck of the wine bottle quite firmly. 'Not one little bit.'

★

Trixi had been sure to arrive in good time. She leaned on the railing and waited uncomfortably as the doors slid open and closed, admitting arriving passengers who were often greeted with broad smiles, hugs and even tears. She wasn't at all sure how she would greet Frank when he appeared. They of course barely knew each other. They had only met for the first time after the death of Nicholas. Frank had been stoic; Trixi tongue-tied.

She checked her phone again. She had given him her number, hadn't she? She couldn't remember. A voice called out to her by name and her heart leapt. But when she looked up it was to see a parent from school waving at her. She smiled weakly and waved back. Seldom could Trixi or any ISN teacher go anywhere in Ndwalowe without being recognised. Sometimes it was quite flattering. Other times it was a pain.

'Trixi?'

Frank was standing before her carrying only an overnight bag.

'Frank!'

Spontaneously, she threw her arms around his neck. He hugged her back. That they were still essentially strangers suddenly mattered not at all. Everything that needed to be said was expressed in their embrace.

They slowly released each other and exchanged smiles that were no longer self-conscious.

'Welcome back?' Trixi's words were more a question than a greeting.

'Yeah, well ... To be honest, I was about ready to come back. You have to, you know, move on.'

They walked out of the arrival's hall towards the short-term car park.

'How's Marta?'

Frank frowned. 'It's hit her pretty bad. It's going to be a while till ...'

'Yeah. Sorry.'

'In fact ... She's not coming back. At least, not for a while. She's with her parents in Frankfurt. I don't think she can face seeing ...' He waved his hands vaguely at nothing in particular. 'This is where ... You know.'

'Of course. I understand. Everyone will. But you? You're okay coming back?'

'Yeah. I need to get back in the classroom doing the job I love.'

'Move on?'

'Yeah.'

Trixi gave him an encouraging smile. 'You know we'll be here for you.'

★

'A wok?' Valli frowned.

'I checked with Pam. She confirmed that he borrowed it and returned it. But she wasn't aware he tried to bring it to The Warren.'

'She must have wondered why you were asking.'

'She did. It was all rather awkward. Obviously, I couldn't tell her what it was all about. I asked her not to mention it to anyone. She just looked confused.'

'And the second time? Simon was meeting Gordon Sipple?'

'That's what he said. Are they friends?'

Valli shrugged. 'I have no idea. I don't know either of them well.'

'Gordon, of course, is gay. Are we to conclude …?'

'Simon?' Again, Valli shrugged. 'If so, would he be stalking Anna?'

'But it might explain why he seemed nervous when Anna found him.'

'Should we ask Gordon?'

'No. We have no business preying into peoples' lives. Trying to protect Anna can't be at the expense of other peoples' privacy.'

'No, you're right. Sorry. So, where does that leave us?'

Peter sighed. 'Well, I can see why Anna thought Simon's behaviour was suspicious but it's all pretty circumstantial. I don't think we can take this much further.'

'Anna will be disappointed.'

'And Simon will be feeling pretty aggrieved. God, what a mess.'

'So, back to square one?'

Peter nodded slowly. 'Back to square one …'

'What did Helen and Larry want?'

'Oh, I didn't tell you, did I? It's actually very sad. They are separating.'

'What?'

'Apparently, things haven't been too good. They agreed they would try to straighten everything out over the holiday but …'

'I had no idea.'

'I think they kept it pretty quiet. But they seemed to have their minds made up this morning.'

'That is sad. They're both good people.'

'It happens to good people too.'

'At least there are no children involved. Is one of them going to leave?'

'No, no. And I'm grateful for that. No, they both want to stay but they can't – or don't want to – live together. They are asking for separate flats.'

'We don't have any empty apartments, do we?'

'No. But I can see their point. One of them has to move out.'

'But they stay working in the same school? Not sure I could do that.'

Peter made a face. 'Me neither. But they are both excellent teachers. I'd hate to lose either of them. We'll do what we can to make this work for them.'

'Agreed. Now Frank's back we are fully staffed again. The last thing we need is a sudden vacancy.'

'Ugh. Don't even think about it.'

✶

The early morning SMS Peter received from Chuck Collins came out of the blue and yet somehow did not surprise.

Peter, I'm just boarding the flight to Joburg. I'm leaving. This isn't right for me. I think I've made a mistake. Best, Chuck.

Best'? thought Peter. *Best? Seriously?*

✶

September

In a given school community, will there be more students or parents? It was a question Peter had never considered until in Hamamatsu there had been a need to alter the school's Act of Endowment and a minimum percentage of the parents needed to cast votes.

'How many parents do we have?' turned out to be a surprisingly hard question to answer. The students could be counted more or less accurately but no one seemed to have any idea how many parents there were.

Guesses were made. 'It'll be about the same, won't it? Average family, two kids, and so on.'

'Only if both children attend this school. And what about single parents?'

In the end, and only after the admissions office had laboriously trawled through every student file and compiled an intimidatingly large Excel spreadsheet, was an answer (if not the answer) arrived at. In a school of a shade over five hundred children, there appeared to be seven hundred and three parents.

It also revealed the complexity of twenty-first century relationships. A boy in Grade Eight was in the same class as his uncle. One father had three children in the school in different grades and each with a different mother.

When Peter had related this story to Mick and Valli, they had both laughed. 'Oh, I think my old school can rival that,' chuckled Mick and explained to Peter about the girl in Grade Eleven whose semester reports were sent not to her parents but her husband.

At ISN, Peter had no intention of requiring Godliver Habulenzi to work through more than six hundred files but, after his experience in Hamamatsu, he surmised that there must be at least eight hundred parents associated with his new school.

So why then, he wondered, did the PTA struggle to scare up even two dozen parents for their monthly meetings?

Most international schools have a parent-teacher association or something similar. Their value to the school waxes and wanes according to who is in charge and how they see the PTA's role. At their best, they can be invaluable. Funds are raised for nice-to-have extras or, discreetly, to subsidise students who might otherwise miss out on excursions and other opportunities. Tea and coffee or, alternatively, beer and wine will be served at appropriate events. New families will be welcomed and perhaps provided with a PTA-produced guide to living in this unfamiliar city. The PTA calendar may include recognition of cultural celebrations from Diwali to Valentine's Day, the Chinese New Year to Thanksgiving. And, as often as not, it will be the PTA that sells school-branded merchandise from baseball caps and T-shirts to water bottles and tote bags.

Sometimes, however, PTAs go bad.

Upon receiving Chuck's SMS from the airport, Peter had called Valli and Mick to inform them. Scheduled meetings were abruptly cancelled, Mick phoned around to arrange alternative teachers for Chuck's classes, and before the school day had officially started they had assembled in Peter's office.

'You're sure he's gone? I mean, this isn't some kind of hoax?'

'Valli, he'd better be gone. If this is a hoax …'

'You called him?'

'As soon as I read the SMS. But he must have turned his phone off immediately.' Peter looked at his watch. 'The flight will be halfway to Johannesburg by now. I'm going to email him. He has to give some sort of explanation.'

'Meanwhile,' said Mick, 'we're now a teacher down. And DP maths isn't going to be an easy position to fill at short notice.'

'Well, let's see what the agencies have on their books. Mick, will you do that?'

'Sure.'

'And this is not public knowledge yet. I don't think we should say anything outside this room until we are absolutely sure. What did you tell the teachers who are covering Chuck's classes?'

'Just that he wouldn't be in today.'

'Good.'

'Well,' said Valli, 'I suppose it solves one problem. If Chuck's apartment is now available.'

'What's that?' asked Mick.

'Oh, I haven't even told you yet, have I? Larry and Helen Roper came to see me yesterday. They are separating. Apparently, this has been coming for a while, though I had no idea …'

'And one of them is moving out so we have to find another apartment,' added Valli.

'Why?' Mick's face was expressionless. 'Why do we have to find them another flat?'

'What do you mean? Because it's in their contract. The school provides accommodation.'

'And we are. We are providing accommodation. They came here as a couple, didn't they? And the school provides them with a flat. One of the nicer ones, in fact.'

'But they don't want to live together any more. One of them – Larry or Helen – will move out.'

'I understand that. I get it. But why is that the school's problem?'

Peter was at a loss. 'What are you saying?'

'I'm saying that everyone who works here has a contract. They expect the school to stick to the contract. So should they. It's not in the budget, is it? Two apartments rather than one. It'll be an unbudgeted cost. And does one of them get to stay in a flat that is really meant for a couple? That's not fair.'

Peter was about to reply but was interrupted by a hesitant knock on the office door.

'Yes?'

Only opening the door a quarter, Chiamaka looked in. 'Peter, I'm sorry to interrupt but Tony Bembel is here. He says it's urgent.'

Peter swore under his breath. 'No, we're busy. Tell him …'

'He says it's about Chuck Collins.'

Mick flashed a look at Valli. Valli flashed the same look at Peter.

'Oh. Okay, send him in.'

Tony entered. Chiamaka closed the door behind him. Peter did not invite his guest to take a seat.

'Tony, good morning. What's this about?'

'I'm not really sure. I have the flat next to Chuck. When I left this morning I found this taped to my door.' He handed Peter an envelope. Peter recognised Chuck's handwriting.

Tony! I'm leaving. Here are the keys to my apartment. Please give them to Peter.

Great to know ya, dude!

Chuck.

Dude? Again Peter found himself as exasperated by Chuck's choice of language as his actions. With an angry sigh, he read out loud the message on the envelope and tossed it to Mick.

'No hoax, then?' offered Mick, tearing open the envelope and removing a small bunch of keys.

'It would seem not.'

Tony coughed awkwardly.

'Oh, Tony. Thanks. Look, please don't say anything to anyone till we've … Till we know for sure. You haven't mentioned this …'

'No. No one.'

'Good. Thanks. Valli, you'd better get on. Mick, let's you and me go and take a look at Chuck's flat.'

Without waiting for a reply, Peter snatched up his car keys and strode out of his office.

★

Anna had received Peter's news about his conversation with Simon Swales with the disappointment that had been expected but also what might have been relief. Much as she wanted to put the whole ugly experience behind her, the thought of at last unmasking her stalker held its own fears. She had thanked Peter and nodded slowly when he tried to assure her that the investigation was far from over.

They had shared a slightly self-conscious hug and then Peter had left her sitting in her classroom. She waited and then locked the door behind him.

★

Julia Ryweyemamu was waiting for Peter and Mick outside Chuck's apartment. She said nothing but her expression asked the question.

'It looks like Chuck has gone,' offered Peter. 'For good. He's returned his keys.' He turned to Mick. 'Okay. Let's see.'

Mick led the way with Julia and Peter following.

'Good grief.'

The scene was chaotic. Boxes of books spilled out onto the floor. Clothes were strewn around, hanging from chair-backs and heaped loosely in corners. Several empty beer bottles lay on the table and in the kitchen. Half a crate of still-full bottles sat in the middle of the living room and an open bottle of vodka stood beside the bed. A suitcase and a pull-along looked as if they had never been fully unpacked in the short time Chuck had occupied the flat. Pizza boxes and KFC wrappers littered the kitchen floor. Unwashed crockery filled the sink and broken glass crunched under their feet.

'Someone left in a hurry.' Mick somewhat disdainfully lifted a T-shirt that was draped over the TV and cautiously sniffed it.

'He has a fine collection of boots,' called Peter from the bedroom.

'*Had*. Had a fine collection. He won't be seeing them again.'

'What happened?' asked Julia, clearly shocked.

'Yeah, well, that's the question, isn't it? What size are those boots, Peter. Would they fit me?'

Peter gave his principal a disapproving look. 'Did you bring the camera, Julia?'

'Yes.'

'Thank you. Then please record all this. We'll leave you the key. Please lock up when you leave.'

'Of course.'

Driving back to school, the two men tried to make sense of it.

'He hadn't even fully unpacked.'

'I think someone said his shipment arrived a week or so ago. Looks like he left with only what he could carry.'

'What would make someone just grab what they could carry and flee the country?'

Mick shrugged. 'Do you think … drugs?'

'Maybe he's schizophrenic?'

'Did anyone here get to know him? I mean, even a little. Were there any clues we should have picked up?'

'Ah, who knows? Anyway, I now have a pretty awkward letter to write. Dear parents. Guess what. Your child's maths teacher has bugg—has resigned.'

'With immediate effect.'

The two men both shook their heads sadly.

One of the first restaurants that Peter had taken Sheila to after her arrival was The Mupundu. It had semi-legendary status in Ndwalowe and reservations usually needed to be made weeks in advance. The décor was restrained and sophisticated without being pretentious or self-important. The lighting by night was subdued and by day an ancient and overgrown garden shielded the patrons from the sun's glare. Raucous laughter, exhibitionism, and coarse language would have been unthinkable at The Mupundu. Its self-assured and dignified presence immediately imprinted itself on those who entered its doors and commanded deference and respect.

'It almost feels like it's a privilege to be allowed to dine there,' Peter had gushed to Sheila.

'You're so full of it,' she had answered. 'The food had better be good.'

It was. It was better than good. It was sublime. Doubtful at first, Sheila had looked dubiously at the menu before ordering a tomato and burrata salad for a starter and a spatchcock piri-piri for her main course. A few bites into her salad, she nodded approvingly. 'Fair's fair …' But the spatchcock had her wide-eyed. 'My goodness. This is extraordinary.'

Peter had just smiled knowingly.

The restaurant was owned and managed by Jenny and Ronald Wintercoat, a Welsh couple who had come to Awanza many years earlier to manage a game lodge that had promptly gone bust (Peter empathised more than most) and who had then decided to try their hand at running their own enterprise. Their vision, their attention to detail, their uncompromising standards, and their unassuming and warm personalities had ensured that the city had embraced them. The Mupundu soon started featuring in upmarket coffee table books, the inflight magazines of some of the airlines that served Awanza, and, regularly, the pages of the Ndwalowe media. Ambassadors and senior diplomats frequented the restaurant. Local celebrities liked to be seen there. The President and visiting dignitaries were occasional guests. And Peter and Sheila became regulars. It wasn't cheap but it quickly became a favourite.

The Wintercoats had two children and both attended the international school. And in spite of running the most celebrated (and expensive) restaurant in Ndwalowe, Jenny Wintercoat still played an active role in the school's PTA. She was a woman quite without affectation whose success in Awanza had not caused her to forget or disown her modest origins in Port Talbot. Peter liked and admired her enormously.

Still, he had no idea why she had made an appointment to see him. *God. I hope they're not selling up and leaving*, he thought.

'Thank you for seeing me, Peter. I know how busy you are.'

'Jenny, don't be ridiculous. It is I who know very well how busy you are. I still think it is extraordinary that you are prepared to volunteer in the PTA. And you know how appreciative I am.'

'Well, that's why I'm here. The PTA.'

'Oh.'

'This can't go on, Peter.'

He had some idea what Jenny was talking about. Initially, he had attended the monthly PTA meetings but had soon started finding excuses not to subject himself to ninety minutes of discussions that were as tedious and occasionally as fractious as they were inconsequential. For several years the PTA had been chaired by an energetic and quietly commanding woman from Tanzania. She led by example, quickly closed down critical and negative talk, delegated effectively, and ensured that the PTA was focussed, efficient and collegial. Alas, her replacement, a well-meaning but meek woman from Italy who had never really aspired to the role, had become the hostage of a small faction that seemed more interested in rewriting the PTA's constitution than in doing any of the association's more traditional work. Each month Peter, Valli and Meena drew straws to see who would endure the discomfort, recognising that someone ought to be there to shoot down the silliest ideas and keep an eye on the deteriorating dynamic within the group. In truth, Peter recognised that he ought to do more than just observe but he felt he had quite enough on his plate and, anyway, these were adults, weren't they?

Weren't they?

'What now?' he asked.

'There was some nastiness on WhatsApp and Shumaila and Izumi have resigned. This keeps happening. The good people just decide they don't need this and they quit. It's tearing the PTA apart.'

'Can I guess who was behind the WhatsApp message?'

'I'm sure you can.'

He did. 'I think I need to speak to her,' he said. It was a conversation to which he was not looking forward.

'Wait. Let me try. She already thinks you're the problem. If it comes to it, Peter, who has the authority to close down the PTA?'

'Really? You think it might come to that? I have no idea. Me? The board? I don't know.'

'Perhaps you ought to find out.'

Peter made a face. 'Okay …'

★

Soon after her arrival in Ndwalowe, Sheila had set about imposing a bit of order on the unruly garden of Plot 274. Bushes had been pruned, plants uprooted, rocks and stones removed, fertiliser applied, seeds planted, and hedges trimmed. The lawn would surely have been cut – had there been a lawn. The best Sheila could do was to slash down the tallest grasses and plan to enquire where a heavy roller might be bought or rented. Like many of her plans, it ended up lapsing.

Sheila had arrived in December, well into the Awanzan summer. Not many weeks later, the rains had come and the garden that she described as "chaotic" (Peter preferred "delightfully disorganised") appeared to become more so by the day. The progress Sheila thought she had been making turned out to be illusory.

The garden didn't seem to be so much fighting her as ignoring her.

'Things just grow,' she complained to Peter. 'Wherever they want.'

'Shocking.'

'You don't care. So long as you have your precious birds.'

Peter had to acknowledge that to be a pretty fair description of his position. Nor had he gained any brownie points when he had quoted W C Fields for her. *If at first you don't succeed, try again. Then quit. There's no point being a damn fool about it.*

Sheila was certainly not a quitter but, as the months passed and she had succeeded in taming only small parts of the estate (as she called it), she had admitted to herself that imposing her will on the flora of this small corner of Awanza would be a long-term project. In the meantime, she tried to accept and even embrace the lack of discipline that had at first dismayed her.

She was reluctantly grateful now that Peter had dissuaded her from grubbing up the banana tree behind the house. And she had to admit that it delighted her to stroll into the garden of a morning to shake the papaya tree and catch a falling fruit that she would then enjoy with her breakfast. Plot 274 was not and never would be an English country garden, far less anything approaching the impossibly manicured and stylised formal gardens she so loved in Japan. But it was, she was coming to appreciate, full of its own colour and beauty. There was an informality about much of what she was discovering in Africa that, somewhat to her surprise, she found she was enjoying and the informality (to put it mildly) of her garden no longer seemed quite such an offence.

★

When the time comes to retire, many international school heads find it hard to walk away from a world of which they have been a part for two, three or even four decades. They are members of a fellowship of educators and administrators who (mostly) speak a common language and share similar priorities and values. (Though whether that homogeneity is a good thing or not is a question seldom asked.) And, although cast far and wide to every remote corner of the globe, the members of this fellowship interact regularly and enjoyably.

Conferences, recruitment fairs, programme authorisation and accreditation visits, regional associations, professional development events and online forums are welcome opportunities for heads to connect, establish relationships and cultivate friendships. School leadership can be a lonely job at the best of times. When one's school is geographically remote or located in a country or culture that presents unusual and unwelcome challenges, the need to seek advice, encouragement or even just sympathy from those doing similar jobs elsewhere, becomes pressing. That heads – and, indeed, international school teachers – commonly move between schools (and countries) every few years means that by the time someone becomes a director or principal or headmaster or whatever title is preferred at their institution, they will probably have worked in half a dozen or so schools on two or three continents. Paths cross and cross again. Friends who met in their first international school as young and inexperienced teachers three decades ago now swap anecdotes and find reassurance that running schools in Cambodia and Cameroon seem to involve addressing much the same problems and possibilities.

And when they do walk away from their final school, many erstwhile heads continue to work, full- or part-time, for recruitment agencies or accreditation bodies. Not a few set themselves up as independent consultants. And it is from the ranks of former international school heads that most of those offering board training or a governance audit come.

'His CV certainly seems impressive,' Carola looked at the list of references on the last page. 'Are these good schools?'

'Oh, yes,' said Peter, 'I know some of them quite well. If these schools recommend him, I'd say that says a lot.'

'But he isn't cheap. Fifteen hundred dollars a day plus expenses?'

'I'm afraid that's what these people cost. I actually know others who charge a lot more.'

'Have you met him?'

'Not met him, as such. But I saw him present at a conference in Yokohama a couple of years back. I was impressed.'

'And the others?'

'Here are their CVs. I think any one of them could do the job. It partly depends on their availability. But my first choice would be Seth Taniel.'

'I like that he has Africa experience.'

'Absolutely. He was in Uganda for eight years. And he was in Morocco too, if you count that as Africa.'

'And where is he based?'

'Maryland. Annapolis.'

Carola grimaced. 'How much will it cost to fly him over?'

'Well, that's another advantage. If we can wait till November he's going to be in Lusaka working with another school. I've no doubt that they'd be happy to split the cost of the flight.'

'That certainly helps. All right. Please check the dates when he could come, cost the whole thing, and we'll put it to the board at this month's meeting.'

'Okay.' Peter hesitated. 'You know that not everyone will be in favour?'

'I know very well, Peter,' Carola pursed her lips. 'But isn't that just why we need this?'

Peter nodded and smiled. He liked it when he and Carola were on the same page.

'While I'm here,' Carola had been going to leave but now remembered something she wanted to ask. 'A board member tells me there's no appraisal process for teachers. Is this true?'

'A board member? Who?'

Carola looked uncomfortable. 'Is it true? We don't appraise teachers?'

Peter sighed.

Schools do what schools do because that's what schools do. Peter had been hearing variations on this theme for many years and he tended to agree. The annual calendar, the traditional disciplines and subjects, exams, reports, all children of a given age in the same class doing the same things, school uniform, and so on. It all seemed so traditional, so unimaginative. And did it work?

Peter liked to approach such issues with a question. 'If you were starting from scratch, is this what you would do?' Very often, the answer was no.

'Carola, we evaluate teachers constantly. We're in and out of their classrooms all the time.'

'That's not what I'm talking about. Is anything documented? Are goals set?'

'It doesn't work.' Peter decided there was no point in equivocating.

'What doesn't?'

'Appraisal. Or evaluation of whatever you want to call it. I've worked in three schools before coming here and I've never found an appraisal system that was worth the time or effort. Most teachers think it's a waste of time too.'

Carola frowned.

Peter continued. 'It becomes a ritual that schools do … because that's what schools do. It becomes formulaic. At its worst, we spend hours having meetings, observing classes – that are almost always artificial because the teacher knows they are being observed – and then more meetings and some form of written report that both parties file and then largely forget about.'

Carola did not look at all happy. 'I find this quite disturbing. I think we all on the board assumed that teachers are accountable. That there is some sort of quality control. That you check if they are doing what they are supposed to.'

'Of course they are accountable. Just as I am accountable to you. And, I might point out,' Peter was becoming annoyed and hoped he wouldn't say something he'd regret, 'that you – the board – spent a great deal of money last year on a time-consuming process to evaluate me that we both agreed was ultimately not very helpful. Correct?'

Carola flushed.

'Nor, of course, did you appraise yourselves. How do you know if the board is doing a good job or not if you don't evaluate yourselves?'

'It was a very busy year. We'll certainly do it this year.'

Peter bit his tongue. He and Carola had never fallen out before.

'But if you are advocating board self-appraisal,' suggested Carola, 'you do agree that an evaluation process is necessary? And valuable?'

'Actually, no. I've seen boards half-heartedly evaluate themselves and it's an even bigger waste of time than teacher appraisal. Do you – do we – need to conduct a formal evaluation to know the current board's strengths and weaknesses? And would we – would the board – be brave enough to admit such weaknesses?'

They sat in a silence that was as unfamiliar as it was uncomfortable.

'Some board members think we should set you annual goals.' It sounded more like a question than a statement.

'Like what?'

'Improving the teacher retention rate.'

'Seriously? We had just four teachers leave last year. For a school of this size, that's hardly anything.'

'It costs a lot to bring in a new teacher. It's better if current teachers stay.' It sounded to Peter as if Carola was simply repeating something she had been told.

'Not if they aren't great teachers. And it's healthy to have some fresh blood every year. Of course, if the retention rate—'

'Not great teachers? But isn't that why we need an evaluation process? To weed them out?'

'But you just told me not to weed them out. I'm meant to give them incentives to stay. The retention rate, remember? Do the members of the board know what they are talking about?'

'I think it's better if we stop this conversation, Peter.'

'Yes. Probably.'

'But I am going to put the issue of teacher appraisal on the agenda for the next board meeting.'

Peter said nothing.

'And board self-evaluation.'

'As you wish.'

'Peter, we need to work together.'

'I know. And I hate it when we don't agree. But I think the board should leave me to run the school.'

This time it was Carola who said nothing.

★

'Valli, we don't have a mascot. Why is that?'

Valli paused what she was doing and looked out of the window in thought. 'I don't know. The same question has occasionally occurred to me.'

'All the other schools do,' continued Mick. 'The American School in Lusaka are the leopards. ISK are the lions.'

'I thought Uganda were the leopards.'

'Er, they are. And Addis and Johannesburg are both the eagles. It gets a bit confusing.'

'What were you in Dar es Salaam?'

'The twigas!' Mick said proudly.

Valli frowned.

'Em, giraffes,' Mick admitted. 'It sounds better in Swahili.'

'Doesn't sound very intimidating. Lions, leopards, eagles … giraffes.'

'Twigas,' Mick corrected her. 'Anyway, I think we need a mascot. I'll speak to Peter.'

'Good luck with that,' laughed Valli. 'Not really his kind of thing.'
'It doesn't have to be. He just has to approve …'
Valli raised her eyebrows.
'… or, at least, not object.'

★

Most cities in Africa will have some version of a club or association open only to expatriate women (and perhaps some locals) that combines a certain amount of socialising with often much-needed charity work. Strangely, similar organisations for men seem not to exist, presumably reflecting an era when those employed on fixed-term contracts in embassies and industries were almost always men and it was their wives who needed to occupy their time and find an outlet for their talents.

At first, Sheila had rather bluntly declined invitations to join the Diplomatic Wives' Association of Awanza.

'I don't define myself as a wife and I'm often not very diplomatic,' she had protested to her husband (to whom neither statement came as news).

But in the necessarily small social circles in which she moved, Sheila came to know and like a number of the women who delivered Christmas gifts to orphanages, took the residents of an old peoples' home out for lunches, and raised money for the children's cancer ward, as well as organising occasional family days and an annual 'Black and Bling' Ball (at the mention of which Peter hurriedly discovered a prior engagement).

She still railed against the name of the association, which she found sorely behind the times, but, without formally joining, she did agree to accompany various friends as they went about their charitable work. She was, she admitted, impressed and often touched.

'Thing is,' she said to Peter, 'it's all a bit WI.'

Not sure why that was necessarily a bad thing, Peter just nodded.

Further invitations to join DWAA were made but Sheila continued to say no, only now rather more politely. Why, one might even say diplomatically.

Until, that is, until she abruptly changed her mind.

★

'I'm not really surprised,' said Valli, reading through the brief letter Peter had shared with her. 'I know she was really disappointed not to get the secondary principal job.'

'I know. I still think it was the right decision but I did feel sorry for Meena.'

'Did she say where she's looking?'

'Asia or the Middle East, I think. She wants to be a bit closer to her family.'

'And she's looking for a position as a principal?'

'Absolutely. And I encouraged her. She did a great job last year.'

'So, now we need to look for a new diploma coordinator. Well, for next year.'

'I actually don't think we need to look very far.'

'Really?'

'Well, it was always on the cards that Meena would move on this year. It's not as if it came out of the blue. Looking around, I think there's an obvious candidate. I think we should offer it to Trixi.'

'Offer it? Has she expressed any interest?'

'No but I think she'd be great. She's one of our most senior and most respected teachers. She's organised. She has a great relationship with the students. She's been teaching the DP for yonks—'

'For what?'

'For ages. She's a senior examiner for English. I mean, she's got it all.'

'Assuming she wants it.'

'I think she will. I'll try and catch her this week to sound her out.'

'But …' Valli frowned. 'We have to advertise all positions internally. It's policy …'

'Oh, Valli. I've come across this before. It's such a waste of everyone's time. Anyway, who else would apply? Den could probably do it but he's head of department already. Amsah, maybe. It really isn't a long list.'

'But you don't know who's interested until you advertise. You have to give people a chance.'

'They may well be interested but that doesn't mean they could do it. What if Gordon Sipple applied? Or Mike Sesriem? Are you saying I should interview them?'

'Yes. It's only courteous. Part of their professional development.'

'But there's no way I'd ever appoint either of them. So we go through the farce of them submitting applications and Mick and I spend a couple of hours or so going through the pretence of an interview and then I give it to Trixi anyway. That's neither courteous nor professional. It's dishonest.'

'Maybe they'd surprise you in the interview. At least, if you went into it with an open mind. Though that doesn't seem very likely.'

'Oh, come on, Valli. Do you think that either Gordon or Mike would be a good fit? Would you appoint them?'

'I'd interview them.'

'That wasn't what I asked.'

Valli pursed her lips but said nothing.

'Okay,' said Peter. 'Look. If Amsah applies, I'll interview her. And Den, I suppose, if he wants to make the shift. But then who takes over as head of science?'

'You have to interview anyone who applies. You can't pick and choose. What message does that send?'

'It sends the message that I know what I'm doing and what the school needs. It's called doing my job.'

Again, Valli said nothing.

'Valli, I may only have been here for a bit over a year but I think I have a pretty good idea of people's strengths and weaknesses. And I was DP coordinator myself for six years. I know what the job involves. I think Trixi would be great.'

'Yes, and then you should appoint her. But only after you give other people a chance too.'

'But what a waste of everyone's time! I mean, when Pep Guardiola gets his team together on a Saturday morning…'

'Pep who?'

'It doesn't matter. When a football – sorry, soccer – manager gets his team together before a match, he doesn't ask who feels like playing in goal. His number one striker doesn't rub his chin and say, "Well, I've always fancied giving it a try. Perhaps I could play in goal today?" The manager knows who his best goalkeeper is.'

'Oh, that's not the same at all.'

'Of course it is. I'm the manager. Or, in an orchestra. The conductor doesn't start a rehearsal asking who would like to have a go at playing the French horn. I could go on.'

'I know you could.' The tone of Valli's voice suggested that she sincerely hoped he wouldn't.

✱

Lower Garstang Police Station was a plain two-storey building that had once been painted white but was now streaked with black and grey. The corrugated-iron roof was rusty, the gates to the compound were missing, and much of the fence that enclosed the property had decayed to the point of collapse. On the dusty lot, vehicles parked wherever the driver hoped to find some shade. People, some in uniform, most not, loitered on the broad steps that led up to a front door that appeared to be permanently open.

Other police stations dotted throughout Ndwalowe were newer and in better condition but Lower Garstang was the closest to both the school and the Corbys' home and it was to this station that Peter had been more than once to have various official documents stamped and apply for the required police clearance form in order to renew his visa.

Inside, visitors would find a long chest-high desk behind which various police officers chatted, stared at their phones, and, when they were ready, gave some attention to the citizens who are waiting to be heard.

Peter was seeing the desk in his mind's eye as Sheila spoke. His wife was animated, angry.

Of the friends Sheila had made since arriving in Awanza, it was Susi Shepherd to whom she felt the closest. They were much the same age and shared similar beliefs and values. Susi and her husband, both Australian, were doctors working for a German NGO advising the Ministry of Health on HIV/AIDS projects. Sheila appreciated the fact that the Shepherds had no children and therefore, and unlike many in Sheila's social circle, had no strong opinions on what was (or, more often, was not) going right at the International School. She appreciated a little less, but patiently endured, Susi's frequent suggestions that she, Sheila, had much to offer the DWAA.

'We'll see,' was Sheila's usual answer. But, increasingly, she felt that sooner or later she would have to say yes.

'It was disgusting, Peter. Just ... shameful.' Sheila stared at the table between them, shaking her head slowly. Usually so composed, she was trembling slightly. Peter took her hand.

'Susi was great,' Sheila continued. 'I don't think I could have handled it so well.'

'And the maid … Charity, did you say?'

'She's just a girl. Can't be more than eighteen. She just stood between us. She seemed more confused than anything.' Sheila shook her head again. 'She was bleeding, Peter. The whole room could see that. Susi asked if we could go to a separate room but the sergeant said there wasn't one. And there were women – policewomen – but no one came to help. So we just stood at the desk in front of – I don't know – eight or ten people and the sergeant slowly took our statement. It was humiliating. Degrading. Susi asked if there was a police doctor on call. They just looked at her as if she was mad.'

'No doctor? Isn't some kind of examination necessary?'

'In the end – when we'd done all we could at the station – Susi called a friend who works at the Central Hospital. We took Charity there. She was still bleeding and big bruises were appearing on her arms. We photographed everything and Susi's friend is going to write a report.'

'Where is Charity now?'

'The hospital wanted to admit her overnight. But she just wanted to get home to her mother. In the end, she agreed to stay so long as Susi stayed with her. We got her mother on the phone and I went and collected her. She's going to stay at the hospital too. God, Peter, you should see where they live …'

'And the police? What do they do now?'

'They will, I am told, "open a case". Whatever that means, I don't know. They didn't seem very interested.'

'Did Charity know him? The young man?'

'He does odd jobs for Susi now and again. The only name they have for him is Joseph. And no one knows where he lives.'

'So we won't be seeing him again.'

'Peter, it was as if they'd never had a rape case before. There was no process. There should have been women officers to deal with it, a private room, a doctor who could be called … It was as if we were reporting a snatched handbag, not the violent rape of a teenage girl.'

Peter squeezed his wife's hand. 'You did what you could …'

'No! It wasn't enough. It isn't enough. This can't be allowed to happen like this. Someone has to do something.'

Sheila pulled her hand away and massaged her face. 'Someone has to do something,' she repeated.

*

The PTA at the International School of Ndwalowe enjoyed the use of two large rooms in the same block as the library, centrally located and conveniently close to the parent car park. One was an unhappy cross between a storeroom and a shop and it was from here that volunteer parents sold school merchandise on Monday, Wednesday, and Friday mornings. The other was a usually cluttered space that had once been a classroom but now served as an office and meeting room. Posters advertising long since forgotten events and a large year planner dominated one wall. Unmatching chairs and tables filled most of the room. Two kettles, a coffee machine, and a microwave sat in one corner, a small fridge and a photocopier in another. Every incoming executive committee had resolved to bring order to the chaos but none had.

It was in this room that Jenny Wintercoat looked for Crystal Moore. She had seen Crystal's Fortuner in the car park and knew she must be around. But the PTA office was empty, although the lights were on and a coffee machine gurgled.

She found Crystal in the storeroom, moving cardboard boxes of T-shirts between shelves.

'Morning!' She did not stop her work as Jenny entered. 'This drives me mad. I mean, how hard can it be? S, M, L, XL, blue, white, PE shirts, T-shirts, polos. It's not hard. The shelves are clearly marked. Why can't people get it right?'

Even if she had wanted to, Jenny had no time to answer.

'I know. Three- to five-year-olds, six to nine, ten to twelve. I get it. There are different ways of doing it. And, do you know, I don't really give a damn. But, whatever we do, surely it's not too much to ask that people follow the system. It's just anarchy.'

'You don't have to do it all yourself.'

'Well, like, do you see any other volunteers?'

'Crystal, that's sort of why I want to talk to you.'

'Oh?' She put down the box she was holding.

'Izumi and Shumaila.'

'Oh.'

'And last month Pernilla and Ajit and Maria Rodriguez in June. That's five good people who have quit.'

'Well, five people. Not sure that I'd call them good. I never saw Pernilla or Maria do much around here.'

'That's not fair. They used to be very active. But the way things have become ...'

'What way?'

'Crystal, it used to be fun being on the PTA. We enjoyed ourselves. There was trust. Now it's just becoming toxic.'

'I don't accept that. A few of us are trying to turn the PTA into something that does more than hold bake sales and sell T-shirts. If the old guard can't cope with that ...' she shrugged. 'Not my problem.'

'Does it have to be so abrasive? So personal?'

'I don't think it's personal. If a few snowflakes burst into tears every time ...'

'Crystal, that isn't what's happening. You know it. That WhatsApp Nyota sent Izumi. That was nasty. And did she have to copy it to the entire group?'

'Then talk to Nyota.'

'I will but we both know why she sent it.'

'Izumi was right out of line at the last meeting. If anyone has made this personal, she has.'

'Oh, that's ridiculous!'

'She's the one who said I shouldn't be on the PTA.'

'No, she said that you didn't understand what a PTA is. That what you want to turn the PTA into is not what the school needs. Or what anyone wants.'

'Her opinion. I have mine.'

'Crystal, we've been over this. We are here to work with the administration.'

'By which, you actually mean for the administration. Why will nobody stand up to Peter Corby?'

'Why would anyone need to stand up to him? This is what the rest of us can't understand.'

'Because the PTA needs to keep the administration honest. Call out injustices. They need to know that someone's looking over their shoulder.

This is the third PTA I've been on. I've learned the hard way. I know what they try to get away with.'

'They?'

'You know what I mean.'

'No. That's the problem. I don't. None of us do. We're not here to fight with the SLT.'

'I'm not looking for a fight. But I expect the PTA to be respected. We are the voice of the parents. The director has to listen to us.'

'About what? He runs the school – him and his team. That's not the PTA's job.'

'The way I see it – and I'm not the only one – it should be a partnership. But a partnership of equals. The PTA doesn't answer to the director.'

Jenny stifled a small gasp. 'Well, who does it answer to?'

'The parents. We are here to fight for their interests. And so long as I'm on the PTA, that's what it will do.'

★

Peter seldom looked forward to board meetings. Rereading the agenda for the September meeting, he felt particularly pessimistic. *Just don't lose it, Peter, okay? Just bite your tongue.*

Possibly because others present felt the same way, or perhaps because Mrs Luhanga had announced she would attend, the mood in the conference room as people gathered was unmistakably tense. In other circumstances, Carola and Peter might have caught each other's eye to flash a reassuring look. This evening neither was making eye contact.

Routine matters were quickly dispensed with and then Carola introduced agenda item D.1 – the Access to Education Act.

'Peter, would you give an update on where we are?'

'Thank you, Carola. We …' Peter coughed. He could feel his throat going dry. 'Sorry. As you know – and as is in the minutes,' he glanced at Mrs Luhanga who was smiling and looking into the middle distance, 'the school and our lawyer, Mr Burger, are liaising with the Office of the Permanent Secretary. We have requested a meeting. As of today, we have received no answer.'

He paused, inviting comments or questions. There were none.

'We have also,' he continued, 'repeated our request for copies of all and any correspondence between the ministry and the school regarding this matter but—'

'It has probably been lost.' Mrs Luhanga spoke without emotion as if commenting on the weather.

Ernesto Mayor choked a little on the coffee he was drinking. Carola, who had been making notes, looked up in surprise. Lazarett, to Mrs Luhanga's left, gave her a quizzical look.

Looking not entirely unhappy at the reactions she had provoked, Mrs Luhanga continued. 'If such correspondence ever existed.'

She looked around the room. Again, no one spoke.

'You must understand,' she said, adopting or affecting a look of regret, 'record-keeping at the ministry is not, um, what one would hope.'

She had clearly finished. Carola, in spite of herself, made eye contact with Peter. Both looked slightly shocked.

'Thank you, Mrs Luhanga,' Carola hoped she was sounding matter-of-fact. 'Peter. Anything else to add?'

'Only that I am reaching out to other private schools in Ndwalowe to see what their experience of the ATE Act has been.'

'Something,' Lazarett interrupted, 'that should probably have been done long ago.'

'Thank you, Peter,' Carola interjected hurriedly. 'We have a long agenda and it looks like there is nothing more we can do with this item until we have a reply from the ministry.'

'Agreed. Let's wait to see what they say.' Mrs Luhanga had never spoken as much in a board meeting and certainly never to such effect. Ernesto looked like he was struggling to contain himself.

Carola hurried on. 'The next item is a staffing matter. Peter?'

'Yes, erm, I sent you all an email about this. In brief, one of our new hires, Chuck Collins, rather abruptly – in fact, very abruptly – left. I received a text message saying he was at the airport. He left his keys with another teacher. When we checked his apartment, he had abandoned books, clothes, personal effects … It was all quite extraordinary.'

'What happened to them?'

'What?'

'The personal effects,' Grant continued. 'What did you do with them?'

'The books we put in the library and everything else – clothes, for example – we donated to an orphanage. And we let the cleaning staff we sent in to tidy up keep some stuff – toiletries and crockery and so on.'

'Good. Carry on.'

'I have written to his email address and we've tried to contact him through WhatsApp and Facebook and so on but we've had no reply. I've been in touch with the agency through which we hired him. I want to know if they know anything and I want our two thousand dollars back.'

'US dollars?'

'Of course. It's the standard fee we pay.'

'And?'

'They don't seem to be able to reach him either and they are very reluctant to refund the money.'

'We must insist!'

'I'm working with them, Lazarett. But they are the best agency out there and we can't really afford to fall out with them. Equally, of course, they want our business in the future. I'm sure we can arrange some kind of compromise.'

Lazarett looked dissatisfied.

'More immediately, Peter, you've found a replacement?'

'Yes, Clyde. Well, a temporary solution. Finding good high school maths teachers is always hard. Getting people with IB experience is still harder. And at next to no notice …' Peter grimaced. 'But we've been a little lucky. One of our parents used to teach at the Technical University here. She's agreed to cover Chuck's classes until Christmas. And she's Awanzan so she doesn't need a work permit.'

'IB experience?' Violet asked.

'No. None. So next month we are sending her to Dubai for a quick introduction to teaching IB maths.'

Lazarett snorted. 'What? And how much will that cost? You said she'll only be here to December.'

'Yes, but it's important that she understands how the IB works.'

'She's a qualified maths teacher, isn't she?'

'Yes. Though for university students and teaching the local curriculum.'

'Oh please! Mathematics is mathematics. How different can the IB be? And after she's been to Dubai, why not just give her the job permanently?'

'Because she doesn't want it permanently and because I'd much rather find someone with solid IB experience.'

'Lazarett,' Clyde spoke gently but firmly, 'I think we need to leave this to Peter – to the director. This is his area of expertise. But Peter, can you prepare a report for the finance committee on what impact this will have on the budget?'

'Yes, of course.'

'Has she started yet?'

'Yes. We managed to bring her in less than a week after Chuck left.'

'And we still have no idea why he left?'

'No.'

'Does this kind of thing happen often?' Ernesto looked at both Peter and Trixi.

'Not often,' answered Peter, 'but I've heard of similar things. International school teachers—'

'Sounds like yet another reason to hire locally!'

Peter shut his eyes and counted to ten. Slowly.

'Lazarett,' Carola tried to keep any emotion out of her voice, 'I think we've had this discussion. We are, after all, an international school.'

'An international school. I still don't know what that means.'

'Then why are you on the board of one!' As soon as he had spoken Peter regretted it.

'Peter!'

'I'm sorry. I'm sorry, Carola. I shouldn't have said that.' Although, as he glanced nervously at the other board members, Peter was not unhappy to see what might have been looks of sympathy on a few faces.

'Madam Chairman!'

'Lazarett, Peter has apologised and we have a lot to get through. I don't want to get side-tracked. But, if I may, I think this leads rather well into the next agenda item. Can we move on?' Without waiting, Carola continued. 'Item D.3. It is proposed that we bring in a consultant to work with the board the better to understand our roles and responsibilities …'

'And maybe even understand what an international school is!' Ernesto made no attempt to hide the sarcasm in his voice. Lazarett glared.

'As I think we have discovered over the past year,' Carola continued, 'being on the board of a school – an international school, I should say –

brings with it certain, um, challenges. An experienced consultant can help us work through such things.'

'Board training. Isn't that what it's called?' Lazarett made his disdain very obvious.

Carola replied patiently. 'I think we've all heard that expression and we agree it isn't wholly appropriate. Mr Taniel prefers to call it a governance workshop.'

'Who?'

'You've seen in your board papers,' Ernesto waved his own for emphasis, 'the CVs and costs of three consultants who are available and who could lead the workshop. Seth Taniel is the one we are recommending. But either of the other two would be perfectly okay too.'

'I've actually looked closely at all three,' said Grant. 'I think what stands out for me is that Taniel has worked in Africa. He knows the context. Oh, and I'm very much in favour of this initiative, by the way. I think we need it.'

Clyde nodded. 'I agree.'

'It's a lot of money …' Violet Sindima cautioned. 'But I would like to hear from someone outside of this room what the role of a board member really is.' She flashed a look at Peter who attempted to remain expressionless.

'Even I think so.'

For the second time during the meeting Mrs Luhanga took her audience by surprise. Peter smiled. This was going better than he had dared hope.

'What are we deciding, Carola?' asked Trixi. 'Are we already voting for Mr Taniel or are we still deciding if we want a consultant or not?'

'Good point, Trixi. Then let's find out. Can I have a show of hands? All in favour of bringing someone in to work with the board.'

Lazarett was the only one not to raise his hand.

'I see,' Carola gestured to Chiamaka Kambani who was taking the minutes. 'Carried. I would have preferred a unanimous decision but …'

'Can the minutes please record that I think this is a foolish waste of time and money. I am certainly not in favour.'

'Thank you, Lazarett. Chiamaka, will you please …?'

Chiamaka nodded.

The other two candidates were briefly discussed but Seth Taniel, although the most expensive, was deemed to offer the most relevant experience. A date in November was agreed and Peter was authorised to make the necessary arrangements.

'We still have one other item …' Carola appeared to be looking at anyone in the room except Peter. 'Lazarett, I believe you …'

'Yes. Thank you. In my business – in fact, in every business I have worked in – it is normal to appraise all members of staff annually. I was astonished when I was informed that this is not the case in this school. Why is the management not doing what I would consider a core responsibility? I am told that teachers have repeatedly asked the Senior Leadership Team to introduce a proper appraisal scheme. Why won't they do it?'

'Wait. What?' Peter had expected most of what Lazarett had said but not his final point. 'No one has asked the SLT for formal appraisal.'

'That is not what I have been informed.' Lazarett looked smug.

'Informed by whom?'

'I am not prepared to reveal my source.'

'Your source? Wait. You have someone in school who … who …'

'Yes. As a board member it is important that I know what is really going on.'

Peter looked around the room at the other members. 'Am I … Does anyone else … This is not right. Surely?'

Grant was the first to speak. 'Lazarett, what are you saying? You don't trust Peter to tell us the truth?'

'And,' added Ernesto, 'Trixi is here as a member of staff. Do you think the board is not being fully informed?'

'I know what I know.' Lazarett folded his arms and leaned back in his chair.

The silence was broken only by Ernesto quietly swearing in Spanish.

'Carola,' Peter's throat was going dry again. 'This has to be addressed. This is fundamental. It can't be right that there is someone in school feeding misinformation to a board member. And it's completely wrong that a board member is apparently trusting his 'source' more than the head of school.'

Again, a silence. Carola looked like she was struggling to know what to say.

'Frankly,' Catherine Mulbarton had not previously spoken but now learned forward, 'I am more concerned about an apparent failure to appraise teachers. Is it true that there is no system?'

'Catherine, I'll come to that but first …'

'I think you're trying to change the subject, Peter.' Violet tapped the table with her pen. 'I agree with Catherine. Why is there no evaluation process for teachers?'

Peter sighed deeply and closed his eyes. He ran his hands back and forward through his hair. He was fighting an urge to stand, shove his laptop into his briefcase, and … But no. He opened his eyes and stared at Violet.

'What is the purpose of appraisal?' he asked. 'It is to help identify where someone who is doing a job can do that job better. In the context of a school, it is to improve teaching practice. Ultimately, the goal is to improve student learning. It's all about the students. It's all about teaching and learning. All teachers can improve. Most would want to improve. Schools therefore have every incentive to help teachers improve. It's good for the teachers, it's good for the students, and it's good for the school.'

'Yes, but …' Catherine attempted to interrupt.

'I haven't finished! Schools – good schools – therefore actively work to help teachers evaluate their own practice. Not once a year but continuously. And there are many ways to do it. In the primary school teachers who teach the same Grade collaborate and observe each other's classes. Peer appraisal, if you like. The PYP coordinator helps teachers with planning. We spend a significant amount each year on professional development, bringing in experts and sending teachers to workshops and conferences. In the secondary school teachers of the same subject regularly moderate each other's marking to ensure they are on the same page. The MYP and DP coordinators work with teachers in the classroom and out of it. In our weekly full staff meetings we always have fifteen minutes or so when someone demonstrates something they have been trying in their teaching or introduce a new app they have found. Oh, and there's the annual Tech Camp each February when our teachers – and, indeed, some of our students – offer courses to their colleagues and to teachers from other schools in the city. Having to stand up in front of others and explain what you do and why is excellent professional development. You cannot do it without having worked out what you really want to say. Questions from the audience will further force you to reflect on your practice.'

He paused as if daring anyone to speak. No one did.

'In the May board meeting, I think it was, I described to you the instructional coaching programme we are introducing. Two of our teachers have been trained to lead it and I think so far six teachers have volunteered to participate. Bit by bit – in fact, quite quickly – we will have most or all teachers enrolled. This is a very active and constructive way to have teachers reflect on how they teach. They are videoed and then they and a colleague – a trained colleague – watch the video and discuss what went well and what didn't. That's just part of the process. And it runs for weeks and months. It's not just me coming into their classroom once a year with a clipboard.'

'It sounds like you don't play any part in the process.'

'Lazarett! You have no idea what I do! Or Valli or Mick. Every day we are working with teachers in one way or another. We are in and out of their classrooms regularly. If there are complaints from parents or students – and, of course, there sometimes are – we meet the teachers to talk everything through. Or maybe we've observed something particularly praiseworthy. The best motivation a teacher can have is a letter of commendation or even just a pat on the back. We know each teacher's strengths and weaknesses. It is nonsense to suggest that there is no appraisal of teachers. It's happening all the time.'

'Then why do we still have bad teachers?' Catherine had looked unimpressed throughout Peter's monologue. 'Appraisal is how you root out the bad teachers. Why aren't you doing that?'

'No. Appraisal is not something you do *to* teachers. It's something you do *for* teachers or *with* teachers. It's constructive, developmental. It's not punitive.'

'So we don't do anything about our bad teachers?'

'I don't accept that we have any bad teachers. We have some really good ones and some who are still …'

'All our teachers are qualified, aren't they?'

'Of course, Grant, but just having a teaching qualification … Look, when I started my career twenty odd years ago, was I a good teacher? I doubt it. Or let's just say that I was probably a better teacher after five years or ten than I was when I started. It's like learning to drive. You aren't necessarily a good driver when you pass your test. It just means that you are probably just about safe to let out on the road without killing anyone. But you only really learn how to drive after you've passed your test. It's experience that counts. Same with teaching. Oh, and while I'm at it, teaching is a pretty idiosyncratic kind of thing. It doesn't lend itself to KPIs and the like. It's like being an actor or a comedian. You know when you see a good one but it's damn hard to teach someone how to do it.'

'Or being a parent.' Trixi looked around the table.

'What do you mean?'

'I think most of us are parents. I am. But am I a good one? I don't set annual goals. I don't have someone observe me once a year to tell me how I could do better. I know very well when I've got it wrong and I try to learn from my mistakes. In just the same way I know when a lesson I have taught has gone well or badly. I don't need Peter or anyone else to tell me.'

'Oh that's ridiculous. It's not the same thing at all.'

'Teacher, parent … You're dealing with people – children. And most of the time you're working without a script. It's not like mending a car or working in a factory.'

'I think …' began Carola hesitantly but Lazarett interrupted her.

'So, the bottom line is we have no appraisal process for teachers. Correct?'

'If you mean we don't waste hours of everyone's time each year having pointless meetings and jumping through artificial hoops, then no. We don't. But if you mean …'

'So, as I said. The management are not holding the school's employees accountable.'

'Wait a minute, Lazarett,' Grant spoke more loudly than he had perhaps intended, 'Peter has just explained that it's a lot more complicated than that. And do you know what? In the High Commission we have moved more towards the kind of model Peter is describing. When I began my career I had an annual performance review and, frankly, it was a waste of time. And do you know what else? The more I think about it, the more troubled I am that you are bringing to the board gossip or rumours from someone in the school who probably has an axe to grind. That's just not on.'

Lazarett and Grant glared at each other across the table. Peter wanted to speak but thought it better to bite his tongue.

'Maybe …' Trixi suggested, 'maybe something for Seth Taniel to address when he comes?'

Ernesto broke the silence. 'I think it better to adjourn the meeting now before … Carola, can we…?'

'Yes. I think you're right. I don't think it will serve any useful purpose to go any further. But there are still matters that we need to resolve. Even if we can't do it tonight. Do we agree? Meeting adjourned?'

As the room emptied, Carola caught Peter's eye. She made a small gesture inviting him to stay behind. Puzzled and with his heart sinking (further), he pretended to consult the agenda one more time until they were alone. She approached him with an expression he could not interpret.

'Carola …'

Without pausing, she wrapped her arms around his shoulders and hugged him tightly.

✱

Peter listened to Jenny, his heart sinking. 'So, not very repentant, then?'

'Defiant. Self-righteous. And I can think of a few more adjectives that I should perhaps keep to myself.'

'Is she … I want to give her the benefit of the doubt. Is she sincere? Does she believe what she is saying? What they are doing?'

'I have to assume so. She's quite zealous.'

'And indifferent to the unhappiness it is causing?'

'I actually think she feeds on that. I think it vindicates her.'

'Jenny, why won't people speak up? About Crystal and Nyota Furaha and the others. They are a minority. Why don't people tell them they've had enough?'

'You get paid to do this job, Peter. You have to suck it up. I have to put up with rude customers in my restaurant. But PTA members are volunteers. They don't need this unpleasantness. So they just quit.'

'But then it just lets Crystal and her little gang win.'

'I know …'

'Jenny, have you read the PTA constitution?'

'Er, probably. But a while ago.'

'Let me show you something.' He slid a document across the desk to her. 'Page six …'

✱

October

'Are you going anywhere over the break?' Valli took another sip from the water bottle she always carried and opened her laptop.

Peter made a face. 'I'm not sure. There's so much going on right now.'

'You must, Peter. If I might say, you are looking a bit frazzled. You're always telling us how we need to take care of ourselves. You should too.'

'Yeah, well …'

'No, I mean it. Things are slowly getting back under control. Frank's back. Heather Mulenga has got Chuck's classes. It sounds like the ATE thing has run into the sand – at least for now.'

'But now the PTA is falling apart.'

'Well, you aren't going to fix that over the October vacation, are you? Go away. Take a break.'

'Maybe …'

'Sorry I'm late.' Mick bustled through the door. His phone, his laptop, a container of coffee, and a large notebook were probably one item, if not two, too many for him to juggle. He almost spilled the lot onto Peter's coffee table.

'Oops. Sorry.'

'Careful, Mick!'

'Sorry. In a bit of a rush.' Mick sat down and made to rearrange his stuff.

'I was just telling Peter he should be sure to get away this break.'

'You should,' Mick addressed Peter. 'You look awful.'

Peter's eyes opened wide.

'Oh, sorry.'

'No, no, Mick. You give it to me straight.'

Valli stifled a giggle.

'And while I still have breath in my ailing body, do you think we could start the agenda? Staff accommodation …'

Mick's smile disappeared.

'I know you don't agree, Mick, but we're putting Larry into Chuck's apartment and Helen will stay where she is. At least until Christmas. A lot will depend on how we replace Mrs Mulenga. I'm guessing it will be an overseas hire.'

Mick Shrugged. 'It's your call.'

'And, of course, Frank is still in one of the three-bedroom houses.'

'I know that, Valli, but I don't think anyone much wants to turf him out right now.'

'No, I'm just saying.'

'But you're right. Depending on any staffing changes that may still happen this year we may need to think again about Frank.'

Peter's phone rang. Scowling, he stood and walked over to his desk.

'Are you and Himari going anywhere for the vacation?' Valli asked Mick.

'Indeed we are. We're going to Cape Town. Our first year in Dar we went there over the October break and it's become a bit of a tradition.'

'Nice.'

'And you?'

'We're not sure. Duke's taking the swimming team to Gaborone for three days so we can't really do much.'

'You won't go with?'

'No, probably not.'

Peter returned and sat down. 'That was Chiamaka. A mother wants to see me this afternoon. Says it's urgent. Susan Lynch. But I thought they'd left, Mick.'

'Ah, they did. At least, they did leave but it was only ever meant to be temporary. An urgent family matter back in the States, apparently. Not great when Kelly's in Grade Twelve, of course, but she's a really smart kid. She'll make it up.'

'How long have they been gone?'

'Almost a month. They got back on Friday, I believe, and Kelly was back in school yesterday.'

'Any idea what the mother wants?'

'No, none.'

'Huh. Dare I hope it's good news? That would be nice for a change.'
'Don't hold your breath.'
'No …'

✱

Boards love strategic plans. A plan running to many pages (if and when they are still committed to paper) full of objectives, measurables, dates, and accountabilities gives them at least an illusion of being in control. Certainly, some things can be planned. The building of a new basketball court by a set date should be achievable (though construction may be accelerated or delayed by fluctuating enrolment or the state of the local economy) but other parts of the plan might better be described as aspirations rather than goals. *The school will attract and retain teaching staff of the highest calibre* is a bold and confident statement of intent. It is also almost entirely meaningless. A more honest statement would be, *we will continue to hire the best teachers we can afford and who are prepared to come and live in this part of the world.* Moreover, the very terms "best" and "highest calibre" beg more questions than they answer.

School heads are often less enamoured of strategic plans. They know schools to be situational and contingent. Unanticipated opportunities arise that should be seized whether or not they feature in the current strategic plan. Alternatively, ideas and initiatives that made sense eighteen months ago may quickly have become redundant. At their worst, strategic plans can become straightjackets that actually inhibit constructive growth and development. Achieving what is written in the plan by the required date can create a spurious sense of progress even when circumstances have changed and more pressing matters clamour for attention.

Peter had encountered his first strategic plan in his school in Germany and had at first treated it with a certain reverence. It sounded so confident, so sure what the necessary goals were and how to achieve them. Summaries of the plan's key objectives, cleverly illustrated with charts, renderings of planned facilities, clip art versions of students and teachers, and subtle use of the school's logo were hung in classrooms, in the corridors, and in offices. Twice a year the board published updates, citing percentages, trends and deadlines met that certainly sounded quite encouraging. And yet, as Peter's six years in Germany passed and the school trundled along, doing what it did and doing it more or less successfully, he came to question what the fuss was all about. Surveys of parental satisfaction returned broadly the same results year after year. The annual IB Diploma scores slowly declined for a couple of years and then began improving again. The staff retention rate remained unchanged, enrolment rose and then fell marginally. The school's financial position neither improved nor worsened. In his final year, and prompted by something he had read suggesting that the idea of the strategic plan had passed its sell-by date, Peter dug out the colourful booklet that had once so impressed him. He read down the list of key targets.

'Achieved ... not achieved ... abandoned ... achieved – but only because we redefined "inclusion" ... achieved, sort of ...'

Even those items that could be said to have been achieved now seemed pretty hollow.

- *Conduct a forensic review of the taught curriculum throughout the school to ensure that it is comprehensive, coherent, and relevant.*

Well, the review had been conducted by a committee of teachers and programme coordinators convened for this purpose and so had been "achieved" but, some minor tinkering notwithstanding, no changes were recommended or implemented. And quite how "forensic" the review had been, no one could really say, although everyone agreed that the word added an impressive sense of purpose. Peter reflected on the hours he and his colleagues had spent gathering evidence and preparing the report. He had to conclude that their time could have been better spent.

Not that Peter disapproved of or disagreed with the sentiment that ultimately underpinned the concept of a strategic plan. Certainly, schools should continuously question what they do, why they do it, and how. And even the most successful schools should always be able to identify areas where improvement is probably necessary and achievable. What Peter questioned was whether a detailed plan was a help or a hindrance in enabling a school to navigate the road ahead of it.

"Life is what happens when you are making other plans." John Lennon may not have been the first to express the thought but he had certainly popularised it. And, thought Peter, it was as true of the life of a school as it was of an individual. He reflected on his own life. Not much of it could be said to have been planned. He had more or less assumed he would be married one day and from quite an early age he had known he wanted to go into teaching. But the actualities? Married to Sheila, living in Africa, and now the head of a school? None of that had been planned as such. He hadn't really seen any of it coming – until it happened. Nor, of course, had the events of his life been completely random. He could hardly call it a plan but he had always had a sense of the direction he wanted his life to follow.

And perhaps that was about as much as a school could ask for. Not a strategic plan but a strategic direction.

*

There were those in the Diplomatic Wives' Association of Awanza who worried that their newest recruit was in danger of rocking the boat.

'We're not really meant to be political, dear,' one had tentatively suggested to Sheila.

'It's not political. It's humanitarian. If there was a major earthquake here, would we do whatever we could? Provide food and shelter and so on? Of course we would. Same thing.'

That Sheila enjoyed the support of Susi, who was widely respected in the DWAA, certainly helped. Moreover, Susi's close and mutually respectful relationship with the Minister of Health, who happened to be a woman, didn't hurt either.

Contacts were worked, favours called in, a few fragile egos massaged and, after what seemed to a frustrated Sheila far too long, a meeting was brokered between three members of the DWAA, a representative of the Ministry of Health, and two members of the Ndwalowe Police Service, including the head of the Domestic Violence Division.

'I wasn't aware the police had a Domestic Violence Division,' Sheila had admitted to Susi.

'I've heard of it, Sheila, but I've never known it to do much.'

'Well, this might be progress.'

'The Minister of Health is a formidable woman when she wants to be. In Awanza, it's all about who you know.'

'Isn't that the case everywhere?'

Susi could only agree.

*

Peter had met Susan Lynch a couple of times. Soon after his arrival in Ndwalowe she had introduced herself at a Thanksgiving event hosted by the US Ambassador and he had subsequently welcomed her as a guest speaker during a weekend seminar for Grades Eleven and Twelve students on gender-based violence. He liked her. She was an educated and principled woman who evidently understood and fully endorsed what a school like ISN was trying to be. He only wished there were more parents like her.

But, as a single parent with a full-time job, she was never one of the mothers loitering around the car park with whom Peter made sometimes enjoyable and slightly flirtatious conversation. Indeed, as he waited for her in his office, he struggled to remember when they had last spoken. Perhaps at the end of year assembly in June when her daughter, Kelly, had won an award for her community service project?

Chiamaka appeared at the door. Without saying anything, she nodded over her shoulder.

'Thank you, Chiamaka. Please show her in.' With every day that passed, Peter was ever more grateful for the discreet efficiency with which his secretary did her job. *Boy, if there's one appointment we got right ...*

'Susan. Hello again. I haven't seen you in – I don't know – months.' They shook hands. Peter waved to the easy chairs.

'Well, as I'm sure you know, we were gone for a while.'

'Yes. An urgent family matter, I'm told. I hope everything ...'

'I think so. I hope so.'

'So, you're both okay to come back?'

'Well, that's the point. The urgent matter wasn't there – back in the US. It was here.'

'Oh?'

Chiamaka quietly appeared at Susan's shoulder. 'Mrs Lynch, may we offer you some tea? Or water or something?'

'That's kind. Yes. Tea, please.'

'Peter?'

'Do you need to ask?'

'You drink too much coffee!' Chiamaka chided. She gave Peter a mock reproachful glare but went off to fetch the drinks.

Peter smiled and gently shook his head. 'If it's not my wife, it's my secretary.'

'You're lucky to have people to look out for you.'

'I know. I am. Now, an urgent matter …?'

'It's about Chuck Collins.'

Now Susan really had Peter's attention. 'Chuck Collins has gone.'

'I know. That's why we are back.'

Chiamaka reappeared with the refreshments. 'Milk, Mrs Lynch? Sugar?'

'No. Thank you. Just as it is.'

Chiamaka smiled and withdrew. Susan took a sip of tea. 'Four years ago, Peter, I was working in Indonesia. Kelly was in one of the international schools there.'

'Oh?'

'Mr Collins was one of her teachers. Only, he didn't go by 'Chuck' then. He was Charles Collins. When I read several months ago in the school newsletter that you'd hired a teacher called Chuck Collins, I never made the connection. Nor did Kelly. Until she saw him here. And he saw her.'

Peter held his face in his hands. 'I don't think I like where this is going,' he half whispered.

'Nothing was ever proven. Mr Collins was suspended while the accusations were investigated but the girls' stories didn't really hang together. It seemed likely that *something* had been going on but Mr Collins forcefully denied everything and, ultimately, there was insufficient evidence. The superintendent told me – in confidence – that he suspected the worst but, without proof, his hands were tied. I applied for a transfer and ended up here. Mr Collins also left that year and went to Korea. Kelly and I tried to put it behind us.'

'And then I go and hire him.'

'When she saw him, Kelly was beside herself.'

'Why didn't you tell me?'

'Tell you what? There was insufficient evidence in the school in Indonesia. All I could bring you was rumours. You couldn't have done anything.'

'And Chuck saw Kelly and … Does the fact that he got the hell out – and sharpish – tell us anything? Confirmation of his guilt?'

'Will we ever know?'

'Good grief.'

'He has gone, hasn't he? For good?'

'Oh, yes. We won't be seeing him around here again. Susan, how is Kelly now? Is she okay?'

'Not really, no. I guess she'd managed to suppress it all from four years ago – she was only fourteen – but seeing him again here …'

'Did you get some professional help for her back in the States?'

'Of course.'

'And would you like me to bring in Jean Coady here to talk to Kelly?'

'I think that would help. Kelly likes Ms Coady.'

'Wow,' Peter tried to digest the news. 'Susan, I think it's probably best all round if we keep this between us.'

Susan nodded.

'I'm glad you're back. Both of you. Thank you. Please … please tell us if there's anything we need to know or do. And please tell Kelly that she's safe. She doesn't have to worry.'

'Is she? Is she safe? Will she ever be?'

Peter opened his mouth but he had no answer.

Although ISN was the only International Baccalaureate and only authentic international school in Awanza (one or two small optimistic and opportunistic schools in Ndwalowe shoehorned 'International' into their names but no one was fooled), there were a number of other private schools in the city that had good reputations. They were all cheaper than ISN and adhered to a southern hemisphere calendar. They also offered the Awanzan curriculum, sometimes augmented with some examinations that bore the impressive (and very marketable) imprimatur of well-known British universities. In August and in January and sometimes in other months, students migrated between these schools and ISN, their parents usually citing fees, curriculum, or discipline. Not a few made the journey more than once and often back whence they had been perhaps eighteen months previously.

'The so-and-so family is coming back,' was a reasonably common item of news in the ISN admissions office.

Just as familiar to Peter's ears was the news that an angry email had been received from an angry mother and that her daughter would imminently be transferring to "a school where there are morals/standards/rules (*)".

(*) Delete as applicable.

Sometimes such students disappeared. Just as often, they didn't. Meanwhile, other angry parents from across Ndwalowe moved their children into ISN, citing much the same concerns. Pity the poor youngsters whose parents never seemed to find what they were looking for.

The half dozen or so private schools that parents with the ability to choose considered reputable had formed themselves into a loose association, the better to liaise with – and sometimes negotiate with – the Ministry of Education. Offering a different curriculum and operating on an August to July calendar, ISN had never been invited to join but early in this new school year a letter for Peter arrived from the Association of Private Schools in Ndwalowe hoping he would attend their next meeting to be held at the Ndwalowe Scientific High School.

Looking for advice regarding the ATE Act, Peter readily agreed to attend.

★

Mick O'Cheney was big (in every sense) and loud (also in every sense) and brought to whatever task he faced an appealing and often inspiring energy. He radiated enthusiasm and motivation. If he had a weakness, it was perhaps that he was perplexed when not everyone shared his excitement about his latest idea. Most colleagues liked and respected Mick but discreetly tried not to be in the room when he was embarking on a new project. Being in the wrong place at the wrong time or foolishly observing, 'Good idea, Mick!' could get you roped into another no doubt worthwhile but time-consuming initiative.

But the students largely adored him and his proposal at a secondary assembly that the school should have a mascot was immediately popular. The stylised logos of other schools in Africa and beyond were projected for inspiration and Mick announced that there would be a competition to nominate suitable animals and then a school-wide vote would be taken.

Earlier, Peter had listened to Mick's ideas with more acceptance than enthusiasm but he acknowledged that the students and many of their parents would probably be in support. Mick excitedly listed all the merchandise that would feature the new mascot from mugs to mouse mats, sun hats to swimming caps, and polo shirts to fanny packs.

'Fanny packs? What!'

'That's what they're called. The little pouch you can wear around your waist.'

'Seriously? Good grief. Isn't it … well, rude?'

Mick shrugged. 'Would you prefer bum bag?'

'Can't we just leave them out? Sell back packs instead?'

'It's just an idea.'

So, with Peter giving a light that was at least greenish, Mick threw himself into the search for a school mascot. Peter tried not to think about it.

International schools are often, and quite rightly, nervous about being seen to respect and celebrate some cultures more than others. The national holidays and customs of the host country will usually be observed but schools risk straying into deep water if and when they identify too closely with traditions that are meaningful to some but not others.

Of course, no such restraint is necessary on the part of individuals or communities. The school as an institution may keep its distance but Chinese families and teachers will celebrate the Chinese New Year, the Irish will dress up for St Patrick's Day, citizens of the United States will gather for Thanksgiving, and religious events will be observed by those for whom they matter. And, rather delightfully in these multicultural populations, invitations to participate will often be extended to friends and colleagues. Some celebrations call for a degree of solemnity; others seem rather more tongue-in-cheek. In Germany, Peter had been both amused and bemused each year when his Australian colleagues prepared a barbeque on the 26th of January each year to which everyone was invited. They stood in the staff car park, often in several centimetres of snow, drinking cold beer and eating over-cooked sausages ("snags", apparently) while someone's music system improbably belted out songs about surfing on Bondi Beach.

Serious expressions of nationalism are uncommon and usually unwelcome in authentic international schools but playful, almost parodic, celebrations of one's identity often amuse and entertain. And, of course, few things bring out the flags and other clichés more quickly than sporting rivalries.

'You couldn't get Mick to come? You'll need someone's shoulder to cry on at the final whistle.' Gordon Sipple grinned as he cracked open another can of beer.

'I think he's more of a rugby man,' answered Kevin Bunratty. 'Anyway, one Irishman is more than a match for three English. And where is number three? He's going to miss the kick-off.'

On cue, the door to Gordon's apartment opened and Mark Langtoft hurried in, a six-pack in one hand and a wooden rattle in the other.

'Bloody hell,' exclaimed Kevin. 'I haven't seen one of these in a long time.'

'It was my dad's. It's become a family tradition to bring it out whenever England play. Every time they score …' He waived the rattle above his head. It made an appalling noise.

'Well, that's a relief. We probably won't be hearing that again tonight.'

'You think? A hat-trick for Kane, I reckon.'

'I hope you've warned the neighbours, Gordon. Kevin can get a bit loud when he's had a few.' Simon Swales slapped Kevin on the shoulder.

'Ezekiel won't mind. Anyway, you should hear the racket he makes when Malawi are playing. And Anna hardly ever seems to be in these days.'

'How's she doing, Mark? You work with her.'

Mark shrugged. 'She's okay, I think. A bit subdued, I guess.'

'There haven't been any more of those notes?'

'She hasn't said anything.'

'I do wonder who it is.' Kevin walked to the window and looked out into the courtyard as if looking for clues.

'I heard a rumour that Genuine's name has come up.' Simon would have preferred to change the subject but he could not resist sharing this piece of gossip.

'I heard that too,' agreed Mark. 'He does have an eye for the ladies.'

'My guess is we'll never know.' Gordon picked up the remote and unmuted the TV. 'About to kick-off, guys.'

'I'm not so sure.' Kevin took a seat. 'I reckon he's been lucky so far. He thinks he's clever. But he'll blow it sooner or later. Come on, Ireland!'

'We'll see. Simon, pass the crisps will you?' Gordon reached out to his friend but Simon wasn't listening. He was staring across the room with a look of intense concentration.

*

Mwakami National Park may be entered at any of three gates located in the west, the south and the east. From Ndwalowe, one arrives at the Livingstone Gate which comprises a dusty and ill-defined car park, toilets (though only for the absolutely desperate), a small and rather dilapidated wall of information boards illustrating the principal mammals, birds, trees and reptiles to be found within the park, and an austere brick office wherein payment may be made and permits obtained. Sometimes there are vendors who have laid out on colourful blankets (which are also for sale) wooden carvings of giraffes, hippos and elephants, small woven baskets, bangles, necklaces, and earrings, and little metal models of the windmills that are to be found on farms throughout southern Africa.

Peter had arrived here more than once to find that no other car in sight and on one occasion had waited for a frustrating half-hour until someone in uniform had appeared, yawning, and rubbing his eyes. On this occasion, however, he was surprised to find three other vehicles already in the car park, a seemingly ancient but ostentatiously well-equipped Land Rover Defender, a Toyota Prado and, much to Peter's disapproval, a VW Polo.

Each journey out of Ndwalowe into the wilder reaches of Awanza had prompted Peter to equip the Beast with another item he decided was necessary – a shovel, an axe, a second spare tyre, a roof rack for the carriage of 20 litre jerrycans of diesel, and a powerful spotlight mounted above the driver's door. The second spare tyre had never been required, the shovel and axe never used, and Peter never allowed the fuel tank to get to the point where the reserves on the roof would be necessary. The spotlight had been employed just once on an unsuccessful night drive to find and identify nightjars. Sheila had wondered if these boys' toys were really necessary but, mindful of her first visit to Mwakami, she had bitten her lip and tolerated each of Peter's new enthusiasms.

'I wonder if we ought to get a small generator,' Peter had proposed once. 'In case we get completely stranded overnight somewhere remote.'

Sheila reflected that even the longest trips they had so far attempted had been from one air-conditioned lodge to another on roads that were either paved or professionally graded and that maps of Awanza accurately indicated where filling stations were to be found, even in the remotest regions seldom more than a couple of hundred kilometres from the last one. Being stranded far from assistance seemed unlikely. She had discouraged the acquisition of a generator and, reluctantly, Peter had agreed.

But, even if a reason to employ his new equipment had not so far presented itself, it pleased Peter to drive a big car with a huge engine and all-terrain tyres (six of them) and, perhaps most importantly of all, that the Beast looked the part. This was a car that could go anywhere.

The Land Rover he was now admiring, which, he now noticed, had German plates, was also the kind of no-nonsense vehicle that you could put your trust in and the Prado he knew to be a credible off-road vehicle.

But a VW Polo?

He had seen such cars before in Mwakami and he found that they rather irritated him. They seemed not to be taking the whole experience seriously. Part of the enjoyment of spending time in the bush was the sense of adventure. He had found roads that had been partly washed away by heavy rains. He had more than once driven up a riverbed. There were lions. There were snakes. There was, he reflected with a frown, black cotton soil. People should go to such places recognising and respecting the wildness they were encountering. Arriving in a car that suggested you were taking a short-cut on the way home from the supermarket seemed quite disrespectful. It didn't seem right to Peter. (And, if he was honest, it made him wonder if he and his 4.2 litre Nissan Patrol weren't just a little ridiculous.)

Mulling this over, he watched Sheila striding to the Park Office and, instinctively, started searching the car park and surroundings for birds. Starlings and sparrows of at least two species were in evidence and he was delighted to see what he was sure was a red-headed weaver. A brown and white flycatcher of some sort appeared and almost immediately disappeared. *A Marico?* And then he saw a lizard. Well, he wasn't sure if lizard was quite the right word. It must have been close to a foot long and was strikingly coloured. The head was blue, the body purplish and the stocky tail yellow. He cursed himself for not having his binoculars to hand and hurried back to the car. Time for the camera or just bins? Then he remembered the book Sheila had given him to celebrate the start of his second year. He rummaged in his backpack.

Scanning the contents page of *Africa's Reptiles South of the Equator* as he marched briskly back to where he had seen the lizard, he tried to remember the little he knew about such animals. They had geckos in and around the house in Ndwalowe, skinks in the garden and even the odd chameleon but something this big and colourful was quite unfamiliar to him.

The lizard had moved from where he first saw it but Peter found it again without trouble. It was conspicuous against the grey dust of the car park. Impatiently, he turned the pages of the section on lizards, all the while watching his prey scuttling short distances before stopping and lifting its head.

It's an agama, he concluded with satisfaction. *But which one?*

No further deliberations were possible as a small stone thudded into the earth just in front of the lizard, raising a puff of dust. The lizard skittered across the car park and stopped again. Another stone landed some way behind it, provoking another nervous sprint. Both the agama and Peter hurriedly scanned the area to see where the stones were coming from.

A young boy of perhaps eight or nine was excitedly running towards the agama, a couple of small stones in either hand.

'Hey! Stop!' Peter made to intercept the boy who darted away. Defiantly, and keeping his eyes on Peter, the boy launched another stone in the agama's direction but it landed far short.

'I said stop!'

The boy did not stop. He ran in a broad arc back towards the parked cars, still carrying his stones. Peter glanced back. The agama, he was relieved to see, had disappeared.

'You!' Peter heard a man's voice. 'What are you doing to my boy?'

The boy was clinging on to a large man whom Peter assumed was the father.

'Don't you threaten my son! Who do you think you are?'

'Did you see what he was doing? Your son?'

'Yes. So what? He's a boy. It was a bit of fun. He didn't hurt the lizard.'

Peter was appalled. 'Well, not for want of trying. He was throwing stones at it.'

'So? It's a lizard.'

Peter gasped. 'You have come here … I assume you are here to enjoy the magnificent wildlife. I'd hope you'd want to teach your son to respect and value these animals. Not treat them as objects for entertainment.'

'You don't tell me how to bring up my son.' The man moved towards Peter slightly threateningly.

Then the boy spoke.

'Mr Corby. We're not in school now. You can't tell me what to do.'

Both Peter and the father stopped, frowned, and looked at the boy.

'You know this man, Vinay? Is he your teacher?'

The boy, still staring at Peter, shook his head. 'He's the director. He tells the teachers what to do.'

I wish, thought Peter. But he said, 'You go to ISN?' The boy nodded.

'You don't know all your students?' The father asked, scowling.

'Well, apparently, you don't know who your son's teacher is.' The two men glared at each other, neither quite as assured as they had been shortly before.

Peter decided it might be prudent to lower the temperature. He held out his hand. 'I'm Peter Corby. I'm the director of the international school.'

The father looked unimpressed.

'Director, or principal, if you like.' Peter continued. 'The head, anyway. I'm sorry. I don't know your name.'

Vinay's father hesitated and then took Peter's hand. 'Gill. I'm Dr Gill. Yes, my son is in your school. My daughter, too. She is in Grade …' He looked at his son.

'Eight, papa. She's in Grade Eight.'

Peter looked over Dr Gill's shoulder. A teenage girl was standing by the Prado and did indeed look somewhat familiar. Beside her, a woman whom Peter assumed to be the mother was holding a mobile phone and had apparently been recording everything.

'Is that your wife?' Peter asked. 'What is she doing?'

'I hope she is recording your behaviour,' said Dr Gill.

'My behaviour?'

'You are behaving very aggressively. My son is only eight.'

'Nine, papa. I was nine last month.'

'Exactly,' said Dr Gill, keeping his eyes on Peter, 'nine.'

'Your son ... I ...' Peter's mouth opened and closed but in the end he just shook his head. He looked at Vinay. 'Please don't throw stones at animals. They are not playthings.'

He turned and walked towards his car. Over his shoulder, he could hear Dr Gill calling to him but he ignored it and kept walking.

On the other hand, he thought. *Yes, Vinay, lions. You can throw stones at lions. Good idea. Get out of the car and see if you can hit a lion.* He walked on, smiling rather grimly.

Then he remembered Nicholas Gillespie and he felt terrible.

It is not necessary in Awanza, or in most African countries, to go to the major national parks to find and enjoy captivating landscapes and engrossing wildlife. Though perhaps not on the scale of the more celebrated parks, many privately-owned estates and lodges offer game drives, seductively comfortable accommodation, fine dining, and the always welcome opportunity to leave one's quotidian worries behind. There will undoubtedly be a pool. There may be a tennis court. Horse riding may be available. But there is often little or no pressure to do anything but loll about with a pair of binoculars or a good book, drinking coffee in the morning, beer or rock shandy in the afternoon, and wine at night.

Tourists from Europe and elsewhere will most likely try to cram it all in. Early morning drives to see leopards and cheetahs; night-time drives to see porcupines and pangolins; perhaps an afternoon visit to an (in)authentic African village. Locals are more likely to spend their days waking late, making few plans, and simply enjoying being pampered for a few days.

Lying on loungers by the pool at the Lion Pride Lodge, Gordon Sipple and Simon Swales were trying to decide if it was too early in the day for a beer.

'What time did Mark say he'd be here?'

'After lunch was the best he could say. It depends how long his business in Ndwalowe takes.'

'I was surprised he agreed to come along.'

'I was surprised you invited him.'

'Well, he seemed to enjoy the football game last week. I actually feel a bit sorry for him. Doesn't seem to have many friends. It won't kill us to give him a bit of company for a couple of days.'

'No …' Simon had that faraway look again.

'You still think …'

'I don't know. But you didn't see his face. He was grinning … smirking. Kevin said he thinks the guy will get caught sooner or later and Mark … It was a kind of "I know something you don't know" sort of look. Very self-satisfied. Mark isn't really like that.'

'You would claim to know him well?'

'No, of course not. Does anyone? But he's always seemed rather … timid. Lacking in confidence. But that wasn't the look I saw on his face that night. It was very strange.'

'Well, let's bring it up again. This evening. See how he reacts.'

'Yeah, maybe. I mean, I don't want to accuse anyone. I know how that feels.' Simon shuddered. His friend stretched out his arm and took his hand.

★

Those with childhood memories of riding on top of an elephant at a zoo or of seeing one performing at a circus will have in their mind an image of something large, of course, but also gentle – docile, even. Encountering an adult African elephant in the wild is an altogether different experience.

'Friendly, we can't get to our tent. There's an elephant standing outside. A big elephant. Really big.'

'Uh-oh. He's back, is he?' Friendly Hausiku, manager of the Quarmby Savanna Camp, looked up from the Land Cruiser engine he was trying to fix. He wiped his hands on a rag.

'You know him?'

'One Tusk. He's been hanging around off and on for a few weeks. He disappears for months at a time then turns up again.'

'Whenever I get close, he flaps his ears and gives me a look.'

'A look?'

'An elephant look.'

'Yes, he'll do that.'

'Can we shift him?'

'How?'

'I don't know. I don't suppose going *shoo* works?'

'You want to shoo away a six-ton elephant?'

'I want to get to our tent. We've been driving all day and we need showers. And a change of clothes.'

'And a cold beer?'

'Yes, but …'

'Then what I suggest is that you and Sheila go to the bar and take your time over a couple of beers – on the house. The more you stand around glaring at One Tusk, the more it encourages him. He'll never wander off with you jumping up and down thirty metres away.'

'Seriously?'

'Elephants are highly intelligent. And they can be bloody minded. They certainly want you to know who's the boss. Know it and acknowledge it.'

'He's doing it on purpose?'

Friendly smiled. 'A few months back, I planted some fast-growing trees – indigenous trees, of course – where everyone parks their cars. I thought they might offer some shade. A day or two later, One Tusk found them. He ripped up everyone. He didn't eat them, he just stomped them to pieces. All we could do was stand and watch. I've got a video if you want to see.'

Peter was incredulous. 'Why?'

'I think he was just showing me whose property this really is.' Friendly was now grinning broadly. 'You don't argue with an elephant.'

Peter sighed. 'Free beer, you say? On the house?'

Friendly laughed. 'Come on. I'll pour it for you myself.'

★

The dining room at the Lion Pride Lodge was a high-roofed thatched building built on the slope above a tributary of the Lowana River. Twelve tables were arranged on two levels, the better to allow all diners to see the broad pool beyond the terrace outside where hippos entertained the guests by day and sundry ungulates came to drink at dusk. The floodlights seemed not to concern the thirsty animals but attracted insects which, in turn, brought the nightjars. They flashed fleetingly in the night sky when the light caught them but were mostly unnoticed by the tourists whose binoculars and cameras were more concerned with the waterhole in the not entirely fanciful hope that a lion or hyena may put in a rare appearance.

Gordon, Simon, and Mark sat on three sides of a table, each with a good view through the open fourth side of the room.

'Jackal?' Simon waved vaguely at something moving quite quickly but cautiously behind the drinking kudus.

'Black-backed. It's the only one we get here.'

'You know about animals, Gordon?' asked Mark.

'A bit. You can't really live in Africa and not pick up some of it. But you've been here for a couple of years, Mark. You must have …'

'Actually, no. Not really. I think this is only the second time I've been to a game lodge. I'm just not … terribly interested.'

'What do you do, Mark?' Simon asked. 'People at school think you're a bit of a dark horse.'

Mark Langtoft flushed. 'I'm not really … I'm a bit of an introvert, I suppose.' He took another bite of his filo pastry starter. 'This is good. I like the mushrooms.'

'Sorry, Mark. I didn't mean to embarrass you. But before the match last week, I don't think we'd ever really spoken. You seem quite into football.'

'I am. I watch a lot of football. Alone, mostly.'

'Well, you should invite people round. We'd come and watch footie with you, wouldn't we, Gordon?'

Gordon Sipple had his mouth full but nodded encouragingly.

'Or Anna,' said Simon. 'You two work together. I'm sure she …'

'Oh, no. I don't think …' Mark had turned bright pink. He stared at his now empty plate. Simon flashed Gordon a look.

Gordon took the initiative. 'More wine, Mark?' He lifted the bottle and poured.

'Anna and I, er … Anna is … I mean, we work together really well. And I like her, of course,' Mark was talking but still staring at his plate. 'But she …'

'Mark,' Simon suddenly felt unusually bold. And abruptly angry. 'What do you know about the blue notes someone was leaving for Anna?'

★

On the morning of their departure, Peter and Sheila hoped to make an early start. Peter had received an unexpected and quite worrying phone call from Simon Swales and wanted to be back in Ndwalowe in time to meet him and Gordon Sipple. They settled the bill the night before, packed as much as they could before going to bed, and set an alarm for just after sunrise.

Listening to the morning birdsong, Peter pulled on his shorts and T-shirt. 'She, I'm just going to move the car round to the end of the path.'

From the shower came an indistinct reply.

He pulled up the powerful zip and stepped out onto the wooden deck. He was looking more or less into the rising sun and lifted his hands to shield his eyes.

From behind him – but what seemed to be alarmingly close – he felt as much as heard an impossibly sonorous growl that almost immediately became an ear-splitting trumpet. Quite involuntarily, Peter collapsed to the floor. He scrambled away from the noise, tried to grab the handrail, succeeded only in breaking a couple of fingernails, and tumbled painfully down the wooden steps.

'Jesus Christ!'

He lay in the dust, rubbing a knee that seemed to be twisted, and looking up anxiously at One Tusk on the other side of the deck.

The elephant contemplated Peter. Peter thought it wise not to move. In any case, he wasn't sure he could.

From inside the tent, Sheila's voice called. 'Peter? What happened?'

'Stay there!' He shouted. 'The elephant's back. Don't come out!'

'What have you done?' Peter heard Sheila shout.

Oh great, he thought. *It's my fault, of course.*

Still One Tusk just stared. Peter looked away. Eye contact seemed imprudent. There was something going on here and he decided that he must stay still and silent. Incongruously, a couple of lines from *Monty Python and the Holy Grail* came to mind. *What are you doing? I'm averting my eyes, oh Lord.* In spite of his predicament, he could not suppress a sardonic smile.

'Are you okay?' Sheila called.

'She. Be quiet. Please.'

The elephant grunted and Peter allowed himself a quick look. A grunt of satisfaction? A grunt of displeasure? A grunt of disdain?

'Bloody elephant,' Peter muttered. 'What do you want me to do?'

One Tusk flicked his trunk in Peter's direction but, as best Peter could tell, it did not seem to be a particularly threatening gesture. Slowly, and painfully, he pulled himself into a more or less kneeling position. But still he stared at the ground and not at the elephant.

'Oh come on, man. Just let us go. You win.' Cautiously, he raised his head and looked squarely at One Tusk. There came another grunt, a gentle flap of the ears, and the elephant stepped slowly to one side. Without another look in Peter's direction, he ambled a step or two at a time away from the tent, his tail flicking lazily.

'Phew ...' Peter rubbed his elbows and knees and tentatively stretched his neck. He was bruised but nothing seemed to be broken. 'She,' he spoke just loudly enough, 'he's gone. I think he's going.'

Sheila's head appeared at the entrance to the tent. She gasped to see Peter lying in the dirt and the bottom of the stairs. 'Are you all right?'

'I think so. He was right there. Just beside the tent. God, he gave me a fright.' Peter stood awkwardly, trying to brush off the dust. They both watched the elephant move slowly away, quite obviously no longer interested in Peter or Sheila.

'I think we should ask for a different tent next time,' said Sheila.

'Or a different elephant.'

★

Odetta Menlyn had spent the October break visiting her parents in Durban. South African by birth, her teaching career had taken her to Singapore and Romania but as her parents grew older and retired to the coast, she chose to move to somewhere a bit closer to them. Ndwalowe, a ninety-minute flight from Johannesburg, was perfect. Much as she had enjoyed exploring Asia and Europe, home would always be the Lowveld where her parents had farmed for so many years and in the familiar landscape of Awanza Odetta felt very much at home.

That the school was probably the best of the three she had worked in internationally certainly helped. She liked her colleagues, considered herself fortunate to have Valli Agnelli as a principal, and greatly appreciated the enormous diversity within the school. Her school in Singapore had been quite British; the one in Romania proudly American. Both were fine schools but she now found herself in a school that described itself as international and, as best she could tell, genuinely seemed to mean it.

Odetta had been hired by John Conway, Peter Corby's predecessor as director. She was initially somewhat in awe of his confident and sometimes brusque manner. He was a man seemingly not possessed of self-doubt, articulate and often witty, if sometimes caustic. It was a brave or foolish staff member who challenged him in a public meeting. Although, quite to her own surprise, that is what Odetta found herself doing. When John authored a new version of the staff handbook with virtually no consultation or input from anyone else, it was Odetta who first wrote him a long memo pointing out inconsistencies, inaccuracies and omissions and then, after receiving a curt reply that amounted to "you do your job and I'll do mine", decided to raise the matter at the next full staff meeting. John had not been impressed (although, with a bad grace, he did agree to amend the handbook) but Odetta won a lot of respect from her peers. Soon thereafter she was elected unopposed as the Chair of the Staff Association, a position, she confided to friends, she intended to use "to keep the director honest".

And now, Peter Corby was the director.

Not quite sure what to expect from his first encounter with the Association of Private Schools in Ndwalowe, Peter had decided to wear a suit and tie. In fact, the day was chilly and he was glad to be wearing a jacket, something he seldom did at work. Then again, was he over-dressed? Would it look to his hosts that he was being a touch self-important? In Japan and Germany a suit would have been expected. But in this pleasingly unpretentious African city in the tropics, shirts were usually short-sleeved and few men wore ties. *Maybe a suit but no tie*, he wondered as he drove through the gates of the Ndwalowe Scientific High School. He had been in Awanza long enough to know that there were those who considered the International School to be elitist, exclusive, and condescending towards not only other schools but the country itself. Sadly, Peter knew that there were a few parents whose children attended ISN who could fairly be accused of such arrogance and condescension. (Even more depressingly, he had occasionally heard such views being expressed by staff members.) Certainly, the school was the most expensive in the country and only rarely would an ISN graduate or their parents consider applying to the University of Awanza or any of the other national institutions of higher education.

Their IB Diploma scores and their parents' chequebooks would send these young people to more prestigious universities and colleges in North America, Europe, Australia, and other destinations of comparable status. But, Peter hoped, his school also valued and taught compassion, respect and even humility. Great emphasis was placed on service learning and many teachers admirably led by example. ISN students were gently reminded that they were indeed privileged but they were also taught that their good fortune did not make them more worthy or somehow "better" than those less fortunate. Of course, just because something has been "taught" does not mean that it has been learned. There were, Peter had to concede, students in his school who looked down on those whose parents didn't drive a Mercedes or Land Cruiser or whose smartphone was two generations out of date. A school is not the only context in which a child learns attitudes and values.

Peter was informed that the meeting was being held in the principal's office and he was ushered down a labyrinth of corridors to a large room. The only occupant was a small woman wearing a simple grey smock that suggested some sort of religious order. She rose and the two shook hands.

'Good morning,' said Peter, looking around the room, 'I was afraid I was going to be late. I'm Peter Corby from the International School.'

'Oh, don't worry. These things never start on time. Sister Helen. Ndwalowe Girls' High School.'

'Pleased to meet you.'

'Ah, you must be Mr Corby. Welcome.'

Peter turned and was greeted by a large man dressed in an electric blue suit carrying a thick folder.

'Mr Ngoma? Thank you for the invitation.'

'It's a pleasure to meet you at last. It's high time we had a closer relationship with your school. How are you enjoying Awanza?' Mr Ngoma's handshake was, to say the least, firm.

'Quite honestly, I'm loving it. So is my wife. We're very happy to be here.'

'Excellent, excellent. I'm so happy to hear that.' He gave Peter's hand a further squeeze. 'Now, Sister Helen, who are we still waiting for? Can everyone make it?'

One by one, the heads of four more schools arrived, greeted each other, were introduced to Peter, and took one of the chairs that were arranged in a

116

rather tight circle. The meeting had been scheduled to start at ten but it was close to half-past when Mr Ngoma announced it was time to start.

Peter made to open his laptop but, on his left, Sister Helen reached out and, quite to his surprise, took Peter's hand. On his right, Godson Mbwena, principal of St Michael's, took Peter's other hand. Everyone lowered their heads.

✹

With Carola unavoidably accompanying her husband to a reception at the State House, the October board meeting was chaired by Ernesto. Peter had rather looked forward to Ernesto running the meeting with a characteristic firm hand but, perhaps a little intimidated by the unfamiliar responsibility, Ernesto seemed to Peter to be allowing Lazarett far too much latitude.

'The school is already well into its second year of operation and no one can argue that we are still in survival mode. It is extraordinary that we are not working in the context of a strategic plan. The management should have been working on this months ago. But it seems they prefer to make things up as they go along.' Lazarett paused, perhaps hoping that Peter would be provoked into a reply. But it was Clyde who spoke.

'Lazarett, I'm not necessarily disagreeing about the need for a plan but I don't think it's fair to blame the management. Strategy is very much a board responsibility. We have not until now asked the management for a strategic plan. Now we are doing so and I am confident that Peter and his team will—'

'Confident? I wish I was confident. I must say I get the impression that Mr Corby does not value the whole concept of a strategic plan. Perhaps because it would hold him accountable. We already know his opinion of appraisal.'

Wow, thought Peter, *you're really on form tonight, Lazarett.* But, after more than a year of unedifying exchanges between them, he contrived to look serenely into the middle distance as if focussed on something far more interesting and important.

'We're not suggesting that we leave the drafting of a strategic plan solely to the management, are we?' Grant looked at Ernesto.

'No, I don't think anyone's suggesting that,' Ernesto hurriedly agreed with Grant. 'My understanding is that these things are best generated through a community effort. We must invite input from all stakeholders. Ultimately it's the board's decision – and responsibility – but a plan will work best if it's informed by …'

'And ownership,' Catherine interrupted.

'Sorry?'

'Everyone must feel some ownership of the plan. We have to get everyone behind it.'

'That's an important point, Catherine. Thank you.'

'But,' Peter could seldom stay silent for long, 'a community-wide exercise isn't a trivial thing. And I wonder if we need to involve some sort of external facilitator.'

'Absolutely. Thank you, Mr Corby.'

Peter was far from the only one present to react with some astonishment at Lazarett's enthusiastic agreement.

'And,' continued Lazarett, 'I think we have the ideal opportunity coming up.'

Ernesto frowned. 'What opportunity?'

'Mr Daniel is coming next month, is he not?'

'Taniel,' said Peter. 'It's Taniel.'

Lazarett ignored him. 'And, if I understand correctly, Mr Daniel is an expert on international schools. What an excellent opportunity to have him lead us through the creation of a strategic plan.'

Grant was frowning. 'But we have already agreed a full agenda for Mr Taniel's visit. Ernesto and I have had several conversations with him about board composition, conflict of interest, the separation of governance and operations …'

'But not strategic planning?' Lazarett shook his head disappointedly. 'An opportunity missed, I can't help thinking. What could be more important than charting the school's direction over the next three to five years? I'm sure Mr Daniel …'

'Taniel!' Peter was sure Lazarett was doing it on purpose but he could not contain himself.

'I'm sure Mr Daniel will be willing to revise the day's schedule and we still have a good month before he comes.'

It dawned on Peter what Lazarett was doing.

'Mr Chair …' normally Peter disliked and avoided such formalities but, if he was honest, he hoped it might serve to wind up Lazarett. 'I think Mr

Snyman is proposing that we abandon the governance workshop we have all agreed we—'

'Postpone!' There was definitely some annoyance in Lazarett's voice. 'Postpone, not abandon. I think it's a matter of priorities.'

'If I may say so,' Violet Sindima gave both Lazarett and Peter reproachful looks, 'I think tonight illustrates exactly why we need a workshop on good governance. Why does every meeting end up being so … so bad-tempered? I'm certainly not in favour of postponing or cancelling Mr Daniel's visit.'

'Tan …' Peter began to whisper but stopped himself.

'Violet, you are absolutely right. And there can be no question of changing the agenda for next month. As Grant says, he and I have spent several hours exchanging ideas with Mr Taniel and I'm very confident that it will be an extremely productive day.'

'Thank you, Ernesto.'

'Productive and, as you say, Violet, sadly necessary.' To Peter's satisfaction, Ernesto appeared to be directing his last comment towards Lazarett. 'But I think the idea of an external facilitator to guide the strategic plan process is worth considering. I'll see what Carola thinks.'

'Perhaps Mr Taniel could come a second time?' Suggested Trixi. 'Or stay longer this time?'

'Why don't we just see how we get on with him this time? Let's not get ahead of ourselves.'

'Small victories,' Peter said to Sheila ninety minutes later as they shared the inevitable post-board meeting bottle of wine. 'You take what you can.'

'So Lazarett's attempt to hijack your consultant's visit failed?'

'Oh yes. Shot down in flames.'

'But there will be a strategic plan?'

''Fraid so. Clyde Arthurs is going to chair a small committee that will propose a process and a timeline.'

'Oh well. Keep kicking the can down the road if you can. Busy day tomorrow?'

'Not necessarily busy,' Peter had a faraway look. 'But it may not be much fun …'

✱

As he turned into the admin car park, Peter was surprised to see Carola's Mercedes. He found her in Chiamaka's office.

'Sorry, Carola. I didn't know you were coming. I thought I'd come in a bit late. Another long and rather tiring board meeting last night.'

'Ernesto told me.' Carola made a face.

'And I had a surreal meeting in the morning with the Association of Private Schools in Ndwalowe.'

'Oh?'

'Honestly, The insensitivity of it. The thoughtlessness.'

'What?'

'Oh, the assumption that everyone present was Christian. We all held hands while someone thanked the Lord and so on. Honestly, it was such a surprise that it was over before I realised what was happening. Probably a good thing or I might have said something I shouldn't. But really … I was actually quite angry.'

They entered Peter's office. He closed the door behind them.

'Peter,' Carola was clearly uncomfortable. 'I've had a letter from a parent.'

'Oh?'

'He's making a formal complaint.' She paused. 'About you.'

'Me?'

'Do you know a Dr Gill?' Carola removed a letter from her briefcase and began rereading it.

'Oh, wait a minute …'

'Father of Vinay? Grade Three?'

'Yes. I know Dr Gill and his son.' Peter shook his head slowly.

'Dr Gill is saying that his son won't now come to school. Apparently, he is frightened to come because of something that happened. Something you said or did? You shouted at him?'

'Carola, let me tell you …'

'And now he's traumatised.'

'Traumatised? That's ridiculous!'

'He says he has evidence. A video …'

'He does. I'm sure he does. I just hope he shows you the whole thing and not some edited version of it. Okay, let's meet him. In fact I insist we meet him. Him and his video. You, me and him.'

'And his lawyer.'

'Seriously? Okay, why not? You, me, him and his lawyer. Bring it on! But first, shall I tell you what happened?'

★

If Peter's day had started badly, he had no great expectation that it was going to improve. He sat in his office chewing his lip, checking his notes, and glancing frequently at the clock. A little before ten the first of his colleagues arrived and then a second.

They sat in silence, no one much looking forward to what was to come.

'Peter?' Peter looked up at Chiamaka who was hovering in the doorway. 'He's here.'

Peter nodded and stood. Mark Langtoft entered; it was impossible to read his expression.

'Mark, thank you for coming. Please take a seat'

Peter started his little speech. 'Mark, I'm afraid I need to ask you a few questions and it's important that there's no confusion afterwards about what is said ...'

Mark looked at Peter. He looked at Julia. He looked at Odetta.

'Oh dear,' he said. 'Am I in trouble?'

★

Sitting in her office, Valli looked at her watch. Peter had probably started his meeting with Mark Langtoft by now. Valli couldn't decide if she was frustrated not to be there or relieved. If Peter's theory was correct, this was all about to get a lot more complicated.

She picked up her phone and punched in a short number. 'Chiamaka? It's Valli. Has Mark Langtoft ...? Oh, good. Could you please call me as soon as he leaves? I want to come over and talk to Peter. Okay, thanks.'

She hung up and stared across the room, lost in thought.

'Things are never simple, are they ...?'

★

In Peter's office, Mark had at first been rather guarded. But Peter, speaking softly and leaning forward in a confiding manner, had reassured him that he certainly was not in trouble but that he, Peter, wondered if he could throw any light on the notes that Anna had been receiving. After all, Peter had said, Mark worked more closely with Anna than anyone. Mark had nodded. Almost casually, Peter had asked Mark for how long he had worked with Anna and other inconsequential queries to which he already knew the answers. Mark had relaxed. The conversation they were having was a chat, not an interrogation. Only Odetta and Julia silently taking notes suggested this was anything more than an informal exchange.

At length, Peter paused, shuffled forward on his seat, and looked intently but, he hoped, not threateningly at Mark.

'Tell me, Mark. Do people talk to you?'

'Of course. People talk to me all the time.' Mark looked at Odetta, nodded vaguely in Peter's direction, and shook his head condescendingly. He was smiling. Odetta remained expressionless.

'People who aren't there, Mark. Do people who aren't there talk to you, Mark?'

'Uh? How can they talk to me if they aren't there?' Another snigger in Odetta's direction.

'All right,' continued Peter gently. 'People who are there but you can't see them. Do they sometimes talk to you? Mark? People you can't see?'

Mark's smile disappeared. 'Maybe.'

'What do they say, Mark?'

'Things.'

'What things?'

Mark said nothing.

'Do they say things about Anna Street, Mark?'

After a long pause, Mark spoke. 'I like Anna. I've told you.'

Peter nodded slowly.

'We all like Anna, Mark. Everyone likes Anna.'

Mark did not disagree. 'Thing is, Peter. Anna likes me.'

On the outside, Peter had remained impressively calm. He spoke to Mark in a matter-of-fact voice. His body language gave nothing away. On the inside, however, Peter was increasingly anxious. He felt something close to panic.

If this really is clinical, he reproached himself, *you haven't the first idea what you are doing. You could make this worse.*

'How do you know?'

'How do I know what?'

'That Anna likes you?'

Mark's smirk had returned. 'Oh, you know. Things she says. Things she does. She gives me looks.'

'Do you ever give Anna things, Mark?'

'Things?'

'Mmm. Flowers, maybe? Or chocolates? Or … letters?'

For the first time, Mark looked uncertain. 'Women like being complimented.'

'What do you like about Anna, Mark? If you wanted to compliment her, what would you say?'

'I know someone who thinks Anna has pretty eyes.' Mark spoke slowly as if trying to remember something. 'And he likes the way she does her hair.'

'Has he told her, Mark? It is a he, isn't it?'

Mark nodded but still looked confused.

'Has he told her? Has he, maybe, given her messages of some sort?'

'Maybe.'

'How do you think Anna felt when she got these messages?'

'Flattered?'

'Do you think so? Might she have been a little upset?'

'Why? It's just compliments. Who doesn't like being complimented?'

'Maybe it depends who is doing the complimenting. Anna doesn't know who this person is, does she?'

Mark said nothing.

'And …' Peter continued, 'when does a compliment become something else?' He slowly opened the folder lying in his lap and removed from it a number of the blue notes.

Involuntarily but very obviously, Mark flinched. Julia could not contain a small gasp.

Peter selected one note and read it out. '*Your boyfriend is a lucky man.* I suppose that's a sort of compliment. Is that a compliment, Mark?'

Again, Mark said nothing.

Peter continued staring at Mark for some seconds. Then he opened another note. 'Is this a compliment, Mark? *At night in bed I dream of running my hands over your naked …*'

'I didn't write them!' Mark blurted out. 'I didn't write those notes.'

Peter was holding his breath. He could hear and feel his heart racing.

'I delivered them,' Mark looked from Peter to Julia and Odetta. 'I delivered them. But I didn't write them.'

'Who did, Mark? Who did write them?'

★

November

Anna Street was listening to Peter and trying to reconcile very different emotions. She felt relief but also disappointment. Bitterness but also, to her surprise, compassion. But mostly she felt confusion and not a little anger. At last, she had an answer. An answer but hardly a conclusion.

'So,' Peter was saying, 'he's on sick leave – though very much against his will – until we can get an appointment for him. Glory has recommended two well-regarded psychiatrists. Trouble is, they are fully booked for weeks ahead. I'm seeing if we can jump the queue.'

'Dr Binney,' Valli added, 'has seen a number of people associated with the school over the years. We have a pretty good relationship with her. We're hoping she'll agree to see Mark.'

'What if he won't agree? You said he was on sick leave reluctantly.'

Peter sighed. 'I've spoken to our lawyer. This is a delicate situation. Employment legislation in Awanza is quite supportive of the employee. If Mark chooses to fight the school … It could get difficult.'

'But he has admitted leaving me the notes!'

'I know. And that's more than enough reason for a formal warning. It seems, however, that it is insufficient reason to fire him. And, of course, he hasn't admitted writing the notes.'

'Oh, of course he wrote them.'

'I'm not sure he understands that.'

Anna screwed up her face. 'How can he not …?'

'That's why we need him to see a psychiatrist,' Valli spoke gently, sympathetically.

'In fact,' Peter said, 'two, according to our lawyer. Before we can take further action. But we'll start with one.'

'Is he schizophrenic? Is that the word?'

'I'm no more qualified to say than you are. But it seems that he hears voices. And he is absolutely insistent that it is his "friend" who wrote the notes, not him.'

'So where is he now?'

'I've told him he must not come to school. Ideally, I'd like to confine him to his flat in The Warren but I'm not sure how I can enforce that.'

'His flat across from mine?' Anna looked sour.

'That's another thing we need to talk to you about.' Valli was sitting close enough to Anna to take her hand. 'It's obviously not realistic that you can both be living in the same place while we sort this out.'

'Obviously, he's the one who should move,' said Peter, 'but if he is … disturbed, I'm worried it may make him worse.'

'So,' Valli continued, 'we want you to … relocate for a little while. Would you be happy sharing with Ruth?'

'She's my best friend. But her flat is hardly big enough for two.'

'We know. But it's not in The Warren. We'll need to talk to the landlord but don't worry about the cost. The school will take care of that.'

'We hope it'll only be for a short time,' Valli added.

'Or, if you both like it, maybe we can make it permanent.' Peter tried to sound upbeat.

'Have you spoken to Ruth?'

'Not yet. Would you rather do that?'

'Yes. If that's okay.'

'Of course.'

'What do we tell people? About Mark?'

'That he's unwell and is taking a few days off. That's all anyone needs to know.'

'And about me and Ruth moving?'

'I'm going to send Genuine around to replace your toilet or something. We'll say there's been a bad leak. We all know that happens in The Warren.'

Anna just nodded.

'The good news, Anna, is that we know who it is. You know who it is. There won't be any more notes.' Valli gave Anna's hand a squeeze.

Yes, thought Anna, *that is good news. I suppose.* So why then did she still feel miserable about the whole thing?

★

'Are we a school or a business?' Peter wasn't sure he'd ever heard this question in Germany but it had certainly been posed in Hamamatsu when questions of investment, development, salary increases and the like had been debated. It was most certainly a question that had been asked, and more than once, during Peter's first year at ISN. To no one's great surprise, Peter and Lazarett Snyman tended to lean towards somewhat different answers.

'We have – to all intents and purposes – just one source of income,' Lazarett had argued in a finance committee meeting. 'We charge fees. We sell a product. Well, we provide a service, if you prefer. Either way, we have customers. We also have costs. And we have employees. I cannot think of a simpler or better definition of a business.'

'I can,' Peter had quickly said. Catherine and Clyde made discreet eye contact across the table and shared the same slightly anxious expression. 'I think it's all a matter of purpose. Why are we here? A supermarket exists in order to make money. A company is answerable to its shareholders. Ultimately, a business is there to make a profit. That's the whole point.'

'Exactly.'

'No, Lazarett, not exactly. Not at all exactly. This school wasn't founded in order to make money for an owner or investors. It was established to meet a need. A social need. Of course, the money has to come from somewhere and that means charging fees. But that wasn't why the school was created. It's not why we are here now.'

'Can schools go bankrupt?' Lazarett shot back. 'Surely only businesses can go bankrupt. And, as we all know only too well …'

'Well, put it this way. If we discovered that the land the school is on would make more money – more profit – if we knocked everything down and built a supermarket or a hotel or a sports centre, would we do it? If we were a business, we would. If maximising our profit – especially if we had shareholders – was our priority, we'd be foolish not to. Close down the school and make more money doing something else. I think it's called return on investment.'

'Peter,' Clyde interrupted, 'you know we don't have shareholders. I don't think that's what Lazarett is saying.'

'Of course. I'm simply trying to make the point that our purpose is not to make money. That's not why we're here.'

Lazarett had snorted loudly. 'So, it doesn't matter if we lose money? We're not a business?' He shook his head despairingly.

Saskia was about to reply but Catherine was quicker.

'I think,' Catherine said reflectively, 'I think I agree with Peter.'

The four other people in the room were quite taken by surprise, none more so than Peter himself.

'Go on,' encouraged Saskia.

'We're both, aren't we? We're a business and a school. But, first and foremost, we are a school. We're a school first and a business second. Does that make sense?'

Similar conversations will take place in most international schools quite regularly. Except in the most exceptional circumstances, costs will rise year on year. Some schools, particularly those where embassies and multinationals provide the majority of the students (and income), may have the luxury of increasing fees annually without much fear of pushback. But where the majority of the parents pay fees out of their own pockets, boards need to be extremely circumspect when announcing increases. So, alternative sources of income will be sought (but very seldom found) and, not for the first time, costs will be re-examined to see where savings may be made.

Peter had agreed with (and been grateful for) Catherine's summary of the situation. He had chosen a career as a teacher – 'teacher' was still what he wrote on immigration forms and anywhere else where his occupation was asked for – but he had to acknowledge that he was also now in charge of a small- to medium-sized business. In fact, according to some sources, ISN was closer to medium than small. Peter found the idea a little alarming.

'I suppose I'm the school's CEO?' he had suggested to Sheila once. Her answer – *Faute de mieux* – had not reassured him.

So, as the school's CEO, Peter understood he had an obligation to keep costs as low as possible. But as director of the school (Educational Director, as he was identified in certain documents), his priorities were more to do with the quality of teaching and learning.

'In *Rio Grande* Ben Johnson rides two horses at once,' Peter had muttered once to Saskia and Valli. 'It scares the life out of me watching him. I can't even ride one horse.'

Neither woman had the first idea of what Peter was talking about.

Over some expenses, schools have little control. Staff can be exhorted to switch off lights and not leave air conditioners running over the weekend, but the monthly electricity bill is what it is and must be paid. Similarly, there will be little room to haggle with the school's provider of health insurance and it costs what it costs. (And it usually costs a lot.)

But how the school manages the annual turnover of teaching staff is something over which it has at least some control. Teachers with many years of experience tend to cost more. Teachers with dependants are certainly more expensive. Some schools reward advanced degrees with additional points on the salary scale. Teaching couples with no children are often cost-effective but schools do not always have two appropriate vacancies to fill at the same time. Another factor can be the frequency with which jobs must be advertised and filled. Depending on the school's benefits package, flying teachers in and relocating them at the end of their contract can be expensive. Also, the recruitment process itself can be costly in both time and money. It is sometimes, therefore, better for a school to offer a retention bonus to encourage staff to stay. A further complication is that schools are often looking not just at what a prospective employee will cost but also their age, nationality, gender and, for better or for worse, ethnicity.

Most international schools will make reference to diversity on their website, in their philosophy statements, and so on. It is important. It is one of the key ways in which authentic international schools differentiate themselves from national schools (and inauthentic "international schools"). Diversity within the student body usually takes care of itself. But achieving comparable diversity among the forty, sixty or maybe a hundred teaching staff a school may employ can be a challenge.

It is a truism that heads will try to recruit the best person they can for the job, regardless of other factors. But if all three teachers of Grade Four classes are white, single, American women in their thirties … Do you really want to hire a fourth or wouldn't it be better to appoint someone who will add a different perspective?

It is, of course, a minefield. Is hiring someone because of their age, gender or ethnicity any worse than not hiring them for the same reasons? Few heads would openly admit that their ideal candidate for a given vacancy would be, for example, an Indian or African woman. But they may be quietly pleased when the strongest candidate turns out to be just such a person.

The best international schools will employ teaching staff from two or three dozen countries and staff photos will show a satisfying mix of genders and ethnicities. Harder to know from such a photograph may be the personal and domestic circumstances of these smiling faces. And while most schools will agree on the most visible signs of diversity, not all will attach the same importance to a balance between single and married teachers and those with or without children.

'But is just makes sense,' Peter had argued in a board meeting. 'I know that teachers with dependants cost more but the alternative is what? A school staffed entirely by single people with no children? I wouldn't want that. I think it is healthy that we have younger and older teachers; singles and those who are married; some who have children and some who don't. And if I find the perfect candidate for a vacancy, do I turn her down because she comes with two dependants?' Peter's question was not rhetorical. He knew of schools where that is exactly what would happen.

Peter was grateful that his predecessors had felt the same as he did and that the school did indeed employ a number of teachers who brought with them spouses and sometimes children. Not that such appointments didn't also bring their own problems …

*

As Jenny Wintercoat read the email that had just come in, she smiled. Then she chuckled. Then she gasped. 'Peter,' she said to an empty room, 'you need to be careful.' She reread the email and again laughed. *You're absolutely right about the PTA*, she thought, *but you perhaps should think twice about putting it in writing.* She hit reply, typed LOL and a couple of appropriate emojis and then sent it. 'But you do make me laugh,' she said. Then she deleted Peter's email.

*

Mike Sesriem and his wife, Jackie, tended to keep to themselves. They attended staff functions only infrequently and their social lives appeared to be limited. Mike's colleagues in the science department respected him as a competent and mostly conscientious teacher of biology but none would have called him a friend. What Jackie did with her days was a mystery. Before they married, she had been a freelance copy editor and it was believed she continued to work, at least part-time. But no one really knew for sure. And, in truth, no one greatly cared. At children's parties, other mothers tried to make small talk with Jackie but it was usually hard work and few persevered for long.

It was therefore a source of puzzlement to many that Mike and Jackie's son, Will, was such a lively and confident little boy. Although only seven, he was a vocal member of the Primary Student Council and, in class, his teacher, Blessing Nyanga, had her work cut out keeping him from dominating each conversation. He was also a generous and kind young boy, popular, and always concerned for the welfare of others. People liked Will Sesriem.

At the beginning of each school day Valli liked to be visible, sometimes in the car park and sometimes visiting classrooms. Many parents of primary-age children chose to deliver them each morning to their teachers, often taking the opportunity to have a quick word, perhaps share a small concern or, rather too frequently, make a complaint. Teachers could usually handle such moments themselves but, especially when she was aware of a situation brewing, Valli made sure she was close by, and ready to intercede if necessary.

Knowing that there had been an incident in Blessing's class the previous day (a lunchtime incident that involved an argument over whose turn it was to feed the pet hamster, an upturned pot of yoghurt, an alleged shove, and copious tears), Valli made it her business to be at the door to the classroom as parents, mostly mothers, escorted their children up the path. Will Sesriem had not even been present when yesterday's spat had occurred and Valli knew that Jackie was never a mother to complain so, as they approached, she greeted them warmly.

'Hello, Jackie. Nice to see you again. Good morning, Will. How are you?'

Will looked from Valli to his mother and then back to Valli.

'Miss, last night my dad hit my mum.' His expression matched the gravity of his words.

No one spoke. Jackie stared at Valli. Valli stared at Jackie.

'It was just after we finished eating …' Will began to explain but his mother, who had turned very pale, seized him firmly by the elbow and hustled him into the classroom.

'Jackie …' Valli called a bit helplessly but she was immediately distracted by a tall and red-faced woman clutching a small boy by the hand.

'Miss Valli, I am very unhappy about what happened here yesterday. Look – my son is in shock. It's appalling that you permit such behaviour!'

'Mrs Lossen, I'm … Could you just give me a minute?' she looked to see where Jackie was. 'I just need …'

'No. I cannot give a minute. I want this sorted now! Miss Blessing,' she called across the room, 'I need you here now.'

★

It would have been a stretch to describe Mick O'Cheney's demeanour as sheepish but his usual ebullience was certainly absent. He sat across the desk from Peter, a single sheet of paper lying between them.

'Honestly, Peter. I really didn't expect this.'

Peter just raised his eyebrows slightly.

'I mean, I was almost certain that Cheetahs was going to win it – by a mile.'

Peter shook his head slowly.

'To be honest, I only left it in as one of the final three as a joke. A bit of a laugh. Never did I think …' Mick's voice tailed away.

'So,' Peter spoke slowly, making an effort to keep emotion out of his voice. 'The students came up with a dozen or so suggestions for a school mascot. They were narrowed down to three finalists and then they voted. Correct?'

Mick nodded.

'And …' Peter indicated the sheet of paper, 'we have a result.'

'Just not the one we were expecting.'

'Really? Really, Mick? How long have you been working with teenagers? You give them a choice between the Cheetahs, the Eagles and the …' Peter swallowed hard. 'The Dung Beetles, and you are surprised when almost eighty percent choose that one? How would you have voted when you were a teenager? I'm pretty sure I'd have been a Dung Beetle kind of guy myself. Much too much fun not to go for it.'

'It did seem to be a popular choice when we announced it.'

'That's another thing. You announced it from the stage in front of the entire secondary school. If you'd quietly brought the result to me first we might have been able to do something. Fiddle the numbers or something.'

'Doesn't sound very democratic.'

'Of course not but look where we are now. Which message do we send the kids – and the whole community? Well, boys and girls, you've voted and we of course respect the result. We will henceforth be known as the Dung Beetles. Or, sorry kids. We don't like the result so we're simply going to override it. You must forgive me, Mick, if I say that I'm not terribly happy with either option.'

'Perhaps if you'd taken more interest in the whole thing …'

'Oh, don't even think of going there! Yes, if I'd known where things were heading I would certainly have stepped in. But this was your idea and your project. You know I don't breathe down your neck – or Valli's. I trust you. Well …'

'Go on.'

Peter thought hard before he spoke. 'I do trust you. I have to – and I want to. It doesn't work otherwise. But … please. Perhaps a little more judgement next time?'

Mick O'Cheney flushed, considered a probably unwise reply, and bit his tongue.

'And after I had dealt with the always theatrical Mrs Lossen – can you believe, she is demanding reimbursement for the cost of the yoghurt – Jackie had slipped out.'

'Oh no,' said Peter. 'Sounds like a job for Lee-Ann.'

'Well, that's what counsellors are for.'

'Just Lee-Ann or do you want to be there too? And Blessing?'

'No, let's not overwhelm the poor boy. Lee-Ann and I can talk to him and then I can brief Blessing.'

'From the little I've seen of Will Sesriem, I think it would take a lot to overwhelm him. Poor kid.'

'Poor Jackie. I wonder what happened.'

Mark Langtoft's absence from school was being explained as sick leave but there were the inevitable rumours. Besides, he had been seen shopping and a few of those who lived in The Warren had knocked on his door to see if he needed anything. They later reported to others that Mark had seemed distant. He was disinclined to talk about the indisposition that was keeping him away from work. Indeed, he seemed disinclined to say much of anything to anyone.

The parents of children in Mark's Grade Three class had initially been sympathetic (even teachers get ill sometimes) but as the second week started with a substitute teacher more of them began pestering Valli to know when Mark would return. There was a growing sense that parents were not being told the whole story. Some trusted that the school knew what it was doing. Others were less generous.

It may reasonably be assumed that someone who is in charge of running a school – an academic institution whose business is (on a good day) the encouragement of intellectual curiosity, the promotion of critical thinking, and the search for truth – would spend much of their working day wrestling with higher order questions and challenges, engaging with the philosophical and abstract, and testing the boundaries of pedagogical practice. Rarely, however, is that the case. Indeed, Peter had a friend who had taken over a school in Malawi and had spent his first day as a school head renegotiating a contract with the firm that emptied the school's septic tank.

Peter thought of his friend as he received Saskia's report.

'The whole campus?'

'Yes, I'm afraid so. The other pipes feed off this one.'

'And it's deep?'

'Very deep. If it's what I think it is, it'll take a day's digging just to reach the pipe.'

'It's happened before?'

'As you know, we get minor pipes bursting quite often. How many did we have last year?'

Peter nodded.

'But,' Saskia continued, 'this is different. We had a huge leak in the same place eight or nine years ago. It took nearly a week to fix.'

'And the water must be cut off?'

'Yes. Everywhere.'

'But how on earth can we run a school with no water? The toilets alone will be a huge problem.'

'We still have the semi-purified water we use for irrigation. What we've done in the past is provide buckets of it in every toilet but ...'

'What?'

'It sorts of works for a while – in an emergency – but it's difficult to keep the buckets full and it can be messy ...'

'And that isn't going to help the cafeteria or the science labs anyway. Hey, if there's no running water in the labs, isn't that a health risk? In case of an acid spill or something?'

Saskia nodded unhappily.

'Sheesh. Just what we need. Okay, Saskia, I need to talk to Valli and Mick quickly but I'm guessing we can manage until the end of the day if you turn everything off now. Can you get the word out? I'll call Glory immediately so the Medical Room can be ready in case ...'

But, thought Peter, *in case what? Gosh, we really don't need this.*

Peter had, as expected, received various emails and phone calls (and even a hand-written letter) regarding his announcement that the school would henceforth compete as the Cheetahs. Other parents had stopped him in the car park (and once in a queue at the supermarket) to make their views known. Staff, too, had opinions and did not hesitate to express them.

His interlocutors fell into two camps.

I am/we are shocked/appalled/disgusted/outraged (and so on) *that the school so callously/cynically/irresponsibly/cravenly* (etc.) *overruled the democratic vote of the student body. What kind of an example do you think you are setting? You are fond of using words like principles, ethics, and integrity. Well, I see no evidence of these noble sentiments here. My son/daughter is dismayed/disillusioned/angry/resentful. How can they ever trust you again?*

Welcome to the International School of Ndwalowe Cheetah hotline, Peter had doodled on a notepad.

If you are calling to say you are appalled, press 1.

If you are disgusted, press 2.

If you are merely disappointed, I don't think you are trying hard enough. Please try again.

If you think we should have stuck with the Dung Beetles, press both your thumbs into your eyes until it hurts.

If you are calling to say that your child is traumatised, first, look up the clinical meaning of the word and then GET A LIFE!

The other group were the usual more-in-sorrow-than-anger brigade.

Obviously, the original vote could not be allowed to stand but how on earth could you get yourself into this situation? Who approved the short list?

Who indeed, thought Peter sourly.

Much to Peter's annoyance, a couple of enterprising students had had T-shirts printed with an (admittedly amusing and impressively fierce) cartoon version of the insect on the chest and **Proud ISN Dung Beetles** written beneath in appropriately dung-coloured lettering. The shirts began appearing around the school, the wearers obviously waiting to see how the school would react. There would be no reaction, Peter informed the staff. The school had already made itself look ridiculous. Let them have their little joke. It will blow over. For his own part, he acknowledged anyone wearing such a shirt with a tolerant but rather tight-lipped smile.

'Dung beetles? Seriously?' Catherine Mulbarton shook her head sadly. 'I've had parents call me,' she added.

'I think most of us have,' sighed Carola. 'But I've spoken to Peter and I think he's handling it well.'

'Well? We wouldn't be in this situation if—'

'I know. I just mean he's handling the fallout quite well. I thought his letter to the parents hit the right tone. I think we need to encourage people to see it all in context. It was a …' She looked for the right word. 'It was a *dummer Fehler*, a blunder, but we have – or we should have – more important things to worry about.'

'The water leak, for one,' agreed Catherine.

'Ugh. That is so annoying. At least … if they can finish it all over the weekend …'

'Being paid overtime!'

'Of course. If they can get everything fixed, we might get away with only two days lost. Yesterday and today.'

'I wonder if Peter has had complaints from parents about it.'

'Oh, I'm sure he has …'

★

'Mrs Maerua, I assure you I do understand your position.' Peter smiled a little weakly at his visitor. 'But I would again invite you to consider the school's position.'

'Oh, I understand that very well. I would call it taking money under false pretences.'

'No, that's—'

'For two days – so far – the school has not provided the education for my two children that I have a right to expect. In fact, this is breaking the terms of our contract.'

'Er, we don't really have a contract in that sense.'

'Of course we do! I pay school fees and the school educates my children. Although sometimes I do wonder at what passes for education in this school.'

'Mrs Maerua, we are talking about two days.'

'So far!'

'Two days out of a hundred and eighty-four. Our policies call for not fewer than a hundred and eighty school days so we are still—'

'And the inconvenience! What am I to do with my children when I have to be at work? Did you think of that?'

'I of course understand that this is inconvenient for everyone. We would all much rather be operating normally. But this is beyond our control. In Germany I remember that we had to close the school once because of snow. And in Japan we had a typhoon that closed …'

'You are describing the weather, Mr Corby. Acts of God. That, I could accept. A burst water pipe is not an Act of God. It is surely not too much to ask that a school – even one as badly run as this one – can maintain the basic utilities. That is why I am entitled to a refund for these two days. I am paying for a service which you are not rendering.'

'But you don't pay by the day. It's an annual fee in the knowledge that there will probably be disruptions of some sort now and again. It's not like renting a hotel room by the hour.'

Mrs Maerua's eye widened in obvious outrage but whether real or feigned, Peter could not tell. 'What are you implying, Mr Corby?'

'I'm not implying anything. Bad example. Look, you rent a car by the day; you don't pay school fees on a day-by-day basis.'

'And where are your teachers? What have they been doing for two days?'

'The fewer people we have in school the better. I'm here with some key admin staff but—'

'So, your teachers get a two-day holiday, my children are denied the education they entitled to – under our constitution, I'll have you know! And I have to pay for it. It's outrageous. I think this has to be taken to the Anti-Corruption Commission.'

'And I'm sure, Mrs Maerua, you are just the woman to do it.' He had bitten his tongue for as long as he could but now Peter could no longer contain himself. He stood. 'If you'll forgive me, Mrs Maerua, I want to go and see what progress the workmen have made on the leak. But thank you again for coming. It's always a pleasure.'

He stretched out his hand. His guest hesitated briefly then raised herself from her chair. She made no attempt to shake Peter's hand.

'I will sleep tonight with a clear conscience, Mr Corby. I hope you can say the same.'

'I shall indeed, Mrs Maerua. Please don't worry about me. Goodbye.'

★

Dr Gill sat on one side of the conference room table, Peter and Carola on the other. The lawyer Peter had been expecting was not present. Dr Gill had explained that, on reflection, he had chosen not to escalate matter "for now". Peter suspected (and hoped) that any lawyer Dr Gill had approached had declined to waste their time on such a matter.

Peter clicked the remote and the large screen on the wall lit up. 'You should be connected now, Dr Gill. All good?'

Dr Gill, fiddling with his laptop, appeared a little flustered. 'Just a minute. Tell me again what I'm looking for?'

'I'm sure we can see it just as well on your laptop, Dr Gill.' Carola hoped she was sounding helpful.

'No, no. I want you to see it … Ah, I think that's it.' The large screen blinked and a slightly out-of-focus image of the car park at Mwakami appeared. Dr Gill hit the pause button.

'I want you to see just what happened. Vinay was just idling in the car park.'

'No, he wasn't idling. He was—'

'Please let me finish, Mr Corby. And then I heard this terrible shouting. I could immediately see that Vinay was scared and, very understandably, he ran to me for protection. It was then that Mr Corby approached in very threatening manner. Fortunately, my wife caught it all on her phone. Here. Look.'

He started the video. In the foreground, with their backs to the camera, Dr Gill and Vinay stood as Peter marched towards them. He waved his arm at something out of the picture and appeared to be saying something.

'There's no sound,' Peter scowled.

'No, I'm afraid the sound wasn't picked up.' Was Peter imagining it or did Dr Gill look a little shifty?

'Then how can Ms Lasser hear what was said?'

'Oh, I can tell her exactly what you said. It was very aggressive. I was shocked.'

'Where's the agama?' Carola asked coolly.

'Agama?'

'The lizard. Mr Corby told me about the lizard. Isn't that an important part of what happened?'

Dr Gill looked annoyed. 'I don't really remember a lizard. I was too busy trying to calm Mr Corby down.'

On the video Peter walked away. The camera turned to Dr Gill and Vinay. There was just a second before the screen went blank but Peter was sure Vinay was smiling.

'Do you see, Ms Lasser? Do you see?'

'I see what you have shown me, Dr Gill, but I'm not sure what it amounts to.'

'But you could see how angry Mr Corby was?'

'I can see he was expressing himself forcefully but, with no sound, I cannot tell what he was saying. Or what you were saying to him. And you have your back to the camera. I can't see your expression at all. And I'm afraid you haven't explained what provoked Mr Corby.'

'Nothing. His behaviour was unprovoked.'

'Really? He wasn't reacting to Vinay throwing stones at an ag – at a lizard?'

'No. Vinay was minding his own business. Which is what Mr Corby should have been doing.' He flashed Peter a furious look.

Carola, now clearly in control of this small meeting, turned to Peter. 'Mr Corby. Would you like to add anything?'

Peter paused and then replied, allowing a little smile to suggest itself. 'No, not really, I have told you what really happened that day and I'm sure Dr Gill remembers it all too – even if it apparently wasn't recorded by his wife. I have nothing more to say.'

'You aren't going to attempt to defend your behaviour?' As he had hoped it would, Peter's little smirk and his calm voice had seriously annoyed Dr Gill.

'Dr Gill. There is nothing to defend. Your video shows me walking up to you and talking for moment or two and then walking away. And you and I both remember exactly what I said and why. I might also point out that I am clearly holding in my hand a field guide to African lizards. Bit of a coincidence, wouldn't you say?'

Carola decided she had better bring matters to a close.

'Dr Gill. I do appreciate you coming here today and it is obvious that this is something you feel very strongly about. I do hope you feel you have had a fair hearing but, in all honesty, I cannot see that how Mr Corby acted and whatever he said was necessarily reprehensible. It is also the case, of course, that you were both on holiday and, as I understand it, Mr Corby was acting in a personal capacity rather than as school director.'

Dr Gill opened his mouth to speak but Carola continued. 'I remain concerned, however, that Vinay is too … upset to come to school. May I suggest that we arrange a meeting between you and Vinay and Ms Agnelli?

I hope and believe that she can offer you – you both – reassurances. I really think it is important that we get Vinay back to class as soon as possible. Don't you agree?'

'Ms Lasser, I am grievously disappointed that you are taking Mr Corby's side in this. As a fee-paying parent, I think I am entitled to the support of the board of directors. I fear I shall have to take this to my lawyers after all.' Dr Gill stood, snapped his laptop shut, and with a slightly trembling hand adjusted his spectacles.

'Dr Gill, you must, of course, do as you see fit but I do hope you will consider the suggestion that you meet with Ms Agnelli.' Carola also stood.

Peter, who had started to enjoy all this, hesitated and then joined them. He tried not to look smug. But he didn't try very hard.

Carola escorted Dr Gill to the door of the conference room, wished him a good day, and turned back to Peter.

'That was *unangenehm* … unpleasant,' she said. 'Does he think we are fools?'

'Some parents …' began Peter. 'I suspect he is someone who is used to getting his own way. Anyway, thank you, Carola. I appreciate your support.'

'Really. We shouldn't have to waste our time on this kind of thing.'

Welcome to my world, thought Peter.

Employment contracts in international schools necessarily and quite properly reflect the laws of the host country but otherwise they tend to be pretty generic. Either within the contract itself (which may then run to a dozen or more pages of discouraging legalese) or in separate policy manuals or handbooks which the contract will reference, entitlements and obligations will be detailed, definitions clarified, expectations listed and the consequences of misbehaviour spelled out. Some new recruits scrutinise each page carefully (which is commonly a depressing experience) while others will scan the contract briefly, shrug, and sign. Either way, it is an important document and neither the school nor the employee would consider entering into a relationship without one. Moreover, in many countries a contract will be required for the employee to be granted a work permit or be allowed to open a bank account. But, once signed and filed, contracts are seldom consulted. They are, however, not forgotten. To some transient teaching staff the contract is what they hope will protect them when their new school turns out to be somewhat less ethical or professional than might be expected. To others, it is the very contract that is the problem, binding them to circumstances that may not be at all what was promised at the time of recruitment. Sooner or later, some teachers find themselves weighing up the benefits and costs of walking away. But 'breaking contract' is not a matter to be taken lightly and there is understandable anxiety about what such a blot on their record might do to their future employment prospects.

And so it was an unhappy and deeply uncomfortable Frank Gillespie who knocked gently on Peter's open door.

'Frank? Good morning. Come in. What can I do for you?'

Frank took a seat across from Peter. 'Thank you. Are you busy? I can come back …'

'No. I've got time. What is it?'

'Peter, I … I have to go. Back to Germany.'

'Oh.'

'Marta is not doing at all well. She won't say much but I've been talking to her parents and they are worried.'

'And you? How are you doing?'

'Not so good either.'

'No. So, what do you mean? Go on leave early?'

'No. I mean go. For good. Leave. Quit.'

'Ah.'

'Peter, I'm sorry. I've never broken contract before.'

Peter made to speak but Frank continued. 'You know I thought we could make this work. That after a few months Marta would come down here again. But … That isn't going to happen.'

'You need to be with your wife.'

'What?'

'Go. You're not happy. Everyone can see that. And if Marta is struggling then you two need to be together. Sometimes we need to remember that this is just a job. Family has to come first.'

Frank looked close to tears. 'Family …'

'Frank. Nicholas is gone. But you still have a wife.'

Now Frank was crying. Peter pushed a box of tissues towards him.

'Frank, I haven't known you long but I know you are a conscientious teacher and a good man. I know this must be tearing you up. I really admired you when you came back, especially when Marta stayed. I know how important the job is to you and how seriously you take it. But your priority is somewhere else now.'

Frank cleared his throat and took another tissue. 'Who ... who will take my classes?'

'I have no idea but that's not your worry. And please don't talk about breaking contract. The school will release you from all obligations.'

Frank almost whispered, 'Thank you.'

'Can I just ask you to see out this semester? Just a couple of weeks to go. It'll give me a bit of time to start looking for a replacement.'

'Yes, of course. It'll take me a little while to wind things up here anyway.'

'Frank, give me a letter explaining the situation and saying you want to go. I'll reply saying what I just said. If anyone asks in the future, it'll be clear that you acted correctly and we parted on good terms. You won't need to worry about your CV.'

'Thank you.'

'How do you want your colleagues to know? Should I write something? Do you want to?'

'Could I say something at tomorrow's staff meeting?'

'Of course. If that's what you want.'

Frank nodded. 'And then I'll tell my classes.'

'I should write to their parents at the same time. They will be concerned.'

'Of course.'

'Frank, you've had a crappy few months. But I want you to know that you'll leave here with everyone's utter respect and admiration. I'm so sorry it worked out this way. But go back to Marta and start a new life.'

Frank stood. Peter did the same and held out his hand. There was a hesitation but no handshake. Instead, the two men hugged tightly.

★

The small committee chaired by Clyde Arthurs had worked with commendable speed.

Great, thought Peter. *Board committees usually take forever to do anything. But when I would actually like one to drag things out, they've finished in a month.*

The committee was recommending the start of a process that would involve all constituencies, be advised by an outside facilitator (yet to be identified), and would result in a school strategic plan to be adopted and implemented no later than the start of the next school year. Examples of plans from comparable schools had been sought and a list of useful websites had been circulated to board members.

'It would be great if we could have the plan agreed sooner,' Clyde was saying, 'but it is important that we get it right. I'd rather wait till June and be sure we have a good plan than rush things.'

For that, at least, Peter was grateful.

'The first stage,' Clyde continued, 'will be to identify key pillars. It should be possible to divide the school's operations into discrete areas and then assess what goals are appropriate for each. Finances is an obvious example. Facilities is another. Staffing may be one.'

'Education?' Trixi tried not to sound sarcastic. 'Isn't that why we're here?'

'Of course. Education is a key pillar.'

'And these goals. They will be measurable?'

'Yes, Lazarett. That is how we will know if we are making progress.'

Peter caught Trixi's eye. They had talked at length prior to this board meeting and knew each other's views on strategic plans. Happily, their views very largely coincided.

'The goals, of course, have to be realistic,' Peter said to the room.

'Meaning?'

'They have to be achievable. And relevant. And ...' he could not help himself, 'I'm not sure that everything a school does lends itself to being quantified.'

Catherine Mulbarton looked displeased. 'Peter, surely there are many areas where we can measure where we are and then set targets. Exam results, for example.'

'Absolutely!' agreed Lazarett. 'Again, Mr Corby, you seem very reluctant to be held accountable. The board needs data – hard data. That's what we are asking for. Measurables. I'll give you an example. What percentage of the school's income comes from sources other than fees?'

Peter knew the answer but Lazarett answered his own question. 'Less than five percent, Mr Corby. Less than five per cent. And what is the management doing about that? Very little, as far as I can see. Would it not be helpful if we could increase the income we receive from other sources? We cannot keep putting up fees for ever.'

'Good point,' Catherine nodded approvingly.

'So,' Lazarett was warming to his subject, 'let's set a goal. Non-fee income should be, let's say, ten per cent – no, fifteen per cent – within three years. That is a clear measurable against which we can hold the management accountable.'

A few heads were nodding. Other faces, Peter was pleased to see, looked doubtful.

'Why fifteen per cent, Lazarett? And why three years?' Ernesto was frowning.

'What do you mean?'

'Where do those numbers come from? They seem rather arbitrary.'

'Why not eight per cent?' added Grant. 'Or twelve per cent over four years? I'm agreeing with Ernesto.'

'Well, it could be eight or ten or fifteen. It doesn't really matter but …'

'Well, if it doesn't matter, why set a figure?'

'Because that is how we will know if we are succeeding or not.'

'Now you've really lost me,' said Grant. 'Supposing we doubled our non-fee income but actually fell short of our notional target. What would that mean? Or we achieved our goal but over four years not three?'

'You don't think we should attempt to find other sources of income?' Lazarett was visibly flushed.

'Of course we should,' said Ernesto. 'I'm just not sure what value having arbitrary numbers and dates add.'

'Strategic directions,' said Peter.

'What?'

'Striving to find sources of non-fee income is admirable. We should certainly do that. But it's a strategic direction, not a strategic plan.'

'Go on,' said Carola.

'I think part of my problem …'

At the word 'problem,' Lazarett snorted.

Peter continued, '… is that a plan sort of implies something that will at some point be concluded. For example, years ago it was decided to build a tunnel under the English Channel. No doubt there was a plan.'

'What—' Violet started to interrupt.

'And they built the tunnel. They achieved it. And then it was done. Is that the kind of thing we are talking about?' Without waiting for an answer, Peter shook his head. 'A few minutes ago, Catherine gave the example of exam results. Well, we only have exams at the end of Grade Twelve and comparing one year with another is … er, often not straightforward. So no, not exam results. But academic standards. The quality of the education we deliver. We absolutely must keep working to improve, to do better. But there will never be an end to it. We'll never sit in a board meeting and conclude that we have achieved the goal of improving teaching and put a tick next to it. Job done. Goal met.'

'Parental satisfaction,' Trixi joined in. 'It's often hard to measure but wouldn't any good school be trying to increase parental satisfaction? But where do you stop? How would you decide you'd met your goal? I agree with Peter. These are directions – strategic directions – and very worthwhile. But I'm not sure they fit into a plan, as such.'

'Then how do you measure your progress?' objected Catherine.

'Does it really have to be measured – quantified, bench-marked? Percentages? Statistics? Sometimes, it's more a case of how something feels. I know of a number of schools – I've visited them – that have very impressive statistics. Exam results, university entrance success, a healthy annual profit. But they are miserable places to work in. Unhappy teachers, cliquish students, cynical management.'

'That's not fair, Peter,' objected Clyde. 'You can have a happy and successful school that still has impressive metrics.'

'I know you can. And I've been to those schools too. I just worry that some schools end up focussing too much on what can be measured rather than what really matters.'

'Exam results and financial security don't really matter?' Catherine spluttered in exasperation.

'Of course they do. But other things matter too. Things that may be much harder to measure. Look, imagine you have a choice of schools. One has an unexceptional academic record – not bad but pretty average. But it has a wonderful reputation for nurturing young people. The kids are happy.

There's no bullying. The sports teams may rarely win trophies but they play with joy and a strong sense of sportsmanship. You get the idea.'

'And the other school?'

'Very impressive exam results each year but it's an exam factory. They grind out the results. It's regimented. Joyless.'

'You make it sound like something out of Dickens.' Grant seemed unimpressed with Peter's argument.

'I know. And perhaps I'm exaggerating for effect but it's not fanciful to see these two schools at different places along a spectrum. Which one would you rather put your child in? I know which one I'd rather work in.'

'Why can't we have the best parts of both?'

'Yes, ideally but …'

'Madam Chairman,' Lazarett sighed, 'are we going to spend all night debating whether data matters or not? We all know it does. Mr Arthurs and his committee have done an admirable job,' Lazarett nodded respectfully in Clyde's direction, 'and we have a clear way forward. Why, one might even say a clear direction.' He smiled at his own wit. Peter did not smile.

'I'm inclined to agree,' said Clyde. 'Look, strategic plans are pretty common in other schools we've looked at. And many of us are familiar with the concept from our own places of work. I hear what you are saying, Peter, but I think we are all smart enough not to focus only on the easily measurable. I can't see how we could have a plan without goals.'

Peter sensed that any further arguments would most likely be counterproductive. He looked at Trixi and almost imperceptibly shook his head. She discreetly nodded.

'Can we then …' Carola looked around the room, 'agree to adopt the recommendation and move to the next stage? Do we need to vote on this?'

It was agreed that no vote was necessary.

'Then we still have one more item of business. Peter?'

'Thank you, Carola. You will all remember the tragedy at the start of the school year. Frank Gillespie's son, Nicholas.'

Heads were nodded solemnly.

'Terrible shame,' someone said. 'Poor man.'

'His wife, Marta, returned to Germany. We all hoped just temporarily. Frank hoped so too. But I'm afraid she isn't coming back. It would simply be too traumatic for her. Frank is terribly conflicted; he's a very conscientious teacher. But he feels he must be with his wife to support her and I agree. He'll stay till the end of this term next month and then join his wife.'

'Who will teach his classes?'

'I don't know yet. I mean, it's not ideal, of course. But we'll make a plan. The staff and the parents will be informed tomorrow.'

'Can we recover any of the money?' Lazarett was writing something on a notepad.

'What money?'

Lazarett looked up. 'We all know how expensive it is to hire teachers – international teachers, as you insist. We flew in Mr Gillespie and his wife and son at the school's expense, didn't we? And we house them and pay for medical insurance?'

Peter was at a loss. 'I'm not sure what ...'

'Surely we are entitled to claw some of that back.'

Others were looking at Lazarett quizzically too.

'Claw what back, Lazarett?' asked Ernesto.

Lazarett returned the quizzical look. 'He's breaking contract. The man has barely been here for four months. And for some of that he was on compassionate leave. It seems this has not been a very cost-effective appointment.' Lazarett sat back in his chair, folded his arms, and fixed Peter with an accusatory stare.

'Lazarett, he lost his son!' Trixi was appalled. 'And he's at risk of losing his wife now. He has to go to her.'

'I'm not disputing that. And it was a terrible thing to happen. But it's really not the school's problem. Well, covering his classes now will be. And it's certainly not the school's fault.'

'I don't believe this.' For once, Peter spoke for most of those around the table. 'Frank Gillespie's life has been turned completely upside down and we are going to ask him to refund the cost of flying him here in July? Really? Where's the humanity? What kind of school are we? How would you quantify that, Lazarett?'

'Peter!' Carola cautioned him. 'Please ...'

Ernesto broke the silence that followed. 'His flight to Germany, Peter. Who is paying for that?'

'At the end of a contract the school flies international teachers home. In the circumstances ... Well, unless anyone here thinks otherwise.' Peter looked and felt suddenly weary.

'In the circumstances, you were going to say?' Ernesto encouraged Peter. 'I hope you were going to say that in the circumstances the school will consider this an end of contract and fly him home. Yes?'

Peter looked gratefully at Ernesto. 'Yes. Thank you. I don't see this as breaking contract. The school and Frank agree that he should be with his wife. Prematurely, and in unprecedented circumstances, I'm suggesting that we release him from his contract. In fact, I'm not suggesting anything. That is what I have told him we will do.' He glared not just at Lazarett but at the whole room. 'This is not a board decision.'

'Quite right,' Ernesto looked satisfied. But he also glanced around the room to see if anyone disagreed.

No one spoke.

'Then,' said Carola at length, 'thank you for informing us, Peter. And would it be appropriate for me, on behalf of the board, to write a letter to Frank thanking him and wishing him … erm, good wishes?'

'Yes, Carola. That would be highly appropriate. Thank you.'

'Very good. I'll draft something.'

'One last thought.' Peter looked at the members of the board. 'It's important to do the right thing. To behave ethically. And to be seen to behave ethically.'

A couple of people nodded.

'The school community has nothing but respect and sympathy for Frank. Doing the right thing by Frank sends an important message. It helps to confirm the school's principles and values. This kind of thing will go a long way with the teachers. I'm talking about trust and morale. We may not be able to measure it,' he paused and tried not to look at Lazarett and Catherine, 'but staff will see how the school is treating Frank and be quietly pleased. Impressed, even. So …' he suddenly felt a lump in his throat. 'Thank you.'

★

Brian Bell entered the staffroom where half a dozen people were chatting, drinking coffee, or playing with their phones. 'Anyone know where Mike is?' he asked.

Larry Roper looked up from his phone. 'A few minutes ago, he was in the library doing some photocopying. Oh dear. You don't look happy. Everything okay?'

Brian said nothing but scowled and left the room. Larry watched him go, frowning.

Mike Sesriem was just leaving the library when Brian arrived.

'Mike, got a minute? There's something I need to ask you.'

'Not really. I'm invigilating a resit in ten minutes and I need to get all this stuff back to my lab. Is it important?'

'Yes. I think so. Rachel Caine just came to see me. She was a bit upset. In fact, she was quite upset. And so am I.'

'Is this about the Model United Nations?'

'Yes. It's about the MUN. You said she can't go?'

'I don't know if you know but I've been trying for ages to get a date when we can visit the National Museum of Anthropology. It's been closed for months. Staffing shortages or some excuse. Anyway, I've managed to book Grade Ten in on the twenty-eighth.'

'But that's when we'll be in Jo'burg. We fly on the twenty-sixth.'

'Which is why she can't go. Anthropology is one of the key units in Grade Ten biology. This field trip is critical.'

'But the MUN is all booked. So are the flights.'

'Brian, the whole class – including Rachel – know that I've been trying to get this trip booked ever since the start of the year. I'm sorry but I can't let her miss it. Look, I've got to go. Sorry.'

Valli entered Peter's office. 'Door?' she asked.

'Closed, please.'

'What is it?'

'Julia has just been to see me. She's had a visit from Crystal Moore.'

'Uh-oh.'

'Indeed. Apparently, Crystal said she was there on behalf of the PTA and insisted that Julia tell her what is really going on with Mark.'

'On behalf of the PTA? It's none of the PTA's business. And Crystal doesn't even have a child in Mark's class.'

'Julia said that it was quite uncomfortable. Crystal was very insistent.'

'She can be.'

'Julia, of course, would give her nothing. Seemingly, Crystal was not best pleased. She'll come and see you now.'

'She won't need to. I'm going to send for her. Bloody PTA!'

★

'You've had quite a month,' Sheila looked at her husband with real sympathy. 'I thought a dinner at The Mupundu was called for.'

'Had? Am having. It's not over yet. There's still the board training to come. Pass the olive oil and vinegar, will you?'

'But the leak's fixed. That's something. And now your naughty teacher has gone.'

'I'm not sure that naughty is exactly the word.'

'You still haven't told me what happened. It was all a bit sudden.'

Their drinks arrived. Peter gulped greedily at his cold beer. 'You're driving, right?'

'Yes. I'll just have one glass. You go on and get sloshed.'

Peter gave his wife a disapproving look.

'So, what's his name? Mark?'

'Mm. Well, he was still refusing to see a psychiatrist. And I wouldn't let him come back to school. It was a bit of a Mexican standoff. And then …' Peter threw both his arms in the air, 'out of the blue I got a call from his parents in England. They live in Bournemouth or somewhere like that.'

'That was a coincidence.'

'Not really. They apparently chat to Mark every week or so. They could tell something wasn't right. They didn't know he'd been suspended but they knew there was a problem. So, they called me.'

'You told them?'

'At first I was a bit guarded. I didn't know how defensive they might be. But it wasn't like that. The more I said, the more they seemed almost grateful. Certainly not angry. Well, not angry with me. They then told me that there had been "issues" in the past. In his last job, in fact. They as good as apologised to me.'

'Wow.'

'They're a really nice couple. Very sensible. And obviously very worried about their son. We agreed that they would talk to Mark. Next thing I knew – just a few hours later, in fact – the father called to say that they had persuaded Mark to come home. The mother was just booking a flight to Ndwalowe to come and take Mark back to England.'

'Sjoe. That'll cost a bit.'

'I kind of got the impression this has happened before. Anyway, I had Valli go and see Mark to see if it was true. She said he looked awful. Seems to have really withdrawn into himself. I actually worried if I should have someone stay with him to be sure that he didn't …' Peter made a face.

'Do you think he might have?'

'Who knows? Anyway, Valli met the mother at the airport yesterday and we booked them into the Hilton for the night. They left on the Brussels flight today.'

'So that's that.'

'Not entirely. We still have to empty Mark's apartment and work out what we'll do with everything. His mother didn't seem interested in shipping it all back to the UK. Plus, of course, I've now contrived to lose three teachers before Christmas.'

'To lose one teacher, Mr Worthing, may be regarded as a misfortune. To lose three …'

'Don't!'

'And you said something about wanting to throttle Chuck Collins?'

'Oh! You mean yet another reason. Yes. Saskia came to me this morning. Chuck was in the school for barely five minutes but he did find time to place an order for calculus textbooks. Expensive ones from the US. It's for a course taken by only some of the higher level students so he didn't need more than half a dozen. But I guess he was planning ahead. He ordered eighteen.'

'A little wasteful?'

'Wait. He filled in the order form including the order code and sent it to the business office. They just processed it as usual. Books from the US always take a while. The order arrived this week.' Peter took another swig of beer. 'Saskia was a bit surprised when the van unloaded fifteen boxes. Chuck had used the wrong code. Not the one for single copies; the one for sets of ten. He didn't order eighteen. He ordered 180.'

'How much …?'

'A little over seven thousand US.'

'And the business office didn't notice when they placed the order? That can't have been in the budget.'

'Saskia is, as they say, looking into it.'

'Oh dear. Can you return them?'

'The supplier says they'll reimburse sixty per cent but we have to pay for the postage.'

'Or, I suppose, just keep them?'

'Mmm. And require all students doing the diploma for the next twenty years to take higher level calculus. Waste not, want not.'

'I think you need another beer.'

Peter seldom argued with his wife.

Peter returned from the bathroom to find Mike Sesriem waiting outside his office.

'Wow. That was quick.'

'Uh?'

'I only asked Chiamaka ten minutes ago to ask you to come and see me.'

Mike looked flustered. 'Oh, er, I didn't …'

'No matter.' Peter opened the door and motioned Mike to enter. 'Take a seat.'

'I was coming to see you anyway.'

'Oh?'

Mike was squirming in his chair. 'Peter, I don't know if Valli told you …' He looked nervously at Peter. Peter said nothing. 'You see, Jackie and I …'

'Yes, Valli told me. She told me what Will said. Lee-Ann is talking to Will. And then I was going to call in you and Jackie – together.'

'Oh, there's no need. It's fine. It was just—'

'Is it, Mike? Is it fine? Look, it's not for me to get involved in marital issues. But when there's a child involved and he seems upset … I can't ignore that.'

'I understand.'

'Do you want to talk to someone? You and Jackie? It doesn't have to be me.'

'No, no. No need. It won't happen again.'

'Valli could talk to Jackie?'

'Peter, can you … Please just let Jackie and me sort this out. Please.'

'Can you promise me to keep Will out of it? We can't have him witnessing any more—'

'He won't. He won't. Definitely not.'

Peter nodded. 'If you need help, Mike, there's no shame in asking for it. Whatever is going on, you know we'll try …'

'I know. And thank you.' Mike was now in a hurry to get out of Peter's office and started to stand.

'Er, Mike. Sit down, please. This wasn't why I wanted to see you.'

'Oh?' Mike sat.

'Brian Bell came to see me.'

'Oh.'

'He was quite irritated. Rachel Caine?'

Mike slumped deeper in his chair.

'The MUN can't be rescheduled and it's all paid for,' Peter continued, 'but could you perhaps find an alternative for her to visit the museum? It's open on Saturdays, I believe. And she's a bright girl. Couldn't she perhaps go on her own?'

Mike could see his position was not a strong one. 'I suppose,' he almost mumbled.

'Excellent. I'll let Brian know.' Peter stood. Mike hurriedly followed. 'Any plans for the holiday, Mike?'

'Yes. We're all going back to Namibia for three weeks. We'll see my family in Windhoek and Jackie's mother in Swakopmund.'

'Good. Then use the time wisely, Mike. It sounds like you and Jackie have things to talk about.' Peter reached out to shake Mike's hand. 'Good luck.'

Mike just nodded.

As Mike left, Richard Cooper entered.

'Peter?'

'Hello, Richard. Come in. What can I do for you? Sit down.'

'Thanks, but I've only got a minute. Now that Frank's going, you'll be looking for a new English teacher?'

Peter sighed. 'Indeed. But at very short notice. I'm pursuing a number of options but I'm not very optimistic.'

'Well, at my bridge club there's a British chap who has recently retired. He's been teaching at the seminary for decades. I don't know if he'd be interested but he might be prepared to do half a year or so till you find someone.'

Peter nodded. 'Well, certainly worth following up. What's his name?'

'Willoughby. Mr Willoughby. I'm not sure if he even has a first name. Everyone just calls him Willoughby.'

'Okay. Thanks. Can you get me his phone number?'

'Of course.'

There was a gentle knock on the door. Peter looked up.

'Peter,' Chiamaka said, 'Mrs Moore is here …'

★

Seth Taniel had seen it all before. He listened as Peter alternated between apologising and ranting.

'Peter, this is what happens quite often. I almost expect it. And there's no call for you to go apologising.'

Peter just shook his head in irritation.

The dates for the retreat had been discussed and agreed and, some concerns over the cost notwithstanding, it had been decided that an out-of-town venue was appropriate. The conference room, it was argued, was too familiar and was perhaps associated with behaviours that at least some members hoped the retreat might expurgate. Another room in school would have been an option but it was felt that getting out of Ndwalowe altogether would help to focus minds. No one would be late because they had to drop their child at soccer practice. No one would spend the afternoon with half a mind on the shopping they needed to do on the way home. Moreover, if they met on a Saturday afternoon and Sunday morning, there would be the opportunity for board members – still, in some cases, virtual strangers to each other – to enjoy a convivial dinner and perhaps massage relationships that could sometimes be rather strained.

A wildlife reserve some two hours north of Ndwalowe had been booked. It offered facilities that were perfectly comfortable but also affordable. (Nonetheless, Carola had still suggested that they share rooms in order to reduce the cost to the school. Much to Peter's relief, it was an idea that had been quickly voted down.) It was also quite remote (something that Ernesto had argued was important psychologically) and, as Peter had confided to Carola, telephone reception there could be patchy: a consideration they both agreed may be no bad thing.

The proposal to make it effectively a two-day retreat had been welcomed with more enthusiasm by some than others but all board members had cleared their diaries and given assurances that they would attend.

As he drove along the flat, graded road (probably rather faster than was sensible), Peter continued to complain to Seth.

'Honestly, I expected better from Clyde. I mean, he's one of the ones who set this all up. "Something at the embassy he couldn't get out of." And at three days' notice?'

'It can happen, Peter,' Seth held the grab bar tight as the car swerved briefly on a patch of soft sand. 'And I had a good talk with him over dinner last night. It was very helpful.'

'And, of course, I'm not surprised that Lazarett found some pretext not to be there today.'

'He's coming for tomorrow's session?'

'So he says but he'll have to make an early start to be there by eight.'

'And who is the woman who …'

'Violet Sindima. Apparently, something's come up that makes it imperative that she gets back to Ndwalowe tonight.'

'So, there will be seven board members this afternoon and seven again tomorrow.'

'A different seven.'

'Yes, a different seven tomorrow morning. Actually, Peter, seven out of nine isn't bad. I've known it much worse. I was at a school in Berlin last month. Just four out of ten members turned up.'

'I wish board members realised that it's a commitment, not a hobby.' Seth's anecdote had not made Peter feel any better about his own board.

Seth winced as the car bounced uncomfortably over a small pattern of rocks. 'Is it far?'

'Ten minutes,' Peter said grimly. If anything, he drove a little faster.

★

'I thought that went quite well.' Carola accepted a glass of white wine from Peter and they clinked glasses. 'Are we the first?' She looked around the bar area.

'I just had a quick shower and changed my shirt. I suspect some of the others are cursing at the dodgy internet or trying to phone home.'

'Mr Taniel seems to know what he's talking about.'

'Definitely. I'm glad we got him.'

The afternoon session had started a little late as the last members had arrived in a cloud of dust and apologies. Of Mrs Luhanga there was no sign. Catherine had been going to give her and Trixi a lift but she had not arrived at the rendezvous and her phone appeared to have been switched off. Peter had hardly been surprised.

'Six,' he said to Seth who just smiled and shrugged.

But those who were present had quickly warmed to Seth Taniel's soft-spoken but authoritative delivery and had willingly and conscientiously engaged with the various exercises, questionnaires, and presentations that had been prepared for them.

'Wish we'd done this a year ago,' admitted Grant to Ernesto at the coffee break. 'I really liked that exercise about which decisions belong to the board, the director, or both.'

Violet Sindima had made her apologies and left a little after four o'clock ('five,' Peter had silently mouthed to Seth) but the others had spent two more productive hours arguing – but constructively – about a draft document Seth proposed as a 'Board Member Job Description.' Almost reluctantly, they had closed the proceedings well after six and allowed themselves just thirty minutes to nip back to their rooms and freshen up before congregating for a pre-dinner drink.

'Yes,' said Carola, 'very successful.' She took another sip of wine.

'For those who are here,' cautioned Peter. 'Where are the other four?'

Carola's smile dimmed. 'Mmm …'

★

Very much to Peter's surprise, Lazarett did indeed arrive for the Sunday session. He was the first person Peter saw when he entered the breakfast room. Moreover, he was sitting drinking coffee with Mrs Luhanga.

'My goodness,' said Peter as he approached their table. 'You must have been up early.'

'Good morning, Mr Corby. Why the surprise? I said I would be here, didn't I? And I was fortunate enough to be able to bring Mrs Luhanga.'

'Good morning, Mr Corby,' Mrs Luhanga gave him a slightly condescending smile.

'Er, yes, good morning to you both. Em, excuse me.' He saw Ernesto observing them from the buffet. 'I must get some breakfast. I'll see you shortly.'

'Well, well,' he said to Ernesto while pouring himself a glass of guava juice. 'I did not expect that.'

'Me neither. I'm not sure if I'm pleased or not. I should be glad they've turned up but …'

'Mmm …'

★

'The thing is,' Seth Taniel was saying to the group, 'very often other parents – and sometimes teachers – will approach you with a concern, or maybe a sense of injustice. They believe that because you are on the board, you will be in a position to help them.'

'Which is correct,' Lazarett sounded very sure.

'Well, yes and no,' said Seth. 'That's what I hope to clarify this morning. We are going to consider a number of common scenarios that will illustrate some of the situations you may have to navigate as board members. If you turn to page seventeen in your workbooks you'll find the first example.'

'I looked at this last night,' said Ernesto. 'Very interesting.'

'Then perhaps you'd read it out loud for everyone.'

Ernesto was happy to.

Last night was the AGM. You stood for election as a parent member and were pleased to be elected.

This morning you are shopping in Checkers and, as you turn a corner, you bump into Grace, a good friend and also a parent at ISN. She hugs you and congratulates you on your election. You thank her.

"This is such good news," she says. "Now we can get something done!"

You ask her what she means.

"Alice Jones. She made our children's lives miserable last year in Grade Five. We both know she's the worst teacher in the school. Now you can do something about it!"

1. *What should you do?*
2. *What should you say to Grace?*

'Thank you, Ernesto. Now—'

'Is she?' Mrs Luhanga asked. 'Is she the worst teacher in the school?'

Seth was taken aback. 'Well, it's only a hypoth—'

'It sounds like they both think so,' said Lazarett. He read from the script. '*We both know* ... Doesn't sound like it's in doubt.'

'So,' Seth attempted to regain the initiative, 'what would you say – as the newly elected board member – what would you say to Grace?'

'I'd assure her that I certainly will be doing something about it. As she says, now I'm on the board. I won't be brushed off with the principal's usual excuses.' Lazarett looked at Mrs Luhanga who nodded approvingly.

Peter held his face in his hands.

'Hold on,' said Grant. 'Who says she's the worst teacher in the school? You are just two—'

'Can I,' interrupted Ernesto, 'can I suggest a different answer?'

Gratefully, Seth nodded.

'As I understand it, a board member in this situation should neither agree nor disagree with what's been said. They should listen without passing judgement, be quite sure they understand what the concern is, and then promise to refer the matter to the relevant person. In this case probably the principal or director.'

'But what if it's already been referred to the management?' argued Lazarett.

'I'm sure it must have,' agreed Mrs Luhanga.

'So all that will happen is more excuses and nothing will be done.' Lazarett shook his head. 'It's unacceptable.'

'I don't think a board member should be defending such a poor teacher.' Mrs Luhanga was becoming quite animated. 'Board members have a responsibility to parents. We are their voice on the ... well, board.'

'Quite right, Mrs Luhanga!'

Seth looked at Peter. Peter looked at Seth. It was going to be a long morning.

*

December

Much as Peter appreciated Carola's diligence and dedication, he sometimes wished she had a 'real' job that might serve to distract her from school matters. It was admirable that she took her role so seriously but quite often Peter felt that she was asking for updates on matters that really should not concern her as board chair.

'She means well, of course,' Peter had said to Sheila, 'but it's like she feels she has to check up on me. There was a serious water leak in one of the toilets and a few days later she called to confirm that it had been fixed. That really isn't the role of the board chair. Doesn't she trust me?'

Once, Carola had tentatively tried to persuade Peter to agree to a scheduled weekly meeting but he had demurred.

'You know that I'll tell you immediately if something serious happens. If we met for an hour or two every week, I'd just be giving you updates on the day-to-day stuff.'

'Is that a problem?'

'It … It risks blurring the line between governance and operations.'

'If I may say so, there are times when it feels like you think the board should be seen but not heard.'

'Carola, I think it's a bit like this. I'm the pilot of an airliner. No, not just the pilot, I'm the captain. I'm sitting in the cockpit with my hands on the controls. I'm flying the plane. Behind me are a few hundred crew and passengers. I have a responsibility towards them. I also have authority. Basically, I make the decisions. Well, I make some of the decisions and certainly the minute-by-minute stuff.'

Carola raised her hand to object but Peter continued.

'But the decisions I take are within a wider framework. Obviously, I'm not flying the plane to New York or Tokyo or wherever because I feel like it. I've been given a destination and it's my job to get everyone there.'

'But the board must do more than choose a destination and leave the rest to you.'

'Of course! You are the air traffic control. Periodically, you tell me to fly a bit higher or a bit lower, a bit faster or a bit slower, change direction … But the point is, you – the board – are not on the plane. I am.'

Carola looked a little frustrated.

'Carola, I'm the one sitting in the cockpit keeping an eye on all my instruments. If engine number two seems to be running a little hot, my co-pilot and I will keep an eye on it but there's no need to report it unless we think it's becoming a problem. I don't call up ATC and tell them I'm switching from the wing tanks to the centre tank. I certainly don't need to inform ATC if some of the passengers are complaining about the food.'

'But we are also passengers. Well, some of us. We are parents too. Aren't we sitting in the back of the plane?'

'Yes. And, as we've said before, in any given situation you need to know whether you are a parent or a board member. And I agree. It isn't always easy.'

'Yes,' Carola said slowly, 'I see what you are saying. That does sort of make sense.'

'The danger – and I know this has happened in other international schools – is that some board members seem to want to be up in the cockpit with me telling me how to fly the plane.'

'And some board chairs?'

'It's not unknown.'

A hint of a smile passed across Carola's face. 'Very well. Carry on, Captain …'

★

Peter sat in his office, his chin resting in his hand. He stared at the screen of his laptop, his face expressionless. Now almost eighteen months into the job, self-doubt was giving way to a sometimes fragile confidence that he could actually run a school. He didn't get it right every time but enrolment was steadily growing, the school's finances were improving, the board seemed broadly satisfied with the job he was doing, and parents were mostly happy. Well, not all parents, of course.

He looked again at the list of emails requiring his attention.

An American parent was objecting to the use of metric units in science and maths classes. "When we return to Ohio, my son will need to be proficient in pounds and ounces, quarts and gallons, yards and miles. Why isn't the school preparing him for that?"

Another parent, and not for the first time, was complaining about flies in the cafeteria. "And please don't remind me again that we live in the tropics. That is no excuse!"

A third, and again not for the first time, was demanding that the guards at the main gate should be armed. "An international school like this, full of embassy children, is an obvious target for terrorists. It has happened elsewhere. It only makes sense to give the guards weapons."

Peter shook his head. The idea of Awanza Security Service guards waving around loaded guns frightened him a great deal more than the thought of terrorists storming the school gates.

He took a slow drink of coffee. Running a school? Was this running a school? Replying as patiently and diplomatically as he could to a never-ending catalogue of parents telling him how to do his job? And yet it seemed to be how he spent far too much of his time.

It's really about people, he thought. *Managing people. Well, managing their expectations. And managing situations, of course.*

Situations. He thought back over the soon-to-be completed first semester. Chuck, Frank, Mark. Was that what running a school was? *Some stuff you can prepare for*, he mused. *The introduction of a new curriculum, for example. But the real job – or, at least, the hardest part of the job – is the stuff that you just can't see coming. That's the real test. How you deal with these things.*

His thoughts were interrupted by a gentle knock on the door. Three teachers, Pam Somerscale, Blessing Nyanga and Maeve Dinckles, entered nervously and pointedly closed the door behind them.

'Peter?'

'Yes?'

'We think you need to know ...'

What Peter needed to know was that Elsa Mattsson was, they were fairly sure, cutting herself.

★

No one had ever seen the staff room looking so colourful. Arranged on tables, stacked on the floor, balancing on top of cupboards, and tucked under chairs were dozens, scores (more than a hundred and fifty, it was rumoured) of shoeboxes, each tastefully (or sometimes eccentrically) wrapped in papers of every colour and design. Some were explicitly Christmassy, some were plain. Some sported cartoon characters (Spiderman seemed popular) and others boasted repeating patterns of kittens, butterflies, or bunnies. Bows and rosettes decorated some. Tiny arrangements of plastic bells and hearts were adhered to others. And all bore a small sticker that included the school logo and a dot that was either red or blue.

Helen Roper and Flo Balgowan viewed the scene with satisfaction.

'Is that it? Or are there more to come?'

'I think Trixi said we should expect a few more from Grade Twelve.'

'Well, they'd better hurry up if we're going to deliver them next week.'

Whatever slightly schizophrenic anxieties the international school might have had about celebrating Christmas, Awanza had no such scruples. Neon holly and angels appeared above and along Ndwalowe's main thoroughfares, Santas (dressed in heavy costumes wholly inappropriate for an African summer) were on duty in the department stores, and from mid-November until well into January shoppers in the Riverside Mall tapped their feet (or scowled) as *Rockin' Around the Christmas Tree* and other perennials blasted out through the muzak system. And at Christmas (whether the name was used or not) a school tradition that stretched back further than anyone could remember was that staff members and classes contributed shoeboxes packed with goodies that were then delivered to the luckiest of the dispiriting number of orphanages around the city.

"Goodies"? To small children sleeping two to a bed and with only cold water to wash in, a bottle of cheap shampoo was certainly a luxury – and a welcome one. Soap, toothpaste, and toothbrushes were also unfamiliar treats. The instructions called for an item of clothing to be included – a T-shirt, a simple dress, a pair of shorts – and each box was to contain a sketch pad and pens or crayons. Healthy foods were encouraged – nuts, dried fruit, biltong – but most teachers couldn't resist squeezing in a bar of chocolate or a packet of sweets. Each child also received a small hand towel and a brief note from the donor wishing the recipient a Merry Christmas.

In truth, it was a small gesture that changed very little but it made all parties feel briefly good and it was celebrated on the school's website and in the weekly newsletter. Many of the local Awanzan parents couldn't see the point while some of the younger expatriate teachers gushed excessively on Facebook and elsewhere about the school's generosity and humanity.

Meanwhile, endemic poverty and institutional neglect and denial ensured that there would be needy orphans for many more Christmases to come.

★

'I told them to come and tell you straight away. I couldn't because I was waiting for Mrs Lossen.'

'Oh, Valli. Don't tell me that's still rumbling on.'

'You know what she's like. A dog with a bone. Anyway, it was right they came to me first but I sent Pam and the others to you immediately.'

'Thanks. Elsa? I'm sorry to say I don't really know her well.'

'A bit highly strung. Borderline bulimic, I suspect. Great fun when she's on form but she can be very up and down.'

'And cutting herself?'

'I think they've only seen glimpses. And she's taken to wearing long sleeves.'

'In the height of summer? If I get complaints from parents, it's usually that teachers aren't wearing enough clothes.'

'Maeve became suspicious when Elsa stopped joining them for their regular saunas. They all used to go together but a couple of months back Elsa began making unconvincing excuses.'

'Hard to hide it in a sauna.'

'Exactly.'

'What do you suggest, Valli?' Peter screwed up his face. 'I have absolutely no experience of this kind of thing.'

'I'm just going to talk to her. Ask her straight out. We have a good relationship.'

'And if she is?'

'It could be worse. There are professionals here she can talk to. If she's willing.'

'Maeve and the others will be discreet, won't they?'

'Oh, yes.'

'Phew, I'm beginning to wonder if I'm running a school or a psychiatric ward.'

Valli thought Peter was being a little insensitive but she could see his point.

'And that's just the teachers. Let's not get started on the parents!'

That also, Valli had to concede, was a fair point.

✱

The prevailing culture in Awanza tended to the hedonistic. Those who had first worked the land lived hard lives in often harsh conditions. Cerebral pleasures were few and entertainment and diversion were more often found in physical activities. These pastimes and traditions prevailed even as the population increased and the first towns worthy of the name began to appear. Hunting remained popular (as he came to know people better, Peter was astonished to learn how many owned guns) and sport verged on an obsession – football mostly in the Black communities and rugby for the whites. And drinking. Everyone drank.

'If our learners have a problem, it's alcohol.' Glory Mthembu had said to Peter shortly after his arrival. Alcohol was readily available (not least in most fridges and parents' drink cabinets) and many children acquired the habit early.

The school, of course, ran classes teaching students about alcohol abuse (and illegal drugs and sex and much else) but Peter often felt they were pushing a rock uphill. His protests to the Ndwalowe Rugby Club after some of its members encouraged and enabled a team of sixteen-year-olds (including many ISN students) to get hopelessly drunk were rudely dismissed. "You don't understand", was the least offensive of the replies he received.

Another cause for concern was that many of the Awanzan parents at the school (predominantly those of European extraction) had grown up on farms or at least in remote and underpopulated parts of southern Africa and had been driving from as soon as their legs could reach the pedals. They seemed to Peter far too free with the keys of their cars and several times he had seen children he knew to be in only in their mid-teens driving through Ndwalowe. The thought of a fifteen- or sixteen-year-old driving at night after two or three beers (or worse) terrified him. But he was sure it happened.

★

Peter enjoyed joking that Sheila had her social life whereas he had his antisocial life. It was certainly true that, of the two of them, Sheila was the more comfortable in company and more easily made, and enjoyed having, new friends. Some months after her arrival in Awanza she had announced that she intended to take up golf and had enrolled for a series of lessons at the Ndwalowe Golf Club. Attending the club three mornings a week, she had soon met and exchanged phone numbers with fellow tyros, accomplished golfers, and those for whom the NGC was more of a social club than a sporting venue. Lunch invitations followed and once she felt confident enough to appear on the fairways, she was never short of someone to join her for nine or eighteen holes.

Never having met a single one of Sheila's NGC friends, Peter nonetheless came to know whose marriage was in trouble, who had experienced a frightening traffic accident, who was struggling with the menopause, and – much to his annoyance – who had children at the International School but nary a kind word to say about it. Sheila was hardly a gossip but it did not seem inappropriate that she would share with Peter accounts of petty crimes, low-level corruption, problems with house staff, and the daily realities of being wealthy (and white) in a mostly poor African country.

During their five years living in Japan, Sheila and Peter had entertained little. Their apartment was not large and their dining table could seat four but, comfortably, not more. But the real problem was the kitchen. There was no oven and there were just two small electric rings. Pasta boiling on one ring and a sauce bubbling on the other was fine but anything more ambitious was a challenge. The addition of a rice-cooker certainly helped and Peter learned how to use it to steam vegetables as well as cook perfect rice every time. (The purchase of this now indispensable item had been an urgent priority for Peter upon his arrival in Ndwalowe.) Always somewhat suspicious of microwaves, Peter had rarely used the one in his small Japanese kitchen, although it did occasionally offer another means of cooking or at least heating. But the preparation of a serious three- or four-course meal was something he never attempted. When they wanted to eat with friends or visitors, they went to one of the many excellent restaurants in Hamamatsu. Individuals and very rarely couples might be invited for a simple dish of this or bowl of that but, in their first five years of marriage, Peter and Sheila never hosted what might be called a dinner party.

And that was something they both rather regretted. Peter may not have been gregarious but he could be sociable – within reason. A convivial evening of fine food and stimulating conversation spent in the company of like-minded friends was about Peter's idea of a perfect social event. No loud music, no rooms full of strangers and certainly no dancing. Dishes that were imaginative but often simple, the exchange of amusing anecdotes and witty aphorisms, perhaps a little Mozart in the background ….

'You're so full of it!'

Sheila sometimes had a way of puncturing Peter's dreams.

As they cautiously and tactfully advocated for increased sensitivity training within the Police Service of Awanza, Sheila and Susi Shepherd had been growing ever closer. Testing the water, the two women and their husbands had met at Alfredo's for a pizza and Peter had been delighted to discover that Brian Shepherd shared his interest in birds. (Sheila had theatrically groaned but was actually quite relieved.) The Shepherds were therefore top of the invitation list when it was decided that there had been enough prevarication and a dinner party was to be held.

Peter had enjoyed the hospitality of Valli and Duke more than once before Sheila's arrival and he was eager to repay their generosity. (In truth, he was also quite keen to have at least two familiar faces around the table.) Invitations were also extended to Jenny and Ronald Wintercoat but they reluctantly declined, saying that the run up to Christmas was their busiest time and there was no way even one of them could get away from the restaurant, far less both.

So the final couple were Carla and Colby Wittering. Carla had started taking golf lessons at the same time as Sheila and they had fallen into an enjoyable routine of playing nine holes every Wednesday morning.

'I've never met her husband but Carla's great fun,' Sheila said to Peter as they prepared the table.

'What do they do here?'

'She doesn't work. I think Colby is with McKinsey.'

'McKinsey? What kind of work do they have in Awanza?'

168

'I don't know. Ask him.'

'I'm really not sure about inviting school parents for dinner.'

'I know. You've said so. More than once. But it'll be fine. Carla never talks about school. Have you ever had a problem with the kids?'

'No. Nothing. One is in Grade Five and one in Grade Seven and as far as I know they are both exemplary.'

'Well, there you are. Nothing to worry about.'

'It's often not the kids that are the problem,' muttered Peter but his wife wasn't listening.

✱

One of the many delights of living in a tropical African country is that the distinction between indoors and outdoors is blurred to the point of irrelevance. Except at night during the coldest months, the air temperature is unfailing balmy indoors and out. Windows are often left wide open, doors too, sometimes. Enjoying a morning coffee or a sundowner at dusk, a comfortable chair on the veranda is likely to be the chosen location. By day, the garden can be admired – whatever the season – and by night the almost invariably clear skies reveal spectacular views of the stars.

Although Peter and Sheila ate most meals at a small table on the veranda, the house did boast a spacious dining room and an ancient and somewhat battered wooden table quite large enough to seat eight. French windows (opened now for the first time by Peter and not without difficulty) gave access to the decking outside and admitted the pleasing scents and aromas of a lush garden at the height of summer.

'You should sit here,' Sheila had instructed Peter, 'I'll be here and that gives our guests the view of the garden.'

'Drinks on the veranda first, right?'

'Of course. Do we have enough ice?'

✱

Sheila and Peter both enjoyed cooking. She particularly enjoyed making starters, salads, sorbets, and soups. Peter leaned more towards wholesome meaty dishes – stews, pies, roasts, and casseroles. Both had their own repertoires of desserts from homely bread and butter pudding and apple crumble to iced chocolate *soufflés* and *zabaglione semifreddo*. And neither would consider a good meal complete without an extravagant cheeseboard.

'We eat well,' pronounced Peter observing with satisfaction the dishes already prepared and those still cooking.

Peter's phone rang. Their first guests were at the gate.

★

Candles flickered in the warm breeze and an eclectic selection of music played somewhere at low volume. Ice clinked in glasses, savoury pastry sticks were munched, and dishes of olives and *crudités* were passed around. More than one conversation was taking place while Peter and Sheila discreetly monitored their guests' drinks, ensuring that no glass was ever quite empty.

All this was observed from the crown of a stout palm standing at the other end of the veranda from the dinner guests. It was observed without concern but with some interest. What was happening did not seem threatening but it was a deviation from the usual routine and needed to be assessed. Due attention was also paid to the tray of a birdfeeder nailed to the branch of an avocado tree. As expected, it appeared to have been charged with a generous scoop of birdseed. An overripe banana slit open lengthways was also inviting. The observer decided he had seen enough and slowly began his descent.

'I love your garden, Sheila,' Carla Wittering was saying. 'Are those lemon trees?'

'We're not actually sure. Some kind of citrus, for sure. And, if I'm honest, the garden probably looks better in the dark than it does in daylight. There's still so much to do. Before the next rainy season I—'

'Eek!' Carla jumped to her feet. 'There's a rat!'

The other guests turned to look where she was pointing.

'There,' she said. 'Running along the handrail.'

They looked. Indeed, a medium-sized rodent was clearly visible, no longer moving but staring hard at the little group of people at the other end of the veranda.

'It's a tree rat,' Peter offered. 'A black-tailed tree rat, I think. Though it could be an acacia rat. They both occur here.'

'It's a rat!' said Carla rather definitively.

'You've seen it before?' asked Brian Shepherd.

'Oh yes. They come every night. There'll be two or three more in a minute. They eat the bird food.'

'You feed them?' Carla was incredulous.

'Well, there's always bird food in the tray. Sometimes we put out extra.'

'They're really quite cute,' said Sheila. 'Beautiful big black eyes.'

'You feed rats?' Carla looked to her husband for support. 'I mean, they're vermin.'

'No, they're not really … rats.'

'You just said they were rats,' protested Colby Wittering. 'Tree rats.'

'Okay, but …' Sheila made a gesture towards Peter.

'It's just a name,' he said. 'I mean, hamsters and guinea pigs aren't rats. These aren't either. They're in the genus Thallomys. I think there's four kinds, in all.'

'You haven't seen them, Carla? In your garden? We have them in ours too.' Valli looked at Duke who nodded in agreement. 'They're quite harmless.'

'Euh,' was the only reply she got.

'You can't encourage rats,' Colby announced to the room. 'That's just ridiculous.' He shook his head disapprovingly.

Peter made to say something but Sheila quickly cut him off.

'Well,' she said, 'we've seemed to have scared him away anyway. Time to move inside, I think. We're having *vichyssoise* to start with. Who'd like some white wine?'

★

Peter had liked Brian Shepherd the first time they met but he liked him even more when, as they were taking their seats, Brian asked about the Thallomys, his interest obviously piqued. Needing little encouragement, Peter hurried to his study and returned with volume VII of *Handbook of the Mammals of the World* – not a small or inconspicuous book. As he turned the pages, looking for the illustration he wanted to show Brian, Peter noticed a few faces turned towards them.

171

'It's a book of rats,' he said loudly, hoping it sounded like a joke but definitely not intending it as such. A few people smiled; Colby Wittering did not.

✱

The *vichyssoise* was followed by *bavarois* of smoked salmon and a mango sorbet. Sheila and Susi were asked about – and complimented on – their work with the Police Service of Awanza. Brian Shepherd and Duke Etheridge discovered a mutual passion for tennis and agreed to play the following week. Valli and Carla were delighted to learn that they were alumni of the same college in North Carolina (though not at the same time) and happily shared recollections and – *sotto voce* – rumours about a member of the teaching staff they both remembered. Peter and Colby, sitting at either end of the table, were rather too far apart to make conversation.

Gratifyingly effusive (and probably sincere) comments greeted the arrival of the Moroccan chicken *tagine* and further appreciative noises were made when a particularly fine Pinotage was opened to accompany it.

'We used to boycott South African wine when I was at university,' Peter announced while admiring the contents of his glass.

'Well, you're making up for it now,' Sheila replied archly.

A cheeseboard was hardly touched ('I told you five courses would be too many!' Sheila had hissed at Peter in the kitchen) but, after a suitable pause, a fine chocolate ratafia ice was enjoyed by all and Sheila took orders for coffee while Peter brought out bottles of grappa, brandy and Amarula.

'Lord, Peter. You're spoiling us!' Valli grinned as she accepted a small glass of grappa.

'Well, we've waited a long time to do this,' Peter said. 'We thought we'd push the boat out a bit.'

'I think my boat's about to sink.' Duke exhaled and patted his belly.

Colby Wittering swirled a generous glass of brandy, took a sip, and said, as much to himself as his fellow guests, 'No doubt parents will be happy to know that ISN staff live so well.'

There was a brief silence. Then Peter spoke. 'Sorry?'

Colby looked up. 'I'm just thinking that I doubt if my high school principal in Chicago enjoyed such fine wines – or probably any wines.' He took another sip of brandy. 'Far less expensive brandies like this.'

Valli was frowning. 'Why? My sister is a high school principal. Not in Chicago but in Asheville. She enjoys a good bottle of wine.'

'And she can afford it?' said Colby. 'Teachers must get paid a lot better now than they did in my day.' His face suggested it was a development that did not entirely meet with his approval.

'Why shouldn't she?' asked Valli, now looking annoyed. 'And why shouldn't we? You seem to enjoy eating and drinking well.'

'I do. And I enjoy a salary that allows me to. Of course, I work hard for it …'

'You don't think teachers work for their money?'

Sheila attempted to change the subject. 'Susi, I was going to ask you…'

'Of course they do,' Colby interrupted. 'But, well, short days, long holidays … Let's just say that some jobs are a lot more demanding than others. And the rewards are correspondingly better. And they should be.' He considered his glass of brandy. 'This really is very good.'

'Your job is more demanding, would you say?' Duke asked.

Colby gave a self-deprecating shrug. 'Well, companies pay a lot to have McKinsey in the building. We add a lot of value.'

'You don't think teachers add value?'

'Now you're putting words in my mouth.'

'Well, you've as good as said you think teachers get paid too much.'

'Not at all. In fact, I have no idea what teachers earn in a school like this. But I'd be interested to know.' Colby turned to Peter. 'What's the answer, Peter? What do teachers make at this school?'

Peter hesitated. Valli and Duke were clearly annoyed and he could feel his own hackles rising. He could not see this conversation ending well. 'It varies, of course,' he said, 'with years of experience. We pay in US dollars and there's a published scale. Then there are stipends for assuming various responsibilities.'

Colby waved his hand impatiently. 'How much?'

'A teacher without much experience would start on a little under forty thousand. But that's theoretical because we probably wouldn't hire such a teacher. And at the other end of the scale some teachers will be in the mid-seventies. The average is probably around—'

'What? That's absurd! A teacher here can make seventy thousand dollars a year?'

'A few highly experienced ones. And I don't consider that absurd at all.' Peter could feel his temper rising quickly.

'How much do you earn, Colby? Tell us for comparison.' Valli also appeared to be trying to control her emotions.

'That's neither here nor there. Anyway, as I've pointed out, I'm a consultant, not a teacher. I think most people would agree that the work I do …'

'Colby,' Carla snapped at her husband. 'I think we need to change the subject.'

But Colby was not to be stopped. 'So, Peter, I'm guessing your salary bill must be enormous. What percentage…'

'Seventy-seven percent. It's by far our biggest cost. It is in every school.'

Colby gasped. 'Then no wonder your fees are ridiculously high. If my company wasn't paying the school fees I doubt if I'd pay myself. Hardly good value for money. It sounds like you need someone to take a look at your business model. You should call me in. Then again, you probably couldn't afford me.' Colby laughed. No one else did.

★

'What an objectionable man.' Peter and Sheila were in the kitchen clearing up, the dinner party having ended rather abruptly.

'Yes, I think you made your opinion clear to everyone. But you're right.' Sheila had been embarrassed by the whole exchange but she had to agree with her husband.

'I thought Valli was going to slap him.'

'Poor Carla looked mortified. She whispered some sort of apology as I showed them out.'

'I actually think that Colby didn't realise how offensive he was being. It was as if he was simply mentioning something so obvious as to be hardly worth discussing. Consultants earn shedloads of money and fly business or first class while teachers are down there with taxi drivers and waiters. God, it makes me angry. The arrogance. The ignorance.'

'Yes, darling. Well, he's gone now so let's just get these dishes finished and we can go to bed. Anyway, Colby's arrogance and ignorance notwithstanding, how do you think our first Awanzan dinner party went?'

'I thought it went very well. I particularly enjoyed the tree rat's cameo. I think we should make his appearance a regular feature when we entertain.'

'That may depend on what you mean by 'entertain' …'

✷

Returning to school on Monday morning, Peter learned that he had not been the only one hosting a party over the weekend.

'So where is she now?'

'In hospital. Mediclinic. The leg's broken in two places, apparently.'

'What is it about this school that makes girls jump out of windows?'

Mick looked confused. 'What …?'

'Oh, you weren't here,' said Peter. 'We had one last year who broke her wrist doing something similar. But this sounds more serious. Diane Costa? I don't think I know her.'

'Grade Ten. Usually quite a quiet kid. I wouldn't have expected this.'

'And what did the mother say?'

'That it happened on Saturday night, she said. She was a bit vague on the details, almost evasive. But Grade Ten kids this morning are all whispering in corners and looking very bouncy. Something happened.'

Peter sighed. 'Well, let's hope she's okay. You'll let me know if you hear anything?'

'Of course.'

✷

For Valli's meeting with Elsa, she had casually suggested meeting for a coffee at the Saturday morning farmers' market, something that ISN staff regularly did and an invitation that would raise no suspicions. They had chatted inconsequentially for a few minutes and then Valli asked if Elsa had any plans for the imminent four-week holiday.

'You still have family in Sweden, don't you? Are you flying home or seeing a bit more of Africa? Pam and Maeve are holidaying in South Africa, I believe. Christmas in the Kruger. Oh …'

175

Tears had started welling in Elsa's eyes.

'Seems like I touched a nerve,' Valli later explained to Peter. 'More than one nerve, actually. Seemingly, Elsa's father left when she was very young and she has never had a close relationship with her mother. Quite the opposite, if I understand correctly. So, going back to Uppsala is never something she looks forward to. But, just to muddy the waters, her mother has been diagnosed with cancer. So, there's guilt.'

'She told you all this?'

'I told you. We have a good relationship. And apparently I remind her of her aunt – whom she does get on with. But there's more. She was very friendly with Blessing, Maeve, and Pam. Well, she still is – or would like to be. But she … oh, it's all very sad.'

'What?'

'Young girls. Am I old enough to call Elsa a girl? Anyway, young women. They sometimes put themselves under ridiculous pressures. Elsa thinks she isn't as good a teacher as Blessing. She's not a pretty as Maeve. And she's not as smart as Pam. She's really messed up.'

'But that's nonsense. She's a very attractive young woman, if I'm allowed to say that. And you tell me she's an excellent teacher.'

'She is. And she knows it's all nonsense. That is, she knows it rationally but emotionally … So she gets mad at herself and then there's more guilt and …'

'And she cuts herself. Did she admit it? Or acknowledge it or whatever?'

'Not at first. Not until I pointed out that she was wearing a long-sleeved blouse and jeans on what was probably the hottest day of the year. I hinted – well, maybe more than hinted that I suspected.'

'And?'

'Yes. She showed me her arms. Hesitantly but, if I'm not wrong, also with a sense of relief. It's not as bad as I'd feared but there's no doubt.'

'Elsewhere on her body?'

'She says not but who knows?'

'And now?'

'Well, she's not in denial. That's a start. She knows she needs help. Trouble is, she won't be able to get an appointment for weeks and with Christmas coming up it'll be even worse.'

'And what is she going to do for the holiday?'

'It'd be great if she could be persuaded to join Pam and Maeve. But I don't know how much I can interfere.'

'Well, they know there's a problem. They brought it to you. And they're concerned. Surely they'd be happy to invite her?'

'They did but she declined.'

'That was then. Look, I don't think you'd be going too far if you spoke to Maeve or Pam and asked them to try again. And suggest it to Elsa. They were friends. They still are.'

'I don't know. Might we just be making it worse?'

Peter thought back to Mark Langtoft. Had he got that one right or had he just been lucky? Indeed, was it even over? Throughout the community there were still rumours and speculation about Mark's departure, some stories close to the truth but others wildly inaccurate.

'I've said it before. It always feels like we're working without a script,' he said.

'Let me talk with Elsa again. We've agreed that she's going to check in with me every day. At least until the holiday.'

'All right. Let me know if I can do anything.'

Sheila's adventures with African wildlife in their Ndwalowe garden and in Mwakami had, she was gracious enough to admit, caused her to reassess Peter's passion for birds.

'I mean, I still think it's ridiculous that you insist that there are different kinds of sparrows. A sparrow's a sparrow, for goodness' sake. But the parrots in the garden are lovely. And what was the amazing bird we saw in Mwakami?'

'A lilac-breasted roller. An LBR.'

'Yes, that was it. What a gorgeous bird.'

So, rather to their mutual surprise, Sheila had agreed to accompany Peter on a little foray to a patch of wetlands on the outskirts of the city.

'There's a gonolek I really want to find. And I'll show you at least one kind of jacana, maybe both of them, if we're lucky. The widowbirds should be coming into plumage too but …'

Sheila let Peter prattle on, barely listening and understanding very little when she did. She looked out of the car window as the houses they were passing became grander.

'Most of the ambassadorial residences are in Sunninghill,' Peter was saying, 'but there are a few here. A lot of the African ones, I believe. And then …' he turned off the street and down a muddy track. 'Here we are.'

A small area of open ground lay between a stand of dense bushes and a sea of reeds that seemed to stretch forever.

'I love this place,' Peter said. 'It's, what, just thirty minutes from the house? But it's really quiet and the birds are great.'

'Is it safe?'

'Well, you don't want to be silly. As I said, don't wear jewellery. And I probably wouldn't bring my big camera here. But, to be honest, I've never even seen anyone else here.'

'How did you find it?'

'Through the bird club. It's on the map of Ndwalowe they produce. Ready?'

Their valuables safely locked in the Patrol, Peter and Sheila set off along a narrow and frequently wet track with bushes on their right and reeds on their left. Both carried binoculars. Peter had a small backpack in which he had various bird books.

'Why do you need more than one book?' Sheila had asked as they set out.

'Because some illustrations are better in this book and some are better in this one. And it's helpful to check both. These two are general guides but this book is just about waterbirds.'

'And the other two?'

'One on mammals and one on reptiles. We might see some of those too.'

Sheila waited until Peter had turned away and shook her head slowly.

They walked for maybe a kilometre, pausing frequently while Peter pointed out various small birds skulking in the reeds. Where the reeds thinned, a stretch of still water was visible. Moorhens appeared and disappeared. 'That's a lesser,' Peter whispered at one point. 'At least, I think it is.'

It's a bird, thought Sheila, by now questioning her decision to spend her afternoon trudging through rather smelly mud. She was about to ask

Peter how much further they were going to go when a man in jeans and a T-shirt stepped out of the bushes before them.

They both stopped, startled rather than alarmed. 'Good afternoon,' Peter ventured.

'Good afternoon, Sir,' the man took a few steps forward. 'May I ask what you are doing here?'

'We are bird watching.' Peter held up his binoculars. 'There are birds here,' he said, perhaps redundantly.

The man frowned. 'I am a police officer.' He produced from his pocket a badge that could really have been anything. 'Do you know where you are?'

'Yes, erm …'

'That is the prime minister's house,' the man said, pointing at a wall Peter could just make out through the bushes. It was at least a hundred metres away. 'This is a restricted area.'

'Oh. I'm sorry. I didn't know. There were no signs …'

'Of course there are no signs. Do we want everyone to know where the prime minister lives?'

'Well, no, but …'

'You should not be here. It is a restricted area.'

'Yes, you said that.' Peter was starting to guess where this was heading.

'It is an offence to be in a restricted area. And with a camera!'

'No, these are binoculars … Look …'

'So, now what?' Sheila stepped forward speaking in a tone that Peter knew quite well.

'There will have to be consequences.'

'All right,' Sheila said. 'Shall we go?'

'Go?'

'Well, I'm guessing we'll have to go to the police station. Shall we give you a lift? I assume you don't have a car.'

Peter worried that she was pushing her luck but she seemed to have the measure of this maybe-policeman. He recalled the confidence she had exhibited on the road to Mwakami. He wished he had half of it.

'You want to go to the police station?' The man was now confused and seemed to have lost some of his swagger.

'It's not what we want to do,' explained Peter, feeling that they were gaining the initiative. 'But if an offence has been committed … Well, you said it yourself. There will have to be consequences.'

'But … We can work it out here. If I take you to the police station …'

'You mean, if we take you.'

'Sheila!' Peter hissed.

'If we go to the police station,' the man continued, 'there will be charge sheets and I will have to fingerprint you and then you will have to appear in court tomorrow …' He made a hopeless gesture to underline the complexity of what lay ahead. 'But if we can take care of it here … If we can sort it out now …'

'But how?' Peter furrowed his brow as if utterly perplexed.

The man looked irritated and slightly impatient as if talking to someone slow-witted. 'We can fix it now. Then we don't need to go to the police station.'

'I still don't …' Peter wondered how convincing his little act was.

'I think we both know what he is saying,' Sheila said to him. She turned to the man. 'Am I right?'

'Six hundred dollars,' he said.

Sheila turned to Peter. 'It's going up. It was only five hundred on the way to Mwakami.'

He ignored her. 'Look,' he said to the maybe policeman, 'we don't have any money. We don't carry money in places like this. We don't have watches, we don't have jewellery. And, you know what? Even if we did, I'm not going to pay a bribe. Sorry.'

The man looked from Peter to Sheila and back again. 'Four hundred …'

'You're not listening. We don't have any money.' Peter spoke slowly.

'Where is your car?'

'My car? It's back there a kilometre or so. But—'

'I will wait here. You go and get the money. I will wait.'

'I told you. I'm not going to pay a bribe.'

'Two hundred.'

What had the potential to be quite a frightening experience was rapidly turning into a farce. Corruption and petty theft were real enough in Awanza but not everyone had the stomach or inclination to carry it off convincingly.

Some hours later, safely home and on the phone to her mother, Sheila had laughed. 'In the end, when he realised we weren't going to give him anything, he kind of smiled as if there were no hard feelings and wished us a pleasant afternoon! Only after he'd gone did my knees begin to wobble. I mean, in the end it was funny but ... Well, I think we were lucky ... No, mum, I won't. I definitely won't be going back there. And I hope Peter won't either.'

Sitting across the room from his wife with a cold beer, Peter felt a range of emotions. He was annoyed that what had become a favourite place was now probably somewhere he would no longer be able to go. And, wryly amused as he was at how the incident had finished, he was also aware that the ending could easily have been very different. He wondered if and when their luck would run out. He knew people who had lived in the country for years and who had never had a bad experience. But he had also met others who had experienced violence. Though in so many ways loving his new life, Peter was periodically reminded that this was, for him, a foreign country in every sense of the word. On balance, he was grateful for such reminders.

★

Mick greeted his visitor effusively. Mick greeted everyone effusively.

'Mr Mendy, come in, come in. How are you?'

His guest did not return Mick's broad smile and only accepted a handshake with obvious reluctance. 'Good morning, Mr O'Cheney.' He took his seat stiffly and declined the offer of something to drink.

Uh-oh, though Mick. *Someone's not happy.*

'Now, what can I do for you today?' he asked. 'My secretary said it was urgent but you wouldn't say what it was about on the phone.'

'I don't talk to secretaries. I talk to principals.'

'Well,' Mick attempted another smile. 'Last time I looked, I was the principal so what's on your mind?'

'I'm Diane Costa's stepfather.'

'Oh. Now, how is she doing? Last I heard from her mother—'

'She's doing as well as we can expect. Her leg is broken in two places.'

'So I understand. Poor girl.'

'The leg will heal – well, the surgeon says – but she is still in shock. We are very concerned. This has been very traumatic for her. And, of course, for her mother. They are both very upset.'

'You have our sympathies, Mr Mendy.'

'We don't want your sympathy, Mr O'Cheney. We want an apology. And we want something to be done!'

'An apology? And what would you be wanting an apology for?'

'For the behaviour of your students on Saturday night! For the distress that their actions have caused my family. It's unacceptable.'

Mick's face registered surprise. 'Saturday night, you say. Now, you're going to have to help me here, Mr Mendy. What happened on Saturday night? Besides the unfortunate Diane breaking her leg.'

'You don't know?'

'I don't know if I know. I don't think I do. Why don't you tell me?'

'Students from this school came to my house – uninvited. They brought alcohol. Diane was beside herself. She pleaded with them to leave.'

'Diane? Where were you?'

Mr Mendy scowled at Mick. 'My wife and I were out. In fact, we had planned to spend the night with my wife's sister. It was her birthday but she lives on a remote farm about two hours from Ndwalowe. Too far to drive back the same night.'

It was starting to make sense to Mick. 'So, you were away for the night and Diane invited some friends around?'

'No! We gave her permission to have one girlfriend sleep over so she wouldn't be alone. Just one! Not the twenty or thirty girls and boys who turned up.'

'Diane told you this?'

'Of course.'

'She didn't sort of organise a wee party in your absence?'

'No. Diane knows we would never have allowed that. She also knows we don't allow alcohol in the house. Not ever.'

'And in the middle of the party she somehow broke her leg?'

'It wasn't a party! Mr O'Cheney, will you let me explain?'

'Please do.'

'On the way to my wife's sister we came across a serious traffic accident. A car had overturned. Three people were injured, one of them a baby.'

'Oh, no.'

'Do you know the C44? Very little traffic. We were the first car to pass in an hour or so. There was no telephone reception. Anyway, it would have taken too long for an ambulance to arrive. So we took the injured family to the nearest town. Tsumwana. Do you know it?'

Mick shook his head.

'There's a police station there. And a clinic. We had to make a statement to the police and they insisted that we take them back to the scene of the accident. Anyway, by the end of it all we had no desire to attend a birthday party.'

'Understandable.'

'So we drove home. We got there at about eleven-thirty.'

Mick could picture the scene. 'And you found …?'

'The house full of teenagers! Many of them drunk. They had even forced Diane to drink alcohol. And she never drinks.'

'Forced?' Mick hoped that his face wasn't betraying his thoughts.

'Diane knows our rules about alcohol. She would never disobey us.'

Mick nodded slowly. 'I'm guessing that Diane was a bit surprised to see you.'

'As I said, she was beside herself. And ashamed. Even though it wasn't her fault. She ran away from us, upstairs, and climbed out of her bedroom window. Then she fell.'

'Why did she climb out of a window?'

Mr Mendy hesitated. 'I think she thought I would be angry.'

'I'm guessing you were angry.'

'Of course I was! But not with her. With these … these louts who were drinking in my house. Uninvited.'

'I'm going to have to find out if that's true or not. It sounds to me—'

'We can meet them together. I want to give them a piece of my mind.'

'Sorry?'

'I want you to call all of Grade Ten together. Now. I want to tell them how disgracefully they have behaved. This reflects very poorly on the school, Mr O'Cheney. Very poorly indeed.'

'Grade Ten? You know it was just Grade Ten? All of them? And no one else? That doesn't sound very likely.'

'I know some of them. I can give you names.'

'Yes, I'd like to talk to anyone who was there – to get the full story, you understand.'

'I've given you the full story. These students invaded my house. When can I see them? Now, please.'

'No, Mr Mendy, I don't think that's going to happen.'

'Mr O'Cheney, I must insist.'

'Sorry. I very much doubt if all Grade Ten students were at your house on Saturday night. For starters, we have around sixty Grade Ten students – many more that the two or three dozen you say were at your house. And if I pull any of them out of class I'll have dozens of angry parents on the phone. And even if some were there ...'

'They were!'

'All right but I do want to understand why they were there. I know you say they were uninvited but—'

'Are you going to let me talk to Grade Ten or not?'

'No, I'm not.'

Mr Mendy stood. 'Then I'm afraid I am going to have to take this to the director. I'm very disappointed that you will not accept responsibility for the appalling behaviour of your students.'

'Mr Mendy, I promise I am going to look into this but I think it may be a bit more complicated ...'

'Good day, Mr O'Cheney. I'm not going to waste any more of my time here.'

★

While Mick was attempting to deal with Mr Mendy, Peter was also trying to navigate his way through a difficult conversation.

'I can assure you, Mr Corby, that a lot of parents are very supportive of this idea. They think it would make a big difference.'

'But, Mrs Furaha, that really isn't the role of the PTA.'

'You mean, it hasn't been until now. But we think the PTA can do so much more. This would be an entirely appropriate way for the PTA to become more involved.'

'I'm afraid I can't agree. Also, there would be issues of confidentiality.'

'Are you suggesting we cannot respect confidentiality?'

'I'm suggesting that if a child has a problem or is in trouble or whatever, that is a matter for the school and the parents. No one else.'

'And we are suggesting that the PTA can be the ideal conduit through which problems can be resolved.' Madeleine Kaminski jabbed the desk between them to emphasise her point. 'Bullying, for example. Parents are often afraid to bring it up for fear of reprisals. The PTA can speak on their behalf.'

'Actually, my experience is that parents have no problem raising such issues. You'll recall that you and I have had a number of conversations about your daughter.'

'Unsatisfactory conversations, I might say, which is why we think that parents should channel their concerns through the PTA.'

'So every time a parent has a complaint or a concern, you are proposing that they should bring it to the PTA rather than inform the school?'

'Yes,' Nyota Furaha nodded. 'We'd like such a system to be formalised and all parents notified. It could start from next month after the holiday.'

Peter shook his head. 'I'm afraid it isn't going to start next month or any month. It is not the role of the PTA to mediate between parents and the school. We have existing systems and policies that usually work perfectly well.'

Madeleine Kaminski snorted.

'Usually, Mrs Kaminski. I said usually.'

'Mr Corby, I am disappointed but I'm afraid not surprised that you cannot see the merit in our proposal.' Mrs Furaha collected her notes and stuffed them into her bag. 'The PTA only wants to help improve the school but you seem to want to block us at every turn. I think you are scared to let others see what really goes on here.'

Peter stood. 'Mrs Furaha, I don't even know what that means but it is no doubt meant to be an insult. So I suggest this would be a good time to stop this conversation. Thank you both for coming, ladies. Now, if you'll forgive me, I have a school to run.'

As she pottered around her delightfully colourful garden, noting where work was still needed but also admiring and appreciating flower beds that were blooming, bushes that were recovering, and a vegetable patch that was ever more productive, Sheila caught herself again marvelling at the butterflies.

So many, she thought. *And such diversity*.

Her attention was caught by one she could not remember seeing before. She remained still, trying to study the butterfly before it flew off, as it

185

inevitably would. It was larger than most, the wings were broad and somewhat pointed and each terminated in what Sheila could only describe as looking like some sort of spike.

'Extraordinary,' she muttered.

But what was really spectacular was the butterfly's colouring. Countless patches of vivid turquoise were set on wings that were otherwise jet black. And, as she stared and inched closer, Sheila made out two tiny spots of scarlet. She shook her head in awe.

Peter can keep his birds, she thought. *I wonder if I can find a book on African butterflies.*

She would soon discover that she indeed could find many wonderful books to help her identify the numerous butterflies (and moths) that she now started to notice more often. She delighted in the dizzying variety of sizes, shapes and colours but took no less enjoyment from their often wonderful names.

Lemon Traveller

Striped Policeman

Dotted Pierrot

Silvery Silverline

Brown Playboy

Dancing Telchinia

Wandering Donkey Acraea

Garden Inspector

She would tease Peter. 'Butterfly names are so much more inventive. You've got boring names like Brown Warbler or Green Parrot. We lepidopterists have Restless Cupids, Night-fighters, and Mother-of-pearls.'

Peter would smile tolerantly. He thought it was a bit premature of his wife to call herself a lepidopterist and he wondered for how long this new interest would last. But he was happy that Sheila had drawn his attention to yet another charming and fascinating aspect of African wildlife. He was finding it, as he would tell anyone who listened, a privilege to live on this remarkable continent.

★

'So, the next thing I know, Flo bursts into my office and tells me to come quick.' Mick gestured, his eyes wide.

'I don't believe it.'

'I know. I thought he'd left the campus but he'd gone looking for Grade Ten kids and found some in the Arts Centre. Maggie was trying to calm him down when I got there but he was in full flow.'

'The kids?' Peter asked.

'They hadn't a bloody clue what was going on. Well, maybe some of them did. They just sat there.'

'How did you get him out?'

'A bit firmly, if I'm honest. All that rugby training …' In spite of the situation, Mick flashed Peter a grin. 'Escorted him – I think that's the word – to his car and made sure he left.'

'Good grief.'

'Then I went back to the drama class and apologised for the whole thing. Of course, by then everyone knew what it was all about and they were mostly having a good giggle. Highlight of the day, for them.'

'I'm going to have to write to him. We can't have this kind of behaviour. And can you find out once and for all what happened at the party?'

'Sure. There are a few kids I know who'll tell me but I think we both know.'

Peter nodded. 'Authoritarian father – stepfather – leaves a girl alone for a night and she seizes the opportunity. He comes home and she panics.'

'And dad is in total denial.'

'And the poor girl has a broken leg.'

'And, I assume, a recently acquired taste for alcohol. Oh, to be young again.'

'No thanks. Anyway, sorry to give you another job but will you please put everything in writing. Just for the record. You never know where these things will go.'

'Will do, boss.'

'And thanks, Mick. Sounds like it was a difficult one but you handled it well.'

Mick looked pleased. 'Thanks.'

★

The idea had been raised but Peter and Sheila had never seriously considered flying back to the UK for Christmas. True, a respite from the heat of an Awanzan summer did appeal but when they thought of December days that were short, dark, and wet, the prospect of endless blue skies even with temperatures in the mid-thirties ultimately seemed more inviting. A holiday in Mauritius or Madagascar had been considered but they had left it too late to book anything affordable. Anyway, there was still much of Awanza they wanted to experience and explore.

Not having children, not being religious, and having spent most of their Christmases together in Japan where the 25th of December was just another working day, the Corbys made little attempt to celebrate or even acknowledge the occasion. Others in Ndwalowe, however, enthusiastically embraced the familiar customs and rituals. Wreaths appeared on doors, Christmas cards were displayed, halls were decked (synthetic holly was available in all the supermarkets), Christmas CDs dusted off, presents wrapped and exchanged, and whatever was traditional to eat in one's country acquired and cooked.

But this was still Christmas in the tropics. Brian and Susi Shepherd had invited Peter and Sheila for dinner on Christmas Day and, having just returned from a wonderful week hiking in the Eronuvulu Mountains and still with a rafting adventure on the Lowana river to look forward to, they had happily accepted. Pre-dinner drinks had been enjoyed chest-deep in the Shepherds' swimming pool (not an experience Peter necessarily associated with Christmas) and the turkey had been cooked outdoors on what Brian called a barbie and two South African guests (thankfully not parents at ISN) insisted was a braai. Moreover, the three couples ate on a terrace dressed in shorts with a fan rotating above them while lovebirds screeched in the bushes and the many flies and mosquitoes were swatted away. Ceramic Christmas trees and snowmen decorated the table and Susi had even procured crackers to be pulled. Sheila wore a pair of antlers and Susi a Santa hat.

'Merry Christmas!' they said to each other but seldom without a giggle or a joke.

It was, Peter later concluded, verging on the surreal and yet one of the most enjoyable Christmas Days he could remember.

★

The school holidays in December Peter had known in England, Germany and Japan had been comparatively brief – usually something like ten or twelve days including Christmas and New Year. In Awanza, however, the holiday stretched for a little over four weeks, something Peter learned was quite common in the southern hemisphere.

'It is, after all,' Saskia had explained to Peter, 'our summer holiday.' It was also the case that expatriates from Europe, North America, and elsewhere who returned to spend Christmas with families wished to get the most out of airline tickets that were not cheap.

For those who chose to remain south of the equator but wished to travel beyond Awanza, there were many options. South Africa was always popular and Namibia was gaining a reputation as an appealing, affordable, and safe holiday destination. Botswana had some remarkable attractions but tended to be expensive. The Victoria Falls excepted, people tended to be wary of travelling to Zimbabwe. In any case, the Falls could as easily be enjoyed from the Zambian side. Further afield, Zanzibar and the great parks of Tanzania and Kenya were only a few hours away. Those who had visited Malawi spoke of it with affection but it seldom seemed to be top of anyone's list. Angola and the Democratic Republic of the Congo appeared not even to be on the list.

But Mozambique most certainly was and Valli and Duke and their two children had rented a beach house on the ocean for three weeks. After a week, Valli had sent Peter a brief message and some photos of a pristine beach, a sea that was enticingly turquoise, and a seafood restaurant specialising in lobster, crab, calamari, sea urchins, octopus, and many other things that Peter did not eat.

But the email she sent a few days later was far more interesting.

Hi Peter

I know it's not your thing but we can't get enough of the seafood here. When we go to the restaurant now we don't even have to order. The staff give us our usual table and just start bringing stuff! Love it!

I'm writing to ask if you know if Lazarett Snyman is on holiday or is he still in Ndwalowe? I only ask because I think I saw him here. In our restaurant. I've only seen him at the graduation last year and the AGM so maybe it wasn't him. But I think it was.

And is he married? Cos the woman he was with did not look like any Mrs Snyman I might have imagined. We weren't the only ones in the restaurant staring! LOL.

A coincidence, eh?

Anyway, I hope you and Sheila enjoyed the Eronuvulus.

Give her my love

Valli

No, thought Peter. *Surely not. How can that be possible?* He had said nothing to Valli (or anyone) about the curious events at the !Kha Makalani Lodge in July but he had indeed pointed out Lazarett to her on at least those two occasions. And, thanks to Peter's regular indignant updates about Lazarett's latest machinations he was certainly someone of interest to Valli.

The old dog, thought Peter. He couldn't decide if he was shocked or, dare he admit it, just slightly impressed. And then he picked up his phone to share the news with Sheila.

★

January

Parents complain. That is just the reality. Well, to be fair, customers complain. And parents – certainly in a fee-paying international school – are customers. Sometimes parental complaints are ridiculous. Sometimes they are mischievous. But sometimes they are valid concerns that the school needs to understand, respect, and respond to.

He may not have considered himself one of life's complainers but Peter himself had nevertheless registered his annoyance with poor service on occasion and he fully accepted that if and when the school erred, parents were entirely within their rights to express their displeasure. In some cases it was within Peter's wherewithal to make good something that had gone wrong and he was not slow to apologise on behalf of the school and, if necessary, personally.

But sometimes things just happen and there's not much anyone can do about it. The Dung Beetles fiasco? Yes, that could have been avoided. (And, nearly two months later, Peter was still getting snarky comments from unforgiving parents.) The burst water pipe? Hard to fault anyone there. Although, as had been pointed out more than once, it did call into question how proactive the school had (or hadn't) been in foreseeing problems and employing preventative maintenance. (But, Peter had wanted to argue on a few occasions, how many parents – or board members – would have thanked him if he had announced that, at very significant cost, the school's entire plumbing system was going to be overhauled just in case a pipe burst? Damned if you do, damned if you don't.)

Norman Collard, exactly a year after he and his wife had stormed out of the director's office, outraged at Peter's inexplicable refusal to rectify a particularly egregious mistake, was again expressing his considerable unhappiness.

'Liora has had three different teachers for IB English and four for IB maths. Are you going to defend that, Mr Corby?'

'Mr Collard, I don't know if defend is the right word. I can explain it but—'

'Ms Cutting and Mr Naismith in Grade Eleven. Then they left. That was regrettable but I have to accept that teachers sometimes move on. Then Mr Gillespie missed the first three weeks of the year.'

Peter raised his hand but Mr Collard continued. 'I know, I know, and it was tragic. But the simple fact is that Liora effectively had no English teacher for nearly a month.' (*Just over two weeks*, thought Peter but he said nothing.) 'And now Mr Gillespie has gone and we have Mr Willoughby. And, if I'm not wrong, Mr Willoughby has never taught the IB before.'

'No, but—'

'And then four – four! – different teachers for maths. Of course, she never really liked Ms Cutting in Grade Eleven and, if you want to know, neither did my wife and I. We never even got to meet Mr Collins before he mysteriously disappeared. Mrs Mulenga seemed conscientious but, I'm going to be blunt, a little out of her depth. And now there's apparently a Mr Pigeon.'

'Who is,' Peter said hurriedly, 'a highly experienced teacher of IB maths. In fact he's an examiner. We were very lucky to get him halfway through a school year.'

'That's as may be but how can there be any continuity? If there's a new teacher every month, how can they get to know the students? You've said in more than one public meeting that effective teaching depends on there being a mutually respectful and trusting relationship between the student and the teacher. How can that happen when teachers come and go willy-nilly?'

'Mr Collard, nobody is suggesting this is anything other than …' he groped for the right word. 'Undesirable. No one would have planned it like this.'

'I have to wonder if there even is any planning in this school.'

Why do parents always do that? Thought Peter. He has a valid concern. I'm sympathetic. But he cannot resist exaggerating and tossing in gratuitous aspersions. And that puts my back up and then I stop being sympathetic and … well, we know how it ended last year.

'It may be some reassurance, Mr Collard, that we insist upon detailed handover notes here. When a teacher leaves, especially if they are teaching an exam class, they prepare a detailed file on what the students have done and have yet to do. Individually and collectively. The teacher who is taking over is very quickly up to speed.'

'Collins? Did he do that?'

'No.' Peter sighed. 'In that case …'

'That's my point. You're just making this up as you go along. Seven teachers for two subjects – two crucial subjects, I might point out – in eighteen months. And that's just so far. What's going to happen between now and May? I dread to think.'

Peter was trying very, very hard to remain professional. 'And that's the point, I think, Mr Collard. We don't know. No one can know. *The best laid schemes o' mice and men gang aft agley.*'

'You what?'

Peter hesitated. 'My wife's Scottish. That was Robert Burns. You know the poem?'

Mr Collard stared at Peter as if he had gone mad. Peter wished he hadn't said it. 'The point is—'

'The point is that my daughter's education is being jeopardised and I want to know what you are going to do about it.'

Ah, here we go, thought Peter. *It had to come to this. It always does. Mr Corby, I'm sure you are aware that a meteorite is heading towards the Earth and is projected to land right on top of this school. AND I WANT TO KNOW WHAT YOU ARE GOING TO DO ABOUT IT!*

'What would you like me to do?' Over the years, Peter had become quite good at injecting a little ice into a simple sentence. He thought this might be a good moment to do so. Well, it made him feel better, if nothing else.

'I would like you to accept some responsibility for the situation we are in.'

Fighting his baser instincts, Peter reminded himself to be professional. 'I do accept responsibility,' he heard himself say. 'I am the head of school and the buck stops here.' In reality, Peter's sentence meant nothing but he had half an idea it might help.

'Well,' said Mr Collard, 'that's something.'

'And actually, Mr Collard,' Peter had had an idea. 'I can do something concrete. And I will. I've worked with the IB for many years. They are not unreasonable people. Many students all over the world have different teachers in Grades Eleven and Twelve. Some schools plan it that way. But what has happened here, to Liora and, of course, other students too, is a bit out of the ordinary.'

Mr Collard frowned.

'Imagine,' said Peter, 'that a student suffers a sudden and traumatic bereavement the week, or even the day, before a crucial exam. It's bound to affect their performance. Schools can write to the IB and make them aware of the circumstances. I don't know how exactly they factor this in when awarding a grade but I'm sure they do. I will write to the IB explaining the unusual …' Peter could see Mr Collard was looking happier so he doubled down, 'in fact, unprecedented churn of teachers for these two subjects. I'm confident the examiners will take this into account.'

'Well,' Mr Collard wasn't about to express gratitude but he had to acknowledge that this was … something. 'And you have confidence in Pigeon and Willoughby?'

Pigeon and Willoughby, thought Peter. *Sounds like a firm of solicitors in Hampshire.* What he said was, 'In their different ways I do, they are both very experienced and they come with excellent references.'

'Very well. But I want you to know that my wife and I are extremely disappointed that the school has allowed it to come to this.'

Quite what the school had and had not "allowed" was not clear to Peter but he just nodded gravely. 'You have made your point very clearly, Mr Collard.'

'Then I won't take up any more of your time, Mr Corby.' He stood. 'Thank you for your seeing me.'

'Thank you, Mr Collard.' Peter also stood. 'I hope you have a good day.'

Mr Collard scowled a little and left.

★

'Good morning, Pearl,' Jenny Wintercoat called across the car park to a woman emerging from an expensive Range Rover.

'Oh, Jenny. Good morning. How are you?'

'Very well, thanks. You?'

'Not bad. Though I don't know how I'll be feeling by the end of this meeting.'

'I know. I wish some of the others were here. I tried to persuade Izumi and Shumaila to come back but … Well, you can't blame them.'

They had reached the door of the PTA meeting room. 'After you,' offered Pearl. Jenny grimaced and entered.

Crystal Moore looked up from her laptop. 'Oh, good morning. I wasn't sure if you were coming or not.' Her expression suggested to Jenny that she'd been rather hoping they wouldn't.

'Oh yes, we're here. Good morning, Nyota, Madeleine.'

Perfunctory greetings were exchanged.

'Kim is coming but she'll be a bit late,' explained Crystal.

'No one else?' asked Pearl.

'Not that I know of.'

'Day was,' said Pearl as she took her seat, 'we'd have a dozen or more at these meetings. I think we had eighteen once. I can remember having to get extra chairs from next door.'

'Well, think of it as quality not quantity,' said Crystal rather sharply. 'Shall we begin?'

'There's no one here from the SLT,' noted Jenny. 'There should be one of them at least. Did you inform them of this meeting?'

'But, Jenny.' said Nyota. 'They never have anything constructive to add and it's always quite obvious they would rather not be here. We will manage far better without them.'

'I don't agree. I think it's important that they are involved in our discussions. Anyway, it isn't our choice. It's in the constitution.'

'Then that's another reason – yet another, I'd say – why we need a new constitution,' stated Crystal. 'It's outrageous. What business do they have interfering in our decisions? We don't sit in on their SLT meetings.'

'That's not the same thing at all,' protested Pearl. 'And they're hardly interfering. I think their advice is often very helpful.'

'Are they advising us or manipulating us?' asked Madeleine Kaminski. 'I agree with Nyota. How are we ever going to hold them accountable if we let them run our meetings and tell us what we can and can't do?'

195

'Sorry I'm late.' Kim Rankin appeared at the door with a big tray of brownies under a tea towel. 'I had to wait till these came out of the oven. I thought you'd all like some.'

'Mmm, the smell! Thank you, Kim.' Madeleine helped herself to a large piece. 'Ooh, they're still warm. Delish!'

'I was just saying, Kim,' Pearl paused to accept a small brownie on a napkin, 'I was just saying that someone from the SLT should—'

'Well, they aren't,' interrupted Crystal, 'and I hope you aren't going to tell me that this meeting is therefore invalid or unconstitutional or something. We are the PTA. We don't need anyone's permission.'

'But we should respect the con—'

'I would – and will – respect a constitution that is fit for purpose. And that's why we are drafting a new one. This current one is a joke. I bet it was written by the administration. Anyway, can we get on with the agenda?'

★

The terrace of the Italian-Awanzan Cultural Centre seemed to be Lazarett's preferred place for informal meetings. Perhaps it's close to where he works, Carola had once thought and then realised that she still had next to no idea of what Lazarett did for a living, far less where.

'I used to love this place,' she said, stirring her latte. 'But I've had too many uncomfortable conversations here. It's rather spoiled it for me.'

'Conversations with our mutual friend?' Ernesto asked. 'Do you know why he asked to meet us?'

'No. I've no idea. He just said he wanted to run something past the chair and vice-chair. Oh, here he is.' Carola waved to Lazarett who had taken a waiter by the elbow and was evidently placing an order.

'He knows what he wants, Lazarett,' commented Ernesto. 'I'll give him that.'

Cursory pleasantries were exchanged as Lazarett took a seat and then he came straight to the point.

'How many more?'

'How many more what?'

'How many more teachers do we have to lose before we decide we have to get involved? The school has lost three teachers in half a year. I can tell you that parents are very worried.'

'Have you any reason to believe we will lose more?' asked Carola.

Lazarett threw his arms in the air a touch theatrically. 'Who knows? Corby recruited two of the three. One was gone within a month and the other by Christmas. Does he know what he is doing? Can we be sure the other two he hired aren't going to abandon us?'

'Why would they?' demanded Ernesto, immediately irritated by Lazarett. 'We all know why Frank Gillespie left. You can hardly blame Peter for that.'

'And,' added Carola, 'we have been told – the board have – in strict confidence, of course, why Mr Collins departed so abruptly.'

'Yes. Collins was a paedophile and Gillespie had a police record but Corby still hired them both and—'

'Oh come on! We know what Frank Gillespie's so-called police record amounted to. I cannot believe you are bringing that up again.'

'Ernesto, I am just saying that I don't have confidence in Corby's judgement. We are into another hiring season and the director tells us there will be up to seven positions to fill. Can we really leave it to him to hire these new teachers?'

'Yes,' said Ernesto very firmly. 'It's his job. An important part of his job.'

'And it's because it is so important that I think we should be involved. Look, even if he conducts the interviews and draws up a shortlist, I think the board – or at least a number of board members – should look at the applications and then make the final decision. I suspect we could also save the school some money by hiring a little more sensibly than Corby managed last year.'

'I wish you would call him Peter or at least Mr Corby.' Carola's expression made it clear that this was another conversation that was at the very least uncomfortable. 'The way you say his name sounds so disrespectful.'

Neither Carola nor Ernesto were surprised that Lazarett made no effort to reassure them of the respect he felt for the school's director.

'I wonder what Seth Taniel would make of this,' said Carola.

'I think we both know very well what he would think. It's an outrageous suggestion. Yes, we've lost three teachers. One in the most tragic of circumstances. Another – not hired by Peter, I might say – turned out to be mentally unstable and whatever Chuck Collins may or may not have got up to in a previous school there was no hint of it when he was hired. The references, his police clearance, the endorsement of the recruiting agency – everything was entirely in order.'

'Ernesto, please! Keep your voice down.' Carola looked around anxiously to see if anyone on neighbouring tables was listening to their conversation.

'The fact remains that under his leadership, we seem to be haemorrhaging teachers.' Lazarett would not be silenced.

'Oh that's ridiculous!'

'It's not just me.'

'Not just you what?'

'I'm not the only one who is worried. Many of the teachers are too. They have no confidence in Corby. They see teachers leaving without explanation and they are worried. Will they be next?'

'Who is saying that?' asked Carola, by now quite alarmed at the direction this conversation was taking.

'Oh, people tell me things. Often, they don't know who else to turn to.'

'Teachers?' asked Carola. Lazarett just shrugged.

'Lazarett,' Ernesto said, 'this is the second time you have implied that you have a source within the school. And you know that several of us are extremely uncomfortable about it. It isn't how it should be done. If you didn't think so before, surely you must have understood what Seth Taniel was trying to show us in November.'

'Mr Taniel who is himself a former school director. Hardly objective. I think we can all work out whose side he was on.'

'It's not about taking sides. We're all on the same side!'

'Ernesto!' Carola gave him a pleading look. Ernesto glanced around the terrace. People were indeed turning to see why voices had been raised.

'I'm sorry,' he muttered. 'But this has to stop. Lazarett, we all know your dismal opinion of Peter Corby. God knows why but it's your opinion and you are entitled to it. But it is my opinion that this negativity, this … campaign to undermine the director is starting to have a direct impact on the successful functioning of the board. This has to stop. Lazarett, I'm saying to your face, I think you should step down from the board.'

'I shall do no such thing. The so-called leadership of the school is weak and incompetent. It is my duty as a board member to say so.'

'Then I'm afraid I'm going to take a good look at the Articles of Association tonight. If board members will not depart voluntarily there are mechanisms to remove them.'

'Ernesto,' Carola failed to control the tremor in her voice. 'Please think very carefully about what you have just said. I can see you are angry but I think we all need to step back and … reflect.'

'Carola, I have been reflecting, as you put it, for too long. Too many board meetings become tense and confrontational. It isn't healthy. It isn't the way it should be. Someone has to put a stop to it. Lazarett, I give you fair warning. I want you off the board.'

'Maybe it is you who should resign, Mr Mayor, since you seem unwilling or unable to see where the school's interests truly lie. We are not on the board to be cheerleaders for an ineffective director.'

'Both of you. Stop it!' Carola stood. 'I'm leaving. I suggest you both do too.' She turned her back on the two men and marched towards the exit, trying hard not to meet the eyes of the by now very curious customers sitting on the terrace.

Ernesto gave Lazarett one last contemptuous look, then rose and went to pay the bill. Lazarett finished his drink, his hand slightly trembling.

★

'Both Pearl and I contemplated just walking out. But then who knows what they would have done without us? It seemed better to stay and argue.' Jenny made a rather hopeless gesture.

'It's appalling that they called a meeting without informing me. Okay, the PTA constitution is pretty useless in many ways but it's unambiguous about what constitutes a formal meeting.'

'I think she's almost hoping you'll challenge her about it. It will somehow vindicate her stance.'

'Well, I won't. But I'm going to make damn sure that any new constitution cannot be simply ignored.'

'And even if we can get some more people to join, or maybe come back, the four of them have quite slyly stitched up the positions on the executive committee – chair, vice-chair, secretary and treasurer. And here Crystal is using the constitution that in other respects is apparently rubbish to justify their actions – filling vacant positions before the AGM in June.'

'Just a bit cynical, would you say? Anyway, what was discussed?' Peter reached for his bottle of water.

'Oh, you'll love this. You are going to get a letter – a formal letter on behalf of the PTA—'

'Or on behalf of four members of the PTA.'

'Exactly. A letter demanding that you explain why the school has lost three teachers in five months.'

'Chuck, Mark and Frank.'

'Yes.'

Peter sighed. 'I could sort of see that coming. When Crystal came to see me in November she would not accept that Mark Langtoft's departure was not a matter for the PTA. She gave me lots of sententious rubbish about how the PTA represented the parents and so they had a right … blah, blah, blah. As I told you then, it was a pretty heated meeting. Or do I mean frosty? Anyway, it was thoroughly unpleasant and I could see she wasn't going to let the matter go.'

'They're just a minority, Peter.'

'I know that very well. But a determined minority of troublemakers can do an immense amount of damage. And I simply won't let them.'

Jenny smiled. 'I know you won't.'

Peter smiled too. 'And you won't either, Jenny. Will you? I'm kind of stuck with this thing but you could just walk away. But you never will. I really admire you for that.'

'Oh, I'm just a spear carrier in this production. You're the one who'll have to slay the dragon. All I can do is support you any way I can.'

'And I hope you know how important that is to me.'

Jenny's smile broadened. 'I hate it how we only ever talk about the bloody PTA,' she said.

Peter nodded. 'We should do lunch some time. I can get away for an hour or two. And any mention of the PTA will be banned!'

'I'd like that. Yes. Let's do lunch. Soon.'

Peter found that the idea pleased him enormously.

★

If The Mupundu was Peter's favourite restaurant for dinner, The Garden at the Westerham Hotel was undoubtedly his first choice for lunch. Photos in the lobby of the hotel and in the bar showed the building as far back as the late nineteenth century. Serious and (self-)important men (white men, of course) in white suits and sporting whiskers of many varieties posed in front of the main door or the tennis court. Ladies sat side-saddle on handsome horses. Servants (African, inevitably) stood awkwardly holding trays of drinks and canapés. In time, vehicles began to feature in the photographs and then men in uniform as the display reached the First World War. And then the Second. But the Westerham had not only witnessed history, it had more than once helped to make it as dignitaries and minor royalty had visited for one ceremonial event or another and later as independence had been fought for and then achieved. And if the hotel was a relic of times gone by, it was also – very much to Peter's satisfaction – something of a symbol for the present development of Awanza. For, much as it described itself on its website as a "colonial gem in the heart of Ndwalowe", ownership of the hotel had for a quarter of a century resided in the Nyirenda family whose anti-colonial credentials over several generations were unimpeachable. The current matriarch, Florence Nyirenda, was never to be seen (at least at the hotel) in anything other than extravagant and extravagantly coloured flowing dresses with puffed sleeves and matching headdress.

'I'm African,' she had once said when being interviewed by the Awanzan Broadcasting Corporation. 'I'm Awanzan. And I'm proudly Wawanza. But this hotel and the people who built it are also a part of our history and heritage. It is my privilege to marry the best of the past and the best of the present.'

Peter knew, or at least knew of, many Black Awanzans whose attitude to the past was not quite so generous.

'Would it be naughty of us to have a glass of wine?' Jenny took the napkin out of her glass and shook it. 'I don't usually drink at lunchtime.'

'Well, I certainly don't. In fact I rarely get lunch at all unless you count a cheese and tomato sandwich at my desk as lunch.'

'Then let's push the boat out and have two glasses.'

'No,' said Peter. 'Let's have a bottle. This is the only place in town that has a Saint Véran in the cellar. It's extraordinary.'

'Uh. You prefer their cellar to ours? I'm hurt.'

'Wait till you taste it. Then add it to your list. Hey, I'm doing you a favour.'

The waitress brought menus and took an order for a bottle of Perrier and a bottle of Saint Véran.

'I haven't eaten here in years,' said Jenny, scanning through the salads. 'Never hurts to check out the competition.'

'You think we have competition? Again, are you trying to insult me?'

Peter laughed. 'Jenny, you know very well you have the best restaurant in the city. But it doesn't hurt to patronise some other establishments now an again.'

'It sounds like you are patronising me,' she said but she was smiling.

The waitress returned. Jenny ordered a lamb's lettuce salad with egg and a grilled tilapia with ginger. Peter, apologising, asked for a prawn cocktail and a cheeseburger with chips. Jenny frowned.

'Oh, come on,' said Peter. 'How often do I get to eat lunch? Let me indulge my plebeian tastes.'

'I thought you were a gourmet. I'm seeing you now in a whole different light.'

'More of a gourmand, to be honest.'

'You drink an expensive Saint Véran with a beefburger? I'm not sure you're the kind of customer we want. I may have to take this up with Ronald.'

'How is Ronald?' The wine had arrived. Peter politely waved away the waitress and poured two glasses.

'Oh,' Jenny looked a little mournful. 'We think his mother is dying. He's gone back to Wales.'

'Oh, no. For how long?'

'Not sure. He only got there yesterday. He'll let me know when he's spoken to the doctors.'

'Oh, I'm so sorry.'

'Peter, she's nearly ninety. To be honest, it would be a relief.'

Peter raised his glass. 'To longevity.'

Jenny clinked her glass with his and took a sip. 'Oh, this is remarkable.' She took the bottle out of the ice bucket and studied the label. 'You're right. I must make a note of this.'

'A wealthy American aunt took me out for dinner once in London and we discovered this. I've never forgotten it.'

'We've had good lives, haven't we?' Jenny was suddenly rather serious. 'I mean, compared to most people. Look,' she waved her arms around the garden. 'You won't find this in Port Talbot.'

Peter smiled.

'And Sheila? She had her doubts, didn't she?' Jenny took another sip of wine. 'But she likes it here, doesn't she?'

'More than she thought she was going to, yes. In fact, I think she's in her element. This training programme she and Susi Shepherd are running for the police. She … she says that translating is all well and good but I think she's always rather envied me my job.'

'A vocation?'

'Sort of. You know. Making a difference. Doing something worthwhile. Rape awareness for policemen …'

'And women?'

'Yes, that too. Officers who may not be highly educated … and this is still a very conservative society …'

'And patriarchal.'

'Often. She and Susi really feel they are getting somewhere. But the more they find out, the more distressing it seems to be. In fact, they're in Mashupawana this week.'

'That's right on the border.'

'I know. It took her and Susi a day and a half driving to get there. I'm not sure there's anywhere more remote in the country.'

'When is she back?'

'Next week sometime. They're leaving it open.'

'So, you'll be eating alone this week?'

'Just me and my tree rats.'

'Me too. Well, without the rats.'

Their starters arrived. A basket of breads was placed between them and a tray of oils and vinegars.

'Good?' asked Jenny.

'I don't know why you and Ronald don't have prawn cocktail on the menu. You're such snobs.'

Jenny rolled her eyes. 'You've always said that one day you'd cook for us, Peter.'

'A rash boast usually made after too many glasses of wine.'

'Well,' Jenny paused. 'Maybe now's the time?'

Peter frowned.

'You're eating alone. Well, you and your rats. And so am I.'

'Don't you have to be in the restaurant? I mean, especially with Ronald not being there.'

'We're closed on Thursdays.'

'Oh yes. I forgot.'

'Well ...?'

'I don't know. What would you like me to cook?'

'Something I won't get at my restaurant.'

'Beans on toast?'

'Sounds lovely.'

'The only problem is that I never know what wine goes with baked beans.'

'Let me worry about that. We have a pretty extensive cellar. Even if we don't have Saint Véran.'

'Right. Then let me, er, let me consult my extensive collection of cookbooks and, er, we'll make it a date. Well, no – not a date – a, a ...'

'A dinner between two good friends. Now eat. Your prawn cocktail is going cold.'

'It is cold. It's meant ... oh.'

★

A large man with a ruddy complexion strode into Peter's office. 'Good morning, headmaster.'

Peter frowned. 'Good morning. But I'd really rather you called me Peter.'

'Oh no. That would be quite improper.'

'Look, Ancaster, I ...'

'And I wish you'd call me Willoughby. Everyone does.'

'But that's your surname.'

'It's my name.'

'Well, that's sort of why I want to talk to you.'

'Oh.'

'You're wearing a gown.'

'And have done so every day of my long teaching career.' Said with pride.

'We don't wear gowns in this school. It's not really who we are.'

'It's who I am,' Ancaster Willoughby said but whether defiantly or almost apologetically, Peter could not tell.

'Ancaster … Ancaster, must you stand? I've offered you a chair. Please sit.'

His visitor sat, but with obvious reluctance.

'Ancaster, let me try to explain.'

As a teenager in England in the 1980s Peter had attended an all-boys school. Within quite recent memory it had been a selective school and had placed great importance on the number of pupils who were accepted annually into Oxford and Cambridge. But by the time Peter entered in 1983 the local authority had required the school to open its doors to all boys in the catchment area (a sister school catered for girls) and the character of the school was changing – not at all to the approval of some of the older staff. At the same time as Peter arrived, the long-serving head (a self-styled 'Cambridge man') retired and was replaced by a young but up-and-coming head who, whatever was written on his degree certificates, probably did not refer to himself as a 'Sheffield man.' More change followed. To the traditional school sports of rugby, hockey and cricket was added football, much to the horror of many 'old boys.' Some of the more arcane school traditions were quietly dropped, rules regarding school uniform were relaxed, and the school song was purged of the most Kiplingesque verses. Most older teachers continued to address the boys – and, indeed, each other – by their surnames only but, increasingly, the younger teachers who were recruited preferred to use first names. Gowns had never been required (except on speech day) but they had been encouraged. Now, that too changed. Peter was aware of none of this. Everything about the school, whether an ancient tradition or a recent innovation, was equally baffling to him. And, of course, he questioned none of it. This was the way his school was and, for all he knew, it was how all schools were. Everywhere.

Except, they weren't. He soon discovered that when he set foot in the first of two schools where he would do his teaching practice. It was a large comprehensive school in the London Borough of Southwark located in an area of social deprivation and high unemployment. That the school he had attended enrolled no girls was alternately a source of regret and relief for the teenage Peter. That all but a tiny handful of boys were white and English wasn't something he had much thought about at all. It just was. But in

Southwark, he found something close to the opposite of his alma mater. Up to a third of the children came from homes where English was not spoken. Well over half were classed as ethnic minorities. Almost a half were entitled to free school meals. School uniform was worn almost ironically and sometimes not at all. There was no school song.

But there were girls. Teenage girls, Peter would discover, were not programmed the same way as teenage boys. In particular when they were in small groups ("packs" Peter started thinking of them) their behaviour could be as mystifying as it was sometimes alarming. Contemplating but certainly not understanding their subtly shifting allegiances and rivalries, Peter wondered if he should be grateful or resentful that girls had been only an occasional presence during his school years. On balance, he rather wished he had learned at a much earlier age about the other half of humanity.

The teachers Peter met and observed, too, were mostly unlike those who had taught him. A surprising number were not even British. Peter shadowed and took advice from teachers whose accents were Australian, South African, and Polish and he was sure that other nationalities were represented. Several teachers were themselves of ethnic minorities. One wore a turban; another a hijab. Gowns were no more in evidence than cricket or rugby. Indeed, the school's playing fields had been sold to a housing developer some years earlier.

Peter spent six confused and confusing weeks trying to make sense of a school that seemed in some sense like a parody of the one he had attended. More than once he took the bus home questioning his decision to become a teacher. Much of the time he felt hopelessly out of his depth. But he also started to experience the moments that can make teaching rewarding, humbling, and, at its best, profoundly satisfying.

Six weeks in a highly selective girls' school in Dulwich completed Peter's teaching practice and less than a year later he was starting his career in a well-regarded and forward-looking school in south Manchester. His sometime assumption that all schools were much the same now seemed embarrassingly naïve. Whatever commonalities there may have been between the four schools of which he now had first-hand experience, he was more aware of the quite significant differences.

All four schools had, of course, been located in England and so taught the National Curriculum. They at least had that in common. But when Peter moved to his first international school in Germany, he discovered not only the International Baccalaureate and its various programmes but also educational practices, beliefs and vocabulary that had been imported, deliberately or otherwise, from other countries, very often the USA. He worked alongside teachers of almost twenty nationalities. Americans, Canadians, and others were to be expected but he wasn't at all sure he had ever met, far less worked with, anyone from Russia or Mauritius before. (And, to his embarrassment, he had to discreetly refer to an atlas to confirm where the latter was.)

If the teachers were diverse, the students were yet more so. No single nationality dominated or came close to doing so. (This, Peter gradually came to conclude, was a key way of identifying an authentic international school. A school where sixty or seventy percent – or even half – of the students were of a single nationality or perhaps culture was not, in Peter's eyes, a true international school.) A further surprise for Peter was that the school enrolled children from the age of three. He had never really thought about (far less questioned) the practice of having separate primary (or elementary as he now learned to say) and secondary (or middle and high?) schools. His training and his experience in Manchester had been with teenagers. What happened to children below the age of eleven was something Peter had been happy to leave as a mystery. Now, as he went about his business in what he had learned was a "K-12" school, swarms of frighteningly little and noisy children ran past him and not infrequently into him. He regarded those of his colleagues who spent all day in classrooms with these unpredictable and, as far as he could tell, unbiddable charges with admiration and awe. Truculent and sulky teenagers he could manage. The thought of dealing with the tears and tantrums of a six-year-old scared him to bits.

Not that the students to whom he taught history did not present him with some interesting challenges. He had taught the Cold War every year in Manchester and it was a topic with which he was very comfortable. In England, however, the classes he taught had not included Russians and Americans, Germans and Czechs, Koreans and Chinese. And when he had taught the tortured history of the Arab-Israeli conflict it had been to boys and girls from Didsbury and Withington, not Damascus and Jerusalem. Apartheid South Africa? He found in his classes in Germany Black Africans from Zimbabwe and Zambia and white Afrikaners from Pretoria and

Pietermaritzburg. As he navigated his way delicately through these fraught topics, he reflected with horror how unthinking and cavalier he had been when broaching the very same issues back in England.

Teaching World War Two to a class that included Japanese and Americans, French and Germans, Italians and Poles, Peter had to ensure that all analysis and interpretation was scrupulously objective and not partisan. He therefore recalled almost with disbelief a conversation with a student early in his Manchester career.

'Sir, which side was Brazil on in World War Two?' he had been asked.

Peter, rather pleased to know the answer, had replied, 'Our side. They were on our side.'

Our side?

Objectivity? Detachment? Distance? As his career overseas continued to force Peter to question and re-evaluate much that he had taken for granted, it gradually dawned on him that an international education (a term that was often employed in his professional life but rarely unpacked) really amounted to an education that was not a national education. British youngsters in Britain being taught the history of World War Two by a British teacher who used expressions like "our side" were not so much learning the historical method as they were hearing and absorbing their national story – at least, a version of their national story.

Peter was just about old enough to remember the Falklands War (as it was known in English, if not Spanish). He certainly remembered a bilious uncle swearing at the television as the announcer had reported Argentinian and British claims of gains and losses giving equal weight to each.

'You're the bloody BBC!' his uncle had shouted. 'Stop saying the Argentinians say this and British say that. You should be saying our boys, our ships!'

At the time, caught up in the patriotic sentiments that were everywhere, Peter had eagerly agreed. Now, he wished he could go back in time and have a conversation with his uncle about objectivity. (Though he doubted he would get very far.)

For eight years in Manchester Peter had taught his classes wearing a suit, or on rare occasions smart trousers and a jacket and tie. It had simply been expected. Female teachers wore skirts or dresses, never trousers, far less leggings. But in his international school in Germany, Peter found that the dress code was far more casual. Polo shirts and chinos were favoured.

Not a few teachers, both male and female, dressed in jeans. No one wore a tie. Nor, of course, did the students wear uniform. It was the first school Peter had ever been in for any reason where uniform was not worn. He was disconcerted. Schools have uniforms. Don't they?

No school uniform did he find either when he took the position of secondary principal at Hamamatsu World School in Japan. What he did find was a strictly enforced requirement that everyone in the school had both indoor and outdoor shoes. Just inside the main doors were banks of wooden shelves filled with whichever pairs of shoes were not currently in use and, upon entering or leaving the building, one pair was exchanged for another. For visitors and anyone whose indoor shoes were at one of the other entrances to the building, a box of green plastic slippers was available. More than once Peter had discreetly shaken his head as he watched a guest of some standing (the CEO of a large company, perhaps) wearing a tailored and obviously expensive suit shuffling uncomfortably down the corridor in ill-fitting plastic slippers.

In the schools Peter knew in England, the children who attended them lived locally. That they attended the schools they did was unremarkable. In Germany, most students were the children of expatriate parents on finite contracts but it was also a school of choice for some German families who wanted their children to have an education in English and in a multicultural context. Again, their choices raised no eyebrows. And now in Awanza it was obvious that such local families as could afford the fees would far rather have their children in the International School of Ndwalowe than any of the under-funded and ill-maintained government schools.

In Hamamatsu, however, it slowly dawned on Peter that the Japanese parents who had enrolled their children in the World School were doing something quite extraordinary. Peter liked Japan. He liked a great deal about it. He certainly appreciated the order, the dignity, and the respect. An inspector on the *Shinkansen*, wearing a smart uniform and white gloves, would check each ticket, offer polite thanks, and, as he exited the carriage, turn and bow to the passengers. Peter tried to imagine something similar happening on a train in Britain. (He didn't try very hard or for very long.)

Writing to friends and family back in the UK, Peter found that he used words like courteous and respectable to describe Japan and its people. It was the safest country he had ever lived in. (Once, in a hurry and with too much to carry, he had carelessly left his laptop on the roof of his car in a municipal car park. When he returned three hours later, it was still there.) And it was, of course, efficient. There was much to admire.

However, as his years in Japan passed and he came to understand his host country a little better, he realised that the many things he appreciated and respected about Japan came at a cost. Crime was almost unheard of, people mostly dressed conservatively, voices were seldom raised, politeness was highly valued. But underlying all this was a sometimes suffocating pressure to conform.

Peter had been introduced to a familiar Japanese proverb. *The nail that sticks out gets hammered down.* German families could put their children in an international school and no one would give their choice a second thought. In Ndwalowe, Awanzan families whose children attended ISN were envied rather than questioned. But in Japan, the act of taking your child out of the Japanese system and enrolling them in a school where they would be taught in English, rub shoulders with scores of other nationalities, learn a foreign curriculum taught by teachers from who knows where, wear no uniform, and not experience the normative education that taught young people how to *be* Japanese amounted to something almost subversive. Peter had Japanese students admit to him that their grandparents and uncles and aunts strongly disapproved of their parents' decision and said so loudly and often.

Peter had worked in four schools in four countries and had visited many more. No two were the same. What mattered in one school seemed not to matter a jot in others. But the best of them, he came to understand, knew what they were and, just as importantly, what they weren't. They knew what they valued and what their priorities were and said so, openly and clearly. All schools teach mathematics and the sciences and the arts and so on. But they also teach children about so much more, sometimes explicitly but just as often implicitly. Subtle signifiers everywhere inform children about acceptable and unacceptable behaviour, gender roles, conventions and rituals, differing cultural values, the exercise of authority, competition and collaboration, tolerance, respect, compassion, patriotism …

'You see, Ancaster … er, Willoughby. The gown, the use of surnames … and I believe you like to be called a master rather than a teacher? And you require the students to stand when you enter the room?'

Ancaster Willoughby nodded.

'It's … We are not that kind of school. There are schools like that, I know very well. But such schools …' Peter tried to choose his words carefully, 'such schools probably espouse other, er, values and expectations. Apart from anything, you are essentially representing a type of educational culture that is … well, British. Or, in fact, English.'

'I am English.'

'As am I. Well, British. But not even five percent of our students are.'

'I dislike that word.'

'Students? You'd prefer …'

'Pupils.'

'Really? I don't even think they use that term back in Britain anymore. I see students referred to when I read the paper.'

'Maybe the paper you read. Not the one I do.'

'Ancaster, you're here for another five months or so – and I'm grateful to have you. Thank you. But can we agree on one thing? A teacher – in your case a teacher of English – teaches, erm … *The Catcher in the Rye, An Inspector Calls*, Shakespeare, and so on. But they also teach, or certainly influence children, in so many other ways.'

'As you said at my interview, headmaster, I will also be teaching works by Nigerians, Kenyans, writers from the Indian subcontinent, South America. The International Baccalaureate requires it.'

'Yes, but that's not what I meant. Let's take names. If you call a student – a boy – Suárez rather than, say, Alberto – which everyone else calls him, you are making a statement about your relationship.'

'I am indeed. He is a pupil and I am his teacher. There should be distance, respect.'

'I would say that respect is earned …'

Ancaster Willoughby frowned. 'A cliché, if I may be so bold, headmaster.'

'Then let's say that respect can be expressed in many ways. And, lest we forget, it works in both directions. Teachers must respect the students they teach.'

Ancaster Willoughby looked like he was going to reply but then thought better of it.

'Look,' Peter felt he was losing this one. 'Can we compromise? Keep the gown, if you must. But I really would prefer it if you would call the st- the children by their first names. Can you do that?'

Later, reporting the conversation to Valli, Peter had begun to doubt himself. 'Really, the guy's only here for half a year. Does it really matter if he wears a sodding gown?'

'I think most people find him rather quaint,' Valli had laughed. 'He's a character. Aren't you always going on about diversity?'

'I think it's because he's so English. This is an international school. It's not Eton College.'

'Where?'

'Doesn't matter. And yes, diversity is good but so is everyone being on the same page. And he's definitely not.'

'Peter, this may be a fight that's not worth having. Just suck it up till June.'

'That's what I'm starting to think. I just hope he doesn't embarrass me.'

And still parents complain. Expressions of annoyance about too much or too little homework (not infrequently from parents of children in the very same class), the quality of food in the cafeteria, a school calendar that fails to take into account the holy days of certain minority religions, the (alleged) disrespectful behaviour of ancillary staff … Any international school head will be able to take this list, nod knowingly, and add many, many more examples of actions or inactions, circumstances or situations, mistakes and missteps that have prompted parents to pick up the phone, draft an email, or demand an appointment, sometimes with justification, sometimes without.

Most things that upset parents can ultimately be resolved to the greater or lesser satisfaction of each party. At worst, they can be kicked into the long grass. But sometimes the two sides are too far apart for any kind of consensus to be possible.

'Mr Laer, thank you for coming to see me. It's always disappointing when a parent chooses to withdraw their child and, if possible, I appreciate the opportunity to talk and find out what we could have done better.'

Peter's guest gazed at him evenly. 'I have no problem telling you very plainly why I have chosen to withdraw my daughter. None at all.'

Mr Laer seemed disinclined to elaborate immediately so Peter continued. 'Well, that will, I'm sure, be very helpful. Your letter simply said that you had concluded that this was not the right school for Maria. That's, um, pretty broad. I wonder if you could give me a few specifics.'

'Mr Corby, I expect a good school to educate children, not indoctrinate them.'

Peter frowned. 'Go on.'

'There were moments in Grade Ten when I wondered what a teacher's true intentions were but I chose to give them the benefit of the doubt. Naïvely, I now think. But now she is in Grade Eleven, there isn't even the attempt to disguise what is going on. Do you not agree, Mr Corby, that teachers should keep their political views to themselves?'

'It ... Well, it depends.'

'It depends?'

'Yes. I mean, Maria is seventeen. In some countries she would be able to vote next year. Maybe she already could in some countries. She's on the verge of becoming – legally – an adult. We wouldn't be doing our job if we didn't expose her and all the other students to some of the dilemmas and controversies that societies are wrestling with all over the world.'

Mr Laer did not look like a man who suffered from self-doubt. 'Whether my daughter is a child or an adult, I want her to make up her own mind—'

'As, of course do we,' interrupted Peter. 'Sorry to interrupt, but perhaps we are actually in agreement.'

Mr Laer looked doubtful. 'Last week,' he said slowly, 'Maria came home and said that her class had been discussing the morality of the death penalty. And I'm sorry to say, the teacher made his own views on the matter very clear. And there have been other examples. Abortion. Women's rights. The so-called climate crisis. Frankly, I've had enough.'

'Are you referring to Mr Matibini?'

'I am indeed. Theory of Knowledge, I believe you call it.'

'Yes, it is a key component of the IB Diploma. And I know exactly the conversation you are referring to because I was there. I was invited to join the debate about the death penalty and was delighted to do so. I thought it was an excellent class. A really good discussion.'

'I'm sure you did. I also understand that you made no secret of your own views on the subject.'

'No, I didn't. But there's a vast difference between explaining and, I hope, justifying one's own opinions and denying that there are other perhaps valid perspectives. Mr Matibini and I were very clear ...'

'Very clear that you and Mr Matibini are liberals. You make a grave mistake if you assume that all the parents in this school are too.'

Peter had met enough ISN parents not to need to have their often conservative inclinations pointed out to him. 'Absolutely true, Mr Laer, and I hope that the school is open-minded enough to respect all views and opinions. You've no doubt heard me say how diversity is at the very heart of a good international school like this.'

'All views? All opinions?'

'Yes. Well, I would suggest there are certain issues where the school does take a position but, I would hope, no parents would find it controversial. For example, the school as an institution and teachers individually obviously have zero tolerance for racism. That could hardly be described as partisan or political ... Oh.'

For two decades Peter's working day had involved interactions with others and their conversations, whether with students, colleagues, or others, were frequently about matters of some gravity, things that mattered. He had learned to read faces, pick up inflections, interpret vocabulary ...

'Em,' he hesitated. 'Would I be right in thinking ...?'

'I won't deny, Mr Corby, that it doesn't help that Mr Matibini is Black.'

Peter's jaw dropped.

'Mr Corby. You tell me how important Theory of Knowledge is. Then why do you allow it to be taught by—'

'Someone who is Black?'

'Well, they aren't the brightest people on the planet, are they?'

Peter threw himself forward in his chair. 'Mr Laer, I ...'

'Oh, go on, I know what you're going to say. But how long have you been in Africa? A year? Listen, I've spent my whole life here. You're—'

'What's your problem? Because Mr Matibini is Black?'

Mr Laer just shrugged.

'I don't know if you know, but João's mother – Mr Matibini's mother – is Portuguese. His father is Zambian – yes, a Black Zambian, of course, but it's a bit like Barak Obama. I have never got my head around this. You have two parents, one Black and one white. And that makes you Black? Why?'

Mr Laer paused. He was not an unintelligent man nor an uneducated one. He looked at Peter with something approaching condescension. 'Do you drink, Mr Corby? Do you drink wine?'

'What?'

'If you mix white wine and red wine, what do you get? And don't say rosé.'

Peter was struggling. What he might have said had the two men been arguing in a pub and what the director of the international school was allowed to say were far apart and he was caught between the two.

'You get red wine, Mr Corby. At least, wine that is, to anyone who looks at it, red. The white is gone. The red dominates. Do you understand?'

'No. No, Mr Laer, I don't understand. I will never understand.'

'I put my daughter in this school knowing that you had brown and Black teachers as well as white. I would have preferred it to be otherwise but this is, people say, the best school in Ndwalowe so I tolerated it. Maria has Ms Nair who is not white but at least she is Indian. Where Ms Naqvi comes from, I have no idea. The others are white and I have no problem with them. But Mr Matibini is—'

'Biracial, Mr Laer. Biracial and surely a wonderful role model for the mixed community that is our school. You do realise that a third of our students have parents of different nationalities? Different nationalities and, often, different ethnicities. I think that is wonderful. It is the future.'

'Well, it's not my future, Mr Corby. Or my family's. Or my daughter's. People should stick to their own kind.'

'But your argument makes nonsense of that. A child is fifty percent white and fifty percent Black? Whose "own kind" is that?'

Mr Laer glared at Peter. 'Zambian and Portuguese, you say?'

Peter nodded.

'Is Portuguese really white?'

★

In the days and weeks following Mr Laer's visit, Peter replayed the conversation over and over in his mind. He was neither ignorant nor naïve. He knew racism existed everywhere. But in the UK and Germany and Japan the racism he had witnessed (and in Japan, he suspected, occasionally experienced) had existed in the shadows. It was euphemistic, subtle, implicit and, no doubt, sometimes subconscious.

But now, he perhaps needed to remind himself, he was in a very different context. Awanza was a post-colonial country on a continent where some memories were still raw. Here, as in many countries south of the Sahara, political parties existed that campaigned for land redistribution, reparations, more aggressive affirmative action, and even the expropriation of property owned by whites. In Awanza such parties remained – for now – on the fringe, the President and his ruling party understandably wary of scaring away investment and talent. But occasionally in Parliament, annually at open-air rallies, and quite often in opinion pieces published in Awanza's admirably free press, the 'them and us' of racially based politics was kept alive. The white community scowled and perhaps told each other it was just a few hotheads but they mostly just kept their heads down. And then they double-checked their burglar alarms and the locks on their doors.

For Peter and Sheila, still relative newcomers to Africa and respectfully mindful of their status as guests in Awanza, such racial tension as they were aware of existed as no more than a barely audible background noise. In their daily lives they saw nothing more than people of various ethnicities going about their business apparently with far more important things to do than worry about someone's skin colour. In shops, at work, in the street, at social occasions, people laughed and argued and conducted their affairs without, as far as Peter could tell, race ever being a factor.

And yet the longer Peter lived and worked in Awanza, the more he sensed that there was still a divide. Peter's dentist was white. His doctor was white. The school lawyer was white. Six out of nine board members were white. The three members of the school leadership were white. The gardeners Sheila had employed to clear the worst of the thickets at Plot 274 were Black but the owner of the company was white. There were restaurants where ninety percent of the customers each evening were white but, of course, all the waiters and waitresses were Black. (Though, to be fair, there were also restaurants where the clientele was delightfully mixed – though the waiters were still Black.) Mixed race couples were not at all uncommon (particularly among younger people) and at lunch time Black and white office workers sat and joked together at Kitzi's and elsewhere. But, of an evening, white families tended to socialise with other white families and, Peter assumed, Black families did the same. He thought back to the dinner party in December. Four white couples. At the time, he hadn't given it a thought. Now, it made him rather uneasy.

He had heard white couples – usually those who had lived all their lives in southern Africa – bemoan the state of public hospitals and schools, the roads, the sometimes unreliable electricity supply and more and there was often an implicit suggestion that things used to be better before majority rule. Few, of course, had memories that stretched back far enough to remember and their complaints and grumbles were mostly anecdotal.

'My late aunt could remember when Garstang High School was a wonderful institution. Now look at it.'

But, of course, such people didn't use government schools or hospitals. Their children attended private schools (or sometimes boarded in South Africa) and everyone had private health insurance. They might have shaken their heads sadly at the run-down state of the Ndwalowe Central Hospital but it didn't cater to the likes of them and Peter had never heard of any white Awanzan campaigning to improve things.

Odd comments had been made in white-only company that had made Sheila and Peter quite uncomfortable but never had anyone expressed openly and unapologetically racist sentiments. Until now.

In one way Peter had been shocked. In another, he thought he should probably have expected it sooner or later. He may not have met anyone like Mr Laer before (at least, not knowingly) but Saskia, a white woman married to a Black man, had recounted stories that had made Peter appalled and angry.

What depressed Peter the most, however, was that the words he had heard had been spoken by a parent at an international school. Racism and all manner of prejudice existed in every society but international schools – the best international schools – were islands of equality, tolerance, mutual respect, acceptance … Weren't they?

But Peter knew he was kidding himself. Most (though not all) teachers in international schools were there, at least in part, because they valued and enjoyed the diversity, the heterogeneity, the chance to travel and meet people of other cultures and beliefs. Most willingly bought into their school's inclusive philosophy and if they did harbour prejudices, they did their best to keep them well-hidden.

The students, by and large, absolutely accepted the multicultural nature of the school they attended. Much as Peter had attended an all-boys and almost entirely white school in England and had thought it entirely normal, the children at ISN and similar schools thought nothing of being in a class where there might be twenty nationalities, half-a-dozen religious faiths, at least two genders, and skin colours of every shade.

But the parents? Some, for sure, expressly chose international schools because of deeply held beliefs about equality, internationalism, inclusion and much else. But others? Peter had seen it in Germany and in Japan but here it Ndwalowe it had been particularly, if depressingly, obvious that what some parents were paying for was simply an excellent education and the school's philosophy, principles and values were of very little importance to them. In fact, though he was reluctant to admit it to himself, it wasn't even an education that some parents were paying for, it was simply a qualification that would get their child up the next step on the ladder.

In his heart, Peter had always known that some parents merely paid lip-service to the school's philosophy. But it had come as a shock to hear Mr Laer so bluntly reject it. How many more Mr Laers were there among the ISN parents, Peter wondered. He suspected the answer, if he ever learned it, might be quite discouraging.

★

The January board meeting began with what was cautiously welcomed as good news. Peter was able to report some movement regarding the Access to Education Act. As he did, several pairs of eyes discreetly looked towards Mrs Luhanga. Her expression, however, remained enigmatic.

'The good news is that Mr Burger—'

'Who?' interrupted Catherine Mulbarton.

'The school lawyer.'

'Ah yes. Sorry. Go on.'

'Thank you. Mr Burger and I were at last able to have a meeting with the Office of the Permanent Secretary. The delay was because they were apparently trying to locate the correspondence that they say was sent to the school in reply to John Conway's letters to the Ministry. Seemingly, they are unable to do so.'

Mrs Luhanga made a small noise that could have meant anything.

Peter continued. 'We have to assume that's good news. Also, they have not thrown out our argument that the school – this iteration of the school – is legally less than three years old.'

'The Ministry has written to the Solicitor General for a ruling.' Mrs Luhanga spoke looking at no one in particular as if merely commenting on the wallpaper. 'Of course, that will likely take some time.'

In the silence that followed, Peter looked at Carola who returned his rather startled look. 'Thank you, Mrs Luhanga,' Carola muttered.

Then Ernesto spoke. 'Mrs Luhanga … Must we call you that? Everyone else here is on first name terms.'

She frowned. 'I would prefer it.'

Ernesto let out an impatient and not very polite sigh. 'All right. Mrs Luhanga, how shall I put this? May I ask if there is anything else you know about this situation that we perhaps should know? You are the Assistant Deputy Executive Director. It was your letter that started all this. You work in the Ministry every day. And you sit on the board of the school.' Ernesto was getting agitated. 'Frankly, Mrs Luhanga …'

Don't say it! Thought Peter.

Ernesto said it. 'Whose side are you on?'

Mrs Luhanga looked distinctly annoyed. Catherine said, 'Oh my!' rather loudly. Grant Guthrie and Clyde Arthurs looked grave. Carola seemed to be struggling for words.

'I have endeavoured to do my duty regarding both the Ministry of Education and the school,' said Mrs Luhanga with some dignity. 'I do not take kindly to having my impartiality questioned.'

'But that's the whole point!' Ernesto could now not contain himself. 'How can you be impartial? You have to be … well, partial to both sides. You wrote us the letter!'

'It is out of my hands,' Mrs Luhanga said rather primly. 'I have nothing further to add.'

Clyde Arthurs leaned forward and motioned at Ernesto, who was about to speak, to be quiet. 'Mrs Luhanga, I absolutely respect the awkward position you are in but I think Ernesto has, well, a point. It does seem to me that you could … that you are in a position to, er, assist the school …'

Mrs Luhanga was giving Clyde her full attention.

'… if you were,' Clyde continued, 'so minded.'

Mrs Luhanga took her time to reply. 'My influence in the Ministry is quite limited.' Peter was not the only one in the room to hear her words and conclude that she was actually saying entirely the opposite. 'I am merely a functionary.' Whatever Mrs Luhanga thought she was, thought Peter, the word 'merely' was most unlikely to feature.

'But,' Carola picked up the question, 'could you perhaps, erm, oil the wheels?' She glanced at Peter to see if she had used the right idiom. He nodded.

'If the board would like me to use what little influence I may have ...'

'Yes?'

'I may, perhaps, be able to represent the school in a favourable light.' Mrs Luhanga was commonly something of a bit player in board meetings; tonight she was centre stage. Moreover, she seemed to be enjoying it.

'I think,' said Carola cautiously, 'we would all be grateful ...' She looked around the room at her fellow board members. 'Perhaps you and the director and I could meet to, er, discuss how we might move forward. Might you have time this week?'

'I will need to consult my diary,' said Mrs Luhanga quite firmly but Peter detected a hint of a smile at the corners of her mouth.

'Of course, of course. But please just let Peter – Mr Corby – and me know when you might be available. We could come to your office if that would make it easier.' Carola looked at Peter who nodded.

'Er, no. There's no need. I'll come to school.' Mrs Luhanga clearly did not want anyone coming to her office.

What's going on? Thought Peter. *What's she up to?*

But Carola was already introducing the next item. Suddenly, no one in the room was thinking about the Access to Education Act.

★

Sheila heard Peter's car in the drive and was waiting for him at the door. 'Well, how did it go?'

Peter shook his head. 'Ernesto has resigned.'

'Oh no.'

They moved to two chairs on the veranda. Sheila already had a bottle of white wine in an ice bucket and two glasses waiting. 'I thought you'd need this,' she attempted a smile.

'More than I usually do,' said Peter, sitting and filling both glasses.

'What happened?'

'Just what I feared. Ernesto read out the relevant section of the Articles of Association and explained why he was proposing that the board should ask Lazarett to resign. God, it was awkward, Carola looked miserable.'

'And the others?'

'No one was enjoying it. Well, maybe Lazarett.'

'He wasn't asked to leave the room?'

'No. The Articles are clear that a board member in this situation has the right to be present. Ernesto made a kind of statement for the prosecution. And I could see that people around the table pretty much agreed with him. Well, sympathised with him. But when they were asked to speak … There was some hand-wringing expressions of regret that it had come to this. Some – you know – well, maybe everyone shares the responsibility for an atmosphere that hasn't been blah, blah, blah.'

'And it went to a vote?'

'Ernesto insisted. There was a long argument – believe it or not – about whether Lazarett himself had a vote but eventually it was agreed that he didn't. Thank goodness. And then he was asked to leave the room. It was a secret ballot and Carola handed out slips of paper. It only took sixty seconds and Carola read out the results. Two votes for him to go, three for him to stay, and three abstentions.'

'Do you know who …?'

'Ernesto himself, obviously, and Trixi said she was going to vote yes but who knows?'

'But it was hardly a vindication for Lazarett, an endorsement. Three out of eight?'

'But only two out of eight voted for him to go.'

'So he stays?'

'He was asked to come back in and Carola told him the result. I think he was a bit surprised by the numbers – two, three, three – but mostly he just looked very smug. And then Ernesto stood up and said that in the circumstances he felt honour-bound to resign. Carola and some others tried to talk him out of it but he just gathered up his papers and left.'

'Angry? Humiliated?'

'Of course. But I think he also felt really let-down. I'll give him a day or two and see if I can get him to come out for a beer. I just felt awful for him. I think everyone did.'

'Not quite everyone, maybe.'

'Ah, yes. And then it got very interesting. Everyone just wanted to get the hell out of there as quickly as possible but Lazarett wanted to say something. Ernesto had gone, he said, but what about the other vote that had been cast against him? Shouldn't that board member now resign too?'

'No!'

'Carola wasn't having it for a second. She said the evening had been painful for everyone and she was bringing the meeting to an immediate end. She was the first out of the door. Everyone traipsed down the stairs trying not to make eye contact. As I was locking up, I could see Clyde and Grant in the car park in deep conversation. Violet Sindima, I think, was in tears.'

'So a board of eight now? Ernesto's gone?'

'One of the best of them. He's going to leave a big gap.'

'A gap to be filled quickly?'

Peter shrugged. 'I don't know. We could. That is, the board could if they want to. But there's no obligation to do so. I'll see what Carola thinks. Maybe they'll just wait till the AGM.' He took another gulp of wine. 'Bloody hell. Bloody Lazarett Snyman.'

Sheila could only offer a look of genuine sympathy.

February

Sheila's attempts to discipline the sprawling garden of Plot 274 were making progress. Unruly lantana and hibiscus bushes that she had cut back quite aggressively had grown again into shapes that Sheila considered more appropriate. Overgrown flowerbeds had been cleared and filled with plants and shrubs of a joyous variety of colours: flame lilies and pavonias, yellow bells and blood lilies, aloes, and proteas. With Abraham's assistance, a rock garden had been rebuilt and a small water feature installed. Peter had wondered silently if it was a little twee but he was happy that it attracted many kinds of bird in search of drinking and bathing water. He had not remained silent, however, when Sheila had again proposed removing the banana plant.

'Why?' he had asked. 'Apart from anything, we enjoy the bananas.'

'I thought it was a bit of a novelty at first but you must admit it's ugly.'

'Rubbish.'

'And people tell me that snakes often live in banana trees.'

'So? We like snakes.'

'No. You like snakes.'

Eventually, Peter's will had again prevailed. But he worried that Sheila had also turned against the papaya tree that was standing in rather spindly isolation. However, after the argument about the banana tree, the subject was not raised.

Sheila had concluded that what had once passed for lawns on three sides of the house were probably beyond recovery and, much to Peter's relief, she ignored (for now) the most remote corners of the plot and the impenetrable hedges that provided cover and habitats for wildlife of many kinds.

But she took great interest in the citrus trees that ran along one side of the veranda.

223

'What are they?' Peter had asked. 'They're a bit big for limes. But they aren't lemons, are they?'

Sheila confessed that she wasn't sure and tried to explain to Peter what she understood of the complicated and contested issue of citrus taxonomy.

'That sounds unnecessarily complicated,' he suggested, cupping in his hand a round green fruit somewhat larger than a golf ball. 'But an orange is an orange, isn't it? And a grapefruit's a grapefruit?'

'You've got a cheek!' Sheila laughed. 'When I point to bird and say "vulture", you insist that there are lots of different kinds.'

'Fair point,' he conceded.

Whatever fruit was growing on the citrus trees was plentiful and juicy. Peter was moved to experiment with a rather successful version of key lime pie and it gave both him and Sheila a ridiculous amount of pleasure to be squeezing their own fruit into their G&Ts. It was therefore a matter of concern when Sheila discovered that something was clearly eating the leaves of their citrus trees.

She fingered half-eaten leaves, turning them over and looking for further evidence. The youngest leaves appeared to be preferred. In some cases whole leaves had gone, leaving only the stalk. Other leaves had been sculpted along one or both edges. And then she separated two adjacent leaves and found what she had been looking for.

In the kitchen, preparing their evening meal, Peter heard what was something between a scream and a squeal. But it was for sure Sheila's voice. He hurried outside.

Sheila was running into the house as he was running out. He was confused to see that his wife was laughing.

'Peter! Come and see this!'

'Are you all right?'

'Yes. Well, actually, I've just been threatened ...'

Peter looked alarmed.

'... by a caterpillar!'

He followed her back to the stand of citrus trees.

'Look!' said Sheila, and, using a small twig, lifted a leaf to reveal what was below. Peter saw a fat green caterpillar nearly the size of his little finger, thicker at one end than the other (the head?), and sporting a couple of brown diagonal stripes. 'He's the culprit?'

'Indeed. But get a little closer. Point your finger towards it.'

'Really?' Frowning, but doing as instructed, Peter leaned towards the caterpillar and lifted his hand. To his astonishment and Sheila's delight (it was definitely a squeal this time), two bright red horns shot out from the caterpillar's head and waved menacingly at him. He jumped back.

'Bloody hell!'

'Isn't he great? A pugnacious caterpillar!'

'Do you think it's poisonous?'

'Why? Are you planning on eating it?'

'Let me get my camera. We need to get some pictures of this.'

'You're making that up,' Valli had suggested when Peter told her the following day. 'A caterpillar with horns?'

'Well, I don't know what else to call them. They reminded me a bit of a snake's forked tongue. The caterpillar retracted them and then shot them out again each time we got too close.'

'And, of course, you identified the species?'

'Yes. Well, Sheila did. She's getting quite into butterflies. The answer appears to be *Papilio demodocus*.'

'Uh?'

'The Citrus Swallowtail butterfly. It's quite gorgeous, actually.'

'But the caterpillars eat your citrus trees.'

'I know. We're struggling now. We hardly want to kill caterpillars or butterflies but they are munching through our fruit trees.'

'So?'

'Well, I do have a plan …'

Peter almost skipped up the stairs to his office and strode happily down the corridor. The long-planned visit by a team of five on behalf of the New England Association of Schools and Colleges had concluded the previous day and at the exit interview Peter had been assured that, a few relatively trivial matters notwithstanding, the team had been impressed and their recommendation would be for the school to be awarded full accreditation status.

He could never quite make up his mind about the value of accreditation. It was a concept unknown to him before he entered his first international school. In Germany, Japan and now in Awanza he had been through the process three times, though all with different accrediting agencies. There were commonalities between all three experiences but also some significant differences. So much, Peter was concluding, seemed to depend on the people who comprised the team. They were practising or sometimes retired teachers and administrators themselves and usually, though not always, with international experience. Some had served on multiple team visits; some were doing it for the first time. Some left their egos behind; some most certainly didn't. (In Japan the chair of the visiting team had arrived on the first morning to announce that the hotel room the school had booked for him was inadequate and so he had upgraded himself to a suite – at the school's expense, of course.)

And that was most definitely another factor. It was up to the accrediting agency to decide how many visitors were required and to choose who they would be. But it was up to the school to cover the cost of their flights (be they domestic, regional, or inter-continental), accommodation, transport within the country, and all meals. Half a dozen people flying in from afar and staying, inevitably, in a better than average hotel for up to four or five nights was not an insignificant expense. In most schools it was a big enough cost to be a separate item on that year's budget.

There was, therefore, a financial cost but the accreditation process also demanded an enormous investment in time. Over many months, committees drawn from the school community considered every aspect of the school's operations from student wellbeing to the condition and suitability of facilities; from how closely the school adhered to its published philosophy to how the board conducted itself; from its admissions policy to professional staff development. Wordy reports were written, each supported by folders and folders (either physical or in pdf form) of evidence. There were templates and deadlines, acronyms and jargon. Many of the hoops schools were required to jump through made sense, others seemed arbitrary, and some just amounted to stating the obvious.

Full accreditation was usually a requirement for a school to be admitted to regional or international organisations and, if not always essential, it was certainly advantageous when schools recommended graduating students to universities.

And yet, had Peter ever heard parents enquire about a school's accreditation status? Had any teachers he was trying to recruit questioned him about accreditation? ISN had functioned for more than eighteen months first with no accreditation (it having lapsed with the bankruptcy and closure of the old school) and until now with only provisional status. But had that really made a difference? Parents still enrolled their children, teachers still accepted jobs at the school, students were still accepted by good universities around the world, and the International Baccalaureate had still authorised the school to offer its programmes. Accreditation had its advocates and it provided schools with a cost-free way to have their staff visit other international schools, an experience that was often as valuable for the visitors as it was for the hosts. But, Peter wondered, was it all ultimately worth it?

Of course, what Peter may have thought about it was largely irrelevant. For better or for worse, any credible international school needs to be accredited. Though just where that need came from, Peter was never entirely sure.

As he turned the corner he saw a small delegation of older students awaiting him. One was studying the framed photos on the wall while the others were engaged in serious discussion. All, however, now stood respectfully as he approached.

'Good morning. Are you waiting for me?'

'Yes, Mr Corby. Do you have a few minutes?' Alana Johanneson was a student Peter had come to know and like a great deal. She was bright and confident and frequently contributed articles to the student newspaper that were articulate, thoughtful, and usually provocative. 'She's the perfect IB student,' Peter had said to Alana's mother once. 'You should be very proud.' The mother's reaction had been a wry smile. 'I will always be proud of my daughter. Though sometimes I wish she wasn't so ... passionate.'

Peter ushered his visitors into his office and indicated the comfortable chairs. 'Please, take a seat.'

The four students sat and Peter took his usual seat. He quickly confirmed that these were all faces he recognised and could even name. He was pleased. Throughout his career he had known school heads who claimed to know every child by name. It had always seemed an improbable boast to Peter but he did wish that after more than eighteen months at ISN he could identify more than a small number of children.

'Thank you for seeing us, Mr Corby.' Peter knew Bandile Links to be an earnest and conscientious student whose mother worked at the South African High Commission. She was a delightful woman who never missed a parent evening or school event and who frequently thanked Peter for the job he was doing. He rather wished there were more parents like Mrs Links.

'Not at all. I'd much rather be chatting to students than staring at my computer screen. What can I do for you?'

'Do you know who Aafiya Abdullahi is?' Alana was usually someone who came straight to the point.

'Er, no. Should I?'

'She is a young woman in Nigeria. She is illiterate and she is a single mother ...'

'Oh, wait. Yes, of course I know. It was just the name I didn't recognise. She has been sentenced to death by stoning. There was a big article in *The Guardian* yesterday.'

'Yes, and we think it's not right.' Alana looked at her three colleagues who nodded gravely.

'Well, good for you. I'm proud of you.' And he was. When writing references for students or, indeed, teachers, Peter had no higher praise than to describe someone as "principled".

'So, you agree?' Bandile seemed slightly relieved.

'Of course. I've always opposed the death penalty in any circumstances. And to stone to death a young woman for falling pregnant is just abhorrent.'

His guests exchanged looks. One or two of them smiled. 'Then, Mr Corby, you'll let us protest? You might even join us!' one of them said.

Peter realised that he knew the girl's name to be Justine but he could not remember her surname. It annoyed him.

'Well, Justine. What do you have in mind?'

'We want to arrange a march to the Nigerian Embassy—'

'High Commission,' Bandile corrected her.

'Yes, High Commission. We want to march there and hand in a petition signed by as many ISN students and teachers – and maybe parents – as we can get. We hope you'll be the first to sign.'

The four students had entered Peter's office rather stiffly but now they were excited and animated. His heart sank.

'Em, I'm not sure that's going to be possible.'

Four faces fell.

'But you agree with us?'

'Yes, Alana, I do. That is, I – Peter Corby – I agree with you one hundred percent. And I think that it's admirable that this is important to you and that you want to do something about it. I really do.'

'But …?'

'But I'm someone called Peter Corby on the one hand and I'm the director of the International School of Ndwalowe on the other. Peter Corby can think whatever he wants. The director of the school doesn't really have that luxury.'

Alana scowled. 'I thought the school wanted us to stand up for what is right.'

'It does. Of course.'

'But the school itself won't do that?'

Peter sighed. 'Alana, it's complicated.'

She snorted. In other circumstances Peter might have reproached her. On this occasion he rather sympathised.

'Alana, we have students here from Nigeria. The High Commissioner has his children in the school.'

'Then he should care what people in the school think about his country!'

'I think it's fine for him to hear what people think – some people. But the school itself cannot really have an opinion.'

'Why not? The school has opinions on all sorts of things. It's against racism, isn't it? And homophobia?'

'Yes, but …'

'Abortion? Female genital mutilation? Antisemitism? Climate change?'

Peter searched for the right words but could find none. Alana was biting her lip and Bandile just looked crestfallen. Justine glared at Peter. The last student to speak, Hope Banda, chose her words with care.

'Mr Corby, is the problem that we are putting one country on the spot? Statements of principle are one thing. Actual real world cases are another?'

Peter looked at her with respect and admiration and perhaps even gratitude. At its best, the education schools such as ISN provided went way beyond the gaining of knowledge and understanding and the acquisition of diplomas and certificates. It allowed and encouraged these young men and women to think, to question, to doubt, to challenge … For every moment when Peter despaired for the future of the planet, there were moments like these that gave him hope.

'Yes. I think that's the point. We can – and do – teach about the appalling injustices of apartheid in South Africa.' He nodded at Bandile. 'That's in the past. No one is going to argue back. But,' he paused, wondering how frank he dared be, 'Well, let's just say there are countries in the world today that are accused of practising something very similar to apartheid. But the school would be in very deep water indeed if it came out and said so.'

'But I can say so. We can say so.' Alana was making a statement, not asking a question.

'Absolutely. And you make me proud when you do.'

'But we can't do it on behalf of the school?'

'Let me give you an analogy. You know I used to teach history? Anyway, Abraham Lincoln has gone down in history as the president who ended slavery. His own personal abhorrence of slavery is not in doubt. He made countless speeches and wrote thousands of words denouncing slavery. There can be no question that he personally detested it. But …'

Peter paused for effect. 'But if you look for it, it doesn't take you long to find Abraham Lincoln saying that if the price of preserving the union was keeping slavery, it was a price he would accept. Abraham Lincoln, citizen, hated slavery. Abraham Lincoln, President of the United States, saw his first duty as the preservation of the union.'

Alana fixed Peter with a look that might have been sarcastic. 'You mean it's complicated.'

'Yes, Alana, it is. And the problem is that very few countries have hands that are entirely clean. I'm British. Do you know much about Britain's history in, for example, the slave trade? The problem of race in the United States? Hindu extremism in India? The Kurds? The Palestinians? Aborigines in Australia and the Māori in New Zealand? The Rohingya? Repression in Saudi Arabia? The Taliban? Where do I stop? I used to live in Japan. Do you know much about the status of women in Japan? And who gets to decide which side of the argument the school is on? North Korea has an embassy here in Ndwalowe. Did you know that? And we have two children from the North Korean embassy. Should the school take a stand on human rights abuses in North Korea? And if yes, why not Brazil? Why not Qatar? We'd end up putting every country in the world in the dock.'

'Maybe we should.' Alana was defiant.

'Or maybe we should promote the values we believe in and let each of us draw their own conclusions about each and every individual case. Look, the school as an institution isn't going to change government policy or social mores in any country. It would be futile. Gesture politics. But, perhaps more subtly, the school can help students to work it out for themselves. Ultimately, that will be much more effective in the long run than making a principled stand and going down in flames.'

This time with perhaps more understanding, Alana muttered, 'It's complicated.'

★

Every month or so, Sheila treated herself to a pedicure. All of the major hotels had spas and she had tried most of them. But Jenny Wintercoat had recommended a small privately run establishment and it had immediately become Sheila's favourite. She had even bullied Peter into going more than once.

Moreover, after almost two weeks of camping with Susi Shepherd in one of Awanza's most remote and underdeveloped corners, she felt that she deserved a little pampering. A pedicure was a given but as she locked her Rav 4 and strolled towards the reception she wondered if she had time to add a massage or even a facial. Still arguing with herself, she pushed open the door and almost bumped into Jenny.

'Oh!'

'Hello there!' The two women embraced warmly.

'Just leaving?'

'Yes,' said Jenny, 'I've just had the most marvellous massage. Needed it too. I didn't know you were back.'

'Oh, yes. A couple of weeks ago.'

'What's Mashupawana like? I've never been to that part of the country.'

'Probably what you'd expect. Run-down, neglected.'

'You were there to work with the police, weren't you?'

'Yes. It's the old story. Unemployment or even just underemployment. Alcohol abuse – the men, that is – and high rates of domestic violence.'

'Rape?' Jenny almost whispered the word.

Sheila nodded. 'But it was actually quite encouraging. The police there were very open to our suggestions. I think they are grateful for anyone showing some sort of interest in what they are up against. Susi and I were able to deliver some training and we managed to get a couple of local doctors involved. They're looking now to see if they can find or build a small facility where rape victims can be received with a bit of privacy.'

'That's encouraging?' Jenny looked dubious.

'I know what you mean. But it's an improvement. It would be great if we didn't need any of this but we do so it's important that we try to do it right.'

Jenny nodded. 'I admire you. You and Susi.'

'Well, you know. It's better to light a single candle and all that. Anyway, how have you been? I haven't seen you in weeks.'

'Oh, busy. As usual. Especially with Ronald still in Wales.'

'Wales?'

'Yes. Didn't Peter tell you? His mother is extremely ill. In fact, we think this is the end. But she's a tough old boot and she's hanging on.'

'And Ronald is there?'

'Yes. He flew up, oh, three or four weeks ago. Each time he thinks maybe he can come back she takes a turn for the worse. He's torn.'

'That must be exhausting.'

'I thought Peter would have mentioned it. That's why he cooked me that wonderful curry. Honestly, if I ever open an Indian restaurant, I'll employ him.'

'Curry?'

'Yes. When you and Susi were away and Ronald … Peter didn't say anything? We had dinner together one night. He cooked.'

'No,' Sheila said. 'He didn't tell me. Was it good?'

'It was lovely. But I wonder why he didn't mention it.'

'Mmm. Me too. I'll ask him.'

★

Like most schools, ISN had grown in fits and starts, adding or renovating buildings and facilities when enrolment was healthy and there existed within the board of the day an inclination to invest rather than save. There was, in theory, an overarching development plan but, as often as not, projects took on lives of their own, driven by the priorities and preferences of successive directors and board chairs. The result was a slightly eclectic mix of architectural styles. The architect who had designed the Arts Centre had evidently been a fan of modernism and its aggressive angles and tinted glass jarred somewhat with the vernacular architecture that was more common across the campus. But it did feature an attractive grove of lemon trees that produced prodigious amounts of fruit each year and the benches that were dotted throughout the grove were popular with teachers at break times.

Flo Balgowan's classroom opened directly onto the grove and she took an almost proprietorial pride in the neat rows of healthy and carefully tended trees. Leaving at the end of each day she never failed to stop and admire the blossoms or ripening fruit according to the season. She was always among the last to go home and she treasured these quiet moments when she alone could admire and appreciate the seductive colours and smells.

The discovery that she was not alone therefore slightly startled and surprised her. There was a figure at the far end of the grove.

★

After his resignation from the board, Ernesto had received a number of messages offering condolences and expressing various emotions from anger to regret. One message, however, he had not anticipated.

As he entered the hotel lobby, he reflected on the numerous other occasions he had spent mornings, afternoons, and evenings there. The Lowana Lodge was close to the school, quite reasonably priced, and always happy to accommodate the school's needs. After board and committee meetings at school it was to the Lowana that members sometimes repaired for a nightcap. Ernesto was a regular at these late evening dos. Mrs Luhanga certainly was not.

She was sitting by the window in the Garden Room, a pot of tea on the table before her. She was admiring the view and did not see Ernesto approach. His greeting slightly startled her.

'Mrs Luhanga. Good morning.'

'Oh. Mr Mayor. Good morning.' She half rose out of her chair and they shook hands a little awkwardly. 'How are you?' she said as he took a seat.

'I'm well, thank you. Keeping busy.'

'That's good.'

'Yes.'

In the silence that followed Ernesto was grateful to see a waitress approaching. He placed his order.

'So …?'

'Yes. Thank you for coming, Mr Mayor. I hope my message didn't take you by surprise.'

'A little, yes.'

'But I've been wanting to talk to you ever since last month's board meeting.' She paused. 'That was very regrettable.'

What was regrettable? Ernesto wondered. His resignation or the attempt to force Lazarett off the board? *And I wonder how you voted*, he thought.

'You really care about the school, don't you?' She continued.

'Sorry?'

'And being on the board. You take that responsibility very seriously.'

'I would hope we all do. Or, in my case, did.'

'I had no idea what to expect when I joined the board.' Mrs Luhanga looked out of the window. A couple of hadada ibis were working their way across the lawn. 'I don't think I realised how important it is. And I was surprised how … passionate some members are. You and Mr Corby especially.'

'And Mr Snyman,' Ernesto could not help adding a third name.

'Yes,' she agreed. 'Mr Snyman. Our meetings are sometimes rather, mmm, confrontational, aren't they?'

'Then, you'll be glad I'm no longer on the board.'

'No! Not at all. I think you are a great loss to the board. It's maybe not a bad thing to have people who speak their mind. Even if we don't always agree.'

'Do we agree about Mr Snyman? You know my views about him.'

'He speaks his mind too and I respect that. I did not agree he should be forced off the board.'

'I see.'

'Mr Mayor …'

'Oh, do we have to do this? Does it have to be so formal? My name, as I'm sure you well know, is Ernesto. I wish you would call me that.'

Mrs Luhanga looked ever so slightly shocked. 'It's a question of respect.'

'You will not be showing me any disrespect if you call me by my first name. I assure you. I really would prefer it.'

Mrs Luhanga hesitated. 'Very well. Then, if you don't mind, my name is Prosper.'

Now it was Ernesto who looked rather shocked. 'Oh. All right. Thank you, Prosper.'

They both smiled a little coyly. Each took a sip of their drinks.

'Ernesto ...' she enunciated the word clearly but perhaps a little stiffly. 'You asked me in the last board meeting whose side I was on.'

'Ah, I apologise if—'

'I was rather offended, I admit. But it made me think. I'm a member of the board of directors. That is a serious responsibility. I'm not sure I had previously thought about it like that.'

'But, of course, you are also employed by the Ministry. That's a responsibility too.'

'Yes. And the school has quite the reputation in Awanza. In the Ministry, we never really know what to make of it.'

'The Ministry doesn't have much to do with the school, does it?'

'All schools in the country have to be approved by the Ministry. Though in the case of ISN, I'm not really sure what that means. Except, when I joined the board I was quite clear that it didn't deserve special treatment and shouldn't expect it.'

'The Access to Education Act?'

'Among other things.'

'And now? You've been on the board for eighteen months. Do you think the school deserves special treatment now?'

'Not special,' she answered slowly. 'But I'm beginning to think it might need ... a different approach. Not special but different.'

'Have you met with Peter Corby and Carola yet? That was proposed at the last board meeting, wasn't it?'

'Yes, I have. We had, I think, quite a constructive meeting. I probably should not say more at this point.'

Ernesto looked annoyed. 'Since I'm no longer on the board?'

Mrs Luhanga looked sympathetic. 'As I say, it's regrettable.'

Flo Balgowan and Francine Defontaine lived in adjacent flats in The Warren, the rather claustrophobic development in which most of the single teachers were housed, and they frequently car-pooled, partly to save petrol money, partly out of concern for the environment, but mostly because they enjoyed a good gossip.

'I got a bit of a fright to be honest. I wasn't expecting anyone to be there. And it was almost as if he was hiding, trying not to be seen.'

'But why would he do that?'

Flo shrugged. 'I don't know. But when he saw that I'd seen him and he stepped out of the bushes to say hello, he was quite awkward. He looked sort of … guilty.'

'A peeping tom? God, it's Anna all over again.'

'No, I'm sure it was nothing like that. But what was he doing there and why did he seem shifty?'

'It doesn't sound like him.'

'No. That's what puzzles me.'

★

The boards of international schools meet a number of times a year, though what that number is varies considerably from school to school. Seldom will they (or should they) meet more than once a month. A few, indeed, meet barely once a quarter. Important decisions are made in these meetings of the full board but much preparatory work is devolved to board committees – some standing committees and some ad hoc as necessary. How many committees there are and what they are expected to do will also vary from school to school. The board treasurer will almost certainly chair a committee keeping an eye on finances and few would question such a committee's importance or value. At the other extreme, however, there may be committees whose purpose and worth are far more opaque.

At the start of the school year Catherine Mulbarton had proposed to the board that it should establish an education committee. Peter's heart had sunk. Such a committee had existed in his previous school in Japan and he had been an unwilling member. He had never really understood what the point of the committee was. Nor, he suspected, did the three board members who attended and who asked of Peter and his primary school colleague endless reports that took hours to write but rarely achieved more than confirming the obvious or providing data that no one knew what to do with.

Peter had carefully and, he hoped, diplomatically questioned the need for an education committee and Trixi had supported him. But two or three board members had welcomed the proposal and no one seemed minded to argue strongly against it. And so it was agreed that such a committee would be established comprising Catherine as chair, Violet Sindima as a member, Peter, and the primary and secondary principals.

They met once a month. At Catherine's insistence, the venue was different each month. The primary library then a secondary science lab. A kindergarten classroom (where they squatted uncomfortably on tiny chairs). The drama studio.

'It will help us to focus,' Catherine had argued. 'Sitting in Peter's office, we risk seeing education as something abstract. We need to remind ourselves that it is real.' In the context of the education committee, Peter frequently found it necessary to bite his tongue.

But sometimes tongue-biting wasn't an option.

They were sitting in one of the language rooms. Large posters decorated the walls. One showed the Palace of Versailles, another the Eiffel Tower. A particularly interesting one comprised a map of France cleverly composed of many and various types of cheese. *Le Tricolore* appeared more than once and the faces of France's 2018 World Cup winning team beamed down from above the whiteboard.

'My daughter takes French.' Violet looked around the room approvingly. 'She says it's one of her favourite subjects.'

'Having a second language is a central part of an international education,' offered Mick. 'As I'm sure you all know, it's an IB requirement right up to Grade Twelve.'

'Having more than one language is taken for granted in most parts of Africa,' said Catherine rather sternly. 'A so-called second language is more or less the minimum. I grew up with Afrikaans and English and I took Xhosa and French at school. I expect you did too, Violet?'

'Oh, yes. Well, in my case it was English and Kiwanza and I took Portuguese in school. And I can get by in Afrikaans and Swahili too.'

With the air of someone who had just won an argument, Catherine turned and fixed Peter with a stare. Peter had no idea what the argument was about and just said, 'Sorry?'

'Violet and I are bilingual.'

'I think Catherine is asking if we are.' said Valli with what might have been a sigh.

'Oh. Right. Well, I'd never claim to be bilingual but I can just about manage in German and I did pick up a little Japanese. I did French at school but only till I was sixteen and I've forgotten almost all of it.'

'So how did you communicate in Germany and Japan?' Catherine sounded vaguely disapproving.

'Em, well, I could manage the basics. Ordering food in a restaurant and that kind of thing. And in Germany a lot of people speak very good English. That was less the case in Japan, however.'

'So you relied on people speaking English?'

'Well, everyone did. At least, everyone where I worked. I was in two international schools, don't forget. Everything was in English. The people I worked with spoke English. My social life was in English.'

Catherine looked unimpressed.

'Swahili, you said?' Mick smiled at Violet and continued, '*Habari ya jioni! U hali gani?*' He grinned broadly.

Violet was briefly taken aback but then replied in fluent Swahili and at some length. Mick's face fell. 'Er, I'm sorry. That was a bit too …'

'And it's not evening.'

'Sorry?'

'You greeted me with "good evening".'

'Oh.'

'Hasn't it been argued that international schools are often bubbles?' Catherine was talking to herself as much as the others. 'Existing within the host country but not really being part of it? Are we a bubble?' She looked around the room.

'It is sometimes a problem,' Peter spoke slowly, carefully. 'And the best schools recognise it and try to do something about it. Community service programmes, for example. Entering local sports competitions. Visiting local sites of cultural significance …' Even as he spoke Peter could see where this was heading. His voice tailed off.

'And all of which happens, I'm guessing, in English,' Catherine enunciated the last word with what sounded almost like distaste.

No one said anything.

'How are our students to engage with the country around them – with the culture around them – if they cannot speak the language? How many of our students take Kiwanza?'

'We only offer it in Secondary,' began Peter, 'and students choose between Kiwanza, French, Spanish and Mandarin. In fact, for a school of our size, we offer an impressive number of languages.' His attempt to sound positive fell a bit flat.

'And how popular is Kiwanza?'

Mick had been hastily tapping the keys of his laptop. 'We have about three or four in each of Grades Six to Eight, a little more in each of Nine and Ten, three in Grade Eleven and one in Grade Twelve.'

'Just four doing the diploma?' Violet was surprised.

'Yes. Each year a number of our Awanzan students take Kiwanza as their language A option. Sometimes they take it with English A for a bilingual diploma.'

'Overseas students don't take it to diploma level?'

'Well, it may have happened in the past but the four current students are all local.'

'Is it viable to run a course for one student? Or even three?'

Peter interrupted. 'It would be a bad look if we dropped Kiwanza. And it's one of the ways we try to burst the bubble.'

'But only for a tiny handful of children. And most of them seen to be locals anyway.' Catherine was becoming increasingly agitated. 'Do any non-Awanzans take the language?'

Mick consulted his laptop again. 'In the middle school a few do, yes. But, the reality is that most parents choose one of the other three languages for their child.' He looked a little mournful.

'So we have children from fifty or so countries and hardly any of them learn to speak the local language?'

There was little Peter could say.

Catherine continued. 'When you worked in Germany, Peter, how many foreign students studied German?'

Peter sighed inaudibly. 'Most of them. In fact, if I remember correctly, it was compulsory until the end of Grade Ten.'

'And in Japan?'

'Most non-Japanese studied it, yes.'

'So, why not here? Why is it important for foreigners in Germany to learn German but we see no need for foreigners in Awanza to learn Kiwanza?'

'I don't know, Catherine. It is something I inherited. It's not something I've thought much about.'

'Evidently!'

'For what it's worth, Catherine,' Mick leaned forward, 'it was much the same in Tanzania. Swahili was offered but only a small number of students opted to take it.'

'And do we think that this is right? Why is Kiwanza not compulsory here? Up to Grade Ten, say?'

'Well, if we were to do that, we'd need to make space on the timetable. Something would have to give. And are you proposing just Secondary or in Primary too?' Peter could see a way of regaining the initiative.

'Why not?'

'Valli?' Peter turned to his colleague. 'Compulsory Kiwanza in Primary?'

'Well, we could do it if we had to but, as you say, what would we cut to make space?'

'And we'd need a lot more teachers,' Mick added.

'But we could do it?' Catherine persisted.

Peter nodded slowly. 'We could. But I think we are missing the key point. My guess is that parents don't want it.' He paused. Catherine frowned. 'Look at the evidence,' Peter continued. 'It's there. It's an option – at least in Secondary. But very few people take it. In Germany it was compulsory but even if it wasn't I think most parents would like the idea of their son or daughter learning to speak German. But, honestly, you're here in Awanza for two or three years – maybe four – and then you and your family will be off somewhere else. Bluntly, what use will Kiwanza be? We sometimes like to tell ourselves that parents in an international school are motivated by some sort of internationalist mindset. Some are, sure, but most see things in much more utilitarian terms. How many students here are pushed by their parents into taking economics in the diploma programme when they'd rather be doing art or music?'

'Should we be giving parents what they think they want or being true to the school's beliefs and philosophy?'

Peter laughed, not unkindly. 'Catherine, an excellent question. Should politicians just follow public opinion – give them what they want – or try to guide them into a better place? An age-old question. Our parents are customers. If you don't give them what they want, they can take their business elsewhere. But, you are right, there are times we should lead and not follow. But we have to choose our battles.'

'And be very circumspect in which battles we do choose.' Mick looked at Peter and nodded.

Catherine looked flustered. 'Violet. You agree, don't you? This is your language and culture we are talking about.'

Violet visibly squirmed. 'Catherine, I can see why you are proposing this and … thank you. But, no. I would not be in favour at all of compulsory Kiwanza.'

'No?'

'Catherine, my husband and I speak Kiwanza with the kids at home. They speak it fluently. They don't need it at school. We certainly don't need to pay these high fees for something we can give them for free. I'd much rather my children learn French – or, in my son's case, Mandarin. These are languages that will benefit them in the future.'

'But don't you think that foreigners should learn the language?'

'It would be nice but I agree with Peter. I don't think many parents would be happy if we made it mandatory.' Violet continued to look uncomfortable. 'My kids love this school. And they have lots of friends from all over. And when they play together—'

'They speak English,' Catherine completed Violet's sentence.

'Yes. And I'm okay with that.'

'Can't we do both?' Catherine looked a Peter.

'What do you mean?'

'Recognise the reality of what parents want but also lead. Set an example?'

'Oh. You mean learn Kiwanza? Me?'

'All three of you, I would say. Wouldn't it send a powerful message if the senior leadership team could speak Kiwanza? Speak Kiwanza to the gardeners, the security guards. To Awanzan parents, even.'

Peter nodded. 'It would. It would be very positive. I'm not arguing. But how long would it take? How many hours a week? And, frankly, is it really a priority?'

'Can you speak any Kiwanza?'

Peter shuffled uncomfortably. 'A few words. Greetings. Thank you …'

'I think you can do a little better than that.' Catherine's suggestion could have been patronising but Peter found that he rather agreed. He'd never be fluent but he could certainly make more of an effort. She was right. And it would be well received in various quarters.

He nodded. 'I think you have a point.'

★

'Hiding in the lemon trees?' Sheila could not stifle a laugh.

'I wasn't hiding.' Peter protested. 'Well, I didn't want to be seen …'

'Hiding.'

'No!'

'Flo must have thought so.'

'She looked … startled,' Peter conceded. 'So I just greeted her, asked how she was doing. You know, small talk.'

'Standing among the lemon trees with a cardboard box in your hand?'

'No. I managed to hide the box.'

'And the caterpillars? Our wee friends?'

'Safely relocated. They can munch their way through the school trees to their hearts' content.'

Sheila shook her head but she was smiling. 'Otherwise, how was your day?'

'Ugh. Another daft idea from a board member. Catherine Mulbarton thinks that Kiwanza should be compulsory throughout the school. And when her idea was shot down she demanded to know why I haven't tried to learn it. You know, sort of setting an example.'

'Good question. Why haven't you? I have. Well, I'm taking classes.'

'And you're a linguist and you have plenty of time on your hands.'

'You didn't learn much Japanese either, did you? Well, not much more than telling a taxi driver how to take you home.'

'*Tsugi no shingoo hidari desu.*'

'Exactly. And considering you spent six years there, your German is not much to write home about.'

'Thank you very much.'

'But that's just you, isn't it?'

'What do you mean?'

It's never been that important to you to fit in. You quite like being an outsider.'

'I've never pretended otherwise.' Peter paused and reflected for a moment. 'You think that me not making much of an effort to learn other languages is – what? Something deliberate?'

'Maybe not consciously but it's sort of a statement, isn't it? This is who I am. Take me on my own terms.'

'And speak English. God, you make me sound awfully arrogant.'

'Not arrogant as such. But you are who you are and you're not usually in a hurry to make compromises. You speak English. You speak it fluently. You can usually express yourself very clearly. You couldn't do that in another language. At least, not until you'd become much more fluent. Speaking only English means you are usually in control of the conversation. And you like that.'

Peter raised an eyebrow.

'Wow,' Sheila continued. I'm enjoying this. I should have been a psychiatrist!'

'Well, doctor, what do think about this? Part of me sort of agreed with Catherine. So I'm going to see Hope Mmusi tomorrow and see if she has a couple of afternoons a week when she can give me lessons. I'm not aiming too high but I do want to be able to say more than hello and goodbye.'

'My goodness. Old dog, new tricks. Who'd have thought?' Sheila laughed.

'Anyway, it's not as if I'm an outlier. How many of our friends can speak Kiwanza?'

'Susi can. She's almost fluent.'

'Well, that's because of her job.'

'So? And Jenny. She speaks Kiwanza.'

'That's two. Who else?'

Jenny … Sheila's demeanour changed abruptly. 'You never told me that you had dinner with Jenny when I was away. In fact, you cooked for her.'

Peter frowned.

'When I was in Mashupawana. I bumped into Jenny today. She told me.'

'I didn't tell you?'

'No.'

'Well, you were in Mashapua …'

'Mashupawana.'

'Yes, there. And Ronald was in Wales and … it was just a spur of the moment thing. I cooked a curry.'

'She said. But why didn't you tell me?'

'I didn't mention it? I thought I had.'

'She came here?'

'Yes.'

They both looked uncomfortable.

'She, you don't think …'

'I just wish you'd told me.'

'I thought I had. Sorry.'

'Okay,' Sheila stood. 'It's nothing. Anyway, I'm going to bed.'

To Peter it didn't sound like nothing.

✱

Shortly after he had arrived in Ndwalowe, Mick had spent a good couple of hours getting to know Valli. They sat in her office, Mick full of questions and Valli happy to tell him how things were generally done at the school. Both were experienced principals and each had their preferred approaches but in truth their differences were minor.

'I try not to spend too much time in my office,' Valli had explained. 'I think it's important to be out there – see what's going on.'

'And be seen! I agree.' Mick tended to be enthusiastic about everything.

'I've actually been doing it for years,' said Valli, 'but I just learned recently there's a name for it. I think it's even taught in business schools.'

'Oh?'

Valli picked up a pen and wrote MBWA on the whiteboard. Mick frowned.

'Dog,' he said.

'What?'

'Dog. It means dog. In Swahili.'

'Really? Oh.'

'What do you think it means?'

'Management By Walking Around.'

'Seriously?' Mick laughed.

Valli looked slightly offended. 'It's a recognised strategy.'

'What a load of nonsense. Why do we need a name for just walking around? I take it it's an American thing?'

'Mick! I find that very offensive.'

'Oh,' His face fell. 'I'm sorry. I didn't think.'

And it was while Valli was managing by walking around that Blessing Nyanga found her to tell her that Jackie Sesriem had appeared that morning with a black eye.

★

On his way to pay a visit to a primary school art exhibition, Peter noticed two colleagues deep in conversation on the other side of the car park. Seeing Genuine Ambadh, Site Manager, and Saskia Kakonje, Business and Operations Manager, in conversation was not unusual but the way they both turned to look at him and Saskia waved to him was ominous. 'What now?' He muttered.

Quick good mornings were exchanged. 'Something up?' Peter asked.

'Genuine is just informing me that the cleaners can't get into the two PTA rooms.'

'Why not?'

'Because, Sir,' said Genuine, 'it looks like the locks have been changed. I just went to check and my master keys don't work either.'

'The locks have been changed? Did either of you know anything about this?'

'Uh-uh.'

'No.'

'But, how … Show me. I want to see this.'

The three of them walked the short distance to the library building where the two PTA rooms were located. Genuine produced a large bunch of keys and offered them to Peter. 'Try it yourself. Either of these two should work.'

But they didn't. Neither key would open either door.

'They've been changed. The bloody locks have been changed. I don't believe it. And what's this?' Peter indicated a large television screen mounted just inside a window. It appeared to be showing a series of photos and short videos of PTA events.

Saskia studied it carefully. 'I haven't seen that before. It must be very new.'

'And it must have cost a bit too,' said Peter.

'Maybe not that much,' said Saskia, 'but I'll find out from Nandeep.'

'And I'm going to have a word with Crystal Moore about these locks. Who does she think she is?' His visit to the exhibition forgotten, Peter retraced his steps back to his office.

He found Valli waiting for him.

'Peter, I think we have a problem. Again.'

'We do. Well, unless yours is the same as mine, we have two problems. What is it?'

'Blessing just saw me. Apparently, when Jackie Sesriem dropped off Will this morning, she had a black eye.'

'Oh, no ...'

'She was wearing dark glasses but Blessing said it was very obvious.'

'She didn't say anything? Jackie?'

'Blessing didn't say but I don't think so.'

'It could, I suppose, be an accident. She walked into a door or something.' But even as he said it, Peter knew that both he and Valli had reached a different conclusion.

'You need to speak to him. Again.'

'I know,' said Peter. 'But this time I want to have a witness. This could get serious.'

'It should get serious.'

'Yes. Of course. You're right.'

'Now, your turn. What—'

'Oh, just that the bloody PTA appear to have changed the locks! The cleaners couldn't get in. Genuine, Saskia and I have just been to check.'

'They can't do that!'

'They can and they did. I'm about to get in touch with Crystal Moore. I'm about up to here with the PT bloody A.'

'Well, don't forget Mike.'

'No. No, I'll attend to both right now. And do you perhaps want to see if Jackie will talk?'

'I doubt if she will but yes, I'll give her a call.'

'This wasn't at all how I intended to spend my morning.'

Valli nodded and even offered a weak smile. 'How often do we say that?'

★

Julia Rweyemamu sat to one side, her laptop open on the table before her. Mike had listened to Peter talking without showing much emotion and certainly no contrition. Peter was getting exasperated.

'Mike, she has a black eye!'

'You've no idea what she's like. The sarcasm. The gaslighting. The accusations. She takes it out on the kids too.'

'When Lee-Ann spoke to Will, he—'

'Of course he would! He's terrified of his mother. She's … She's … Peter, you just don't know.'

'Did you hit her?'

Mike glanced at Julia who was quietly typing. 'She … I'd had enough, Peter. She provokes me.'

'Did the kids see it?'

'Sally was asleep. But Will …'

'We're going to have to talk to Will. Well, not me but Lee-Ann and probably Valli or maybe Blessing. This is a child protection issue, Mike.'

Mike closed his eyes and shook his head slowly.

'Mike, in North America or Europe – and maybe elsewhere, I don't know – I'd have a statutory obligation to report this to social services. Here I'm not so sure but Glory and Lee-Ann tell me there's a Mother and Child Unit at the Central Hospital. It deals with domestic violence. They seem to have some confidence in it.'

'Peter, don't, please. Please. It isn't necessary.'

'It is necessary. You have a wife with a black eye and a seven-year-old son who … well, I don't know what he witnessed but it can only have been very upsetting. Don't you see? What choice do I have?'

'Peter…'

'Look, I don't know you well and I barely know Jackie at all but something is wrong here, you must see that. For the school's sake – and for your sake – this has to be taken seriously.'

Mike stared at the floor. Peter noticed that his hands were trembling.

'You and Jackie need help. You need to talk to someone. I'm telling you this and I'm going to tell Jackie too.'

'Can we just ...' Mike spoke still staring at the floor. 'Can we just keep it between us?'

'Well, we'll be as discreet as we can but if your wife's walking around with a black eye ... People will talk.'

'We had counselling once before, back in Namibia.'

'And?'

Mike made a vaguely hopeless gesture. 'Okay. All right. We'll try it again,' he said. 'If I can get Jackie to go.'

'Do. Please. And do it soon.'

The look Mike gave Peter was poisonous.

Carola and Peter had arranged to meet to discuss how to proceed with the ATE Act in the light of what appeared to be conciliatory moves by Mrs Luhanga. Their own meeting with her had been surprisingly constructive and Ernesto had called Carola to describe his conversation with her at the Lowana. But by the time Carola arrived at Peter's office and Chiamaka had brought her a small pot of tea, there were other, still more urgent matters on the agenda.

A copy of *The New Awanzan* lay on the coffee table between them.

'Catherine wants her expelled.' Carola sighed.

'Oh, that's ridiculous.'

'Bringing the school into disrepute and all that.'

Peter looked again at the article.

Student Protest at the Nigerian High Commission

Alana Johanneson (17), a citizen of New Zealand and a student at Ndwalowe International School, chained herself to the railings outside the Nigerian High Commission yesterday. She was protesting about the sentence meted out to Aafiya Abdullahi, an unmarried mother, who is due to be stoned to death. The case has been widely reported internationally. Miss Johanneson was freed after about an hour. A police spokesman confirmed that officers had been called to the Nigerian High Commission but suggested that a formal charge was unlikely. "She has been issued with a warning," he said. The Nigerian High Commission was approached for a comment but declined.

'I'm not sure this doesn't actually cast the school in a good light,' he said. 'No one was hurt, no damage was done, and anyway, they got the school's name wrong.'

'Have you spoken to her mother?'

'Yes. She couldn't decide if she was furious or proud.'

'Have any other parents been in touch?'

'Not yet. But a few of the usual suspects will probably want to have their say.'

'So, is this a school matter? Will there be consequences? I've told you what Catherine thinks. On the other hand, Grant called me when he saw it and he thinks the whole thing is hilarious.'

'Well, Mick and I had a quick chat about it. The school's name – well, the old name – does appear in the paper. But, again, how bad is it for the school? To be honest, my inclination is just to let it blow over. Let's not do anything to breathe more life into what is really a pretty minor thing. What I will do is write to the Nigerian High Commissioner to assure him that Alana was not acting on behalf of the school blah, blah, blah. My worry is that he will demand some kind of action on our part.'

'I know him. Well, Horst knows him better than I do. All the ambassadors know each other. I'll maybe give him a call myself and see what his mood is.'

'Thanks. Apart from anything, we have other things to worry about.'

'You said something about the PTA? What are they up to now?'

Peter made a face. 'Two things. They have unilaterally changed the locks on their doors. So now the cleaners can't get in and, more importantly, there's a safety aspect. In an emergency we need access to every room in the school. I called Crystal Moore and she was defiant. I pointed out that the doors are school property. Her answer was that everything behind the doors is PTA property. She implied that the PTA doesn't believe the school can be trusted not to play fast and loose with the stuff they store in there. She specifically mentioned the beer and wine they have but that's in a locked fridge and we certainly don't have a key to that.'

'Has anything ever been stolen?'

'Not that I'm aware of. But they probably wouldn't know anyway. I understand their record-keeping is pretty chaotic.'

'You mentioned two things?'

'Oh, I think this is even more serious. They've installed a large LED screen in one of the windows. I thought it would be expensive but it turns out that these things are surprisingly cheap. But I still wanted to know how much it cost so we asked the business office. Any time the PTA spends money, it must be approved by the PTA treasurer or chair and counter-signed by someone from our accounts office – usually Nandeep Agarwal. But when we asked him, he knew nothing about it. The payment hadn't gone through his office.'

'Are you sure they bought it? Maybe someone donated it.'

'Oh, I'm sure. I called the bank. It turns out they – the PTA – have changed the process for authorising payments. Now the treasurer and any one of the other three members of the executive committee can approve purchases.'

'So they've taken the school out of the loop?'

'Yes.'

'And didn't inform you?'

'No.'

'Do they have the authority to do that?'

'I managed to speak to someone quite senior at the bank and apparently they do. It's a PTA account, not a school account. They can manage it any way they want.'

'But they should have asked you. Or at least told you. Or even just Saskia or Nandeep.'

'That isn't the way they work these days. Crystal keeps saying that the PTA needs more independence. She sometimes uses the word autonomy.'

'But it's just a school PTA. How can they possibly be independent? It makes no sense.'

Peter shrugged. 'They're completely out of control.'

'So now what? We have to get the doors fixed at least.'

'I think I'm going to have to get Faansie Burger's advice. I can see this thing escalating. It could get very damaging.'

'So the school is going to pay for legal advice as to how to deal with its own PTA?'

'I know. It's absurd.'

Carola shook her head sadly. 'Well, with all this going on, it's perhaps as well that we may not have to worry about the ATE Act.'

'Oh, I'd forgotten all about that. Mrs Luhanga ...'

'Or Prosper, as Ernesto now says she wants to be known.' In spite of herself, Carola flashed Peter a sly smile.

'I can't work her out.'

'No, but she seems to be a bit more amenable now.'

'Well, let's see what happens at the next board meeting. I do hope it's less dramatic than the last one.'

'*Ja, hoffentlich!*'

Even Peter's German was good enough to understand that.

Peter's visit to Faansie Burger had given him the clarity he needed but not the answer he wanted. Valli and Mick were also finding it hard to understand.

'So, the PTA isn't in fact answerable to the school? Have I understood that correctly?' Mick leaned forward, frowning.

'Correct. It is a wholly separate entity under Awanzan law. Faansie asked me to think of it like a club run by volunteers. A swimming club. A bird club. If there is a bank account and some sort of board, it exists in its own right.'

'It sort of makes sense,' said Valli. 'I guess it's about responsibility, accountability.'

'But,' argued Peter, 'the bird club I belong to only exists because ... well, it's a bird club. That's the whole and only point. The PTA, however, only exists because of the school. It has no purpose or reason to exist other than the school.'

'What if ... forgive me for saying this,' Mick chuckled mischievously, 'what if the school went bankrupt? I mean, obviously not. Who ever heard of a school going bankrupt?' Neither Peter nor Valli were finding this particularly funny. 'Sorry, I just mean, if the school – any school – closed down for any reason, would the PTA still exist?'

'A PTA but no school?'

'Yes.'

'It sounds ridiculous but if I understood Faansie correctly, then yes. Until and unless the members of the PTA decided to close it down, it would still exist.'

'But if the school was closed, the PTA wouldn't have any members, would it?'

'Guys,' Valli sound slightly irritated, 'this is all very interesting. Schrödinger's PTA and all that but what matters is that we seem not to have any authority over the PTA. You don't, Peter. And nor does the board of directors.'

'Yes,' agreed Peter.' You're right. I suppose in the back of my mind I thought that if it came to it I could just tell the PTA what to do. Or even close it down. Seems that isn't the case.'

'We could evict them,' said Mick.

'What?'

'If they aren't part of the school, what are they doing occupying two precious rooms? Tell them they can have their silly meetings but they must have them elsewhere. Off school premises.'

'And that would help the situation how?'

'Well, if they're declaring war. We have some moves too. Or, I know, charge them rent!'

'Mick, I think it better if we don't escalate this thing. I think Crystal Moore and her gang are looking for a fight. I don't think it's in anyone interests to give them one.'

Mick looked disappointed.

'There is one thing,' Valli looked thoughtful. 'You can't tell the PTA what to do, Peter, and nor can the board. But the members can. And I know a lot of parents and teachers are not happy with how the PTA is behaving.'

'Unhappy enough to do something about it? Most of them just seem to walk away.'

'I think we could rustle up enough people to mount some sort of challenge. A vote of no confidence, or something.'

'Mmm. I like that. Let me talk to a few people and see what we can do. Yes, good idea.'

Peter was thinking it was time he and Sheila had dinner at The Mupundu again.

★

March

If Peter had been delighted to recruit Jonathan Pigeon as the permanent replacement for Chuck Collins, Jonathan was no less pleased to have secured a teaching position at short notice. He had more than a dozen years of teaching the IB Diploma under his belt including long stretches in two highly regarded international schools in Europe and yet his recent applications had been getting him nowhere. Explaining why he had left the Netherlands to return to his native New Zealand only to be heading overseas again barely three months later involved sharing at least some details of a hasty, ill-advised, and ultimately humiliating marriage proposal that he feared made him look rather flaky. He also suspected that at least one of his referees might be doing his cause more harm than good.

Indeed, he would never see it but in his file a confidential email from his former director acknowledged and commended Jonathan's "excellent rapport with students" but lamented that his "essentially unserious nature" sometimes inclined him to "whimsy". Peter wasn't altogether sure that an "unserious nature" was necessarily a bad thing and was no stranger to whimsy himself. Much more to the point, he desperately needed to appoint a maths teacher with substantial IB experience and was quite prepared to risk that Jonathan Pigeon might turn out to be a bit of a clown.

In fact, Peter had quickly warmed to his latest appointment, rather admiring Jonathan's sometimes irreverent attitude to authority and convention. Jonathan too found his new school very much to his liking. Both men would have described the arrangement as a win-win.

*

Carola had a fine understanding of her role as board chair. A critical friend to the head of school. The arbiter of intra-board disagreements. Someone to keep an eye on the big picture. It could be exhausting.

'It's Lazarett again,' she was explaining to Peter.

'What now?'

'He's suggesting that the two principals – Valli and Mick – attend board meetings.'

'Oh? Should I assume this is some sort of implicit criticism of me?'

Carola declined to answer.

'Because if it is,' Peter continued, 'I think he's shot himself in the foot. In Hamamatsu I attended board meetings as secondary principal. So did the primary principal. I believe the same was true in Germany. In fact, I think the business manager attended too. It's really not uncommon.'

'So, you don't object?'

'Am I allowed to? This is a board decision.'

'Correct. But before I put the idea to the whole board I wanted to know what you thought.'

'Thank you, Carola. I appreciate that. No. I have no objection. I'm rather in favour. I'll be happy to have Mick and Valli there.'

'And Trixi? You don't think it might get a bit … unbalanced? Four members of staff?'

'I can't vote. Nor will Valli or Mick be able to. So, it's still only one of us who can. And that's fine. It's how it should be.'

'Do you think they'll want to attend?'

'Valli and Mick? It's really not up to them. If the board decide that they need to attend then they will. I'm sure.'

'So, you're okay if I make this proposal to the whole board?'

'Absolutely.'

Sometimes Carola and Peter parted with things unsaid. Sometimes they parted with a conspiratorial smile.

★

Jonathan Pigeon made friends easily. He was confident and likeable, sociable and gregarious. Somewhat half-heartedly, the school assigned to new teachers a "buddy" who would answer their questions and guide them through the first few weeks. Jonathan's buddy was Brian Bell, also from

New Zealand, and the two men immediately discovered they had much in common, not least a mischievous sense of humour.

★

Nominally, Brian Bell was on break duty. In fact, he and Jonathan Pigeon were engaged in a good-natured argument about rugby.

'I'm just saying I'd rather go to a Heartland match. The skill level may not be the same but it's far more authentic. It's much closer to the rugby you and I used to play.'

'I still do. There's a decent club here in Ndwalowe. You should come.'

A short, rather serious looking student approached the two men and hovered a discreet and deferential distance before them.

Jonathan turned to him. 'Samir? Do you want something?'

'I'm sorry, Mr Pigeon. I don't want to interrupt.'

'That's okay. What is it?'

'My last test, Mr Pigeon. I only got sixty per cent.'

Jonathan nodded sympathetically. 'I know. What are you going to do about it?'

'I studied. I mean, I did. I really did. I always do. So why aren't I getting better grades? I know I deserve better.'

'You "deserve" better?'

'Yes. Are you sure your marking is correct?'

Brian stifled a laugh.

'Well, Samir, I hope so. I have been teaching IB maths for a decade or more,' Jonathan winked at Brian.

'You know that maths is not just about the right answer?' continued Samir. 'How you get the answer is important too. Do you take that into account when you grade?'

'Thank you, Samir, I am aware of that. I am an examiner, you may recall.'

'But you are still not giving me the right grades.'

Jonathan studied the boy. 'You want higher grades?'

'Of course.'

Jonathan nodded thoughtfully. 'How badly?'

'What?'

'How badly do you want to get your grades up? And how high? Seventy per cent? Higher?'

Samir frowned. 'I ...'

Jonathan leaned closer to Samir and lowered his voice. 'How old are you, Samir?'

Samir's frown deepened. 'I'll be eighteen next month.'

Jonathan nodded again. 'You're not a child, Samir. You know how the world works. You don't get something for nothing. Isn't that right, Mr Bell?'

'Absolutely.' Brian agreed. 'You scratch my back ...'

'Eh?'

'You do something for me and I'll, er, do something for you. Except I can't in this case, 'cause you don't do economics. But if you did ...' He tapped the side of his nose. Samir hadn't the first idea what that meant.

Jonathan somewhat theatrically looked up and down the corridor and confirmed that no one was in earshot. 'You can get higher grades, Samir. I can make that happen.' He winked.

'I'll leave you two to discuss this. I'm meant to be on duty.' Brian flashed a grin at Jonathan and sauntered off down the corridor.

Jonathan watched him go. And then turned his attention back to Samir.

★

There had been no board meeting in February and Carola was not sorry. January's meeting had been bruising and the routine five-week gap between meetings had been even more welcome than usual. Moreover, she was somewhat optimistic that the imminent meeting might, for once, pass off without voices being raised and tempers being lost. In fact, much as she lamented the departure of Ernesto Mayor, she did admit to herself that he was one of those who sometimes raised the temperature and his absence, at least in that regard, might be beneficial.

She had been wondering for a few days if Mrs Luhanga would reintroduce herself as Prosper following her morning tea with Ernesto. In fact, the situation was not to arise as Mrs Luhanga (Prosper?) had informed Carola that she had urgent business in the south of the country and would regrettably have to send her apologies. Carola and Peter when she had told him both suspected that her absence was contrived so that they could speak

256

more freely when they reported back to the board the surprisingly constructive meeting there had been between them.

'If she really is easing off on the ATE thing, she may not much want to be at the meeting where she could be questioned,' Peter had suggested. 'Easier, in fact, to let us deliver the news.' Carola had agreed.

Other items on the agenda, besides the usual reports, were progress on the strategic plan (which, Peter had noticed with some satisfaction, seemed to have stalled), discussion about which model to use (and when) for a board self-evaluation exercise, and Lazarett's proposal that the two principals should attend board meetings.

'That won't be controversial, will it?' Carola had sought Peter's reassurance.

'I can't see why. I can't see anyone objecting.'

And nor did they. Barely an hour after calling the meeting to order, Carola checked the agenda one more time to confirm that nothing had been missed and asked if there was any other business.

'That's a record,' smiled Grant. 'I make that ...' he glanced at his watch, 'one hour and eight minutes. We must try and do that more often.' He closed his laptop and began gathering up his papers.

'If you don't mind, Mr Guthrie ...' Lazarett gestured to Grant, 'I do have one item of AOB.'

'A quick one, I hope,' said Grant, still smiling. 'Let's not jeopardise the shortest meeting on record.'

Lazarett ignored him but spoke to Carola. 'Madam Chairman, I need hardly remind everyone that at the last board meeting, one of our members chose to resign. So we now have a board of eight.'

'Er, yes.'

'I think that's a vacancy that ought to be filled. The board may in fact number up to twelve. Nine, it would seem to me, is the minimum to ensure effectiveness and efficiency. Consider tonight. Mrs Luhanga's absence means we are just seven. Barely half of what the Articles of Association permit.'

Carola acknowledged that Lazarett had a point.

'But we're only three months away from the AGM,' said Clyde. Unlike last year, there will be elections. I'm stepping down, for one. And there may be others. I think that's the time to look for new members.'

'No doubt that will happen in June but if we have an outstanding candidate now, why wait?'

'Do we have an outstanding candidate?' Peter frowned. 'Do we have any candidates?'

'We, Mr Corby?' said Lazarett. 'If you don't mind, this is a board matter. A matter for the voting members of the board.'

Peter flushed. Carola shot him a look that implored him not to say anything. 'It sounds to me,' she said to Lazarett, 'that you have someone in mind.'

Lazarett looked pleased and produced from his briefcase a number of copies of a curriculum vitae. He distributed them around the table, rather pointedly not giving Peter one. 'Highly experienced,' he was saying, 'a very strong financial background and excellent managerial skills. I've worked with him myself. Very impressed. Oh, and he has two children in the school. I think he'd be an ideal board member.'

'Is he interested in joining the board?' Grant was studying the CV.

'Oh, yes. He's actually quite keen.'

'Shouldn't this go before a nominations committee? If we had one?' Clyde tossed his copy of the CV onto the table. 'We're going to need one for the AGM anyway.'

The discussion continued for a few more minutes but Peter was barely listening. He could now see the name on the first page of the CV Clyde had discarded.

It was Colby Wittering.

★

The knock on Peter's door was hesitant. Peter looked up from the magazine he was reading and greeted his visitor.

'Jonathan. Come in. Take a seat. Do you know this magazine?' He held it up to show Jonathan the cover. '*International School.* Lots of interesting stuff. Actually, I've published a few things in it. Book reviews. That kind of thing.'

'Yes,' said Jonathan. 'I know it. I published a small piece myself about ToK in maths a year or two back.'

'Really? I must look it up. Good for you. I think it's great when teachers write for publication. It really makes you stop and think about what you do and why. Doing it is one thing. Explaining it to someone else is quite another.'

Jonathan just nodded.

Peter frowned. 'Are you okay, Jonathan? You seem a bit ... down?'

'Not really but, er, I think I should tell you ...'

'Yes?'

'Mr Hamid came to see me this morning.'

'Mr Hamid?'

'Father of Samir in Grade Twelve.'

'Oh yes. I know Samir. Bit of an oddball, isn't he?'

'Yes. Something like that.'

'What did Mr Hamid want?'

Jonathan took a deep breath. 'He wanted to know how much money he would need to give me to improve Samir's grades.'

There was a long silence. At length, Peter said, 'Say that again.'

'He wanted to bribe me. Well, he didn't use the word but he made it pretty clear that he is prepared to pay whatever it would take to get Samir better grades.'

Peter was wide-eyed. 'And why would he say that?'

'Because ...' Jonathan swallowed, 'I may have given Samir the impression that, erm, that kind of thing was, erm, possible.'

'Seriously?'

'It was a joke, a prank. Samir was doubting my marking and I just wanted to tease him a little. I never thought he'd take it seriously.'

'Sound like his dad did.'

'Mr Hamid got rather annoyed when I said it had all been a misunderstanding. He said he was going to take this up with you. So I thought I'd better ...'

'I see. So, Mr Hamid is going to come and complain to me that a teacher won't take a bribe? That should be interesting.'

'I think he's more likely to complain that I gave Samir the idea in the first place.'

'You think? And do you think he maybe has a point?'

'I really didn't think Samir would ...'

'What did you think he'd do?' Peter shook his head. 'I don't want to generalise but some of our students, and their families, come from cultures where ... well, let's just say where relationships tend to be transactional.

New Zealand is famously one of the least corrupt nations in the world. But I'm not sure your sense of humour travels very well.'

'I'm sorry.'

'Well, let's see what Mr Hamid finds reasonable grounds to complain about. If he questions your judgement, I'm not sure how I'm going to defend you.'

'Yeah. I understand. Sorry.'

'And I think you should probably have a discreet word with Samir. Make it very clear that it was a joke that went a bit too far.'

'I will.'

'Oh, and be aware that I'll need to tell Mick. In case some of this reaches him.'

'I suppose so.'

'Oh, don't look so glum, Jonathan. I'm sure you'll make bigger and better blunders than this in your career. I can assure you that I have.'

'Is that meant to cheer me up?'

'During my training in London, I was in a pretty rough school. I had no idea what was going on. Completely out of my depth. One afternoon I was trying and failing to control a class of sixteen-year-olds. I'm afraid I lost it. Before I knew what I was doing, I just yelled at them, *Will you shut the ... up!*' Peter paused but Jonathan had no difficulty guessing the missing word. 'I really thought that was it. My career would be over before it started. Funny thing is, it worked. They did shut up. Well, a bit. And as far as I know, it was never reported.'

Jonathan smiled. 'I can remember doing something similar.'

'How often have I said to people that there's no script? Teaching includes a bit of acting, a little theatricality. But you're up there on stage without much support. If it's acting, it's improv. And that can go anywhere. Well, if you're not careful.'

I take it you'll be explaining all this to Mr Hamid?'

'I'm not sure they have improv where Mr Hamid comes from but I'll see what I can do.'

Jonathan stood. 'Thank you, Peter. I'm sorry.'

'Just don't be so bloody stupid next time, will you?'

Jonathan winced a little. 'I'll try.'

★

Parent-teacher conferences. Parent evenings. Three-way conferences. Whatever they are called, the school calendar will include occasions where parents will meet some or all of their children's teachers. Different schools will employ different models. Perhaps all the teachers are seated at tables arranged around the walls of the gym. It's all conveniently centralised but confidentiality can be a problem. Or perhaps the teachers are to be found in their teaching rooms and parents must crisscross the school grounds, consulting a simple map if necessary. Often parents are given appointments and a fixed number of minutes with each teacher. Sometimes, it's first come, first served. If the event is in the evening, teachers may be meeting parents without a break for anything up to three hours after a full day's teaching. Parents too, of course, are likely to have completed a day's work. Everyone is tired but at least parents usually don't need to miss work to attend. Alternatively, teaching is cancelled for a day or part thereof and the appointments can be scheduled throughout the morning and afternoon. But that can make it awkward for working parents to attend and what is to be done with the children who are not in school while their parents are?

In truth, there is no ideal system and every year in every school some parents will express their dissatisfaction with whatever arrangements the school has made. Teachers too may voice their unhappiness, particularly if there are unresolved childcare issues. Quite commonly, and especially after a change of leadership, schools will switch from one model to a different one only to try yet another just a few years later.

It would be fair to say that most teachers neither enjoy nor look forward to these events. The allocated ten minutes is both too short and too long. When there really is a conversation to be had, it is usually only possible to scratch the surface. And when there's nothing much to be said, parents ask pointless questions to fill the silence and teachers give anodyne answers. So, when a meeting between parents and a teacher is notable, the chances are it's for the wrong reasons.

During parent-teacher conferences (as they were known at ISN), Peter tended to work in his office, hoping for a parent to pop their head around the door to tell him how happy they were but knowing that any parent who sought him out would more likely be wanting to register a complaint. Now and again, he would take a stroll around the school to see how things were going. He would exchange a few pleasantries with parents he enjoyed meeting or duck down corridors or into the first empty room to avoid those he didn't.

It was after such a brief tour of the school that he returned to his office to find two parents waiting for him. He knew them somewhat. The mother held some position within the Delegation of the European Union. What the father did was a mystery.

'Mr and Mrs Connolly,' he greeted them. 'What can I do for you? Please come in.' He pushed his door open and ushered them in.

'Thank you for seeing us,' began Mrs Connolly. 'I know you must be busy on days like this.'

'Never too busy to talk to parents. That's what today's all about. How's Amber doing? I hope you are getting positive reports.'

'Yes,' Mrs Connolly looked her husband who nodded. 'Mostly pretty good. She seems to be coping with Grade Eleven.'

'I'm glad to hear it.'

'But we do have one concern.'

'Oh.'

'We were particularly anxious about English,' explained Mr Connolly. 'What with Mr Gillespie leaving at Christmas …'

'And missing several weeks at the start of the year,' added his wife.

'Yes, that too. So, we were very much looking forward to meeting Mr Willoughby.'

Uh-oh, thought Peter.

'Amber seems to like him. She says he is passionate about literature. You see, Amber is too.'

'You never see her without her face in a book.' Mr Connolly's pride was obvious.

'Well, that's excellent,' said Peter. 'I'm glad it's going so well.'

'Well, that's what we thought too.' Mrs Connolly frowned. 'Until Mr Willoughby said it was a shame.'

'A shame? What was a shame?'

'He said Amber was obviously a bright girl who needed to be stretched. But he didn't think it would happen here. At ISN.'

'What?'

Mrs Connolly took a deep breath. 'His exact words were, "this is not an academic school".'

Peter could feel his hackles raising. 'He said that ISN is not an academic school?'

'He did. Those were his very words.'

'Well,' Peter exhaled, 'that's a new one. I need hardly say that I don't agree with Mr Willoughby. I should also point out that he's only been here for a few weeks. Nor can I immediately guess what he means by "not academic". Exam results aren't everything but our IB results compare pretty well with comparable schools.'

'That was our impression too. But it's a bit of a worry to hear …'

'You're absolutely right, Mrs Connolly. And I'm very grateful that you brought this to my attention. Clearly, Mr Willoughby and I are going to have to have a conversation.'

★

At much the same time as Peter was talking to the Connollys, Richard Cooper was greeting the next names on his appointment list.

'Ah, Mr and Mrs Snively, come in. Oh …' He was a little surprised that they were accompanied by an obviously elderly lady with features that suggested south-east Asia. Married to a Jordanian himself and after many years working in international schools, Richard found peoples' identities more than averagely interesting. He gave his unexpected visitor another glance. Thai?

'This is my mother,' said Mrs Snively quite sharply. 'She doesn't speak English.'

Then, why is she here, wondered Richard but he smiled and invited his guests to take a seat.

'Now,' he said, 'Solomon …' His smile disappeared. 'I'm glad we have this chance to talk. When we met earlier in the year, I informed you that his work really was not satisfactory.' He consulted his notes, 'I noted that homework was frequently late and he commonly seemed distracted in class.'

'You called him lazy!' Mrs Snively spoke with considerable emotion.

'I did? That isn't really a word I like to use, but if you say so. Anyway, I'm sorry to have to tell you that matters are no better now. We are approaching the end of Grade Eleven and Solomon has very little to show for all these weeks. We'll be starting coursework soon and it is imperative that he starts to make an effort.'

Richard shifted in his seat and waited for a response. There came none. 'Mr Snively?' he said. 'Any thoughts?'

Solomon's father would not make eye contact but his lips were pursed tightly. He said nothing.

'Mrs Snively? Have you anything to say?'

'Oh, I have plenty to say but it's better that I don't!' She crossed her arms and turned away.

Richard looked from one guest to another a little hopelessly. 'Mr Snively, you must …'

All he got was a glare.

Granny? What about you? Richard thought of asking but wisely decided not to. 'Well,' he started, 'if there's nothing to say …'

'You know they don't like you.' Mrs Snively snapped at him.

'I beg your pardon.'

'The students. None of them like you. And they don't understand what you are trying to teach.'

'Really?'

'Yes. Every night they are on their devices talking to each other. It's so frustrating. The parents, too. We've talked to lots of parents who feel like we do.'

'Is that so? Well, that's odd. You are the …' Richard thought for a moment. 'You are the eighth set of parents of Grade Eleven students I've talked to tonight. No one else has said anything. They all seem perfectly happy with how things are going. Of course, their children are putting in the effort, concentrating. It's no wonder they are doing well.'

'In the last report you called Solomon immature. He was so upset.'

'I'm afraid his attitude in class is often … Look, he giggles. He passes silly notes to other students. This is Grade Eleven. He is taking the IB Diploma. But I'm afraid he often behaves like a much younger child. He needs to grow up.'

'See! No wonder he is discouraged.'

Richard tried a different tactic. 'You must have seen most of Solomon's teachers tonight. What have they been saying?'

Mrs Snively waved her arms. 'Absolutely fine. They say that Solomon is making excellent progress. It's just economics. Just you.'

'I see. Mrs Snively, you must realise that we talk to each other. In fact, we have fairly regular meetings to share with each other how students are doing. Have you met Ms Nair yet tonight, the diploma coordinator?'

Mrs Snively shook her head.

'Well, I hope you are going to. I can only tell you how he's doing in one subject. She will give you the bigger picture and, from what I understand, Solomon is failing pretty much across the board.'

'Failing? Failing! How dare you? It is you who is failing!'

Richard shook his head sadly. 'Mrs Snively … Mr Snively … I can only give you my professional assessment of how things are going. If you are not prepared to hear …' He looked at them. They glared at him. The grandmother smiled benignly.

'Then,' he stood, 'then there really doesn't seem much point in continuing this conversation.'

No one moved.

'I'm saying that we have nothing more to say to each other. Thank you for coming. Let me open the door for you.' He walked across the room and did so.

As he closed the door behind them, Richard muttered, 'Oh, Lord. Some parents …'

✱

The Connollys had gone and Peter was scribbling notes on a pad when a voice said, 'Mr Corby, do you have a minute?'

He looked up. 'Of course. Mrs …?'

'Snively. And this is my husband, Ethan, and my mother.' They entered his office.

'Good evening, it's a pleasure to meet you. You have a child in …?'

'Grade Eleven. Our son, Solomon.'

'Oh, yes, I know him. He's in the basketball team.'

'Yes, he is. He loves his sports.'

'That's wonderful. You know how we believe in an all-round education.'

'Well, that's why we are here. In so many ways Solomon is doing very well. He loves the school.'

'Always good to hear.'

'But there is one area, one subject …'

'Yes?'

'We're not happy, Mr Corby. Not happy at all.'

'Oh, dear. What is it?'

'Solomon is in Grade Eleven and one of his subjects is economics.'

'With Mr Cooper?'

'Exactly!' For the first time that evening a member of the ISN staff heard Mr Snively's voice.

'I see. Well, actually, I don't. What's the … What's the problem?'

'We had an appointment to see Mr Cooper. At eight-twenty. Fifteen minutes ago.'

'And?'

'We went in and …' Mrs Snively began tearing up. Her husband put a reassuring hand on her shoulder. 'We went in and … All we want is the best for our son, Mr Corby.'

'I'm sure. Like any parent. So, what … What happened?'

'We still don't know, Mr Corby. We asked Mr Cooper a few questions about how Solomon was doing …'

'The usual.'

'Yes. And then Mr Cooper began screaming at us. I don't even remember half of what he said. Then he stood up and threw the door open and yelled at us to leave.'

'Oh, my goodness.'

'My wife is still in shock.' said Mr Snively, 'You can see.' He put a protective arm around his wife's shoulders.

'Er, yes. I can see she's upset.' Peter looked at Mrs Snively who was by now sobbing and then glanced at the grandmother who was staring beatifically into the middle distance. He looked at his watch. 'I'm not sure we can do anything tonight and, anyway, maybe we should all take a few hours to cool down. Can you come and see me tomorrow morning? Say 9am?'

'We should both be at work,' said Mr Snively. 'But this is important. We'll be there.'

'Very good. And I'll ensure that Mr Cooper is too. I'm so sorry.' Peter stood.

As his guests left the office, Peter fervently hoped that Sheila had a good bottle of white on ice.

★

Teaching at ISN started at 7:30am. Newcomers to Awanza were often surprised by the early start but it was quickly explained to them that the practice dated back to the days before air conditioning. Indeed, many rooms in the school were still not air-conditioned. Moreover, many businesses and offices across the city opened at much the same time so it was helpful for parents to be able to drop off their children on the way to work. Starting teaching at 7:30 meant that teachers were expected to be on school premises by 7:00. For some, this was a daily challenge (in truth, Peter was often one of them) but the admirably disciplined regimes of others saw them in their classrooms (or at least the staffroom) well before the notional deadline. Peter knew Richard Cooper to be someone who was invariably punctual and, after dropping his briefcase in his office and surprising Chiamaka with an unusually early greeting, he quickly made for Richard's classroom.

The door was ajar but Peter still knocked gently as he entered.

'Richard, good morning. Sorry to barge in on you like this.'

Richard had been rearranging the chairs and tables that had been moved to accommodate the previous night's visitors but now turned and greeted Peter. 'Well, hello. You're a stranger in these parts. At least, this early in the day.' He glanced at his watch to confirm that it was still just a few minutes after seven. 'Is there a problem?'

'Richard, the last family I talked to last night were the Snivelys ...'

'Ah. Yes, I had that pleasure too. What did they want?'

Peter briefly outlined the accusations he had heard less than twelve hours earlier. 'I have to say, Richard, it doesn't sound like you.'

'I should hope not! But thank you. Shouting at them, they said?'

'Yelling and screaming, I think were the words they used.'

'Good grief.'

'And then you threw them out.'

'No, I explained that we had nothing further to say to each other and I invited them to leave. Politely, I hope. Well, firmly but politely.'

'All right. Anyway, I told them I'd look into it and I've asked to meet them – and you – at nine this morning. Sorry, I didn't check if you are teaching or not.'

'I'm not.'

'Good. Then please come to my office a little before nine and we'll try to defuse this.'

'Did you get the granny too?' In spite of the situation, Richard was smiling.

'I did. What was all that about?'

'Safety in numbers? Do you know where Mrs Snively is from?'

'Yes. After they'd gone I checked the database. Mr Snively is from the US and his wife is Vietnamese.'

'She's a hard one.'

'What is her beef?'

'Their boy, Solomon, is an indolent little toad. She seems unable to accept that and does not like it when it's pointed out.'

'And you pointed it out?'

'Not in quite those words but yes. As, I'm sure, did my colleagues but of course she would not admit that.'

'The original tiger mum.'

'Mmm.'

'Oh well, let's see what happens. See you at nine.'

★

Peter found Ancaster Willoughby waiting for him in Chiamaka's office.

'Miss Kambani said you wanted to see me, headmaster.'

Oh, for goodness' sake. Just call her Chiamaka, you pompous clown, thought Peter. 'Yes.' he said, 'You got the message?'

'I did.'

'Good.' They entered Peter's office and the door was closed.

'I only have a few minutes, headmaster. I'm teaching first period.'

'Then I'll be quick. I'm given to understand that you said to a couple of parents last night that the school is not academic.'

Ancaster reflected for a moment. 'Yes, that's right. The Connollys.' He did not seem at all perturbed.

'Why on earth would you say a thing like that?'

Ancaster looked confused. 'Well, I wouldn't have thought it was a particularly controversial opinion. The school doesn't necessarily aspire to being academic, does it?'

'Of course it … Why would you say that?'

'Oh,' Ancaster raised his arms as if what he was about to say was obvious. 'For a start, the school is not selective. As best I can see you accept anyone. So long as they can pay.'

'No, we're certainly not selective. We're inclusive and proud of it.'

'Exactly. And there's no uniform. That has always been a red flag for me. Schools without uniform cannot be taken terribly seriously.'

Peter gasped.

'And,' Ancaster continued, 'not unconnected to the lack of uniform is a certain …' he paused. 'I don't want to say lack of discipline. Let's just say informality. I don't find the pupils disrespectful as such. But they exhibit a … yes, informality that I find inappropriate.'

Peter struggled to find the right words.

'So, headmaster,' Ancaster looked at his watch. 'I really must go. But you can see why the school's expectations of students rather mitigate against the likelihood of them seeking academic excellence.'

'No, Ancaster I don't.'

'Oh, I don't mean it as a criticism. I'm sure the school has many wonderful attributes. But one could hardly speak of it in the same breath as some of the best academies that I – and I'm sure you – have experienced in our careers.' He stood.

'Ancaster. One minute. You have your views and I doubt if anything I say will change them. But I will not have you denigrating the school to parents. Or to anyone.'

'I wouldn't say I did denigrate the school. I merely—'

'You sowed doubt in the minds of two parents. The parents of an exceptionally bright young woman who will, I'm sure, get a forty plus diploma. That is at least one definition of academic excellence.'

Ancaster looked at his watch again. 'Headmaster, may I? One hates to be late.'

'Yes. You must go. But please think about what I've said.'

'I shall.' Ancaster hurried out of the door. 'Good morning, headmaster.'

★

Richard discovered the Snivelys in the corridor outside Peter's office.

'Good morning,' he said with as much sincerity as he could muster. Mr Snively did not speak. His wife pointedly turned her back on him. The granny appeared not to have been invited. Richard just sighed.

Peter's door opened and Chiamaka came out, holding an armful of folders. 'Oh.' She turned back into the office. 'Your visitors are here,' she said.

Richard heard Peter's voice and Chiamaka indicated that they should enter. She stood aside and then pulled the door closed behind them.

★

'Richard? Shouting at parents and throwing them out of his room? That's not the Richard Cooper I've come to know.' Mick was hearing about the meeting with the Snivelys.

Valli was too. 'Solomon was in Grade Five in my first year. The family have been here for a long time. I remember the mother being a bit over-protective then. Actually, more than a bit.'

'And the boy? Solomon?'

'Devious. Always good at shifting the blame to someone else.'

Mick concurred. 'When Meena gets all the DP teachers together to see how the kids are doing, his name always comes up. Shifty.'

'Good,' said Peter. 'Well, not good, obviously, but I'm glad I took Richard's side this morning.'

'I understand it was quite a short meeting,' Mick grinned. He could usually be guaranteed to see the humour in most situations.

'Well, I didn't really know how to handle it. Their accusations didn't make any sense but there were no independent witnesses. All I could do was ask Mrs Snively to reiterate what she told me last night. And, boy, she did. She even implied that Richard had been swearing at them.'

'Ah, no,' said Mick. 'I have never heard Richard utter a curse word.'

'However much he may have wanted to this morning. But, in fact, he handled it brilliantly. Mrs Snively had her say – at some length, I may say. And I sort of listened and looked serious. Then, when she'd finished, I said, "Mr Cooper, would you like to say anything?" And Richard just looked calmly at each of them and said, "No, not really." They both sort of crumpled. I think they'd come expecting and maybe wanting a big argument. Richard just seemed to treat the whole thing with disdain.'

'The moral high ground.'

'Something like that. I made some probably inane comments about an unfortunate misunderstanding and how what we all had in common was wanting to help Solomon achieve his best and so on and so on. Then I thanked everyone for coming. I think I even said something like, "I'm glad we were able to sort that out" – God knows why – and then they all left.'

'Much ado about nothing.'

'Isn't that usually the case?'

As is often remarked, there is no simple, easy, or universally accepted definition of what people call an "international school". Whatever their name, many have an unmistakable national accent, usually American or British (for which read English), sometimes Canadian or Australian, and very occasionally something else. Schools overseas teaching in German, French, Swedish, Japanese and other languages will rarely call themselves international. They are usually delivering their national curriculum and will generally employ their own nationals as teachers.

But there do exist schools that sincerely aspire to being authentically international. Peter would have described ISN as such a school. When asked to justify his claim, he could employ some reasonably convincing arguments. There are so-called international schools, he might argue, where all the senior leadership team are of the same nationality, whereas at ISN he was British, Valli was American and Mick Irish. Ah, but, a devil's advocate might reply, you are all white, you all come from the Global North, and you are all native speakers of English. And Peter would have to agree. But, he might counter, the PYP coordinator, Modesty Molefe, was from Botswana, Larry Roper, the MYP coordinator, was Canadian and Meena Nair, the DP coordinator, was Indian. Six senior positions in the school and six nationalities. The devil's advocate might nod and further acknowledge that two out of the three coordinators were from the Global South and were not white but the English language still seemed to dominate. Well, it's the language of the school, Peter might point out. And, before the advocate could question why an authentic international school would teach only in English, Peter would hurriedly draw attention to the fact that out of the six senior positions he had listed (held by people of six nationalities, he would repeat), three were held by men and three by women. Are you saying that gender equality is an indication of internationalism, his interlocuter might ask. Well, Peter could reply with some confidence, let's just say that schools that genuinely aspire to being international must believe in diversity, equality and inclusion and must lead by example. So, "international" actually means Western and liberal, might be the next question. And, in his heart, Peter would have to agree.

Schools, such as ISN, and school leaders, such as Peter, might strive for an identity that was deserving of the signifier "international" but the evolution of international schools since perhaps the 1920s and certainly from the early 1960s did not happen in a vacuum. Schools have to start somewhere and, inevitably, they will borrow, and maybe adapt, that which already exists. Moreover, the growth and development of international schools was often encouraged, guided and to a not insignificant degree financed by the half dozen or so regional associations that emerged from the late 1950s under the watchful eye of the Office of Overseas Schools, itself a branch of the U.S. Department of State.

Acknowledging the influence of these regional associations but also quite simply as a result of the critical mass of schools that made no apologies for being American rather than international, the kind of schools that Peter had worked in and visited had come to adopt a fairly uniform vocabulary and set of practices. In England, Peter's school had Years; in Germany, Japan and Awanza, there were Grades. Accreditation was a concept unknown to Peter before he moved abroad but by the time he arrived in Ndwalowe, he understood it to be a given in all international schools (almost always, it turned out, by one of three American accrediting bodies). Graduation at the end of Grade Twelve (and sometimes at other watershed moments in students' careers) was another unexpected novelty. And in the international schools he came to know he discovered that counsellors were ubiquitous.

Quite what counsellors did or were for took Peter a little while to understand. Nor did his own experience with a counsellor get off to a great start. In Germany, a Grade Twelve student had tried Peter's patience by repeatedly missing deadlines and then making solemn promises that were never kept. Eventually, in exasperation, Peter had informed the student that she would not be welcome in any of his classes until she submitted all the outstanding assignments. He then steered her to the door and closed it

272

behind her. Evidently, she took her plight to the counsellor who then wrote Peter a brief message.

Peter, Claudia Werner came to see me just now. She is in tears and is obviously traumatised. I'm busy immediately after school but I'd like you and Claudia to come and see me at four o'clock so that I can decide how we should go forward from here. Bethany.

Peter was incensed. *'So that I can decide how we should go forward from here,'* he quoted to a colleague. 'Who the hell does she think she is? And "traumatised"? Children in Afghanistan seeing their parents killed before them are traumatised. You can't be traumatised because your teacher has told you to do your bloody homework!'

His colleague had nodded in sympathy. 'You'll find that most students who pass through Bethany's hands are deemed to be traumatised.'

Relations between Peter and Bethany were never better than strained. But he had more respect for the counsellor he found in Hamamatsu World School and by the time he arrived in Awanza he could see how, with discretion and sensitivity, counsellors could play a valuable part in any school's broad mission to ensure the wellbeing of children. (And, Peter came to learn, it was certainly not unknown for their teaching colleagues to turn to counsellors in moments of stress or anxiety.)

Peter had inherited two counsellors at ISN. There was some overlap but, mostly, Lee-Ann Gardner worked with primary students and Jean Coady with secondary. If he was honest, Peter didn't really know what they did all day but whenever he looked in on them, they appeared to be consoling, advising, encouraging or sometimes chiding. Not, of course, that he would open their door when the more serious and confidential conversations were taking place. At least, and thankfully, very few of the students they worked with were ever described as traumatised. He did worry sometimes that children were being referred to a counsellor a bit too freely and had suggested to Valli and Mick that teachers ought to be able to manage what seemed to him fairly minor behavioural issues. They tended to agree but weaning some teachers off the easy option of involving a counsellor proved difficult.

One thing that Jean Coady did that Peter thoroughly approved of was to establish and manage a team of peer counsellors. These were secondary students whom she had trained to spot when friends were struggling and were learning what best to say or do. It was an excellent way of encouraging empathy and compassion and Jean would say that over the course of a year she could see students visibly maturing. It also, of course, helped to nip in the bud unhappinesses that might otherwise escalate.

Her peer counsellors met once a week at lunchtime to share experiences and hear a few more words of wisdom from Jean herself. They brought their sandwiches and drinks and sat in an informal circle. Peter was sometimes invited to attend and rather enjoyed doing so. He did not join them in the circle but took a seat towards the back of the room from where he could follow the conversation but quickly be forgotten by the students. He learned a lot about these boys and girls as they recounted incidents where they had managed to do some good – and where they had been less successful. He learned about what was trending (as it were) in the school and, slightly guiltily, he heard some interesting comments about this or that teacher.

But the moment he knew he would always associate with Jean's peer counsellors came one lunchtime as he sat in the corner watching the latecomers arrive and Jean sorting a bunch of handouts she was going to be referring to later. He became aware that three boys sitting with their backs to him were arguing. It appeared to be good-natured but firmly held opinions were obviously being expressed. Had he not listened closely, he would have assumed the argument was about football or TV programme or some popular singer.

'But it wasn't,' he explained to Sheila that night. 'It took me a minute or two to realise what they were on about. And I couldn't believe it. These boys – who were all about fourteen or fifteen and sitting in a modest African city – were arguing about which of Frankfurt, London or Paris airports was the best. They were talking transfer times, shopping options and business class lounges, for God's sake! I'd barely been in a plane at their age.'

'Which London airport?' laughed Sheila.

'That's another thing! They were distinguishing between Heathrow and Gatwick! Zurich got a mention, Amsterdam. I was making Airfix models at their age. They're flying around the world in business class!'

'International schools …' said Sheila and laughed again.

'Many of these children want for nothing materially,' Peter had once been told by a veteran of the world of international schools. 'But many are deprived emotionally. Wealthy and successful parents with modern lifestyles. It's easier to buy the child a new iPhone than to read them a bedtime story.' And Peter had come to recognise the truth in these words. *Yes*, he thought. *I'm not sure it's such a bad thing to have these counsellors.*

★

School websites can be tricky things. They are there to both provide information and impress. But sometimes what they reveal is not what was intended.

Valli had once received an application from a teacher working in a prominent and well-regarded international school in Europe. She had taken a look at the school's website and, out of curiosity, had read the profiles of the director and principals to see if she knew anyone there. What she read surprised, irritated, and embarrassed her.

Mark graduated from UNC (go Tar Heels!) and has advanced degrees from LSU and Northwestern. He started his teaching career in Augusta, GA and before coming to Europe was a superintendent in Springfield, MO.

'I understand it,' she complained to Duke that evening, 'and you understand it because we are American. But what message is this sending to others? We are an American school run by Americans for Americans? But they aren't. They are the leading international school in a major European capital city!'

The website of the International School of Ndwalowe was not as flashy as some but did a reasonably honest job of describing the school as it really was. Much was made of the great diversity of nationalities to be found in the school community – a number that fluctuated almost monthly as students came and went but which was seldom less than fifty.

Under the 'Who we are' tab, a page was dedicated to diversity, liberally illustrated with photographs of smiling children of many ethnicities, approving endorsements in several languages, and a world map across which coloured pins of different sizes indicated which countries were represented at ISN. The page was bordered top and bottom, left and right, by rows and columns of national flags. A version of the page had been carried over from the old NIS website and Peter had paid it very little attention. It was colourful, attractive, and well-intentioned but, in Peter's opinion, a little superficial.

Peter's belief in the importance of diversity was unshakeable. When he spoke or wrote about his school he emphasised how it was able to bring together people and peoples of many different cultures who proved every day that they could coexist, working and playing together in an atmosphere of mutual trust and respect. He often employed the term 'international mindedness' and if, like many people, he struggled somewhat to define exactly what it meant, he nevertheless argued that aspiring to it was important, admirable and, indeed, essential.

He celebrated the school's diversity at every opportunity but he had some sympathy with those who argued that it was sometimes reduced to "flags, foods and fairs". Children wearing their national costume made for some pretty pictures in the yearbook and the sweet and savoury delights proudly served at the school's annual International Fayre were enjoyed by everyone, but wasn't all this, Peter worried, just perpetuating clichés and stereotypes? Japanese women wear kimonos. Scottish men wear kilts and eat haggis. The Belgians survive on a diet of waffles. A little knowledge is a dangerous thing, it is said. Sometimes Peter thought that "a little knowledge" was all that his students were being given.

Of course, as he was invariably reminded by Sheila and Valli whenever he aired such concerns, he was "a miserable old killjoy" (Sheila) and "full of it" (Valli). And Mick's attitude to the whole debate was made very clear when he came to school on St Patrick's Day wearing a green bowler hat, a false ginger beard, and trousers embroidered with about a million shamrocks.

(Upon seeing Mick, Peter had locked himself in his office but the students found it hilarious and a number – most without the slightest connection to Ireland – announced that next year they would do the same.)

But even Peter would have agreed that if you are going to do "flags, foods and fairs", you may as well do it right.

Which, it transpired, was why Mrs Maerua was sitting in his office this March morning.

'Mr Corby, I want to know why you have so little respect for Africa,' she began.

Peter was accustomed to conversations with Mrs Maerua including an accusation, though he was not always sure what he was being accused of or why.

'I assure you, Mrs Maerua, I have the greatest respect for Africa. I consider it a privilege to live here.'

She harrumphed. (A good harrumph or two could always be relied upon in conversations with Mrs Maerua.)

'Well, you wouldn't think so from the school's website.'

'Peter frowned. 'What is it about the website …?'

'Why are there so few African flags?'

'Flags?'

'Mr Corby, have you even looked at the school's website?'

'Mrs Maerua, of course I have looked at the website. In fact, I keep a close eye on it to ensure that it is accurate and up to date.'

'How many nationalities does the school currently have?'

'Em, I don't know exactly. It changes quite often but …'

'But it will be on the website, won't it? That will be up to date?'

'Well, it should be. I'd need to check when Mrs Habulenzi last updated the page but …'

'And they will all have flags?'

Peter began to see where this was going. 'You are referring to the page on our website that celebrates diversity?'

Another snort. 'Well, it celebrates something but I wouldn't call it diversity.'

They were sitting on the comfortable chairs at the far end of Peter's office but he now stood and went over to his desk. He opened the school website on his laptop and found the page in question.

'Fifty-one, Mrs Maerua. We have fifty-one nationalities represented in the school.'

'And are there fifty-one flags?'

Peter looked at the border of flags. His heart began to sink.

'Mr Corby. Can you put it up here?' She indicated the large screen mounted on the wall of his office. 'Then we can both see it.'

He did so, but already he could see the problem.

'Are you good at identifying flags, Mr Corby? Can you recognise them?'

'Yes, Mrs Maerua. As it happens, I think I can identify most flags.'

'Then kindly list all the African flags that you can see.'

He sighed. 'Mrs Maerua, I think I can see the problem. And … you are right.' The words rather stuck in his throat but she was right. She was absolutely right. The collection of flags appeared to make very little sense. And the more Peter looked, the more arbitrary it seemed. The flag of Denmark appeared three times, the Japanese flag twice. He saw the flags of small countries from which he was sure the school had no students (Bhutan?) but was unable to spot the flags of Canada, Italy or Australia. And Africa, much to Peter's tight-lipped annoyance was represented by just South Africa, Kenya, Nigeria, Botswana, Ethiopia and what he thought was either Ghana or Senegal. Even worse, he realised that there was no Awanzan flag. He wondered if Mrs Maerua had noticed that.

'And there isn't even the flag of Awanza, Mr Corby!'

'No,' he said. 'I can see that. I will, of course, have someone attend to it immediately. Thank you for bringing it to my attention.'

'There is, of course, the British flag.' She pointed to the screen.

'Sorry?'

'You're British, aren't you, Mr Corby? I see you made sure you had your own flag there.'

'In fact, Mrs Maerua, I had nothing to do with which flags were included and which not. Until today, I hadn't even looked closely.'

'So you say.'

Mrs Maerua was uniquely skilled at getting under Peter's skin. Insinuations were her stock-in-trade. She usually affected the demeanour of a skilled barrister wearily extracting a confession from a slippery but slightly dim defendant.

But experience had taught Peter not to take the bait so he simply said, 'It is important that the school respects all nationalities equally. I will take a personal interest in ensuring that our website does that.'

'Just the website?' Mrs Maerua's sharpest barbs were usually the briefest.

'No, obviously not just the website. And I am absolutely sure that if you spot any other areas that need attention I can count on you to tell me.'

'I would much prefer it,' she said sadly as she rose to her feet, 'if you and your staff would at least try to see that the school lived up to its stated values without parents having to point out its many and obvious failings.'

Peter also stood. 'I do not accept that our failings are many and obvious but no school is perfect and we will continue to try to achieve the high standards we all aspire to. Thank you again for coming.' He opened the office door and courteously invited her to pass through it.

'Many and obvious, Mr Corby. Many and obvious.'

'Goodbye, Mrs Maerua.'

Peter sat in Valli's office enjoying, as he always did, the sound of small children playing happily outside. He thought of his own office a couple of hundred metres away on the first floor of the administration block and with a view not of the school but of the neighbouring garden centre. Not for the first time, he wondered if he should relocate closer to where teaching and learning were happening. But, as always, he had to conclude that rather little of his day-to-day work had much to do with teaching and learning. He still liked to think of himself as a teacher but the reality was that he was the manager of an SME that just happened to be a school.

With that depressing thought in mind, he turned to Valli who was reading something on her laptop. 'Do you know what this is about?'

'Just that she wanted to see us both together. My guess is that she's going to tell us she's leaving.'

Peter nodded. 'It was right to give her an extension. Time to make up her mind. I'm still hoping she's staying.'

But Anna Street was not staying and that was indeed why she had asked for the meeting.

'Are you sure this is what you want to do?' Peter asked after Anna had announced her decision.

'No. I'm not sure at all. I've really enjoyed my time here. Well, most of it. But something has changed. It's not like it was.'

'That's understandable.'

'I hoped that I could, you know, move on. But there are just too many triggers. Perhaps I shouldn't have moved back to The Warren.'

'You tried,' said Valli. 'That was all you could do.'

'I'm really sorry to be creating a vacancy so late in the year.'

'Oh, don't worry about that. As you know, we've had a few unexpected vacancies this year,' Peter almost smiled. 'We managed then and we'll manage now. But what about you? Have you started looking for jobs?'

'Yes,' said Anna rather guiltily. 'Though I haven't actually applied for any yet. In fact, I wanted to ask you both a favour. If I'm not taking liberties.'

'Of course not. What can we do?'

Anna reached into the folder she had been carrying. 'Obviously, I'll tailor the letter to match each school but this is my template of an application. And this is my CV.'

'Résumé,' said Valli with a little sigh.

'CV,' said Peter. He took two copies of each. 'Sure. We'll take a look at them and see if we can give you some advice. Any idea where you are looking?'

'Actually,' said Anna, 'when I accepted the job here, my mind had been set on something in Europe. I never intended to come to Africa. Oh, I'm so glad I did but this time … this time it has to be Europe.'

'Okay, well there are plenty of great schools in Europe. But there are a few dodgy ones too. It's entirely up to you but once you have a school or two in mind … Well, Valli or I may know something about it …'

'Or know someone who works there,' interrupted Valli, 'so don't hesitate to ask our advice.'

Anna began to tear up. 'I was dreading this meeting. But you've both been so kind.'

'We want what's best for the school. But, of course, we also want what's best for everyone.' Peter looked at Valli who nodded in agreement.

'To be honest,' she said, 'helping people develop their careers is one of the most enjoyable parts of our job. And sometimes that means moving on. Have you thought of applying for PYP coordinator positions?'

Anna looked surprised. 'No, I hadn't.'

'Well, you should. You have more than enough experience and I think you'd be great.'

'All right. Thanks.' Anna looked slightly flattered.

'Anna, you know we are so sorry to see you go, especially in these circumstances. But we do understand. We'll help you any way we can.'

This time the tears did come. Anna stood. She gave Valli a tight hug and, after just a brief hesitation, hugged Peter too. 'Thank you. Thank you,' she mumbled. And then she left.

After the door closed behind Anna, Peter said, 'Bugger! I know we could see this coming but I still hate to lose her. She's an excellent teacher.'

'I know. But it is what it is. Now, we had better move quickly if we're going to replace her for next year.'

Peter was reading Anna's letter. 'I hope she gets something too. It's a bit late in the cycle.'

'Oh, she will. She's good. And we'll obviously give her great references.'

'Hmm,' said Peter. 'She's thirty-two, Thirty-three next month. I would have thought she was younger than that. She certainly looks younger.'

'How do you know?' Valli frowned.

'Her CV,' Peter waved it at Valli. 'Her date of birth.'

'She's put her date of birth on her résumé?'

'CV.'

'They're not the same thing. But, either way, you don't reveal your age.'

'Why not? I always do.'

'Well, I don't. And in the US, employers aren't allowed to ask your age.'

'Really? But once you start putting down qualifications, it won't be hard to work out how old you are. I got my first degree in 1994. That gives people a pretty good idea of how old I am.'

'Only if you mention the year.'

'Uh?'

'What matters is that you have a Bachelor's or Master's or whatever. It doesn't matter when you gained it.' Valli now looked at Anna's CV. 'Oh, no. She's included a photo.'

'So?'

'You don't. You just don't. Bluntly, it can disadvantage some candidates. If you're a person of colour or old or something.'

'Well, Anna's not going to have a problem. This is actually a lovely photo. She's very pretty.'

'So, you'd give her a job because she's pretty?'

'No, of course not. But it's not going to count against her.'

'But you can see how a photo might count against you?'

'No. Not really, You know very well, that I value diversity. That means gender, nationality, ethnicity, age … I need as much information as I can get when I'm interviewing. It could actually be to your advantage if you are Black or older or whatever.'

'She's put down that she's single, too,' Valli was shaking her head in disapproval.

'Good! We want to know if teachers have dependants or not. It's important.'

Valli gave up reading and tossed Anna's documents onto the coffee table. 'Well, it's up to her but I'm going to advise her to take some of this stuff out.'

'Won't it rather depend on what kind of school she's applying to? When I get CVs without a date of birth or indication of marital status and so on, it immediately puts me off. And I cannot be alone. I know I'm not.'

'But there will be schools that will be surprised and not want to get that information.'

'Well, more fool them. For once, I'm inclined to have sympathy with the "political correctness gone mad" argument. You're applying for a job and you won't reveal your age or gender or marital status? That's nonsense.'

Valli looked seriously annoyed.

'All right,' said Peter, 'maybe if you're applying for certain jobs. If you're going to sit on a checkout till in a supermarket, it probably doesn't matter if you're married or not. Or your gender or, within reason, your age.'

'That sounds a bit elitist.'

'You know what I mean. But if I interview someone called, say, Lesley and offer them a job, do I need to wait to I collect them at the airport to discover if they are male or female, twenty-five or sixty-five, with three kids or none?'

'You're being ridiculous.'

'Well, I'd need to know all this stuff sooner or later and, I will insist, before any job offer is made.'

There was an uncomfortable silence.

'Look,' said Peter. 'At least ask Anna to bear in mind that some schools may not want this information but others will expect it. Whatever your own opinions, you'd be doing her a favour.'

Valli gave Peter the briefest of nods.

★

Once a quarter, Richard Cooper went into his branch of the Ndwalowe Bank to transfer funds to a small portfolio of pension funds in the UK and elsewhere. He followed closely the markets and, just as importantly, exchange rates and he liked to think of himself as an astute investor. The sums involved were not huge and it was as much a hobby as a serious investment in the future but it amused him and, to be fair, his assets were steadily appreciating.

Humming contentedly, he stepped out of the bank onto Independence Avenue and strolled in the direction of his car. Some yards ahead, Richard noticed, a man in a suit waiting at traffic lights was studying him closely. He looked familiar. The lights changed but the man did not move. Then Richard recognised him. It was Mr Snively.

Richard hesitated then resumed his progress up the avenue. He had nothing to apologise for. As Richard approached him, Mr Snively turned and began walking towards him. Richard scowled and braced himself for an argument.

But Mr Snively wanted no confrontation. He held out his hand. 'Mr Cooper,' He almost whispered. 'I'm so sorry. My wife … It's better not to argue with her.'

Richard was momentarily flummoxed. Then he stepped forward and took Mr Snively's outstretched hand.

You poor man, thought Richard. *You poor man.*

★

April

They had slipped into a comfortable routine. Sundowners on the veranda where, at dusk, they watched the Thallomys tree rats descend to raid the birdfeeders. Insects attracted by the wall lights were greedily snapped up by geckos. (The species, Peter announced, was Turner's Tubercled Gecko. 'It's a gecko,' Sheila had stated with finality.) If they were lucky, they would hear nightjars calling. The haunting 'cow-wow' of the Freckled Nightjar was most common but now and again Peter tried to convince himself that he was hearing the call of a Fiery-necked Nightjar too. Sheila did not have an opinion on the subject.

But they both held, and were not shy to express, strong opinions about the large brown moths that settled on the rims of their drinks and brazenly poked their proboscis into the wine (preferably red).

'Bloody moths!' exclaimed Peter as he waved away from his glass not one but two. 'This is your fault, She. You're the so-called lepidopterist. You don't catch my birds doing this.'

Sheila quickly placed coasters on top of both glasses and laughed. 'They're persistent wee buggers,' she said. 'Oh, look, there's one in your salad.'

'And these are the ones …?'

'Yes. You be careful not to get it on your skin. It burns. You know what they're called in Afrikaans?'

'Not sundowner moth?'

'No, that's the English name. In Afrikaans it's a *pismot*. But I'm afraid I'm much too much of a lady to translate that for you.'

'That's okay. Even with my famously limited language skills I think I can work that one out.'

Peter took a sip of wine and quickly replaced the coaster. Somewhere what sounded like an owl hooted, though Peter had no idea what species it was. He sighed happily. Life was good. *Pismots* notwithstanding.

✷

Cassie Farmer appeared in Peter's doorway.

'Hello. What's up?' he asked.

'I just sent you something. I thought you'd want to see it.'

Peter refreshed his emails. 'It's from Mrs Furaha,' Cassie explained. 'She told me to send it to all parents.'

But Peter wasn't really listening. He was reading the brief document with increasing incredulity and irritation.

'*The PTA plays a crucial role in the efficient running of the school*. No, it doesn't! What's she on about?'

He read on. '*A key responsibility of the PTA is assisting the management in the drafting of policies*. What? *Remember that the PTA is YOUR voice. Assert your democratic right*. Democratic right? The school isn't a democracy. This is outrageous.'

'They are inviting all parents to a meeting ...'

'I see that. *... where the PTA's new constitution will be introduced*. Oh, really? I don't think so.'

'So, I shouldn't send it out?'

'No! Certainly not. And please forward me Mrs Furaha's email. I'm going to write to her.'

Cassie hurriedly returned to the reception.

✷

From: pcorby@isn.edu.wz
To: Nyotafuraha1@awanzacom.wz
Subject: PTA communication to parents
Dear Mrs Furaha
I have just been shown the text of a message I'm told you wish to have sent to all parents. I am writing to inform you that I cannot approve this. The text contains a number of inaccuracies.

I am also surprised to learn that a revised PTA constitution has apparently been approved. Please allow me to draw your attention to Clause 4.4.1 of the current and still valid constitution.

4.4.1 All major decisions within the PTA must be taken in consultation with the Educational Director. Major decisions are defined as:
i The disbursement of large funds;
ii The dissolution of the PTA;
iii Amendments to the PTA constitution.

I am aware that there has been some discussion about amending the current constitution but I have certainly not been included in such conversations.

For what it's worth, I am of the opinion that the current constitution is in need of revision. But the process needs to happen in accordance with the process set out on page six of the current version.

I should be very happy to meet with you and the other members of the Executive Committee to discuss this.

Sincerely

Peter Corby

★

Peter had wasted no time apprising Carola of his opinion of Colby Wittering.

'I've met him. He's odious.'

'Odious?'

'Er, objectionable. Rude. Obnoxious. He has a very low opinion of the school. And he thinks teachers are paid far too much. He probably thinks I am as well. Ask Valli and Duke. They met him too.'

'Where was this?'

'I'm sorry to say at my house. Sheila knows his wife. We had a dinner party. It didn't go well.'

'But you saw the reaction of the other board members when Lazarett introduced him. They seemed quite enthusiastic.'

'Some of them, maybe. But Clyde made a good point. We're going to have elections and, I assume, nominations at the AGM in June. It's normal for boards to have a committee to manage that kind of thing.'

'A nominations committee, did he call it?'

'It's called different things in different places but yes. Let's establish one and let it solicit nominations and vet candidates. Colby Wittering can put his name forward if he wants. It can all wait till June.'

But it couldn't wait till June.

★

From: Nyotafuraha1@awanzacom.wz
To: pcorby@isn.edu.wz
Cc: Crystalmooreinawanza@gmail.com; kim@rankinfamily.wz;
kaminskim72@gmail.wz
Subject: Re: PTA communication to parents
Dear Mr Corby
Your email of yesterday refers.

The Executive Committee of the ISN PTA acknowledges your offer to meet regarding the constitution of the said association. It further welcomes your agreement that the previous version was no longer fit for purpose.

As a courtesy, the Executive Committee will be happy to share a copy of the new constitution with you. Any observations you may have will, of course, be considered but please note that the precise wording of the constitution will be a matter for the Executive Committee only and its decision will be final.

The Executive Committee would further ask you to reconsider your puzzling decision not to distribute the message that was recently submitted to the school office as we are not aware of any "inaccuracies".

With kind regards
N. Furaha
PTA Vice-Chair

★

The accident could have been much worse. As Peter was pulling out of the school drive after a long, late and tedious finance committee meeting, an old Toyota Corolla travelling at speed and with no lights suddenly appeared through the windscreen wipers. Had Peter stamped on the brakes even a second later, the car would have smashed into him. As it was, it scraped alarmingly down the passenger side of the Beast and was dragged to the left and onto what was, thankfully, bare ground. Peter uttered an oath, yanked on the handbrake, and jumped out into the rain.

A young man was awkwardly climbing out of the Corolla. There appeared to be no other passengers.

'Are you all right? Do you speak English?' Peter made to grab the young man who looked like he was going to faint.

'Yeah. I'm okay. Thanks.' The man made eye contact with Peter and then looked at Peter's car. 'Sorry.'

As is always the case in Africa, a small crowd was immediately gathering. They appeared to be no more than curious but Peter was glad to see that one of the school security guards had run over to him.

'It's Jacob, isn't it?'

'Yes, Sir.'

'Can you call Mohammed Bukhari and tell him what happened? I'd like him to come, if he can.'

'Yes, Sir.' He dialled a number.

Peter turned back to the other driver. He was sitting on a tree stump and looking very pale. Peter could feel his own legs getting a bit wobbly too. He joined the other man on the stump.

'You okay? Really?'

'Yes, Sir. I'm not injured.'

'Don't call me Sir. I'm Peter.' He held out his hand.

The young man took it. 'Lucky.'

'Sorry?'

'My name. It's Lucky.'

In spite of the situation Peter had to let out a laugh. 'Well,' he indicated the two cars, 'I guess we've both been lucky.'

Jacob approached Peter. 'I'm calling Mr Bukhari, Sir, but there's no answer.'

Peter swore again. 'Okay. Keep trying, will you?' He turned to Lucky. 'Let's get out of the rain. My phone's in my car anyway.'

The passenger door wouldn't open so Lucky sat in the back behind Peter while he made his call. 'Saskia? Sorry to call so late. Look, I'm all right but there's been an accident …'

Watching the small crowd disappear back wherever they had come from, Peter briefly explained the situation to Saskia. Once reassured that Peter really was unharmed, she offered what advice she could.

'You really need to have the traffic police there. But after nine and in the rain … Well, I wouldn't hold your breath.'

'I don't have that number. Could you …'

'Of course. Give me a couple of minutes.'

They sat in the dark and the rain. Even Jacob had now disappeared. His heart was still thumping but Peter felt strangely calm. It was almost as if he had known that something like this would happen and he was almost glad to have got it out of the way. Not, of course, that something similar – or worse – couldn't happen again.

'Water?'

He passed a bottle back to Lucky who took it gratefully. Peter's phone rang.

'I called Traffic. As I suspected, they said they'd send someone in the morning. Is your car drivable?'

'Good point. I don't know. But I think so. His too, from the look of it. There's a lot of torn and bent metal but I think we can both drive.'

'And you're sure no one is injured?'

Peter looked at the rough ground where Lucky's Corolla was now sitting. By day, the area was occupied by vendors cooking and selling street food. Had the accident happened earlier, some of them would now be under Lucky's car.

'Yes. No one. A bit shocked. Shaken. But uninjured.'

'All right. Then call me if you need anything else and get home safely. I'll see you in the morning.'

'Thanks, Saskia. I appreciate it.'

He leaned back over his seat. 'Did you hear that, Lucky? The police will come tomorrow. Can you be here? Quite early I'm guessing. Oh, I'm the principal here. At this school. This is where we'll meet.'

Lucky looked a bit forlornly at his car. 'You're the principal?'

Peter tentatively started the engine. All seemed in order. 'Can your car go, Lucky?'

Lucky's car started but the steering seemed as wobbly as Peter's legs.

Peter leaned in through Lucky's side window. 'Look, I think we can get it onto the school grounds behind the gate. It'll be safe there.' Jacob had reappeared. He and Peter guided Lucky as he crabbed and edged the car off the waste ground and down the school drive. A horrible grinding noise came from somewhere but the car was moving.

'Don't worry about getting it to the car park,' Peter said to Jacob. 'Just inside the main gate will do. And keep an eye on it.'

Lucky emerged from his car for the second time. If anything, he looked still more distressed.

'You're sure you're okay?' asked Peter, genuinely concerned for the young man's state.

'I'm fine. But I have no money …'

'Ah,' said Peter. 'Taxi money. Of course.' He pulled out a small wad of notes. 'Where do you live? Is it far?'

'Not far. No.'

'A hundred?' said Peter. 'More? You need to get back here tomorrow morning.'

'A hundred and fifty.' Lucky seemed quite sure.

Peter gave him the money. There was no thank you.

'Oh, I need your number,' said Peter. 'You have a phone?'

The two men exchanged numbers. 'Okay,' said Peter. 'See you tomorrow. About eight, I suggest.'

Lucky nodded. *Strange*, thought Peter. *I should be bollocking him for driving at night in the rain with no lights but I almost feel sorry for him. My car belongs to the school. We have full insurance. Ultimately, it's no big deal. But I wonder what his circumstances are.*

Peter left Lucky talking in Kiwanza to Jacob and returned to the Patrol. He began to rehearse what he would say to Sheila.

★

Seeing the damage to his car in daylight made Peter still more grateful that he and Lucky had both walked away from what could have been a very serious accident. And seeing Lucky's Corolla looking more abandoned than parked just inside the school gate was another sobering reminder of the previous night's drama.

Mohammed Bukhari, the school's transport manager, was waiting for Peter. The two men walked around the Patrol, sucking air through their teeth, tutting, and fingering some of the torn metal.

'You were lucky,' said Mohammed.

'You've looked at the Corolla?' Peter asked.

'Mmm. Your car can be repaired but I think that one's a write-off. Does he have insurance?'

'I've no idea.'

Lucky, of course, did not have any insurance. He did at least have a driving licence although Sergeant Mposi had frowned and given Lucky a stern look when he had examined it. Not for the first time in Awanza Peter felt there were things going on of which he had no understanding.

They were sitting in the conference room, Peter, Mohammed and Saskia on one side of the long table and Sergeant Mposi and Lucky on the other. The policeman was tall, smartly dressed in the uniform of the Ndwalowe City Police and with a rather stern demeanour. Lucky, slouched beside him, looked uncomfortable and somewhat overwhelmed, though whether it was because of the presence of the sergeant (with whom Lucky had exchanged a few quiet words in Kiwanza) or the imposing surroundings of the conference room Peter could not tell.

'Both cars will need to be examined by an officer from the Traffic Directorate.' Sergeant Mposi was making notes on a large pad of yellow paper. 'And I will need you both to show me exactly where the offence took place and make statements.'

Offence? Thought Peter. *Offence?*

'Your car,' Sergeant Mposi looked at Peter, 'can be driven to the depot. The other will have to be examined here. I shall make arrangements.'

'When can we get the report?' asked Peter.

'Report?'

'The report we need from you to take to our insurance.'

'There will be no report.' Sergeant Mposi looked challengingly at Peter. To his right, Peter could hear Mohammed sigh deeply.

'But we need the report from the police in order to claim.' Saskia was evidently trying to sound calmer than she probably felt.

Ignoring Saskia, Sergeant Mposi addressed Peter. 'You moved your vehicle from the scene of an accident. That is an offence.'

Lucky had also moved his vehicle but Sergeant Mposi didn't seem to be worrying about that. Of course, nor did Lucky have any insurance to claim.

'If that is so,' Peter spoke slowly, trying to choose his words with care, 'then, of course, that must be dealt with. But surely that is a separate issue. The accident itself must still be documented.'

'Will your insurance pay for his car?' The sergeant indicated Lucky who looked rather startled.

Peter looked at Mohammed who frowned. 'I don't know. That may depend on whose fault the accident was. Won't it?'

'Oh, it was your fault.' Sergeant Mposi made some more notes on his pad.

'What? You haven't even seen where it happened!'

'Do you want a report? The report will state that it was your fault.'

There was another sigh from Mohammed. He laid his hand on Peter's arm. 'Peter, can I have a word with the sergeant alone, please?'

'No.' It was suddenly clear to Peter where this was heading. 'Mohammed, do you know where the Traffic Directorate depot is?'

Mohammed looked very unhappy but nodded.

'Then we will go there right now. In my car. Perhaps someone there will do their job.'

'Peter …' cautioned Saskia.

Peter stood. Lucky, startled, also jumped to his feet.

'Sergeant Mposi, are you going to give us a report or not?'

The sergeant now looked a little less cocksure. He did not answer directly. 'I think you must now show me where the accident happened.'

'And then?'

The sergeant looked around the room as if he hadn't heard Peter's question. 'We will go now,' he said and stood.

✱

'He was trying to find a way to stay in the game.' Peter handed Sheila a glass of wine and took a seat beside her on the veranda. 'He knows that there's money in this if he can play his cards right.'

'So you showed him where the accident happened?'

'At first he said that Saskia and I didn't need to come. Mohammed could make my statement for me.'

'What?'

'I know. Anyway, I insisted. He took only a cursory look at the site of the accident and then we moved to the shade of the guard house to make our statements. He didn't seem much interested in Lucky's details but he asked me all kinds of questions.'

'You have money. I assume Mr Lucky doesn't.'

'Indeed. Oh, and the sergeant was not at all happy when he asked me for my religion. "Why none?" he demanded. I think in the end he wrote Christian. And then we all piled into my car and drove to the depot. Well, Saskia went back to her office but the rest of us went.'

'That must have been a jolly drive.'

'Stoney silence. And then when we got there, Sergeant Mposi told us to wait and disappeared into the building. So we waited. And waited. And waited. I was just about to go and complain to someone when he reappeared. The officer who inspects vehicles was sadly not available. We need to take the car back tomorrow.'

'There's only one officer for that kind of thing?'

'Of course not. It was just another ploy. Anyway, I don't need to go. Mohammed will take it. He's given me one of the school Land Rovers to use till the Patrol's fixed.'

'And will there be a report?'

Peter shrugged. 'Eventually, there will have to be. But I wonder how many hoops Sergeant Mposi will make us jump through first.'

★

From: pcorby@isn.edu.wz
To: Nyotafuraha1@awanzacom.wz
Cc: Crystalmooreinawanza@gmail.com; kim@rankinfamily.wz;
kaminskim72@gmail.wz
Subject: Re: PTA communication to parents
Dear Mrs Furaha
Thank you for your reply.

You suggest you are unaware of what I termed 'inaccuracies' in the message you wish to be sent to all parents. Please allow me to quote from the draft you submitted.

"A key responsibility of the PTA is assisting the management in the drafting of policies."

That is not the case and has never been the case. There are two classes of policy within the school.

<u>School policies</u> are decided by the administration. Examples would be that Primary School children must wear hats outside or that children may not play on the jungle gym without adult supervision.

Examples of <u>Board policies</u> would include maximum class size, admissions criteria, and an inclusive recruitment policy.

In neither case should the PTA be expected to be consulted. That has certainly not been the school's practice hitherto.

To send out your message as it is drafted would be to spread misinformation. I am sure you would not wish the school to do that.

Returning to the revision of the PTA constitution, you refer to the "previous version". I'm afraid I was not here in 2014 when the constitution was last updated; that would be the "previous version". What I do have before me is the <u>current</u> version of the constitution which will remain in force until (and if) a revised version is accepted by two-thirds of PTA members present and voting at a special meeting convened for said purpose. Allow me to quote from page 6 of the constitution.

9.2.2 The constitution can be amended by a special meeting called for that purpose provided that two weeks written notice must be given of any proposed changes and that these are agreed to by 2/3 of the present and voting members in good standing.

No such meeting has been held and the message you wish to be sent to all parents does not include details of any proposed changes.

You will understand, therefore, that the message is, in effect, unconstitutional.

I reiterate my offer to meet with the Executive Committee of the PTA to discuss how we move forward from here.

Sincerely,

Peter Corby

*

Most board decisions are taken in full board meetings. But it is not unknown for decisions to be taken after video conversations or impromptu and informal meetings and then be formally minuted at the next board meeting. Such exchanges had resulted in the board agreeing to establish a nominations committee to be chaired by Clyde Arthurs. It would seek nominations to the board that would be decided by elections at the Annual General Meeting in June. But Lazarett had continued to promote the candidacy of Colby Wittering and no members had felt strongly enough to argue. It was therefore agreed that on an evening in the near future all voting board members who were able to attend would meet Colby at the Lowana Lodge for a get-to-know-you with a view to deciding if he should be invited to join the board. Peter wasn't sure if he wanted to be there or not. Well, he certainly did want to but, when Carola tactfully raised the question, he acknowledged that his presence may not have been either appropriate or constructive. In any case, only voting members were invited so Peter had no option but to stay away and wait for either white or black smoke to be signalled.

Rather than sit at home and stew (and no doubt drink too much wine) he suggested to Sheila that they ate out at Alfredo's (where he could stew and drink too much wine).

*

Peter listened to Mohammed's report with exasperation. For two days running, Mohammed had taken the Patrol to the depot and on each day he had been left to hang around the dusty car park, kicking his heels and waiting for someone to show any interest in him. Various excuses had been made – when anyone bothered to tell him anything, that is – but no one expected Mohammed to believe them and, of course, he didn't. Sergeant Mposi had been glimpsed a couple of times but he had only spoken to Mohammed once.

'He said he thinks Lucky's car can be repaired,' Mohammed informed Peter with a sceptical frown. 'But it will take a while for the insurance to pay up so he was suggesting that we – I suppose he means you – just give Lucky an amount of money so he can get it fixed.'

'Hah. And how much of that wad of money will end up in Sergeant Mposi's back pocket?'

Mohammed nodded unhappily. 'I think he knew there was no chance. He was just sort of trying it on. Nothing to lose, I suppose.'

'But he's got a bloody cheek. Of course it will take for ever for the insurance if he doesn't give us the report. Anyway, what is happening to Lucky's car? It's still sitting there looking terrible.'

'I'll move it to the workshop. I'll get it towed, if necessary.'

'Okay, thanks. Hasn't Lucky been in touch?'

'No. Nothing.'

'And have the police even been to look at it yet?'

Mohammed shook his head.

'I'm not going to pay a bribe, Mohammed. I won't do it.' Mohammed just nodded. But he kept his thoughts to himself.

Violet Sindima always liked to arrive at any given appointment not only on time but, as far as possible, seriously early. It was a way, she thought, of showing respect. Equally, she was sadly and uncomfortably aware of the opinions of many (white) foreigners regarding the time-keeping habits of Africans. How often had she bit her lip and forced a smile as Europeans or Americans made allegedly humorous comments about 'African time' or 'Awanzan time'? She was determined that such accusations could not be levelled at her.

Nonetheless, however early she thought she would be, she found in the Members' Room of the Lowana Lodge a tall, sharply dressed man drinking what appeared to be a cocktail and surveying the largely empty room around him.

'Mr Wittering?' Violet approached him with some confidence but also ready to be disabused.

'The very same,' he boomed. 'And you are?'

'Violet Sindima. I'm a member of the board. The board of the International School of Ndwalowe.' She added, probably unnecessarily.

'As indeed will I shortly be! What can I get you to drink?'

'Oh, just a bitter lemon,' said Violet, 'I'm driving.'

'Well, so am I,' said Colby. 'Let me put something a bit stronger into that for you.'

Violet's objections were drowned out by the arrival of Lazarett Snyman. 'Mr Wittering, I'm so glad you are here. Thank you so much for coming.'

The two men shook hands about as forcefully (and painfully?) as Violet had ever witnessed but she was then relieved that the drink that was delivered to her by a charming waiter all in white contained no alcohol.

Quite quickly, the other members arrived, introduced themselves and ordered drinks, alcoholic or otherwise. Only Prosper Luhanga appeared to have forgotten the date.

They sat in an alcove beneath equestrian prints and medieval maps of something that almost resembled a version of Africa.

'Mr Wittering,' began Carola, 'as I'm sure you know, the current board,' she waved at her colleagues sitting around a circular table, 'assumed the responsibility of governing the school about two years ago when the previous school—'

'Went bankrupt.' Colby interrupted.

'Indeed. And all, well, most of that board resigned.'

'How could that happen? I mean, bankruptcy doesn't come out of the blue. Where were the controls?'

'As Hemmingway said, it comes gradually and then suddenly,' said Grant with a grin.

'Bullshit!'

If Colby had wanted to gain the attention of his audience, he succeeded.

'Mr Wittering?' Carola could feel her control of the occasion quickly slip away from her.

'The board. The previous board, they failed in their responsibilities. My wife and I had just arrived in Awanza. I managed to attend one AGM just a few weeks after I took up my position here but it was obvious that the educational director had the board in his pocket. There were a few half-hearted questions from the floor about the school's cash-flow situation but the board just shut them down and the board chair – not you, Mrs Lasser, of course – pushed on like there was no problem.'

'Did you attend last year's AGM, Mr Wittering?' Clyde asked.

'Colby, please. Yes, I did and I thought it was pretty amateurish.'

'Oh?'

'Had anyone actually prepared for the AGM? There were questions from the floor that no one could answer. More than once you had to ask the educational director. That's never a good look. The board runs the school, not Peter Corby.'

'Actually …' Catherine began to argue but Colby cut her off.

'And that evening is a metaphor for the whole school. When the board is weak, the educational director can get away with whatever he wants. We saw that with Corby's predecessor. What was his name?'

'John Conway,' someone said.

'Yes, him. He is the one who bankrupted the school. Where was the board? Where was the oversight?'

Grant was starting to get annoyed. 'We can assure you, Mr Wittering—'

'Colby.'

'Colby, this board is well aware of its responsibilities and that includes, of course, holding the director accountable. Last year we spent a significant amount of money conducting a three-sixty evaluation of Peter Corby.'

'I remember. I completed the parental questionnaire – which, I might say looked like it had been put together by someone doing it for the first time. If you're going to spend all that money, at least get a professional.'

Grant made to protest but Colby continued.

'And what ever happened to that so-called evaluation? I never saw the results.'

'We didn't share the results with the community. That was never—'

'So it was just hushed up? Can I see a copy now? Or when I join the board?'

'It wasn't hushed up at all!' Trixi could no longer contain herself.

'I'm sorry,' said Colby. 'I didn't catch your name.'

'Trixi. Trixi Villiers.'

'Ah, yes. You're the teacher, aren't you?' Colby looked at Carola and shook his head. 'This isn't right. It's a conflict of interest.'

'What is?'

'You can't have a teacher on the board. This isn't Germany. There's no worker participation here. Or, there shouldn't be.' He turned back to Trixi. 'I'm sorry but you really shouldn't be here.'

'Actually,' said Violet, clearly agitated, 'I very much value Trixi's contribution to board discussions. I think she brings a valuable and unique perspective.'

'Thank you. Violet,' said Trixi. 'And if being a teacher on the board is a conflict of interest, why is it not a conflict of interest to be a parent on the board?'

'Oh, that's facile. The parents are the customers. The stockholders, if you will. This is their school. Not the teachers'.'

'But the teachers have a stake in the school too. It's their livelihood.' Even Clyde, normally very composed, now had a tremor in his voice.

'Teachers are employees. Period. They are not a constituency, they are a commodity. And, as I understand it, in this school quite an expensive one. When did the board last review salaries?'

'We look at salaries every year when we prepare the annual budget. Our financial situation is steadily improving but it was felt that a rise could not be justified this year.'

'A rise? Are you joking? When I'm on the board we are going to conduct a thorough review of what the correct market price is for teachers in a school like this. It will be a simple matter to collect data from other schools and other comparable businesses. My impression is that the school is paying way over the odds. I think you'll be surprised at the savings we can make.'

Lazarett had said nothing until now but he nodded at Colby and muttered, 'Exactly. Good.'

'And how much do you pay Peter Corby?'

'That's … confidential,' said Carola.

'Well, I'll take a look once I'm on the board. My guess is you're not paying enough. Well, enough for someone like Corby, probably, but if you want to attract the best talent, you have to compensate them accordingly. Does he get an annual bonus? Linked to performance?'

'Mr Wittering—'

'Colby.'

'Mr Wittering,' Carola repeated, 'I don't wish to be rude but I think my colleagues and I have heard as much as we need. We are grateful for your time but I wonder if you would now leave us to confer.'

'Oh.' Colby Wittering was not used to being dismissed. 'Shall I … shall I wait?' He gestured towards the bar.

'No, there's no need. We will certainly be in touch shortly. Thank you again.' Carola rose and held out her hand. Colby stood and took her hand.

'Thank you all,' he looked around the table. 'I'm looking forward to working with you. I think we'll be a great team.'

No one spoke.

★

Peter was surprised to receive a phone call from Mohammed. He wasn't sure why but things seemed to be happening. Since Peter frequently had no idea why things did or didn't happen in Awanza he was quite pleased to hear than an African could be just as confused. An hour later Mohammed called again with the excellent news that an officer had appeared, inspected the Patrol, taken a statement from Mohammed, and filled in a lengthy form.

'He says we'll have the report next week.'

'Really? Wow. I don't know what's changed but that's excellent. Well done!'

Peter hung up and set off down the corridor to tell Saskia the good news. He met her coming in the other direction.

'Saskia, good news!'

'You think so?'

'What?'

'I was just coming to see you.' She handed Peter an official-looking envelope. 'This was just delivered by hand.'

Peter started opening it but Saskia couldn't wait. 'You must appear at the Central Police Station at eight am on Monday.'

'What? Why?'

'Because you've been charged.'

'With what?'

'Reckless driving.'

'What? I haven't been charged. Not with reckless driving or anything.'

'It says there you have,' Saskia pointed to a short sentence in bold letters. Peter also saw the name of Sergeant Mposi as the "Arresting Officer".

'Arrested? Charged? I haven't been arrested or charged. This is a farce! It was an accident. It wasn't even my fault.'

Saskia looked sympathetic. 'What was your good news?'

'Oh, Mohammed's on his way back to school. Someone turned up at last and inspected the car and we'll have a report next week.'

Saskia paused then smiled. 'Clever.'

'Uh?'

'You think it's a coincidence? Suddenly they inspect the car and at the same time you are charged with reckless driving?'

The penny dropped. 'Uh-oh. If they can't get me one way, they will another.'

''Fraid so.'

Peter sighed. 'Do I need a lawyer?'

'Probably not. But someone should go with you. Mohammed, I suppose.'

'Oh well. Another one for the book.'

'What book?'

'The book I'm going to write. Though I may wait until I'm safely retired.'

✱

'So what happens on Monday?' Sheila seemed to be almost enjoying Peter's nightly updates.

'I have no idea. Is this what's called an arraignment?'

'I'm not sure. Isn't that when you are charged?'

'But the letter says I've already been charged. Which is, of course, nonsense. Anyway, Mohammed and I are off to the Central Police Station first thing on Monday.'

'How exciting!'

'Sheila. I'm being arrested. Or I've been arrested. Who knows? I might be chucked in a cell. You could be shoving meals for me through the window bars by this time next week.'

'Oh, it's hardly *Midnight Express*. They don't even want to lock you up. They just want to squeeze a few dollars out of you.'

'I'm glad you think so. Please remember our short time together with affection. I'm going to write my will.'

✱

'Lazarett was, as you can imagine, peeved.' Trixi was reporting back to Peter.

'Peeved? I'm sure there are better words than that!' They both laughed.

'He tried to give us a long lecture about how we were missing a great opportunity but he was wasting his time. It was six against one.'

'No abstentions?'

'Oh, no! No one had any doubts. Wittering would have been a disaster on the board. No one else would have been allowed to have an opinion. Or even speak.'

'Imagine what Ernesto would have made of him!'

'I only wish Ernesto had been there. There would have been fireworks.'

'So, no pay cut for you?'

'Or pay rise for you! Or for whoever comes after you.'

'He actually said that?'

'Oh, yes. You're probably being paid too much but we ought to be paying a lot more to ensure that we get the best.'

'Logic, for want of a better word, that seems to apply at senior level but not on the shop floor.'

'He does work for McKinsey.'

'I continue to wonder how much Colby makes. You know that Valli asked him but he wouldn't reply?'

'She told me about the dinner party,' said Trixi. 'I think the word she used was 'blowhard.' Having seen him at the Lowana, I'd say that's pretty accurate.'

'Has he been informed yet?'

'If not already then imminently. Carola said she'd write to him.'

'Oh, well. Then he and Lazarett can go out for a beer and drown their sorrows. Looks like we dodged that bullet.'

Peter raised his hand for a high five. Trixi was happy to oblige.

★

From: Crystalmooreinawanza@gmail.com
To: pcorby@isn.edu.wz
Cc: Nyotafuraha1@awanzacom.wz; kim@rankinfamily.wz;
kaminskim72@gmail.wz
Subject: Obstruction of legitimate PTA business
Dear Mr Corby

On behalf of the Executive Committee of the PTA, and with its full support, I am writing to register in the strongest possible terms our frustration that you continue to obstruct our attempts to modernise what I think you agree is an outdated association.

We have spent many hours attempting to redefine the PTA's role within the school. The PTA can be and should be a critical voice giving parents a forum through which to contribute to a continuous program of school improvement. No one knows the strengths and weaknesses of the school better than the parents whose children attend ISN every day. It is outrageous and unacceptable that you continue to raise legalistic and petty objections that are simply designed to delay and impede the sensible reforms we are proposing.

Please be informed that I shall be requesting an urgent meeting with the Chair of the ISN Board of Directors to register the PTA's intense frustration.

I am very sorry to have to take this action but I'm afraid you leave us no option.

Yours
Crystal Moore
Chair of the ISN PTA

★

Peter and Mohammed were standing in a small ground floor office that was badly in need of renovation. Dark, grubby marks surrounded the light switch. Two of the windowpanes were cracked. A single bare bulb hung from the ceiling. Enormous heaps of dog-eared manila folders leaned against walls, many of them spilling their contents onto the floor. A faded poster exhorting citizens to report corruption was tacked to a wall.

Since being ushered into the room, they had not been offered seats, possibly because there weren't any. Before them were two aged, battered and unmatching desks behind each of which sat an officer in uniform. One was reading *The New Awanzan*. The other, a sergeant, was busy with his phone. Neither gave their visitors the slightest attention.

Peter was itching to say something (probably something unwise) but sensed it would be better to follow Mohammed's lead and say nothing. It was, Peter reflected, a bit like the time he, then a spotty teenager, had been sent to the headmaster's office for some infraction or other – having the top button of his shirt undone or some such. Except, of course, the headmaster's study had looked nothing like this.

The newspaper man chuckled and attempted to interest the sergeant in something he had just read. Without looking up from his phone, the sergeant just grunted. Perhaps looking for a more responsive audience, the officer folded his paper, stood, stretched, and pushed his way past Peter and Mohammed and out of the office.

'You have been charged with reckless driving?' The sergeant was still looking at his phone but appeared to be addressing Peter.

'Sorry?'

The sergeant put his phone down and pulled towards him a manila folder. 'Mr Peter Corby?'

Peter nodded.

'Then you have been charged with reckless driving.'

'Not that I know of. When?'

The sergeant scowled. Mohammed quietly whispered to Peter, 'it's better if you just agree. Just say yes.'

Peter shrugged but that seemed good enough for the sergeant.

'Then you must appear at the Ndonboli Magistrates Court this afternoon. Do you know where it is?'

Peter looked at Mohammed, who nodded.

'And I need you to surrender your driving licence.'

Very reluctantly, Peter pulled out his wallet. 'Can I have a receipt?'

'Why?'

'Why? Because I want to see it again.'

The sergeant's face clouded. 'Of course you'll see it again. After the prosecution. And no, we don't give receipts.' He snatched the licence from Peter and made a note in the manila file. 'One o'clock. You need to be there at one. You can go now.' He did not look up.

Peter glanced at Mohammed who nodded gently and began pushing Peter towards the door.

★

Ndonboli Magistrates Court turned out to be a horseshoe of single-storey buildings around a small courtyard of bare earth. Mohammed and

Peter joined the crowd of people milling about fairly aimlessly and then Lucky's smiling face appeared at Peter's side.

'Oh, hello. Are you being prosecuted too?' Peter asked.

'No, no,' said Lucky, 'I'm a witness.'

Peter just sighed. 'Of course you are.'

Lucky and Mohammed made idle small talk while Peter took a look around. Two small courtrooms occupied one wing. Each had a raised judge's bench at the back, tables for the clerks before the bench, a witness stand, and rows of pews for those awaiting justice. One court was empty but in the other a judge was sitting in session wearily working his way through what looked like a long list of misdemeanours. As Peter watched through the open door and through the windows that had bars but no glass, a succession of cowed and round-shouldered defendants rose, muttered a few words in response to the judge's brisk questioning and received their sentence with a deferential nod of the head. A constant stream of police officers entered and left, some carrying papers, most just chatting to each other or buying newspapers or packets of nuts from the urchins who sold them in the courtyard. Outside, people stood or sat everywhere. Rows of benches, sheltered from the hot sun by a corrugated-iron roof, were one option but most squatted in the shade of the buildings or wandered to and fro, talking, laughing, arguing and occasionally making what seemed not very hopeful enquiries of the police who in turn dismissed them with obvious lack of interest. No one seemed to know what was happening but all had long ago acquired the Awanzan habit of waiting and no one seemed surprised or particularly agitated. Waiting in Awanza is not a question of patience or stoicism. It is to assume a state of passivity. I am here because I am here. I may as well be here as anywhere else. Something may happen here or it may not. Life will go on in any case. There is nothing I need to do. Nothing I want to do. Nothing I can do.

As the only white face among hundreds, Peter drew a few mildly curious stares but, in truth, he was ignored by most. He returned to Mohammed and Lucky who had been joined by a third man who was trying to make animated but seemingly inconsequential conversation. Lucky smiled annoyingly. Mohammed looked bored.

'What are we waiting for?' Peter asked.

'The prosecutor,' Mohammed said with a sigh. Peter found himself a cool spot in the shade, leaned back on the wall and opened the magazine he had sensibly brought with him.

An hour passed. Peter caught a glimpse of the sergeant who still had, Peter hoped, his driving licence but he quickly disappeared again. A distraction was provided by the arrival of a large truck that backed cautiously into the courtyard and was then loaded with men (there were apparently no women) brought from the holding cells. Several policemen stood in attendance, one with a large shotgun, and the prisoners emerged one at a time to clamber onto the tailgate and into the cage on the back of the truck. Many adopted a jaunty, defiant gait. Some looked thoroughly scared. All were watched by the assembled crowd who evidently enjoyed the spectacle and who looked on with amusement and little evidence of sympathy. The process took a while and a surprising number of men were squeezed into what seemed an inadequate space. Those close enough to the sides clutched the thick mesh for support and stared back at those outside. Some catcalls were passed in both directions and then the truck drove off with its human cargo of losers.

Mohammed was nudging Peter in the ribs. 'We need to go in now,' he said.

Nothing seemed to have happened so Peter didn't know how Mohammed knew but he followed him into the empty courtroom. Others were filing in too and they joined them on the pews. A few officials shuffled papers at the front but paid them no heed. They sat. They sat until a policeman appeared and motioned them back outside. He directed them to the benches Peter had noticed earlier and told them to wait. They waited.

A second truck appeared and yet more miscreants were brought out into the bright sun, blinking and staring their defiance at the police or hanging their heads in trepidation. Peter joked with Mohammed that he'd be on the next truck and made him promise to return his simple possessions to his grieving wife. His colleague laughed but the look in his eye suggested that he was not altogether sure how this thing was going to play out. From where they sat Peter could look into the courtroom and he was encouraged to see the morning's sergeant take his place beneath the judge's bench. But although other officials came and went and both words and papers were exchanged, they seemed no closer to starting the process. And when they were at last summoned it was not to face the officer with whom Peter had spoken in the morning but to take their places on the benches in the other courtroom, now empty, as the judge appeared to have run out of people to fine or send away in the truck.

Mohammed and Peter sat between men who joked with each other or stared into the distance, preoccupied and reflective. All seemed to be defendants and all quickly lapsed into a respectful silence at the arrival of a police officer. He gestured at Mohammed who rose and went to him and was then ushered out of a back door. Peter waited, increasingly curious, in a strangely detached way, to discover what would happen. Behind him, the convicted continued to fill the second truck, its engine running and its dirty exhaust filling the air with an acrid smell. Mohammed returned looking conspiratorial. He sat beside Peter and leaned close, speaking softly.

'Okay. Here's what happens,' he began. 'You're going to be fined a thousand Awanzan dollars. But you have to hand over three thousand. You give it to me and I'll give it to the police.'

'A bribe?' Something told Peter it had always been going to end like this.

'Yes.'

'And what's the alternative? What if I don't pay?'

'Then we'll sit here till four-thirty when the court closes and they'll send us home.'

'And we'll have to come back tomorrow?'

'Exactly.'

'And the next day too?'

'Possibly.'

'Okay.' For nearly two years in Awanza Peter had been pleased to say that he had never paid a bribe but that proud record was dashed in an instant and two syllables. Almost (but not quite) amused, he passed Mohammed the money – discreetly – and watched him sidle off to the waiting policeman. Again they both disappeared out of sight.

Mohammed returned with instructions.

'The magistrate will ask you if the account of the accident is correct. You must say yes. She'll then ask how you plead to the charge of reckless driving and you have to say guilty. She'll write for a few moments and then ask you if there are any extenuating circumstances. You say that this is your first offence in Awanza and that you have a wife and family who depend on you.'

'Do my tree rats count as 'family'?' Peter whispered.

'Just say it. She'll then write some more and then fine you a thousand dollars. I've got it here out of the three thousand. Okay?'

'Whatever you say.'

They sat in silence until Mohammed tapped Peter on the shoulder. 'Looks like you aren't the only white man here.'

Peter looked where he was pointing and indeed saw another white man in the courtyard discussing something with a couple of policemen. He looked about Peter's age and well dressed. Peter was curious to know what had brought him here and wondered if they would have an opportunity to talk. It was therefore with a mild shock that he abruptly realised that the man had emerged from the cells and was being politely steered by the police into the now full truck. His white face then appeared among the many Black ones peering out through the mesh that covered the windows and shortly after that the truck drove away.

Peter still had no serious expectation that he would not be going home that night to Sheila but the sight of a white man being driven off to gaol gave him a shock. He decided that he wanted this thing over and done with.

Mohammed's policeman reappeared and read out a list of names. Peter's was on it and he took his place in a line of naughty schoolboys being taken off to see the headmaster. They were marched down several corridors and lined up outside a closed door. Silence had fallen on those who had previously been garrulous.

Knowing it was probably foolish, but not much caring, he took out his mobile phone and began writing a text message to Sheila.

Am waiting to see the Magistrate. Money has changed hands and ...'

Yet another sergeant tapped him on the arm and he started. He nodded for Peter to follow him and, quickly slipping his phone into his pocket, Peter joined him halfway down a dark corridor and out of anyone's earshot.

'You know what to do?' The sergeant asked.

'What?'

'You know what to say? Just say yes to everything and tell her that you have a wife and family who depend upon you. Okay?' He smiled and patted Peter on the shoulder encouragingly. Did he wink?

He returned Peter to the end of the line and opened the door to the magistrate's office. She was a large rather self-important woman wearing a black gown over a smart business suit. As they filed in she did not look up from her papers but exchanged a few terse words with her clerk, also female, and a uniformed policeman who was presumably going to prosecute. He was not Peter's acquaintance of the morning and he wondered if he would again see his driving licence. He counted eleven other accused and he was the twelfth. They were crammed into an undignified huddle in a room where half a dozen people would have been snug and where they now numbered fifteen. There was the tropical smell of bodies that are always sweaty – Peter's being one of them.

The clerk selected a manila folder and read out the details on the cover. One of Peter's peers mumbled and stepped forward as best he could in such a confined space. He and the magistrate exchanged a few words in Kiwanza. She sighed and looked disapproving. Brief notes were made, sentence was passed and he was removed by a waiting officer. A second manila folder, a second contrite-looking defendant and a second application of summary justice. And then it was Peter's turn.

He noticed that his case number was 2018/261/Nd. It was written on the folder in ballpoint along with his name and a few other details. He was amused to see that Sergeant Mposi had been unable to bring himself to record Peter's atheism and that next to 'religion' he had indeed written 'Christian.' His case apparently merited the involvement of the prosecuting officer and the magistrate passed him the file from which to read. He read in English, nervously and with frequent mistakes. For the second time that day Peter listened to Sergeant Mposi's not altogether accurate version of the circumstances that had brought him to this interesting juncture.

As the officer read, the magistrate made some notes. She had not yet looked at Peter and nor did she as she asked, 'Is that what happened?'

It still stuck in the throat but he did the needful.

She wrote a few more comments but from where he stood he could not read them.

'And you accept the charge of reckless driving?'

'Er, yes. I do.' (If his fingers were crossed behind my back, did it still count?)

She again busied herself with her notes.

'Have you anything to say before I pass sentence?'

Peter wondered if he was keeping a straight face but tried to sound convincing. 'Em, this is my first offence in Awanza and I have been here for nearly two years. And I have a wife and family. They depend upon me.'

The magistrate had presumably had more practice than Peter at this kind of thing and she nodded gravely before writing some more.

He was then sentenced.

'In view of the extenuating circumstances I fine you one thousand dollars. Failure to pay will result in a prison term of four months. Will you pay the fine?'

(Four months in prison or the equivalent of forty quid? It seemed absurd but then Peter reflected that very many of the people appearing before the magistrate very possibly had no way of raising such an amount. If he had started to feel smug and arrogant, he now felt something closer to shame.)

'Yes. I will pay.'

Still without her eyes having met Peter's she made a final entry in her notes and waved him away.

His latest police sergeant escorted Peter back whence he had come.

'Did it go all right?' He asked with a smile as they walked.

'Yes, yes – everything was fine.'

'I told you it would!' he said as if it was he whom Peter had to thank. 'Now, what about me? Can you help me with my transport?'

Peter had already descended from the moral high ground and crossed the Rubicon so what the hell? He stuffed his hand in his pocket and pulled out the first banknote he found. It was two hundred dollars. The sergeant seemed well pleased.

Mohammed rose to greet him. 'Well?'

'Exactly as you said. I've been fined a thousand Awanzan dollars. Let's pay it and go.'

Mohammed went to a window to pay Peter's debt to society and then Peter noticed the sergeant who had taken his driving licence now sitting under an awning passing the time of day with other officers. He approached him and indicated Mohammed over his shoulder receiving the necessary receipt.

'May I have my driving licence now?'

With something approaching a smile and a show of politeness the sergeant unzipped a side pocket of a battered briefcase and handed it over. Peter thanked him, they shook hands, and he returned with Mohammed to the school Land Rover.

'I wonder if the police will really give the magistrate a thousand,' Mohammed mused.

'Is that what they said?'

'Mmm. A thousand for them and one for her.'

'Well, she spoke her lines as instructed. I don't believe that was a coincidence.'

They drove in silence for a few minutes and then Peter said, 'It doesn't have much to do with justice, does it?'

Mohammed shifted uncomfortably and looked out of the side window. 'No, not much …'

From: pcorby@isn.edu.wz
To: Crystalmooreinawanza@gmail.com
Cc: Nyotafuraha1@awanzacom.wz; kim@rankinfamily.wz;
kaminskim72@gmail.wz; bodchair@isn.edu.wz
Subject: Re: Obstruction of legitimate PTA business
Dear Mrs Moore

You might be on stronger ground if you had chosen to share with me examples of "the sensible reforms we are proposing". To date, I have seen none.

And if you consider my insistence that the current PTA adheres to the terms of the current constitution to be [quote] "legalistic and petty", then might I ask why you are bothering to draft a revised constitution since you presumably do not expect it to be respected either?

You are correct. I do believe the current constitution to be poorly drafted, ambiguous, and incomplete. We are in full agreement that the school would be better served by a revised document. But I must insist that I, as the Educational Director of the school and in accordance with Clause 4.4.1 of the current constitution, be fully involved in the revision process.

In the meantime, you are, of course, entirely within your rights to take your case to the Chair of the ISN Board of Directors. You will see that I have copied her here and please note that I have forwarded to her the previous correspondence between Mrs Furaha and myself.
Sincerely
Peter Corby

May

Many international schools (though some may rather unkindly call them so-called international schools) deliver what is effectively a national curriculum or perhaps that of a State or Province. Indeed, the International School of Ndwalowe (or Ndwalowe International School as it then was) had for a time used curriculums from Ontario and later Ohio. But, like many schools around the world, it had adopted first one, then two, and then three of the programmes of the International Baccalaureate Organisation. All three of Peter's international schools had been IB World Schools. He would have been deeply reluctant to work anywhere else.

And for schools that offer the IB Diploma in the final two years, the month of May means only one thing: exams.

On the same days and at the same times (allowing for time differences around the world), something like 150,000 students in about 150 countries open their exam papers, swallow hard, and discover what they can recall of what they have spent two years studying. The exam schedule runs for about three weeks, with the diploma coordinator or their designated deputy solemnly retrieving each session's exam papers from a safe that is required to be securely situated behind as many locked doors as possible. At ISN the safe was in a small windowless room located between Peter's office and Chiamaka's. The only door to the room was behind Chiamaka's desk and she was accustomed to Meena Nair, DP coordinator, apologetically squeezing past her three or four times a day to retrieve exams or lock away completed papers.

'Morning,' Meena smiled as she entered Chiamaka's office.

'Morning. Busy today?' asked Chiamaka.

'Three this morning and two this afternoon,' Meena waved at Chiamaka a small bunch of keys including one that must have been fourteen or fifteen centimetres long. 'Then we won't be needing these again till Monday,' she said.

'Has the first week gone okay?'

'So far. We've had a couple of kids arrive late – we do every year – but nothing serious.'

'Do you think we'll get an inspection this year?'

'It seems likely. I honestly thought they'd send someone last year. The school being in one sense new, and all.'

'We don't get any notice, do we?'

'Oh, no. That's the point. Someone will just turn up at Cassie's desk and announce that they are from the IB and want to see our arrangements – where the papers are kept, where the students take the exams, and so on. It happened in my first year. We got in trouble for not having signs telling people to be quiet. But the drama studio is virtually soundproof anyway. But we do it now, of course.' Meena looked at her watch. 'Hey, I'd better get going.'

With one of the smaller keys, she unlocked to door to the secure room and entered.

★

Peter passed the letter back to Carola. 'Pretty much what I expected,' he said.

'Her argument appears to be that since everyone agrees that the current constitution—'

'Or 'previous,' as they like to call it.'

'Yes, I noticed that. Anyway, the constitution is unfit so let's just ignore it and adopt a new one. Oh, Mrs Furaha said they would send you a copy. Did they?'

'No, of course not. Just like they promise they will send me the minutes of meetings but never do. Meetings, I might say, that I am meant to be invited to but they don't do that either.'

'What is it they want?'

'Power. They want to have a say in how the school is run. Crystal once said something about a three-way partnership between the board, the school administration, and the PTA.'

'But that's absurd.'

'And now,' Peter indicated the letter, 'they want the board to overrule me and let them get on with their revolution. Have you shared it with any other board members?'

'No, and I'm not going to. It's addressed to me so I will reply.'

'Saying …?'

'Saying that as far as I can see the current – not previous – the current constitution is quite clear on the process to adopt a new one and I suggest they adhere to it.'

'Good. Thank you.'

'But your problem won't go away.' Carola frowned.

'I know. But a lot of people are fed up with Crystal Moore's antics and I know for a fact that there are moves afoot to bring this to a head. If the PTA have gone rogue and won't cooperate then we may be better off without one.'

Both Chiamaka's and Peter's offices opened onto a corridor but there was also a communicating door between the two. As Peter was talking, a noise emanated from behind the door that could only be described as a wail. Peter scowled and made to open the door. Before he could, it was flung open and Meena rushed into his room. Behind her, Peter could see Chiamaka looking quite shocked.

'What is it?'

'The key!' said Meena. 'The safe key. It's snapped.'

'What? How …'

'I'd just taken out this morning's papers and was locking the safe. And the key just snapped.' Meena held out a stub of what had been the key. 'The rest of it is still in the lock.' She looked pale.

'So we can't open it?'

'It is open. I was just locking it when it snapped.'

'So we can't close it?'

'No.'

'Let me take a look. Oh, Carola. Sorry about this. But we'd finished, hadn't we?'

'Yes, we're done. I'll get out of your way. Good luck.'

The safe was old, about the size of a small fridge, and extremely solid.

'They knew how to make them in those days,' admired Peter as he squatted to inspect the damage. The door was closed but, as Meena had said, not locked and it easily swung open to reveal the neat stack of exam papers within. 'That's not good,' said Peter rather unnecessarily.

'Peter, I need to go and start the exams,' Meena was clutching to her chest the morning's papers.

'Yes, of course. Get going. We'll see if we can sort this out.'

The fieldtrip Mike Sesriem had arranged to the National Museum of Anthropology in November had been very successful. So much so that two of his students had elected to base a major coursework assignment on a number of the artifacts they had discovered there. A return visit to the museum was proposed.

'Since I'm no longer teaching Grade Twelve, I have the whole morning free so, with your permission, Mick, I'll take them down in one of the school cars. Shouldn't be more than a couple of hours.'

'Just clear it with the teachers whose classes they'll be missing.'

'Of course.'

Chiamaka had locked the secure room door but was still under strict instructions from Peter not to leave her office.

'If you need to go to the toilet or something, call me or Saskia or someone,' Peter had instructed her. 'I know the door is locked but I want someone there at all times until we get the safe fixed. It would be just our luck to have an inspection now.'

When asked about a reliable locksmith, both Saskia and Genuine had recommended the same small family business. 'They've done lots of odd jobs for us over the years,' Saskia had said. 'They're pretty reliable. I'll look up the number and give them a call.'

'Be sure to say it's urgent. We must get this sorted today.'

'I know. I will.'

Jenny put down her phone and scribbled something on a list in front of her. 'Pernilla says she'll be happy to sign,' she said. 'I think that takes us to twenty.'

'And there's still many more we can approach. The more we can get, the better.' Pearl Figueira was scrolling through the contacts on her phone. 'Teachers too. I mean, it's the P – *T* – A, isn't it? They're members too.'

Jenny reflected for a moment. 'I'm not really sure. The constitution is pretty vague on that. Can they vote at the AGM? I can't remember.'

'Well, teachers with children can, of course. We should at least get some of them.'

'Oh, absolutely. Crystal will try to make this out to be some sort of coup by a few disaffected ex-members. Let's not give her the chance. The broader we can make this thing, the stronger our position we be.'

'Have you shown Peter Corby the letter yet?'

'Oh, yes. Well, the first draft. He and I took it to the school lawyer yesterday, just to be sure.'

Pearl made a face. 'It's ridiculous we have to do this.'

'I agree. But I think the last straw was the International Fayre last month. I've never seen such a poor PTA effort. It was embarrassing. And a lot of people noticed.'

'I think Crystal was making a point. She thinks the International Fayre is beneath her.'

Jenny nodded. 'Well, let's just make a point of our own.'

★

To Peter's relief, the locksmith was there within the hour. He whistled when he saw the safe and muttered something about making no promises but he had with him an impressive set of tools and other implements that Peter was at a loss to identify. Genuine was instructed to stay with the locksmith, ostensibly to 'help' him but in reality to ensure that the contents of the safe were not touched. Somewhat optimistic that the morning's drama might not turn out to be a major one, Peter returned to his office.

★

The first schools to include the prefix 'international' in their name were founded in 1924 in Geneva and Yokohama but they remained members of a very small club until well after the Second World War. It was in the late 1950s and particularly the early 1960s that parents in far flung corners of the globe began to identify the need for alternatives to whatever educational options existed locally. The chosen language of instruction tended to be English and the teachers who were employed most commonly came from anglophone countries. Many such schools grew over the years into significant and in some cases prestigious institutions. But almost all began life as modest, almost amateurish operations sometimes staffed by, and almost always governed by, volunteers who, if they were honest, would have admitted to making it up as they went along. Depending on the laws of the host country, these schools were almost invariably established as non-profit entities governed by boards usually composed of parents of children in the school, representatives of the diplomatic community, and sometimes local worthies. Most schools were happy just to break even each year and if a surplus was generated it was used to improve the school in whatever way was deemed best. The parents, in a sense 'owned' the school but they were not shareholders and no dividends were ever paid. International schools were there to meet a need, provide a service. No one thought of international schools as a way of making money.

Until they did.

More often than not, Peter's lunch was a sandwich taken in front of his laptop any time between 10am and 3pm but on Fridays the cafeteria prepared rather wonderful curries. His mouth watering as he thought of the dal makhani he knew would be waiting for him, he was walking across the car park when his phone rang.

'Hi, Saskia.'

'Peter, I have good news. And, I'm afraid, bad news.' Saskia sounded a little nervous.

'Uh-oh. Give me the good news.'

'The locksmith has just left. And he managed to get the broken key out of the lock.'

'Oh, that's fantastic. So now we can lock it.'

'Er, no. That's the bad news. We can't lock it.'

'Why not?'

'Because the key's broken.'

'I know that but what about the spare?'

There was a silence.

'Saskia,' Peter said. 'Please tell me there is a spare.'

Another silence.

'Right,' said Peter grimly. 'Wait there. I'm coming back.'

There would be no dal makhani for Peter that morning.

★

Cassie Farmer was sealing the morning's completed exams in a DHL envelope when Mike Sesriem marched into reception.

'Hello again. Here's the key back. Someone might think of putting petrol in the car. It's pretty low.'

You, of course, wouldn't think of doing that, thought Cassie. She took the key and returned it to the relevant drawer.

'And you'd better give this to someone. Someone in the business office, I suppose.' Mike handed Cassie some sort of document in a slim plastic sleeve.

'What's this?'

'A parking ticket, as far as I can make out. It was under the windscreen wiper when I got back the car.'

'Where did you park?'

'Oh, you know what the centre of town is like. It's impossible. But I found a spot just outside the Central Bank. It's only a short walk from there to the museum. Anyway, give it to Saskia. She'll know what to do. See ya.'

★

'Saskia, if I can't trust you, who can I trust?' Peter was genuinely upset.

'Peter, I knew there was no spare. I mean, there used to be one but I can't remember what happened to it. But I was pretty sure that Mr Coetzee would be able to give us a new key … or even repair the broken one. But he said the safe was so old that he couldn't help.'

'Then put in a new lock? The door was open. Surely, he could have done that?'

'Again, he said it was such an old model that nothing he has in his workshop would fit. Anyway, most safes today have combination locks.'

'So now it's,' he looked at his watch, 'almost 1pm on a Friday and all the IB exams are sitting in a safe without a lock?'

'Behind three locked doors and an alarm system.'

'Yes, but I can assure you that won't cut any ice with some officious IB guy who turns up in the next half-hour. I've done it myself. I've been an inspector. It's mildly exciting. You arrive at some unsuspecting school out of the blue and flash your badge – except, of course, there isn't any badge – and complete a long and rather excessive checklist. It's quite unforgiving.'

'And our students could be, what, delisted, or something?'

'Actually, no. Bark and bite and all that. The IB can be … what was the word I used? Unforgiving. But they are deeply – and admirably, I might say – reluctant to punish the students when the school is at fault. I'm completely torn. Do I report this to the IB and throw myself on their mercy? Or do I cross my fingers and hope they never find out?'

'Well, there's been no breach of security so far. The exam papers are all there and untouched.'

'And I've never heard of an inspection over a weekend. How soon could we get a replacement safe here?'

She looked at her watch. 'One pm,' she said. 'We might even get one today. There's really only one supplier in town. Let me go and call them. It won't be cheap.'

'Of course not,' said Peter. 'Of course not.'

The envelope waiting on Peter's desk was clearly of high quality with embossed logos and, when he opened it, subtle watermarks on the several sheets of paper within.

He read with some puzzlement …

Dear Dr Corby

It is a pleasure to write to you. Your reputation precedes you and I am honoured to make contact with someone as accomplished as you are in the field of international education. I can only say what a privilege it will be to meet you in person.

I am writing on behalf of the Prince's Academy of International Schools (PAIS) of which I am certain you have heard.

To date, we have fourteen schools in twelve countries (Tanzania, Uganda, Ghana, Senegal, Kenya, Malawi, Sri Lanka, Thailand, Laos, Vietnam, Brunei, Indonesia) with a combined enrolment of almost eight thousand students. Our annual turnover is close to $18,000,000.

We are very selective in the schools that we consider for our portfolio, so I hope that you will consider it an honor that we are interested in opening discussions with you about adding the International School of Ndwalowe to the PAIS family.

I am very conscious that this approach will have come, as they say, "out of the blue" and I entirely understand that this is something you will need to discuss fully with your board of directors.

Should you, however, wish to discuss the possible acquisition of the school and your personal future role within a revised managerial/leadership structure, please be reassured that I will of course be available 24/7 and our conversations will, I hope I need not say, be completely confidential.

Please find enclosed the last year's financial statement and our vision navigator covering the next five years. (Note in particular the emphasis on growing our footprint in Africa.)

I very much look forward to hearing from you.

Sincerely

Todd Noble

Vice-President, Acquisitions

Peter wondered what on earth a vision navigator was but he leafed through the papers he had been sent. There were bar charts illustrating the growth in enrolment and income over the last five years, the inevitable photographs of students in goggles and suspiciously white lab coats, a site map of what was presumably their flagship school in Thailand, more photographs of impressive sports facilities, and numerous glowing endorsements from happy parents. Of the Prince, whoever he was, there appeared to be no sign.

Mr Noble was correct. Peter had heard of PAIS. It was one of a number (a growing number, unfortunately) of businesses that bought, or sometimes built from scratch, international schools which they then ran strictly for profit. In their defence, they had deep pockets and could usually invest serious sums of money in facilities or – something else they were good at – greatly improve marketing. But their reputation within the international community of teachers and administrators was not good. Terms of employment often looked attractive until you examined the small print and those who had worked in such schools told stories of style always triumphing over substance. 'Cynical' was a word Peter had heard used more than once.

Whatever reservations Peter may have had, he knew he would have to take this offer to the board. He wondered how they would react. He also wondered how ISN had ended up on Todd Noble's radar.

★

'Tomorrow? A Saturday?' Peter wasn't sure if this was good news or not.

'I pushed for today,' said Saskia 'but they said we should have placed the order before ten if we wanted same day delivery.'

'You did explain the urgency of the situation?'

'I tried. I'm not sure they think of exam papers as being quite as valuable as, say, wads of US dollars.'

'Oh, well. If that's what it is … that's what it is. Do you think we should station one of the guards in the admin block overnight?'

'I think that would be simply drawing attention to the fact that we have a problem.'

'You're right. You're right. Maybe I should sit in the car park all night.'

'Oh, Peter, you're getting this way out of proportion. Listen to yourself!'

'You think? Sorry. It's just a bit of a nightmare scenario.'

'Well, here's another one. Well, not a nightmare perhaps but … well, you decide.' Saskia handed Peter the parking ticket Mike Sesriem had turned in a couple of hours earlier.

'What's this?'

'Read it.'

'Oops,' said Peter. 'Was this you?'

'No, of course it wasn't me. It was Mike Sesriem this morning. In one of the school cars.'

'So, why do you have it?'

'Because Mike seems to think that the school will pay it. He's also ignoring the fact that the driver must report to any police station within thirty days to have points added to their licence.'

'Have you talked to Mike?'

'No. He gave this to Cassie and then skedaddled.'

'We don't pay these things, do we?'

'No. People can use school cars on school business but it's up to them where they park. Same as if they are caught speeding.'

'Then please send for Mr Sesriem and disabuse him of his … let's say optimistic assessment of the situation.'

'I shall.'

★

'Okay,' said Jenny. 'Thirty-five. That's a pretty good number. Even Crystal can't explain that away. Who are you still trying to contact?'

'Ajit's phone seems permanently on voicemail and Maria isn't picking up. But I'm sure I can get them.'

'And teachers?'

'Trixi Villiers and Jackie Sesriem are in. And I had a very good chat with Catherine Mulbarton. She's really annoyed with what the PTA has become. She used to be the PTA Chair, you know?'

'No, I didn't. But she's on the board. That will help.'

'It won't hurt.'

'Now, let's see what Crystal Moore makes of this.'

★

'But, Saskia,' Mike looked quite pained, 'I was on school business. I was taking two kids to an important appointment at the museum.'

322

'I know. But you are the one who chose where to park and you got yourself a parking ticket.'

'But what was I to do? The staff at the museum are not known for their customer friendliness. I had an appointment at ten. Turn up even fifteen minutes late and they won't want to know.'

'And you are forgetting that you need to present yourself to a police station within thirty days to have your licence—'

'Oh, come on! I've lived here for six years. I don't have blemish on my licence. Hit me with a few points and my insurance will go through the roof.'

'I'm sorry, Mike,' not that she sounded particularly sorry, 'but what do you propose we do?'

Mike thought. 'Couldn't someone else go to the station and say they were driving? Someone who wouldn't mind getting a couple of points?'

'Like who? No one wants points on their licence. And you're asking someone to lie to the police?'

'A white lie. The police don't care who was driving.'

'No, Mike. You have to pay the fine and you have to go to the police station. I suggest you do it quickly and get it over and done with.' Saskia pointedly pushed the parking ticket across her desk. 'Here, this belongs to you.'

Peter didn't spend the night in the car park but the following morning he was very relieved to watch the new safe being unloaded and, not without difficulty, manhandled upstairs and into the secure room. Meena was on hand to transfer the papers to the new safe and Saskia appeared too.

'Phew,' said Peter as they watched the truck disappear out of the school gates. 'That's a weight off my mind. Of course, now we probably won't get an inspection.'

But he was wrong.

A man in a suit and with a visitor's badge approached Cassie's desk. 'Good morning,' he said. 'My name's John Furness. I'm from the IB.' He handed her his business card.

Cassie's heart leapt a little. 'Oh. This is the, er … You're here to …'

'I believe the DP coordinator is a Ms Meena Nair? I'd be grateful if you'd tell me where I can find her.'

'She'll either be in the exam room or her office. Shall I call her?'

'If you would be so kind.'

Meena was indeed in her office but hurried to the reception to greet their visitor.

Introductions and brief pleasantries exchanged, John told Meena what of course she already knew. 'I'll want to observe a full exam session but first I need to inspect where the papers are stored.'

'Absolutely,' said Meena. 'Please follow me.'

As soon as they were out of sight, Cassie dialled Peter's number and he was waiting for them outside his office.

'Good morning.' He held out his hand. 'I'm Peter Corby, the director.'

'John Furness. We've met.'

'Really?'

'Yes. It was at the conference at the University of Bath where you were delivering a paper on why Japanese parents in Japan choose international schools. I spent several years working at Hiroshima International School and I found your talk fascinating.'

'I remember. You urged me to publish my research.'

'And you did. I saw it in the JRIE last year. Congratulations.'

'Thank you. So, what are you doing these days?'

'Retired, I'm happy to say. My wife and I now live in Cape Town so the IB tend to use me for these little jobs in southern Africa. Speaking of which,' he turned to Meena, 'the exam papers?'

'Of course. In here.' She led the way. Peter followed, silently offering thanks to the God he didn't believe in.

'The building has an alarm system, I assume?'

'Yes. It's turned on every night.'

'So, there's the front door, the door to your secretary's office, and this door. That's three. That's good.'

'And this is the safe.'

'Oh, that's excellent. A very solid model. And a combination lock too. Very good.' He was making notes on a clipboard. 'You won't believe it,' he said, 'but there are still schools using safes with keys.' He noticed the old safe. 'Like that one.'

'Oh, we don't use that for anything terribly valuable,' Peter gushed. 'As you say, that's an old model. We have this beauty for our exam papers.' He patted the new safe affectionately.

'Have you any idea how easily the keys to these old safes can snap?' Peter tutted. 'Can you imagine?'

'Unprofessional, I call it. Anyway, then, that's all fine.' John Furness returned the clipboard to his briefcase. 'Now, the exam room. Nice to see you again, Peter. Keep up the good work.'

'Yes,' said Peter. 'Good to see you too, John. Take care.' The two men shook hands. As she escorted John down the corridor, Meena turned back and flashed a smile at Peter. He just shook his head. 'Phew ...'

*

John Furness had been and gone. He still had to submit his formal report to the IB but he had assured Meena that everything was in order. Indeed, "flying colours" were invoked. Meena had quickly shared the good news with Peter.

'What a carry on,' Peter said. 'Imagine if he'd come on Friday afternoon.'

'Well, happily, he didn't,' said Meena, 'and we did nothing wrong. All's well that ...'

Peter's phone rang. 'Sorry, Meena. I should take this.'

'No problem. I'll catch you later.' Meena left his office.

'Hello, Peter Corby. Who is this?'

The voice on the line was immediately recognisable but strangely hesitant.

'Mike? Mike, is that you?'

*

An important job in any school is the creation of the annual calendar. In fact, much of it writes itself as the arc of one school year is very much like another. But no two years are ever quite the same. Public holidays must be observed and, although they may fall on the same date each year, they won't fall on the same day of the week. If the school is open on a Monday, for example, but will be closed on a Tuesday, the opportunity may be taken to work a long weekend into the calendar. Of course, that 'lost' Monday must then be made up elsewhere. Wherever the location of the school, Easter, which may occur in either March or April, will probably be respected and in many schools other religious and cultural festivals will claim their place on the calendar. Over these dates, the school has little control but it can choose when to schedule staff professional development days and the dates of such holidays as occur during the year. Creating a calendar isn't, in the end, a particularly challenging job but embarrassing mistakes can be made without a keen eye for detail.

At ISN, Peter tasked the two principals with working up the first draft. He then cast his eye over it and sometimes made suggestions. Then it was published internally so that all staff could have their say (and for those with sharp eyes to point out anomalies). By the time it was made available to parents (always a good year in advance), it was probably about as good as it could be.

Valli and Mick were politely disagreeing about the timing of the professional development days when teachers would be in school but students wouldn't.

'They can't all be on Fridays or Mondays.' Valli objected.

'It's much better than having them midweek and this way parents can take a long weekend, if they want.'

'If I had my druthers—'

'Eh?'

'If I had my druthers.'

'You don't have your druthers? Why not? What happened to them?'

'What are you talking about?'

'I have no idea. What are *you* talking about?'

'My druthers. You don't know that expression?'

'Not at all. I assume it means, if I had my way.'

'Exactly.'

'Then why not say that?'

'I did. If I had my druthers.'

'Two countries divided by a common language,' laughed Mick.

'That's the US and England.' Said Valli. 'You're somewhere in-between.'

'Isn't that the truth! Ireland in a nutshell.'

They went back to arguing about dates.

★

Both Sheila and Peter had spent more time in Lower Garstang Police Station than either would have chosen but never had Peter driven onto the dusty parking lot with a greater sense of foreboding.

He slammed the car door shut and strode up the steps to the reception. He observed the usual throng of people, some in uniform, most not. Police officers entered and departed through various doors, usually carrying documents or bundles of manila folders, but they paid very little attention to the Awanzan citizens forlornly trying to interest someone in their problems. And in the corner, slumped on a bench, was Mike Sesriem.

Mike noticed Peter but quickly looked back at his shoes. Peter started to walk towards him but a sergeant took his elbow and asked, 'You have come to represent the defendant?'

Defendant? thought Peter. *Represent?*

'I am the principal of the international school,' Peter said trying to sound important but not disrespectful. He wished he was wearing a tie. 'Mr Sesriem here works at my school. He is a teacher.'

The sergeant nodded. 'Good.' He indicated one of the grubby doors. 'In there ...'

Mike stood and the sergeant ushered his guests into a small office. There was a table and two battered chairs but no one sat.

'Mr Sesriem came with a parking ticket,' began the sergeant. 'He wanted me to understand that he had been on important and urgent school business otherwise he would not have parked where he did. Is that true?'

Peter hesitated. 'He was on school business, yes.'

'But not important and urgent?'

Peter could think of nothing to say. He made sure not to look at Mike.

'As I thought,' said the sergeant. 'But Mr Sesriem was quite insistent.' He stared at Mike as if inviting him to speak. He didn't.

'And so I explained to Mr Sesriem that even if his business was urgent, it still did not justify parking in a forbidden zone. The laws of Awanza are

327

quite clear and must be observed by everyone.' It was obvious what the sergeant meant by everyone. 'I then asked for his licence and that is when … Mr Sesriem, perhaps you would like to tell your principal what you did, what you said.'

Mike looked utterly miserable. 'It was really a misunderstanding.'

'It was no misunderstanding.'

'I wasn't really … I mean, I can see why you thought …'

'"Can't we just settle this here?" is what you said, is it not? "Just you and me". And then you took out your wallet.'

'To pay the parking ticket!' spluttered Mike.

'"And do we really have to go through with the points on my licence?" I have a very good memory, Mr Sesriem. Are you denying that you said that?'

Mike said nothing.

'And by then, you had several banknotes in your hand.'

'To pay the parking ticket.' This time Mike barely mumbled the words.

'I don't think so, Mr Sesriem.'

No one spoke. Mike looked ashen.

'Sergeant,' Peter began, no longer trying to sound important but genuinely wanting to be respectful. 'To the best of my knowledge Mr Sesriem has lived and worked in Awanza for six years and in all that time he has never committed an offence.' He looked at Mike who nodded weakly. 'But now he has most certainly committed one offence and it is clear you believe he has committed a second. Perhaps we could separate the two. There is absolutely no question that he will not pay the parking ticket and, of course, accept the points on his licence. That matter we can – and will – settle in full right now.'

'Mr Sesriem,' said the sergeant. 'Do you agree? Or do you still—'

'Yes! I mean, no, I will pay.'

'And the points?'

'Yes. Yes, of course. I mean I never …' The words died in his throat.

'Which leaves us with the second matter,' said the sergeant looking back at Peter.

Peter nodded. 'It does. And I'm afraid I have nothing to suggest. You must decide what … what we do.'

The sergeant was a tall man with a bearing that Peter later described as military. His voice was authoritative without being intimidating. He had a short beard flecked with silver and eyes that were kindly.

You'd make a good teacher, Peter found himself thinking.

'You are both educated men,' said the sergeant. Peter wondered where this was heading. 'The offence we are discussing is an extremely serious one and the punishment is invariably severe.'

Mike gave an involuntary shudder.

'But I'm going to be honest with you. It is also notoriously difficult to prove in the absence of a witness. And today there were no witnesses.'

Peter began to understand what the sergeant was saying. At least, he hoped he did.

'I fear a court case would be unsatisfactory for both parties. Whatever the outcome, I assume it is an experience you would not wish to have, Mr Sesriem. And,' the sergeant looked at the card Peter had given him, 'Mr Corby, I very much doubt if you would want the school's name to be in the papers – as it assuredly would be.'

'I would not.'

'And for my part … I repeat, in the absence of a witness, I am not at all sure that we could obtain a conviction. But I hope, Mr Sesriem, that the last hour has given you food for thought. Whether you did or didn't today, I hope it is not something you would ever think of doing in future. You may not be as fortunate a second time.'

Mike looked rather wide-eyed. 'No, it isn't … I mean, I wouldn't …'

'Good.' The sergeant pushed the door open and shouted loudly, 'constable!' An officer hurried across the reception.

'Yes, sergeant.'

'Mr Sesriem here has a fine to pay and he must surrender his driving licence.'

'Yes, Sergeant.'

As Mike followed the constable, the sergeant put out his hand. 'Goodbye, Mr Sesriem. I hope you will reflect on what I said.'

They shook hands with Mike muttering, 'I will, I surely will. Thank you.'

Peter made to follow but the sergeant put his hand on Peter's arm. 'Ah, no, Mr Corby. You and I aren't quite finished.'

He closed the door again.

★

Peter had sent a copy of the letter from PAIS to Carola who had immediately approved his suggestion that scanned copies be sent to all board members for discussion at the next meeting. She also asked him to prepare a small presentation on whatever he knew or could find out about PAIS.

'And examples of other similar business. You say there are a few?'

'There are three or four big players but there are more and more entering the market all the time.'

'You sound like you don't approve.'

Peter shrugged. 'It doesn't matter what I think. I'm just rather attached to the model of an independent not-for-profit international school. There's something rather noble about it. And I suppose I don't really believe that anyone should be making a profit out of delivering education. Education is ... sacred.'

'Noble and sacred. I don't often hear those words when we are discussing schools.'

'Look at the people who invented the IB in the late 'sixties. They were idealists and visionaries, not businessmen. They didn't set up the IB to make money out of it. They didn't take shares in it. But, my God, if they had done, they'd be rich by now.'

'I take it you are not in favour of this offer from PAIS.'

'Actually, I really don't know. My initial reaction is what I've just shared with you. But none of us know the details yet. They seem to have a lot of money. And we don't. A million US could make a huge difference to our facilities. But I'm sure it wouldn't be the school it now is.'

'They'd change the culture?'

'I've known it happen. Look, we are very proud of our learning support department. We are committed to being a fully inclusive school so we take a fair number of children whose needs are ... not mainstream. We have full-time and highly trained learning support teachers. But they cost money. SAIS could just say no to any more enrolments and close learning support down – or, at least, significantly downgrade it. That would improve the bottom line but it would profoundly alter the kind of school we are. And that's just the first example that comes to mind.'

'Maybe make the school selective rather than inclusive?'

'Why not? That would improve our annual exam results and that in turn would help marketing. There's an obvious logic to it. If your aim is to make money.'

'And ours isn't?'

'Our aim, as I'm sure you know and I think you agree, Carola, is to provide the best education we can for the broadest range of students. We have bills to pay so we want to at least cover our costs and if we can generate a surplus to plough back into the school, that's all well and good. Think back to the people who founded this school. Their priority was not to turn a profit.'

Carola nodded. 'You're right, of course, but things change.'

'They do. But not always for the better. Anyway, I'm going to ask Ernesto.'

'Ernesto? Ask him what?'

'He's a venture capitalist. At least, I think that's what he calls himself. His firm goes looking for opportunities like PAIS. He'll at least know how this kind of outfit operates. He may have some advice for me.'

'It can't hurt, I suppose.'

'Meanwhile, I'll get copies of the letter off to all the members. I do wonder how they will react.'

'I think we can guess how at least one of them will.'

Peter agreed. He did not find the thought reassuring.

Mike and Peter had driven back to school in their own cars but Mike had strict instructions to go straight to Peter's office.

'But I'm teaching,' Mike had protested feebly. 'I was only free before break and I didn't think it would take long at the police station.' He looked at his watch. 'I'm already late.'

'My office!' snapped Peter. 'I'll call Mick and have him cover your class. You're actually quite a bit late by now. He probably already has.'

Mike was waiting in the corridor when Peter arrived. Chiamaka appeared at the door to her office. 'Peter …'

'Not now, Chiamaka. Sorry, but not now.' He almost shoved Mike into his office and slammed the door behind them.

'What the … What the hell were you thinking of? Trying to bribe a police officer. A sergeant.'

'Oh, come on. You've never heard of a bribe being paid before. In this country? Have you ever done it?'

Peter scowled but didn't answer.

'Anyway, I wasn't—'

'Oh, of course you were. He knew it, you knew it.'

'Then why did he let me go? That stuff about not being able to win the case in court. That's BS. Anyway, what did he want with you? He shut the door and you must have been in there three or four minutes.'

Peter said nothing.

'You didn't …?' said Mike. 'I mean, after all that …'

'Mike, if I could fire you over this, I would. I cannot tell you how furious I am. Can you see the headlines? *International school teacher convicted of offering a bribe?*'

'Except, I wouldn't have been convicted, the sergeant was saying. I'm beginning to think I should have stuck to my guns. I have points on my license now and—'

Peter almost felt the urge to punch Mike. 'You have no bloody idea, do you!'

Mike suddenly had a thought. 'You won't …' he said, 'you won't tell Jackie, will you?'

'I will,' said Peter. 'I absolutely will. If I ever hear of you hitting her again.'

'Oh, that's got nothing to do with it.'

'Mike, you touch your wife again and I'm going to bring all hell down on you. No, you don't know what Sergeant Akolo and I said behind that closed door but I can assure you that he knows who you are and won't need much incentive to bang you into one of those police cells at the back of Lower Garstang Police Station. And from the little I've seen, you really, really don't want to be there.'

Mike glared at him. 'You have no right—'

'What I do and don't have any right to do is neither here nor there. And if there is a fallout when you are banged up and it reflects badly on the school, then so be it. Perhaps we can play the 'doing the right thing' card. Either way, you're stuffed and we just have a PR thing to manage. Do you feel lucky?'

'Oh, God, you're bloody Clint Eastwood now.'

'Mike. I'm going to be straight with you. It's May. The recruitment season is long gone. But if you resign now and disappear … I can't say I'll give you a glowing reference but nor will I scupper your chances. As a colleague, you're …' he hesitated. 'Well, let's just say you're not a bad classroom teacher. My advice would be to move on, learn from all this, have a fresh start. Maybe you and Jackie can have a fresh start. But I really don't want you here anymore.'

'I have a contract for next year.'

'I know you do. And I'm not about to put the school before the Labour Commissioner. But ask yourself, is it really in anyone's best interests for you to stay? Your interests? The school's interests? Your family's interests?'

'So, you're firing me?'

'Contractually, as you point out, I have no right to do so. Let's just say that I, as director, am giving you career advice.'

Abruptly, Mike looked deflated. 'Jackie's leaving anyway.'

'What?'

'She's going back to Namibia and taking the kids. I was going to tell you.'

'And you?'

'I don't know. She doesn't want me to come. She's got a job in Windhoek. They'll live with her sister to begin with.' He looked away and bit his lip. 'She's leaving me, Peter.'

Peter found it hard to feel much sympathy. 'Maybe it's for the best.'

'So, now I have no wife and no kids and you're telling me I have no job. Oh, but I do have a criminal record.'

'It's a parking ticket, Mike, though you nearly managed to give yourself a serious criminal record. And, as I said, you do have a job. Unless you choose to leave.'

'But you won't give me a contract beyond next year, will you?'

'It seems unlikely.'

'So, I either go now or in a year?'

'That's about the size of it.'

Mike nodded. 'Then, I suppose I'll let you know. Can I go now?'

'Yes.'

'Quite the morning …'

As soon as Mike had left, Chiamaka put her head around Peter's door. 'Mr Burger called. He wants to know if you have time to meet him today. He says he's free after two.'

'Do I have time? Honestly, after the morning I've had so far, my head is spinning. Do I have any appointments this afternoon?'

'No. So I told Mr Burger you'd be there.'

Peter laughed. 'Thank you, Chiamaka. I'm glad someone knows what they are doing – what *I'm* doing!'

'Coffee?' she asked.

'Gin?'

'Coffee.'

Peter wasn't sure if her voice reminded him of his wife or his mother.

★

Appointments with Faansie Burger inevitably meant that the school was grappling with a problem of sufficient gravity to require legal advice and yet Peter looked forward to them. Partly, he enjoyed Faansie's cheerful demeanour but mostly it was because he seemed quite skilled at making said problems go away.

'Thanks for coming, Peter. I always prefer face to face to talking on the phone.'

'Couldn't agree more. What have you got for me?'

'Two things. I've been over the letter you and Mrs Wintercoat brought in. I've made just a few tweaks but essentially it's perfect. To the point and firmly rooted in their constitution. Have you got the necessary signatures?'

'Last I heard, they had two or three dozen.'

'Splendid. Then I'd say you're good to go. Do let me know what happens.'

'I will. And the other thing?'

'Oh, I received a letter today. Hand-delivered.' Faansie leafed through the many sheets of paper on his desk. 'Ah, here it is.' He passed it to Peter.

'Ministry of Education?'

'Read on.'

Peter did so. A smile crossed his face. 'That's it? End of story?'

'It appears so.'

Peter read part of the letter out loud. '*After further consideration of your letter of 26ᵗʰ February and following a review of the pertinent legislation, the Solicitor General has advised the Ministry that the International School of Ndwalowe is exempt from the terms of the Access to Education Act of 2015.* Exempt? Not just because we are less than three years old but just … exempt? Forever?'

'That's my reading of it.'

'No reason is given.'

'Sometimes people don't want to put too much in writing.'

'I wonder if Mrs Luhanga will know more.'

'I'd put money on it. Whether she'll share it with anyone is another matter.'

'So, that's it? I can report this back to the board and that's the end of the matter?'

Faansie nodded. 'I'll write to the Ministry to acknowledge receipt of their letter but, otherwise, case closed. Glad we could get a result.'

Driving back to school, Peter tried to remember what had been on the day's to-do list when he was shaving that morning and how little of it (i.e. none) he had achieved. 'Oh well,' he said to himself. 'I suppose it's never boring.' Not that he would have objected to a little boring now and again.

The constitution of the ISN PTA (the *current* constitution as Peter insisted on calling it) included the following two items.

11 SPECIAL MEETINGS

11.1 Special Meetings must be announced by the Executive Committee upon the receipt of a written request by not fewer than twelve (12) members.

11.2 Discussion and voting at a Special Meeting is limited to the issue(s) for which the meeting was requested.

11.3 Special Meetings requested by members must be convened within twenty-one (21) calendar days of receipt by the Executive Committee.

13 DISSOLUTION

13.1 The ISN PTA may be dissolved by a 2/3 majority of those members present, in good standing, and voting on such a resolution at a Special Meeting called for that purpose.

13.2 Any resolution to dissolve the ISN PTA shall contain the necessary instructions regarding the disposal of the assets of the PTA.

13.3 Notice of such a Special Meeting must be made to the membership no less than twenty-one (21) calendar days prior to the date of the meeting.

Both were included in the letter delivered to the Executive Committee of the PTA and signed by a little over forty members. Also included was a terse paragraph stating that it was the opinion of the undersigned that the PTA as it was presently constituted no longer represented the interests of the membership and was responsible for the deterioration in the relationship between the PTA and the school administration. A Special Meeting was requested at which it was proposed to dissolve the PTA.

Those who had signed the letter (and many who had not but were sympathetic to it) waited for the response.

'Why,' said Peter to Sheila, 'I've even seen parents huddled in the car park talking about it, all very clandestine and *sotto voce.*'

'Parents gossiping in the car park? Whatever next?'

'I never thought I'd live to see the day.'

But Peter, if he was honest, was also impatient to see how Crystal Moore and her small band of devotees would reply.

'What if they don't?' he had said to Valli. 'What if they then ignore it?'

'Then I think you'll be paying another visit to Mr Burger,' she had replied. 'But really. What an utter waste of time. The PTA is meant to be supporting us.'

And then the reply came. It was addressed to the entire school community and was sent to Cassie for distribution. On this occasion, Peter saw no reason to object.

To all parents and staff of the International School of Ndwalowe

Last week the Executive Committee of the PTA received a letter purporting to come from a small number of members. It requested the Executive Committee to call a Special Meeting (as per Clause §11 of the

336

old constitution), the purpose of which would be to vote on the dissolution of the PTA.

The old constitution is widely considered to be no longer fit for purpose. We are pleased to note that the Educational Director himself is of this opinion. Indeed, a clear example was to be found within the letter we received which cited both Clauses §11.3 and §13.3, each of which contradicts the other.

The Executive Committee has devoted many hours to drafting a new constitution that will – at last – accurately reflect the essential role that the PTA plays in the life of the school to which we are all committed. We look forward to sharing the new constitution with the school community at an early opportunity.

In these circumstances, we see no purpose in convening a meeting that would only serve to distract from the more important business at hand.

Please be assured that we will continue to work tirelessly to represent the interests of the parents whose children attend ISN.

Sincerely,

Crystal Moore, PTA Chair
Nyota Furaha, PTA Vice-Chair
Kim Rankin, PTA Secretary
Madeleine Kaminski, PTA Treasurer
Cathy Kemp, member at large

The reply was more or less what Peter had expected and, indeed, hoped for. Faansie Burger had predicted what the response would be and now briefed Peter on the next steps.

'The Executive Committee is now in violation of its own constitution. It cannot choose whether or not to act upon receipt of such a letter. It is obliged to. The constitution is unambiguous. You, as director, are an *ex officio* member of the Executive Committee – whether they inform you of meetings or not – and so you, as Educational Director and *ex officio* member of the Executive Committee, now have the right – in fact, the duty – to call the special meeting they are refusing to call. I've taken the liberty of drafting the message you should send to the community. I'll send it to you today.'

Having read Faansie's draft back in his office, and not without an almost childish sense of excitement, Peter had forwarded a suitably

337

formatted version on school letterhead to Cassie with instructions to send it out to everyone. His only concern was the passing of time. Depending on which of §11.3 and §13.3 were deemed to take precedence, holding the meeting before the end of the school year would be a close-run thing. Attempting to hold the meeting once school had closed and everyone had departed for their winter/summer holiday was a non-starter. And setting a date early in the new school year risked forfeiting the momentum Peter could feel building.

Moreover, there was still another board meeting to manage – the last of the year before the Annual General Meeting in June.

Peter couldn't decide if he wanted another two or three months to tie up loose ends or for the school year to end tomorrow.

Both, was his not very helpful conclusion.

✶

Carola was usually but not always the first to take her seat in the conference room. Peter's office was just down the corridor but he was often one of the last to arrive. The other members arrived in no particular order, took the best seats, and helped themselves to hot or cold drinks and snacks that were either sweet or savoury but were certainly unhealthy either way.

But on this occasion, Carola made sure that she took her place at the head of the long table before there was any chance of anyone else arriving. She poured the flask of hot water onto a rooibos teabag and hesitated over a chocolate biscuit before deciding against it.

She looked around the room, studying again the framed photographs that now seemed so familiar. She had been attending board meetings in this room for more than two years and for most of that time she had been chairing the meetings. It seemed hard to believe. She could see where she had been sitting when the then chair had solemnly announced that the school was technically bankrupt. Other, more recent, memories of minor dramas came to mind but she shook her head. Board members, parents – even Peter Corby and Lazarett Snyman, she found herself thinking – were well-meaning and educated people. So, why did board meetings so often become bad-tempered? Was it her failure to keep control? And did she really want another year (or more) of this?

Her thoughts were interrupted as the door to the conference room opened and five women entered. Carola, a secret but passionate aficionado of old westerns, immediately had an image of the little deputation running Claire Trevor out of town in *Stagecoach*.

'Er, hello,' she said. 'Are you in the right place?'

'This is where the board meetings happen, isn't it?' As Crystal Moore spoke Carola recognised her.

'Mrs Moore,' she rose to her feet. 'Yes, there will be a board meeting shortly and—'

'And we are here to observe,' stated Nyota Furaha. 'That is how it works, isn't it?'

'I … I don't know. We've never had observers before, as best I can recall.'

'Board meetings are public events, Mrs Lasser. All ISN parents …'

'And teachers,' interrupted Cathy Kemp.

'Yes, all members of the community are welcome to attend board meetings. I'm sure I read that somewhere.'

'It's called transparency,' said Crystal Moore, helping herself to a bottle of water and taking a seat at the far end of the table.

'Then,' said Carola, trying to regain the initiative, 'you are very welcome.'

Some not very subtle whispering between the five members of the PTA notwithstanding, there followed a silence that Carola found very unsettling. Eye contact was briefly made and she attempted to smile but she knew how unconvincing it was.

'Anyone,' she whispered. 'Please, anyone.'

'Anyone' turned out to be Catherine Mulbarton who strode into the room, started to greet Carola, and then noticed the visitors.

'Oh, hello. Mrs Kemp, isn't it? We've met. I'm sorry. I don't know your friends.'

Introductions were quickly made and Catherine's manner swiftly changed. 'Oh, the Executive Committee of the PTA?'

'The very same,' said Crystal. 'I believe your signature was on the letter we received a couple of weeks back.'

'It certainly was.' Catherine looked defiant.

Again the door opened and Grant Guthrie and Clyde Arthurs entered.

'Evening, all …. Oh.'

'We have some observers tonight,' Carola explained hurriedly. 'I believe it is within the, er, rules.'

Again, introductions were made, hands shaken, and the best seats competed for. Board members gathered towards one end of the table, the five visitors towards the other. By the time Peter arrived, his preferred seat had been occupied and there were no more packets of crisps to be had. He settled for a packet of peanuts and a bottle of sparkling water and dubiously played with a chair he knew to be unreliable.

'I had a bad feeling about this,' he later recounted to Sheila a little after midnight and a bottle of Pinotage.

Chiamaka and the remaining members arrived, chairs were shuffled sideways to accommodate the unusual numbers present, and Carola attempted to bring the meeting to order. But just as she looked at her watch and indicated to Chiamaka that proceedings were about to start, the door opened one more time and Colby Wittering entered.

'Good evening,' he spoke as if they had all been waiting for him. 'ISN board meeting, I believe?'

Various heads nodded.

'Very good. Most of you know me. For those who don't, my name is Colby Wittering. I have children in Grade Five and Grade Seven.' He looked at more than a dozen faces. 'We seem to have quite a crowd tonight.'

'Good evening,' a few voices muttered.

Colby looked around and saw a spare chair slouched against the wall. 'I guess this will have to do.' He pulled it forward and squeezed himself in between Trixi and Violet, neither of whom looked best pleased.

Colby beamed at the others in the room. 'Right. Let's get going.'

Carola was looking distinctly unsettled. 'Well, thank you, everyone. This is the last formal board meeting of the year and I—'

'Sorry, Carola, I hate to interrupt but we seem to have … what would they say in the Houses of Parliament? Strangers present.' Grant made a limp gesture towards the other end of the table.

'Observers, Grant. Parents of children in the school. Our meetings are open and observers are … welcome. Is that not so, Peter?'

Peter was going to answer but Colby was first to speak. 'You're asking the director? The educational director? Sorry, but who's running this meeting? You are the chair. You're in charge of this meeting. Not him. You don't ask him how to proceed. You tell him!'

'Of course, but …' Carola was as flustered as he had seen her.

'Madam Chair,' Peter could seldom be bothered with what some considered appropriate etiquette but he thought it might be to his advantage on this occasion, 'my understanding of the Articles of Association is that parents and employees are indeed welcome to attend meetings of the board of directors but they attend strictly as observers. In other words, they may observe, they may witness, but they are not at liberty to join in with discussions unless they are expressly invited to do so. Is that not the case?'

He looked around the room. Several board members who Peter was quite sure had never studied the Articles of Association in any depth nodded in agreement.

'Correct.'

'Absolutely.'

'That's my understanding too.'

'Then,' said Carola, 'if that's clear to everyone …' She turned to Chiamaka. 'I make it six minutes past.'

Most board meetings in most schools are divided into two sessions. The first is 'open' and observers from the community are welcome to attend. Routine and uncontroversial matters are attended to in this session. But items that are confidential or in some way sensitive are discussed in a 'closed' session, sometimes called an executive session, and such observers as may be present will be politely asked to leave.

As usual, proceedings began with the minutes of the previous meeting held on 16th April where it was noted that Valli and Mick were attending for the first time. This was met with a frown from Colby.

'You have the director and a teacher and now both principals?'

'Mr Wittering …'

'That's ridiculous. They almost outnumber the real board members.'

'Mr Wittering,' Carola tried again, 'as I think was made clear, and I say this respectfully, observers are not invited to contribute to the discussion.'

Colby Wittering was not someone used to hearing the word no. 'So, fee-paying parents must stay silent while the entire administration of the school—'

'But, of course, you don't pay fees, do you? Your company pays.' Valli could not help herself.

She earned a sharp rebuke from Carola, 'Ms Agnelli!'

'Well, I pay my daughter's fees and I think parents should be allowed to speak,' Cathy Kemp said. 'I remember at the AGM last year the board didn't seem to want to hear what the parents thought. It's disgraceful.'

'Ladies and gentlemen!' Carola rarely raised her voice but she certainly did now. 'The protocol has been explained and it is not for those present to either agree with it or disagree with it. It is what it is. Members of the school community are welcome to attend but they are not welcome to contribute to the discussion. May I please ask that we have no more interruptions.'

Glares were exchanged across the table but no one spoke.

Carola consulted her agenda. 'Clyde, the strategic plan committee.'

'Thank you, Carola. I'm afraid the committee hasn't found time to meet since the last board meeting. I was travelling and one of the other members was in hospital for a minor operation. I know I said last month that our deadline was still achievable – just – but I'm afraid that is no longer the case. It looks like we will have to have the consultation phase at the start of next year. I'm sorry.'

'Being on the board isn't a hobby.' Colby Wittering's words hung in the air. 'I can see now why you didn't want me. Scared that someone would hold you all to account.'

'Mr Wittering, I must—'

'Oh don't worry, Mrs Lasser. I'm going.' He pushed his chair back noisily and stood. 'I've seen enough. But I can assure you I will be standing for election at the AGM. You are having elections, aren't you? You'd better. It's time the school had some competent people in charge. Good night.'

He didn't bother to close the door. In a rather stunned silence, Grant stood and gently pushed the door shut. 'Well, anyone else want to make a grand exit?'

'I think most of us would like to make an exit, grand or otherwise.' Mick gave a little chuckle. 'You didn't tell us that board meetings were this lively.'

'Oh, it's never dull, Mr O'Cheney.' Catherine sounded weary. She turned to Carola. 'This might be as good a time as any to inform you that I won't be standing for re-election. I think two years is about all I can take.'

'Oh, Catherine …'

'There will be vacancies?' Crystal asked.

'Two by the look of it,' Lazarett answered her. 'And we still have an existing vacancy to fill so three. Unless, of course, we decide to expand the board which I personally think would be sensible. Then we could have four or five new members.'

'Excellent,' said Crystal. 'Perhaps the PTA could have a permanent place on the board.' She looked at Nyota who nodded approvingly.

'Mrs Moore, if you don't mind, we still have a long agenda to get through.' Carola looked at her watch. 'We really must get on.'

'Is the PTA on the agenda?'

'The PTA? No, why?'

'I would have thought in the current situation the board would want to step in. The administration appears to be orchestrating a campaign to discredit the PTA. I cannot believe you are going to permit that.'

'Is that why you are here?' Clyde was still smarting from Colby's jibe. 'To pursue this ridiculous squabble? I think it is clear to everyone in the school what is going on and I might say that the board are fully behind the educational director. I am not a parent but I know many people who are and, without exception, they are tired of the PTA trying to arrogate to itself extraordinary powers and authorities.'

'Well said!' Catherine patted Clyde on the arm.

Crystal Moore was rather taken aback. 'We are here because the director seems to want to abolish the PTA. I can only speculate why. And I had hoped that the board might intervene. Whoever heard of a school without a PTA?'

'It's not unknown,' said Trixi. 'There are alternatives. And, frankly, anything would be better than what we currently have.'

'Does no one here think the director should be accountable?' Crystal was quickly losing her swagger.

'He is accountable,' Carola looked the length of the table at Crystal. 'He is accountable to the board of directors which is as it should be. He is not accountable to the PTA. Nobody is.'

★

'And with that,' Peter said, 'Crystal Moore and her merry band departed, trying to maintain their dignity but in reality with tails firmly between their legs. Violet was in tears. She's a personal friend of Cathy Kemp and I think she found the whole thing particularly awkward.'

'You talk as if I know these people,' said Sheila. 'Which one is Cathy Kemp?'

'Oh, just a parent. She made a few waves last year. She is definitely not a member of my fan club.'

'You have a fan club?'

'They prefer to keep a low profile but, believe it or not, there are a few parents who think I'm not doing an altogether terrible job.'

'And the board?'

'Oh, I'll never win Lazarett over and I miss Ernesto but most of them seem to think I'm doing all right.'

'Well, they gave you a new contract.'

'Months ago. You're still happy we're staying for two more years?'

'Yes. Yes, I am. I like it here. I'm glad we came.'

Peter smiled. 'And now, darling, it's gone midnight and I'm back at work in less than seven hours. Bedtime.'

He blew out the candles.

★

June

To no one's great surprise, Lazarett had been the most enthusiastic about the approach from PAIS.

'I don't know anything about them and we must obviously conduct due diligence,' he had said, 'but, in principle, I think this is a very interesting and potentially beneficial proposal. Even before the bankruptcy, the school was never wealthy. And, although we are breaking even now, it will be many years before we have the resources to invest in the facilities I think we all agree we need. I know there are those who argue that we are a school and not a business but I think this approach from PAIS demonstrates that in the modern world schools are indeed businesses. And, as I understand it, with the right management structure, they can be quite profitable. Mr Corby has lectured us more than once on the, I daresay, honourable history of independent and not-for-profit international schools but, let's be frank, such schools may have been appropriate in the nineteen-seventies and eighties but we are now in the second decade of the twenty-first century.

'The market has been shown to be the best compass for guaranteeing efficiency and customer satisfaction. That is no longer in question in industries all over the world from retailing to transport. Why should the provision of high-quality education be different? We know already that there are parents in Ndwalowe who are more than willing and able to pay for the best available education for their children. There is no doubt that the demand is there. I would almost say that we would be negligent not to investigate further an opportunity that appears to have been dropped into our lap.'

No one else had been quite as supportive as Lazarett but the general feeling was that the board should at least invite Mr Noble or whoever to explain in a bit more detail what PAIS could offer and what the implications would be for the school.

Peter, as requested, had made a presentation to the board about what he had been able to discover about PAIS and about other chains of for-profit international schools. He had endeavoured to be objective but he could not hide his misgivings. He had, however, been pleased that the other three experienced educators in the meeting had broadly echoed his reservations. Trixi had even announced, 'I worked in one of these schools in Qatar. My husband did too. They are cowboys. Sup with them at your peril.'

Nevertheless, it had been agreed that a committee, chaired by Lazarett, would contact Mr Noble and decide what the next steps would be. Peter had asked to be included on the committee, a proposal that Lazarett had strenuously resisted, but Carola and a clear majority of the board had overruled him.

'Of course, the director should be involved in the discussions. Who else knows more about the school?'

'But any final decision is the board's alone,' Lazarett had insisted.

'Of course. We rely on the director to give us expert advice but it is the board that must make such key decisions.'

Even Peter couldn't disagree with that.

'Ah, that's interesting,' Ernesto had said when Peter had shown him the approach from PAIS. 'My firm considered investing in international schools a couple of years back. It was more my partner's thing than mine but I know he held discussions with a few such businesses. I've no idea if PAIS was one of them.'

'Did you? Did you invest?'

'No. In the end, we decided against it. It just takes too long to see a return. Seven or eight years, typically. That suits the business models of some investors but we tend to go for quick wins.'

'Could you find out about PAIS for me? I've no idea if this proposal will go anywhere but it might and if it does, I'd like to know who we're getting into bed with.'

'I'm sure the board will conduct due diligence before signing anything.'

'Oh, for sure. But you're a professional and some of the board members are, well, a little naïve. Plus, the board treasurer is not necessarily someone I trust. Have you met him? His name's Snyman.'

Ernesto scowled. 'Point taken. Look, I don't know what I can discover, if anything, but I'll certainly ask around.'

'Thanks.'

✱

Chiamaka appeared at Peter's door. 'Peter …'

Before she could speak she was shoved aside by a burly man followed by a tiny woman about half his size.

'Mr Corby?'

'Yes.'

'My name is Gerson Swart. This is my wife, Minni. I daresay you know our daughter, Missie.'

'No, I'm sorry to say I don't. I …'

'She's in Grade Ten. She isn't even sixteen.' Mr Swart was trembling with emotion.

'Mr Swart, Mrs Swart, please take a seat. I can see you are clearly upset. What is it I—'

'You don't know?'

'I'm sorry. I have no idea …'

'Our daughter, Mr Corby, is pregnant. She is going to have a baby.'

'Oh.'

'*Oh*? Is that it?'

For a fleeting second Peter wondered if they were accusing him of being the father. 'Oh, dear,' he said, 'And …'

'And your counsellor knew but chose not to tell us, her parents.'

'Ms Coady? I find that hard—'

'No, not Ms Coady. The other one. Ms Gardner. She knew but didn't tell us.'

'Oh,' said Peter. 'I was certainly not aware of that and I can fully understand your annoyance. Please … take a seat.'

'*Annoyance*? I can assure you that I feel a great deal more than annoyance.'

'I'm sure. I'm sorry,' said Peter. 'What … When?'

'Yesterday. Missie was late home and her excuses made no sense. My wife eventually got it out of her.'

She almost certainly wanted to tell her mother one way or another, Peter thought.

'What did she say?'

'She said that she went to Ms Gardner a few days ago because she thought she might be pregnant.'

'You didn't know?'

'Of course not! And yesterday morning – at school – Ms Gardner gave her a pregnancy test.'

'And it was positive?'

Mr Swart nodded. 'It is clear to me, Mr Corby, that Ms Gardner is seriously at fault. She had no business going behind our backs. Look what she's done.'

It seemed to Peter that young Missie Swart and whoever the father was were the ones responsible for the current situation but nor was he sure he could defend Lee-Ann.

'We love our daughter! If she is facing the biggest challenge of her short life, we, her parents, should be the ones beside her, holding her hand. Not some probably well-meaning but innocent young woman out of some Midwestern college.'

'Mr Swart, I'm not going to defend Ms Gardner's actions and I will most certainly speak to her but I think what matters here is Missie. Is she in school today?'

'Of course not.'

'Does she not want to come?'

'We don't want her to.'

'Because …?'

'We think the father is a boy in this school,' Mrs Swart spoke for the first time.

'You think? But you don't know?'

'She won't tell us but we have a pretty good idea.'

'What a mess,' said Peter. 'I'm so sorry.'

They sat in silence. Mr Swart's anger appeared to have dissipated somewhat.

'I suppose she was only trying to help,' muttered Mrs Swart. 'I mean, this isn't her fault, Ms Gardner.'

Her husband flashed her a furious look.

'Why don't we speak to her?' said Peter. 'Missie obviously trusts her and whatever happens going forward Ms Gardner may be able to help – not that I'm defending or condoning her actions yesterday. But let's hear what she has to say. What do you think?'

'I'm very unhappy with what she did,' Mr Swart was scowling again.

'I know you are and I understand. I do. But all the adults in Missie's life now need to work together to do what's best for her. Let me see if Lee-Ann can join us.'

★

Lee-Ann was, by anyone's standards, still young and, by chance, had indeed graduated from a college in the Midwest but she was far from innocent and quite experienced enough to let Mr Swart vent without interrupting him.

'You had no right to keep it a secret! She isn't even sixteen. She's a child. We are her parents.' The more he spoke, the more it seemed he was almost blaming Lee-Ann for the pregnancy. Peter was impressed by how calmly Lee-Ann listened to Mr Swart, maintaining eye contact, and gently nodding now and again. At length, he burned himself out. 'I'm really not happy about this.'

'Lee-Ann,' began Peter, 'perhaps you could tell us how this all came about. How do you even know Missie?'

'I coach the girls' basketball team.'

'Oh, of course you do. I'd forgotten.'

'And I've come to know Missie quite well. I'd say we have a pretty good relationship.'

'When did she tell you? When did she tell you she was pregnant?' Mr Swart still wanted to establish Lee-Ann's culpability.

'Well, she didn't know she was pregnant but she thought she might be. She told me three days ago.'

'And you didn't tell us?'

'As a counsellor—'

'Oh, don't give us that confidentiality thing. She's fifteen!'

'What I told her was that she must tell her parents. I told her that if she didn't, then I would. Yes, I generally have to respect the confidentiality of what students tell me but I have to use my judgement. And, as you say, she's only fifteen.'

'So, what happened yesterday?'

'We had arranged that I would give her a pregnancy test.'

'I can't believe this. You think you have the right to do this? Without telling her parents?'

'Mr Swart, my responsibility is to the student. In this case to Missie.'

'But you were going to tell Mr and Mrs Swart, weren't you?' Peter realised he had no idea what the protocol was in such situations. Or even what the law said.

'Because the result was positive, yes. I told her that she must tell her mother as soon as she got home or I would have to tell her – tell you, Mrs Swart – today. She sent me an SMS last night saying that she'd told you.'

'And you believed her?'

'Well, she did tell you, didn't she?'

'So,' Peter said, 'just to be clear. If the result had been negative, you wouldn't have said anything? Is that right?'

'I would have strongly urged Missie to tell her parents that she was sexually active …'

Mr Swart winced as Lee-Ann spoke.

'… but I probably wouldn't have said anything if she really didn't want me to.'

'Don't you have a legal obligation to inform the parents?' Peter asked. Lee-Ann seemed quite sure of herself but he could absolutely see Mr Swart's point of view. 'If I had a teenage daughter, I'd want to know. Or …' he quickly added, '… a teenage son.'

'If they're sixteen or over, there is no obligation to inform the parents.'

'But she isn't,' repeated Mr Swart. 'She's only fifteen.'

'Yes, and the law says that I must inform the parents but only if the age difference between a minor – in this case Missie – and the father is more than three years.'

'You know who the father is?'

Lee-Ann hesitated, 'No, I don't know. Not for sure. But Missie certainly gave me to understand that it's a boy of her own age. Or close to.'

'We'll get it out of her,' said Mr Swart.

Lee-Ann ignored him but turned to Mrs Swart. 'Mrs Swart, if I may, I think it may be time for a mother-daughter conversation.'

'And I'll have a father-daughter conversation with her,' growled Mr Swart, 'But it might be a bit one-sided.'

'Gerson, please. Miss Gardner is right. Last week Missie was a little girl. Now … Well, there's no going back. Whether we like it or not, things have changed.' Mrs Swart turned to Lee-Ann. 'Would you help me? I mean, have the conversation with Missie. She obviously trusts you. I'd like us to do it together.'

'Oh. Well, if that's what you want, I'll be happy to help.'

'Thank you.'

'So,' Mr Swart raised his voice. 'That's it? Mr Corby, you aren't going to do anything? You're defending Ms Gardner?'

'Believe it or not, Mr Swart, but this is a first for me. And I've been teaching for more than twenty years. I know teenager girls do get pregnant but I've never had to deal with it until now. My initial impression is that Ms Gardner acted, um, appropriately. But, as I say, I have no detailed understanding of what usually happens. But, please be assured, I'm going to convene a meeting just as soon as I can with Ms Gardner and Ms Coady and, thinking about it, Ms Mthembu, the school nurse. I wish the circumstances had been different but, now that this has come up, I want to talk to my colleagues so that we are all on the same page. I want to be sure that the school does the right thing. For everyone. For the students and the parents.'

'Huh,' Mr Swart scoffed. 'All well and good but a bit late for Missie.'

'I know and I'm sorry. But please know that whatever happens with Missie now, the school will give you all the support it can.'

'And when I find out who the boy is? And I will.'

'Let's cross that bridge when we get to it. For now, we need to focus on Missie.'

There seemed nothing more to say.

'Mr and Mrs Swart, I'm so sorry this has happened but I want to thank you for letting me know …'

'Because it sounds like she wasn't going to.' Mr Swart waved rather contemptuously at Lee-Ann.

Peter ignored him but addressed both parents. 'You both must work with your daughter to find the best way forward. But if you want Lee-Ann to help in any way, I know she'll be more than happy to do so. And I really hope you will allow Missie to return to school tomorrow. Pregnant or not, she belongs here.'

'But for how long?'

'For as long as you and she want, Mrs Swart.'

'Even when …'

'Yes. I may not have had to deal with this situation before but that doesn't mean I haven't thought about it. There are schools where pregnant girls are forced to leave. I don't intend that ISN is that kind of school. Missie is going to face major challenges going forward. The last thing she needs is the school adding to them.'

'Other parents …'

'Oh, I have no doubt. But you let me deal with them. It's at times like these that we find out who really believes in the school's values and who just pays lip-service to them.'

Which is also true, he thought unhappily, *of board members.*

★

The dinner party in December having been a success (well, the concept, the food, and the ambiance, if not the outcome) Sheila and Peter had dared to invite a few more friends around for canapés, sundowners, Sunday lunches, bar-be-ques, and – for the lucky few – tree rats.

A long-awaited coup was at last getting both Ronald and Jenny Wintercoat to take a night off and join the Corbys for dinner. Peter had initially thought of preparing two or three curries. But, upon further reflection, he had thought it might be altogether better not to. So, the menu consisted of roast red pepper soup, a lamb cassoulet and, all four diners being British, a lemon meringue pie.

'I've got to be honest,' he said to his guests, 'it's a bit intimidating cooking for professional restauranteurs. Never mind the proprietors of the best restaurant in town.'

'Shall I tell you a secret?,' said Ronald, 'I can't even boil an egg. Jenny can about find her way around a kitchen without a map but even she would not claim to be more than a workaday cook. Isn't that so, darling?'

'You're too kind,' said Jenny. 'But fair enough. Businesswoman of the year, maybe, but BBC MasterChef, never! Anyway, Peter, you sell yourself short. This soup is delicious.'

'Oh, it's a very simple recipe.'

'Don't you just hate it when good cooks always say that?' Ronald affected genuine outrage.

'Thank you anyway,' Peter laughed.

'So,' Jenny said, 'year two – for you, Peter – draws to a close. It's flown by, hasn't it?'

'It certainly has. But it's far from over. The AGM next week and the meeting to wind up the PTA the next week. Just a day before the end of the school year.'

'And a PTA AGM,' said Ronald. 'Didn't you tell me that was overdue?'

'Oh, that was weeks ago,' said Jenny. 'Yes, they were meant to have one but then with the motion to close down the PTA they just refused. I think they know how badly it would have gone for them if they'd tried to go ahead.'

'And I'm hearing rumours that at the board AGM Colby Wittering is going to try to force through some sort of motion of no confidence.'

'Colby Wittering?'

'A parent. He works for McKinsey.'

'Here? We have McKinsey people here in Ndwalowe?'

'Well, at least one. God knows what he does. But he put himself forward to join the board. He thinks very highly of himself.'

'And he doesn't like tree rats,' said Sheila, rather to the mystification of Jenny and Ronald.

'And?'

'And the board said thanks, but no thanks.'

'Ooh, er. I bet Mr Witterling—'

'Wittering.'

'Well, I guess he wasn't best pleased.'

'You could say that. He then crashed a board meeting and … do you know what he reminded me of? Donald Trump. Self-important, boorish, rude …'

'Oh, that's Trump on a good day. He can do much better than that.'

'I think Colby was just warming up. Let's see what happens at the AGM.'

'But for a vote of no confidence, he'll need supporters – a constituency. Does he have friends among the parents?'

'I have absolutely no idea. But—'

'Right. That's it!' said Sheila with finality. 'You promised me no school talk tonight. Enough's enough.'

'You're right. Sorry. Jenny, your glass is empty. Let me …'

✱

Ernesto's partner, Hanno Scheppmann, recalled negotiating with PAIS.

'Seemed like a pretty well-run outfit,' he told Ernesto. 'Based in Dubai, if I remember rightly.'

Unfortunately, the discussions having gone nowhere, all relevant correspondence and notes had long since been deleted. But it did afford Ernesto an opening and he had set up a video call with Todd Noble.

Each man introduced himself and it took no time before they realised, almost inevitably, that they had mutual acquaintances.

'You know Lisa? Hah. She and I worked together in Singapore when I was with BlackRock. And how did you meet Kanan?'

'He was advising a start-up we were putting money into in Kenya.'

'And how did that work out?'

'Very well. I'm hoping we can work with him again.'

'Good man, Kanan. Very sharp. Anyway, how can I help you?'

'Well, as I explained in my email, my partner, Hanno Scheppmann, talked to some of your people about three years back.'

'Yes. I wasn't here then but there are people here who remember him. It's a shame we couldn't make it work.'

'Yeah, it didn't happen then but we're once again looking at the education sector. It's obviously booming.'

'Absolutely. We have a number of acquisitions pending that we think will be very lucrative. It's a good time to get in.'

'As I'm sure you know, our own focus is on Africa. Certain economies here are thriving and there's huge potential for growth.'

'That's pretty much our conclusion too. We see Africa as a key growth market in the next five years or so.'

'So you are looking at schools in Africa?'

'Oh, we're looking at schools everywhere.'

'Any particular places in Africa?'

'Ernesto, you know I can't go into details but let's just say that we have identified a few schools that would fit our portfolio.'

'Of course, of course.' Ernesto nodded. And then he showed his hand. 'Todd, I'm going to be straight with you. You know we are based in Awanza?'

'I do.'

'And my daughter attends the international school here.'

'Really? I didn't know that. Does she like it?'

'She loves it. And, as a parent, I'm very happy with it too.'

'I'm very glad to hear that.'

'And to be honest, that's one of the reasons we are turning our thoughts back to investing in international schools.'

Todd said nothing.

'You see,' Ernesto continued, 'there's a rumour here that PAIS are talking to the school. The International School of Ndwalowe.'

'Oh? I wonder where you heard that rumour.'

'Oh, this is a very small town. Everyone knows everyone. And,' Ernesto paused for effect, 'I used to be on the board of the school. Until quite recently, in fact.'

'Is that a fact? So, you, er, you know the current members of the board?'

'All of them. Of course.'

'Hmm. Interesting.'

'Todd, I'm just going to ask. Are you in discussion with ISN?'

'And, as I said, Ernesto, you really wouldn't expect me to answer that. But let's just say we were. For the sake of argument. If ISN was a school we might have an interest in, what could you bring to the table?'

'Well, obviously, any proposition made to the school – a takeover, a partnership, investment, whatever – would ultimately be the board's decision. I know the director, Peter Corby. It might be helpful for you to know that he would not be in favour of any involvement by PAIS.'

'He's said that?'

'Not in so many words, but I know him. He's, er, not a great fan of the free market.'

'Bit of a lefty?'

'Sort of. And his voice will carry some weight. But I'm sure there are others on the board who would be much better disposed towards the PAIS offer.'

'*Offer*? We're very far from making an offer.'

'Of course. Of course. But when – if – such an offer were forthcoming … how can I put this … might there be certain incentives …? I mean, my understanding is that although PAIS – or whoever – may own a given school, there might remain in place a board of some sort to provide some veneer of local autonomy. That's right, isn't it?'

Todd was still wary. 'It's not unknown.'

'And although the board members of international schools are unpaid volunteers, the members of a board reporting to Dubai would be … remunerated in some way?'

'Every school is a bit different but that is one model, yes.'

'So, it might not be … Well, it actually would be a good thing if you had someone who had influence. I mean, someone to whom the other board members would listen.'

Todd said nothing.

'Wouldn't it?' Ernesto persisted.

The two men were more than three thousand miles apart but the miracles of technology allowed Ernesto to see Todd Nobel's smirk. 'But we already do …'

★

Peter liked to position himself each morning and afternoon where he could observe cars arriving and departing, unloading or collecting students, and parking where they ought to or ought not to. Parents and students said they liked to see him and it got him out of the office for twenty minutes or so. In truth, it was one of the more enjoyable parts of the day. So it annoyed him when a phone call or some other inconvenience delayed him. He would then hurry downstairs, try to make it through the reception without being waylaid, and …'

'Mr Corby! There you are. You need to come quickly.'

He recognised the mother who had grabbed him by the elbow but he couldn't recall her name.

'Mrs … What is it? What's wrong?'

'I'll show you. Come.'

She turned and jogged out of the admin building and towards the car park. Peter followed.

'There!' she said. 'Look!'

The car park included a number of elevated islands where pedestrians could stand safely and against which cars would park. Large flowerpots were strategically placed to dissuade drivers from squeezing into forbidden nooks and corners. Not a few of them bore the scratches and scars that confirmed that they had done their jobs rather successfully. The islands were connected by raised walkways painted in irregular stripes of black and white, the busiest of which were policed by teachers in high vis waistcoats. But on the margins some walkways were unattended and it was to one of these that Peter's agitated mother was leading him.

'See?'

Peter did see.

A large BMW was parked on the walkway between two other cars.

'It's her. That woman. She's done it before!'

Peter looked to where she was pointing. 'Oh, no,' he said. He had only exchanged words with Mrs Emangweni once, more than a year ago when her car had been quite badly damaged by an inexperienced guard closing an electronic gate too soon. She had not taken it well.

She was now striding towards him and mouthing something he couldn't quite make out until she got closer.

'… and she should mind her own business! She's always trying to get others in trouble.'

'Mrs Emangweni,' Peter attempted not to sound too accusative, 'this is your car?'

'Yes. It is.'

'Well, I'm sorry but you really can't park there. This is …'

'There was nowhere else. The car park is full. Anyway, I was only sixty seconds.'

'You've been there for at least seven or eight minutes!' the first mother objected.

'And what's it got to do with you? You should keep your nose out of things that don't concern you.'

'These things do—'

'Ladies!' said Peter. 'Please. Can we keep our voices down. There's no need to escalate this. Mrs Emangweni, I'm going to ask you to move your car. You are blocking the walkway.'

'I will if this woman gives me an apology. Who does she think she is? This isn't a colony anymore. We are in charge now.'

Oh Gawd, thought Peter. *This is getting silly.*

'Are you saying that because I'm white?' The nameless mother glared at Mrs Emangweni.

'I'm saying it because you still think you make the rules here. And you don't.'

'Well, the bottom line is that in this school I make the rules, Mrs Emangweni,' Peter was increasingly eager to bring this to a close. 'And one of them is that cars don't park on the crossings. So, I'm asking you again, please move your car.' A small crowd was gathering.

'This isn't your country either, Mr Corby. You are a guest here and you'd be well advised to remember that.' She shoved her way between Peter and the other mother, fiddling for her car keys.

The other mother put her hand on Mrs Emangweni's shoulder. 'Just wait a minute. I don't think you should talk to Mr Corby like that.'

'Oh!' Mrs Emangweni reacted as if she had been shot. 'That's assault! You saw that, Mr Corby. She assaulted me.'

'Oh, for goodness' sake. This is getting ridiculous.'

'What's her name? This white woman. What's her name? I am going to press charges.'

Peter shook his head. 'I don't know. I only know you because ...'

'I might have known you'd take her side. This is discrimination.' This time successfully, she barged past Peter and into her car. Muttering inaudibly, she reversed quite recklessly into the stream of departing cars. Horns sounded and some drivers looked quizzically and perhaps accusingly at Peter. The BMW accelerated away towards the exit.

International schools, small or large, independent or part of a chain, not-for-profit or greedily for-profit, must have some form of legal standing in the country where they operate. They might be established as a company or perhaps a trust. Some are registered charities; some are wholly owned by wealthy individuals. But if they are to employ people, seek accreditation and authorisation by local and international bodies, pay tax or enjoy tax-free status, enter into contracts with service providers and municipal utilities, and much else, they will be required to have and adhere to a document that defines sundry duties and responsibilities, competences and liabilities, protocols and regulations, relationships and conventions. The International School of Ndwalowe had adopted a very lightly edited version of the Articles of Association that had served the old Ndwalowe International School until its abrupt and untimely bankruptcy. It had been readily acknowledged that the Articles were in need of substantial revision and at the start of the new school's second year of existence such a task had been identified as a priority. But boards have lots of priorities and the establishment of a nominations committee in April was as much progress as was made. Even then, it had not met until May and its first meeting had been overshadowed by Colby Wittering's attempt to bully himself onto the board.

'He would in any case have to be elected at the AGM, wouldn't he?'

'No, Catherine, some members are appointed and some elected. It's in the Articles.'

'I'm trying to remember what happened two years ago.'

'Two years ago we were dragging ourselves out of bankruptcy. I don't think anyone was too worried about constitutional niceties. There was just general relief that we could scrape together a board.' Trixi recalled the dramatic events of almost exactly two years previously.

'You were elected, weren't you? By the staff?'

'Yes.'

'And you will be again?'

'I don't know, Catherine. I'm happy to do another term but it'll depend if anyone else wants to stand.'

'It's all in the Articles,' Clyde tapped the thick folder lying before him. 'The staff must vote three working days before the AGM so that the result can be announced and the board ratify it.'

'Gosh, this is all very legalistic,' said Catherine. 'But I suppose it's necessary.'

'Anyway,' said Clyde, 'are we all agreed? We can put out the invitations for nominations?'

'We're only just going to meet the deadline,' said Trixi. 'So, yes. Let's get it done. You two won't be on the board but next year I think we need to get this sorted much earlier.'

No one disagreed.

★

Peter was recalling Saskia's words from a year ago.

'Former general in the army. Former politician. Rumoured to be the richest man in Awanza. Definitely not someone you want to make an enemy of.'

That last part made his throat go dry. In Peter's brief experience, corruption in Awanza meant slipping a few banknotes to someone in uniform. But he had heard enough stories – not least about some of the parents whose children attended his school – to know that the bigger fish played the game by different rules. Only a few months earlier *The New Awanzan* had published what Peter thought were unnecessarily gory details of what appeared to be the contract killing of a wealthy Angolan. Two young men were swiftly apprehended and charged. The murder had been clumsy – amateurish, even – but the guy was still dead.

And how big a fish was Mr Julius Emangweni? Peter wondered.

Former general in the army. Former politician. Rumoured to be the richest man in Awanza.

The biggest fish Peter could think of was the whale shark but, despite its alarming name, he knew it to be more or less harmless. Unless you were a small fish.

Awaiting Mr Emangweni's arrival, Peter felt very small indeed.

★

Some international schools have boards that are comprised entirely of parents elected by parents. Very few schools have boards that do not include any parents but many see merit in including expertise from beyond the school's orbit. To make this possible, boards often have the authority to appoint members, though their constitutions usually stipulate the acceptable ratio between appointed and elected.

For two years at ISN no one had given much thought to who was elected and who was appointed. And when they did, the situation was not as clear as would have been hoped. Carola had agreed to be chair of a new board at the heated meeting called in the immediate aftermath of the bankruptcy. But had she been elected or appointed? Trixi, Catherine and Violet had all been there and tried to recall the exact sequence of events. They agreed that no vote had been taken.

'It was more by acclamation, I suppose,' Trixi had suggested.

'But Catherine and I were elected,' Violet insisted.

'And Ernesto too?'

'No,' said Carola, 'I invited him onto the board a little later.'

'So he was appointed?'

'I suppose so.'

Another issue was the status of Clyde Arthurs and Grant Guthrie representing the US Embassy and the British High Commission respectively. Clyde was stepping down (in fact, he was returning to Washington) so was it an expectation that his replacement must be nominated by the Embassy? No one, least of all Clyde, was sure.

Lazarett had been recommended by the Official Receiver and after a meeting with Carola had agreed to join the board. But did the chair acting alone have the authority to appoint or did it require a decision by the whole board?

And quite how Mrs Luhanga had ended up on the board was a further complication. Her appointment had been insisted upon by the Ministry of Education. But where did that fit into the Articles of Association?

At length, it was decided that Carola and Violet would stand for re-election at the AGM. Trixi would be re-elected by the staff (no one seemed inclined to stand against her) and Grant, Lazarett and Mrs Luhanga would be re-appointed. Two more members would be elected from among the parent body and then the new board would make two further appointments, one of which may or may not be a representative of the US Embassy. A board of ten including equal numbers of elected and appointed members was agreed to meet the school's needs and it certainly satisfied the Articles of Association.

'Anyway,' said Grant. 'It's all pretty arcane stuff. As long as we're happy, I can't imagine any parents caring very much.'

Most of those present nodded in agreement.

★

Peter had been informed that Mr Emangweni would be coming to see him a little after twelve. In Peter's book parents requested appointments rather than announcing when they were coming but given what he knew of his visitor it seemed unwise to antagonise him.

Keeping a nervous eye on the wall clock, Peter tried to distract himself with the minutes of last year's AGM but his thoughts kept returning to the ridiculous altercation in the car park. *Assault?* Did Mrs Emangweni seriously consider what happened an act of aggression? And was she really going to press charges? It was ludicrous but with such an influential husband, might a court or a judge be sympathetic to her complaint? And what if it got into the papers? He could see the headlines.

Perhaps still more worrying was the implicit accusation of racism. What had she said? *This is discrimination.* Peter groaned and saw in his mind still worse newspaper headlines.

Chiamaka appeared at his door. 'Peter. Mr Emangweni …'

Peter stood as his guest strode into his office. Chiamaka quietly closed the door behind him.

Mr Emangweni wore an obviously expensive suit, presumably expensive sunglasses pushed back on his head, and when he extended his hand to Peter he revealed what was assuredly a ridiculously expensive gold wristwatch.

'Mr Corby,' he said as they shook hands, 'it's very good of you to see me at such short notice.' He was smiling.

'Not at all, Mr Emangweni,' he motioned for his guest to take a seat. 'This is an issue that needs to be dealt with promptly. I'm sure neither of us wishes for it to escalate further.'

Mr Emangweni frowned. 'I'm sorry …'

'I'm sure your wife has told you about the incident in the car park.'

Mr Emangweni's frown deepened. And then he threw his head back and laughed. 'Oh, that? Yes, she did mention something. But I didn't take it seriously. She's always imaging some sort of slight or insult. Please don't give it another thought. She gets all worked up but then it all blows over. She's probably forgotten about it already.'

'So, that isn't why you are here?' Peter wasn't sure if he was relieved or slightly frustrated.

'No, not at all,' Mr Emangweni laughed again. 'This is more of a business meeting.'

'Oh?'

'I hear you are selling the school. I might be interested.'

★

The board, in their collective naivety, had been quite taken aback during the last AGM. Carola, for one, was determined that wouldn't happen again.

'I still can't understand the anger, the insinuations. My goodness, we're all parents. We all want what's best for the school,' she complained to Peter.

'You mean, we're all on the same side?' he had answered.

'Yes!'

'That's not the way the world's going, Carola. Brexit in my country, Trump in America. Consensus has become a dirty word. It's a weakness. You choose your side and you fight for it.'

'In a school? How can there be sides?'

'Or on a board?'

Carola nodded sadly. 'Do I really want another year – or two – of this?'

'Well, let's see who's elected. If you and Violet are re-elected there will be at least two new members and then we – oh,' Peter feigned an apology, 'I'm sorry, the board – the *voting* members – can appoint two more. Do you think we could get Ernesto back?'

'I've asked him. He always says no.'

'We – sorry, you – could appoint him.'

'But only if he agrees. And if Violet or I are not re-elected?'

'Oh, come on. You will be.'

Carola did not look convinced. And, in reality, Peter wasn't entirely sure either.

✳

Peter had heard of schools where it was almost impossible to achieve a quorum for the Annual General Meeting. 'Surely, that's a good sign,' people had argued. 'We can be sure they would be there if they were unhappy.'

So, as the auditorium filled and extra chairs were hurriedly brought in from storage, Peter's heart sank. *Unhappy?* He wondered.

He did not have long to wonder.

Carola brought the meeting to order and was almost immediately challenged by a voice from the floor. It was a familiar voice.

'Madam Chair,' began Colby Wittering, 'forgive me but I am unacquainted with the conventions and protocols of these meetings. Would you allow me to raise a point of order?'

'A point of order?'

'Yes, if you wouldn't mind.'

'Well, I'm not sure …'

But Colby Wittering pressed on. 'You, Mrs Lasser, are conducting this meeting as Chair of the Board of Directors of the International School of Ndwalowe, are you not?'

Carola looked puzzled. 'Yes, I am.'

'And the gentlemen and ladies sitting with you on the stage are the members of the board of directors, are they not?'

'Yes. Of course.'

'By whose authority?'

'I'm sorry.'

'We are, as I understand it, here tonight to elect a new board of directors as defined in the school's Articles of Association.' As he spoke he consulted a copy of the Articles. Those close to him could see it was heavily annotated. 'The procedure is quite clear. What is not clear is just what happened two years ago. By what authority were you elected – or appointed – chair? And then how did these other members assume their positions?'

'Mr Wittering—'

'Mrs Lasser, I have to say that this calls into question the whole legality of the past two years. I'm thinking that on behalf of the parent body we may need to seek guidance as to whether or not the school has met its statutory requirements under Awanzan law. I need hardly remind you how serious the consequences would be if it turned out that it had not done so.'

'Wait a minute.' Ernesto rose from his seat near the back of the auditorium and called across the room to Colby Wittering. 'This is ridiculous. I am a director of two companies here in Awanza and until January I was a member of the school board. We are a Section 21 not-for-profit company under the Companies Act of 2004. The directors' names are all registered. I would never have agreed to be on the board if it wasn't properly constituted.'

'Ah, but was it? How did you get to be on the board. You were elected, I assume?'

'No,' a hint of doubt crept into Ernesto's voice. 'I was asked to join the board.'

'Asked? By whom?'

'By Car…. By Mrs Lasser, the board chair.'

'And with what authority did she invite you?'

'With the authority vested in me as chair of the board, Mr Wittering.' Carola was certainly speaking with authority now. 'In this very room in April two years ago, before a large meeting of parents and staff – and, I might say, at a meeting attended by and witnessed by the Official Receiver – I was asked to assume the position of chair. I had been a member of the previous board. In fact, I was the only remaining member of that board. The school had gone bankrupt. There was no board. Until we adopted the previous school's Articles of Association – the document you are holding in your hands – and that was many months later, there was no constitution to follow. Essentially, we – everyone in this room that night – were creating a school from nothing. Many of you here tonight,' she looked around the room, 'were here two years ago. Is this not so?'

Peter was delighted when Carola's question was met with a spontaneous round of applause.

'Hear, hear!' Someone shouted. 'Well said.'

Colby Wittering looked rattled but he was standing his ground. He waved his copy of the Articles of Association. 'May we at least know which members were elected and which appointed?' he shouted.

'Sit down!' Peter turned his chair but could not see who had called out. 'Shut up!' came another voice.

'And,' continued Colby, 'in the circumstances, might it be appropriate for those who were appointed to put themselves forward for election at this meeting? Just to resolve any outstanding doubts?'

Behind Carola, Clyde Arthurs stood. 'No. The ballot papers have been printed already. We received five nominations and four of them will be elected – or re-elected – tonight.'

'You cannot accept nominations from the floor?' Colby made a show of consulting the Articles. 'Section Six, page nine … The Articles appear to be rather silent on this matter.'

Clyde looked a little uncertain. 'I think you are correct that no mention is made of accepting nominations from the floor but by implication, if nominations must be received no less than ten days—'

'By implication? I don't think implication is good enough, Mr Arthurs.'

Again, someone from the back shouted, 'Sit down!'

But then there was another voice.

'If nominations can be made from the floor, I would like to nominate … I'm sorry, is it Mr Wittering? I think he would be an excellent board member.'

Crystal Moore was standing. Beside her Nyota Furaha almost immediately called out, 'I second that!'

Colby looked surprised but not unhappy. 'Perhaps we should take a vote of those present to see if nominations from the floor should be accepted.'

'No!' Ernesto was on his feet again. 'The rules are perfectly clear. The names of those standing for election and the names of the proposer and seconder were published a week ago – as per the Articles. Their CVs have been made available and each candidate will speak briefly tonight. For goodness' sake, man, you're the one who wants it done by the book. Now you are suggesting that we ignore our own constitution?'

'Gentlemen! This has gone on long enough.' Peter was not sure he had ever heard Carola shouting before. Her microphone boomed and whistled. 'Mr Wittering, you have made your point. I am now asking you to sit down.' She glared at Colby. Around the room there were murmurs of approval. He opened his mouth but then thought better of it. Then, still clutching his copy of the Articles, he started edging along his row of seats and towards the exit. A number of parents began a slow handclapping.

'Good God,' Sheila had said later as Peter recounted the night's events. 'Are these people adults?'

'I think Carola was thinking the same thing. She very quickly and rather sternly put a stop to it. She was quite impressive. And then she very firmly told Crystal Moore that there would be no nominations from the floor. That got another little round of applause.'

'And the rest of the meeting?'

'Bit of an anti-climax, actually.'

'Your friend, Mrs Maerua?'

'Not a peep. I was a bit disappointed.'

'I bet you were. And the elections?'

'Oh, Carola and Violet were re-elected and we have two new members – Eadie Reutlinger who is Swiss and George Woolrych who is British. I don't really know either of them but they both spoke well. I'll get to meet them properly next week. Carola has invited everyone to The Mupundu for dinner.'

'Wow. Is she paying for that or the school?'

'We're each going to pay for ourselves. You can imagine how it would look if the school paid for a meal for a dozen people at the most expensive restaurant in the country. And it's a chance to say goodbye to Catherine and Clyde. I think the school is going to pay for them. A nice gesture.'

'And so your second year draws to a close. Are you happy?'

'More or less,' Peter poured himself another glass of wine. 'I seem to have spent most of it filling unexpected vacancies. And now I need to find a replacement for Mike Sesriem.'

'He's definitely going?'

Peter nodded. 'Oh, and we still need to wind up the PTA.'

'Seems fair. They've been winding you up all year.'

'Oh, and people seem to be queuing up to buy the school. That will be the first item for the new board.'

'And you have a pregnant girl in Grade Ten.'

'Yes. It's never dull, is it?'

'Well, I think you're doing a great job.'

Compliments from his wife were sufficiently infrequent to make Peter question his hearing. 'Really? You think so?'

'I'm not in school but it seems to me you're doing pretty well. Most of the time.' She laughed. 'And I don't know if you realise it, but you are loving it.'

Peter reflected. 'Yeah. I am. Good days and bad days, of course, but yes. I think I'm lucky.'

The clinked their glasses. And then Sheila pushed the cork back in the bottle.

★

The meeting to wind up the PTA turned out to be a non-event. About two dozen parents and staff attended but not one of the Executive Committee was present.

'Too humiliating?' Mick wondered.

'I thought they'd put up more of a fight,' Peter said.

'Well, the vote was unanimous. So now we have no PTA. One less thing to worry about, I suppose, but it does leave us with a few more things to deal with.' As always, Valli was pragmatic.

'Selling school stuff?' Peter said. 'Saskia has a plan. It will at least get us through the next few months. Until we decide what will replace our errant PTA.'

'They still have to hand over their assets.'

'And keys.'

'What an appalling waste of time an effort. Crystal bloody Moore. I wonder what she'll do now.'

'She's going to want to be on the board, I bet.'

'Well, she'll have to wait another twelve months. And how many votes will she get?'

'They said that about Trump.' Valli looked mournful.

'You're joking.'

'Never say never.'

★

Sitting in his office on the last day of the teaching year, Peter thought back to that day twelve months previously. He felt the same cocktail of emotions. Some sense of pride at what had been achieved, a sincere sense of relief at bullets that had been dodged, irritation and frustration at pratfalls that need not have been, and, if he was honest, a certain bitterness that people who should have known better had actively made his life harder.

Carola's sad complaint echoed. *Surely, we're all on the same side?* Peter would have liked to think so but he increasingly felt that his assumptions through childhood, university, and employment had been at best optimistic and at worst naïve.

People are fundamentally good, aren't they? Sure, everyone has their little prejudices and bigotries but, ultimately, we all agree and accept that there are essential rules, standards, principles … Lying and stealing is wrong. There is such a thing as the Truth. Isn't there? If you see a fellow human being in need, you don't pass by on the other side.

Peter had been born in the 1970s and had attended school in the eighties. As a young man in the nineties and into the next millennium he had witnessed what he thought of as progress. Not least with his background as a student and then teacher of history, he could trace the progress of social movements that campaigned for civil rights, racial equality, gender equality and much else. Too often, it felt like two steps forward and one back but the tide of history was unmistakable. Women and Black people (good grief, Black women!) were reading the news on British television. Openly homosexual people were increasingly prominent – and accepted – in public life. Things – "things" – were getting better.

And then they weren't.

The IB Diploma course includes a course called Theory of Knowledge. It is well-meaning and mostly quite valuable but those who teach it sometimes struggle to find exactly the right tone, the right words. It is intended to provoke, to challenge, and to inspire. But when should the teacher's own preferences take a back seat? Peter had taught ToK in both Germany and Japan. He thought he would be good at it. But he gradually came to doubt himself.

It had come to a head when he had proposed something to a class of seventeen- and eighteen-year-olds.

'Ultimately,' he had said, 'you can divide the world into two kinds of people. Those who see life as competition and those who see it as cooperation. It's actually very simple. Those who believe in competition believe that they need to win, to get ahead, to take whatever advantages they can. It's a game – no, it's a contest. You either grab what you can or someone else will. Those who prefer cooperation believe in sharing, in striving for some sort of equality, in making sure that everyone has at least the basics – accommodation, food, health care, education, and so on. Fairness, mutual respect. Trust …'

Children had taken the message home. Parents had complained. The words 'socialism' and 'communism' had been thrown around and Peter had been reproached.

'And if I had been quoting Jesus …?' he had argued.

His well-known atheism had been invoked against that argument and he had decided to bite his tongue.

So, schools pay lip service to various ideals but, in reality, they will often bend to meet the wishes – the prejudices – of parents. That is, parents – the customers – those who pay their fees (mostly) and keep the school going.

Peter really didn't want to be ending the year with such pessimistic thoughts but …

'Peter?'

He looked up. It was Ernesto Mayor.

'May I?' He asked but, without waiting for an answer, he slammed the door shut, took a seat and pulled it close to Peter's desk.

'It's Lazarett, Peter. He's trying to sell the school.'

'What?'

'It's Lazarett. PAIS didn't find ISN. He approached them. He contacted them and offered the school for sale.'

'How do you—'

'I'm in. They think I'm on their side. They've opened up.'

'But how can he sell the school?'

'He can't, obviously, but if he can talk the board into it, he'll cream off a decent percentage for himself. He's their man on the inside.'

'No, even Lazarett—'

'Yes, even Lazarett. Especially Lazarett!'

'But ...'

'There are no buts. Why do you think Mrs Luhanga has suddenly become so pliant?'

'I don't ...'

'Because if the school was about to be hit by the ATE Act it would be a much less attractive proposition. She's in on this too.'

'So, she drops the ATE thing and—'

'Exactly!'

'Is anyone else implicated?'

'I don't think so.'

Peter took a further moment to digest the news and then reached for his phone.

'Okay if I bring Carola in on this?'

'I would strongly recommend it.'

Peter dialled Carola's number.